Praise for

THE BOAT PEOPLE

"*The Boat People* is a burning flare of a novel, at once incendiary and illuminating. With a rare combination of precision, empathy, and insight, Sharon Bala has crafted an unflinching examination of what happens when the fundamental human need for safety collides with the cold calculus of bureaucracy. In the best tradition of fearless literature, it shatters our comfortable illusions about who we really are and reveals just how asymmetrical the privilege of belonging can be. This is a brilliant debut—a story that needs to be told, told beautifully."
—Omar El Akkad, author of *American War*

"Timely and engrossing. . . . This is a powerful debut."
—*Publishers Weekly*

"This wise and compassionate novel is an intimate portrait of one of the great humanitarian crises of our time. Its power lies in its breadth, for it examines not just those who come to our country seeking refuge, but also those who determine their fate. As such it implicates us all in the ongoing crisis."
—Shyam Selvadurai, author of
The Hungry Ghosts and *Funny Boy*

"This earnest debut novel forcefully explores the issues surrounding immigration. . . . Deeply moving and nuanced, *The Boat People* asks what price a country is willing to pay when public safety comes at the cost of human lives."
—*Booklist*

"*The Boat People* is a powerful, gripping moral drama told with deep compassion and humanity. Sharon Bala takes us behind the headlines about refugees and asylum seekers straight into the beating hearts of unforgettable human beings. A timely tale and a beautiful, remarkable debut."
—Lynne Kutsukake,
author of *The Translation of Love*

"A multifaceted debut novel. . . . Cinematic details transport us to a tension-rich drama. . . . Bala moves fluidly from past to present, mixing memories with current crises. . . . Such juxtapositions build and maintain suspense all the way to the last line, where readers are left hanging, as if justice is in our hands."   —*BookPage*

"*The Boat People* is a beautifully crafted story with a big heart. This novel has an urgency and relevance that cuts to the bone and will resonate with readers of all stripes. Bala offers no easy answers and no political posturing, but her magnificent storytelling will leave readers wondering about their own convictions, asking themselves, 'What would I do? What would I have done?'"   —Michel Stone,
author of *Border Child*

Sharon Bala

THE BOAT PEOPLE

Sharon Bala lives in St. John's, Newfoundland. She is a member of The Port Authority writing group. *The Boat People* is her first novel.

www.sharonbala.com

THE BOAT PEOPLE

THE

BOAT

PEOPLE

Sharon Bala

ANCHOR BOOKS
A Division of Penguin Random House LLC
New York

FIRST ANCHOR BOOKS EDITION, DECEMBER 2018

Copyright © 2018 by Sharon Bala

All rights reserved. Published in the United States by Anchor Books, a division of Penguin Random House LLC, New York. Originally published in hardcover in the United States by Doubleday, a division of Penguin Random House LLC, New York, in 2018.

Anchor Books and colophon are registered trademarks of Penguin Random House LLC.

The Library of Congress has cataloged the Doubleday edition as follows:
Names: Bala, Sharon, author.
Title: The boat people : a novel / Sharon Bala.
Description: First edition. | New York : Doubleday, [2018]
Identifiers: LCCN 2017020049
Subjects: LCSH: Refugees—Canada—Fiction. | Fathers and sons—Fiction. | Domestic fiction. | BISAC: FICTION / Family Life. | FICTION / Cultural Heritage. | FICTION / Legal. | GSAFD: Legal stories.
Classification: LCC PR9199.4.B3565 B63 2018 | DDC 813/.6—dc23
LC record available at https://lccn.loc.gov/2017020049

Anchor Books Trade Paperback ISBN: 978-0-525-43246-3
eBook ISBN: 978-0-385-54230-2

www.anchorbooks.com

Printed in the United States of America
10 9 8 7 6 5 4 3 2 1

This book is for my parents,
Mohan and Swarna Bala.

We may have all come on different ships,

but we're in the same boat now.

—MARTIN LUTHER KING JR.

THE BOAT PEOPLE

Mahindan was flat on his back when the screaming began, one arm right-angled over his eyes. He heard the whistle and thud of falling artillery, the cries of the dying. Mortar shells and rockets, the whole world on fire.

Then another sound. It cut through the clamor so that for a drawn-out second there was nothing else, only him and his son and the bomb that arched through the sky with a shrill banshee scream, spinning nose aimed straight for them. Mahindan fought to open his eyes. His limbs were pinned down and heavy. He struggled to move, to call out in terror, to clamber and run. The ground rumbled. The shell exploded, shards of hot metal spitting in its wake. The tent was rent in half. Mahindan jolted awake.

Heart like a sledgehammer, he sat up frantic, blinking into the darkness. He heard someone panting and long seconds later realized it was him. The echoing whine of flying shrapnel faded and he returned to the present, to the coir mat under him, back to the hold of the ship.

There were snores and snuffles, the small nocturnal noises of five hundred slumbering bodies. Beneath him, the engine's monotonous whir. He reached out, instinctive, felt his son Sellian curled up beside him, then lay down again. The back of his neck was damp. His pulse still raced. He smelled the sourness of his skin, the raw animal stink of the bodies all around. The man on the next mat slept with his mouth open. His snore was a revving motorcycle, so close Mahindan could almost feel the warm exhales.

He put his hand against Sellian's back, felt it move up and down. Gradually, his own breathing slowed to the same rhythm. He ran a hand through his son's hair, fine and silky, the soft strands of a child, then stroked his arm, felt the roughness of his skin, the long, thin scratches, the scabbed-over insect bites. Sellian was slight. Six years old and barely three feet tall. How little space the child occupied, coiled into himself, his thumb in his mouth. How precarious his existence, how miraculous his survival.

Mahindan's vision adjusted and shapes emerged out of the gloom. The thin rails on either side of the ladder. Lamps strung up along an electrical cord. Outside the porthole window, it was still pitch-black.

Careful not to wake Sellian, he stood and gingerly made his way across the width of the ship toward the ladder, stepping between bodies huddled on thin mats and ducking under sleepers swaying overhead, cocooned in rope hammocks. It was hot and close, the atmosphere suffocating.

Hema's thick plait trailed out on the dirty floor. Mahindan stooped to pick it up and laid it gently on her back as he passed by. Her two daughters shared the mat beside her; they lay on their sides facing each other, knees and foreheads touching. A few feet on, he passed the man with the amputated leg and averted his gaze.

During the day the ship was rowdy with voices, but now he heard only the slap of the electrical cord against the wall, everyone breathing in and out, recycling the same stale, diesel-scented air.

A boy cried out in his sleep, caught in a nightmare, and when Mahindan turned toward the sound, he saw Kumuran's wife comfort her son. With both hands grasping the banisters, Mahindan hoisted himself up the ladder. Emerging onto the deck, inhaling the fresh scent of salt and sea, he felt immediately lighter. From overhead, the mast creaked and he gazed up to see the stars, the half-appam moon glowing alive in the sky. At the thought of appam—doughy, hot off the fire—his stomach gave a plaintive, hollow grumble.

It was dark, but he knew his way around the ship. A dozen plastic buckets were lined up along the stern. He squatted in front of one and formed his hands into a bowl. The water was tepid, murky with twigs and bits of seaweed. He splashed water on his face and the back of his neck, feeling the grit scratch his skin.

The boat—a sixty-meter freighter, past its prime and jerry-rigged for five hundred passengers—was cruising through calm waters, groaning under the weight of too much human cargo. Mahindan held on to the railing, rubbing a thumb against the blistered rust.

A few others were out, shadowy figures keeping silent vigil on both levels of the deck. They had been at sea for weeks or months, sunrises blurring into sunsets. Days spent on deck, tarps draped overhead to block out the sun, and the floor burning beneath them. Stormy nights when the ship would lurch and reel, Sellian cradled in Mahindan's lap, their stomachs tumbling with the pitch and yaw of the angry ocean.

But the captain had said they were close and for days they had been expecting land, a man posted at all times in the crow's nest.

Mahindan turned his back to the railing and slid down to sit on the deck. Exhaustion whenever he thought of the future; terror when he remembered the past. He yawned and pressed a cheek to raised knees, then tucked his arms in for warmth. At least here on the boat they were safe from attack. Ruksala, Prem, Chithra's mother and father. The roll call of the dead lulled him to sleep.

He awoke to commotion and gull shrieks. A boy ran down the length of the ship calling for his father. Appa! Appa! There were more people on the deck now, all of them speaking in loud, excited voices.

The man they called Ranga stood at the railing beside him, staring out. Mahindan was dismayed to see him.

Land is close, Ranga said.

Mahindan scanned the straight line of the ocean, trying not to blink. Nearby, a young man stood on the rail and levered his body half out of the boat. An older woman called out: Take care!

After all this time, finally we have arrived, Ranga said. He grinned at Mahindan and added: Because of you only, I am here.

Nothing to do with me, Mahindan said. We all took our own chance.

Mahindan kept his gaze fixed on the horizon. At first he saw the head of a pin, far in the distance, but as he kept watching, the vision emerged. Purple-brown land and blue mountains like ghosts rising in the background. The newspaperman came to join them as the slope of a forest appeared. Mahindan had spoken to him a few times but could not recall his name. Someone said he had been working for a paper in Colombo before he fled.

We will be intercepted, the newspaperman said. Americans or Canadians, who will catch us first?

Catch us? Ranga repeated, his voice rising to a squeak.

But now there were people streaming onto the deck, squeezing in for a view at the railing, and the newspaperman was jostled away. Mahindan edged aside too, relieved to put distance between himself and Ranga.

There were voices and bodies everywhere. Women plaited their hair over one shoulder. Men pulled their arms through their T-shirts. Most were barefoot. People pressed up around him. The boat creaked and Mahindan felt it list, as everyone crowded in. They stood shoulder to shoulder, people on both levels of the deck, hushing one another, children holding their breath. The trees, the mountains, the strip of beach they could now make out up ahead, it all seemed impossibly big, unreal after days and nights of nothing but sea and sky and the rumbling of the ship. Nightmares of rusted steel finally giving way, belching them all into the ocean.

Sellian appeared, squeezing himself between legs, one fist against his eyes. Appa, you left me!

How to leave? Mahindan said. Did you think I jumped in the ocean? He picked his son up in the crook of one arm and pointed. Look! We're here.

The clouds burned orange. Mahindan squinted. People shouted and pointed. Look!

There was a tugboat in the water and a larger ship, its long nose turned up, speeding toward them, sleek and fast, with a tall white flagpole. The wind unfurled the flag, red and white, majestic in the flaming sky. They saw the leaf and a great resounding cheer shook the boat.

The captain cut the engine and they floated placid. Overhead, there was a chopping sound. Mahindan saw a helicopter, its blades slicing the sky, a red leaf painted on its belly. There were three boats now, all of them circling the ship, a welcome party. On the deck, people waved with both hands. The red-and-white flag snapped definitive.

Mahindan gripped his son. Sellian shivered in his arms, from fear, from exhilaration, he couldn't tell. Soon Mahindan was shaking too, armpits dampening. His teeth clattered.

Their new life. It was just beginning.

Inshallah, Mr. Gigovaz

Gigovaz's Subaru was idling at the entrance of her low-rise when Priya came down from her apartment at 4 a.m. A police cruiser had pulled up alongside and both drivers had their windows lowered like characters in a cop show.

Standing under the shabby green awning, Priya tugged on the building's door to make sure it had locked before walking out toward the curb. Wind blew the rain sideways, the drops bouncing in tiny white splashes off the asphalt. The cop pulled away as she climbed into Gigovaz's car.

Nice area, he said.

Priya didn't know how to reply and said nothing as they drove east on Hastings past hobbled shopping carts and vacant storefronts, sleeping bodies huddled in doorways. She held her travel mug with one hand and fumbled the seat belt into the buckle with the other.

Gigovaz had the radio tuned to an easy-listening station.

Avishai Cohen, he said.

The name meant nothing to Priya, but since she hadn't wished Gigovaz good morning, she said: It's nice.

He nudged the volume up and Priya took it as a sign she was exempt from small talk. Rain thrummed a steady beat against the roof. The inside of the car smelled like stale coffee and wet dog. Big Mac wrappers were crumpled into paper cups. There was a pilled blanket stretched across the backseat, a fine layer of dust on the dashboard, and a ziplock of Milk-Bones on the floor, half the biscuits crushed to crumbs. It was her first trip in Gigovaz's car and Priya was thoroughly unsurprised.

The rain let up as they drove south past Richmond. In the distance, there were container ships and construction cranes, golden dots of light shining through the fog. On the radio, a three-tone melody announced the national news. The refugees were the lead story.

We took control of the vessel twelve nautical miles off Vancouver Island, a spokesman for the Royal Canadian Mounted Police said. The migrants were taken into custody and we are now conducting a deep search of the ship.

The news reader cut in: The ship bore no visible flags or numbers—a sign, officials say, that those aboard were hoping to enter Canada unnoticed.

Gigovaz turned off the radio. A massive cargo ship with hundreds of people, he said. I'm sure that was their plan—to slip in unnoticed.

At the ferry terminal, they were waved into line behind a blue Camry. A Canadian flag was taped to the antenna, waggling in the breeze. It was properly morning now, the sky a mild gray. The lot was nearly empty, only a few commuters out on this holiday Wednesday. Gigovaz rolled down the window to wipe the side mirror and Priya did the same, then dried her hand on her skirt and stifled a yawn.

Today was supposed to be about sleeping in, eating pulled pork pancakes, and watching the Canada Day fireworks from the beach at Kitsilano. Today was not supposed to be about refugees and Gigovaz and an O-dark-hundred commute to Vancouver Island.

———

Gigovaz had been comatose in a staff meeting two days earlier when Priya first spotted him. The partners at Elliot, McFadden, and Lo were congratulating themselves over five columns of numbers on a PowerPoint and Priya was leaning against a wall at the back, ignoring her pinched toes and thinking about an affidavit she was trying to track down, when she noticed Gigovaz, slumped into a chair, chin on chest, a mug dangling off his fingers. In a room full of crisp pinstripes and sharp ballpoints, Gigovaz looked blurred at the edges, soft folds overflowing in every direction.

McFadden said, Billable hours rose 47 percent, and the room exploded in a round of applause. Gigovaz startled awake and Priya found herself staring into a squinted pair of bleary eyes. She turned away and started clapping, but a moment later, when she snuck a peek, Gigovaz was still watching her.

Later, he caught up to her in the elevator and made her labor out the syllables of her last name.

Raja, she said.

Raja, he repeated.

There were half a dozen people in the elevator and no one else was speaking.

Say-kar.

Say-kar.

An.

Rajakaran, he said.

Raja-*se*-kar-an, she corrected.

Her own name sounded foolish to her, all the individual syllables rendered embarrassing and meaningless by repetition.

You're Sri Lankan? he asked.

I'm Canadian, she said, standing up a little straighter.

Gigovaz turned a dimpled hand over itself in the air and said, Yes, yes. But your family is originally from Sri Lanka, right?

The elevator stopped and one person got off.

Yes, she said. They were ten floors away from her desk and every single button on the side panel was lit up.

Tamil? he asked.

Yes.

She compressed her lips and clasped her hands in front of her. Gigovaz was senior counsel, but there was also a chocolate smear on his collar. It was difficult to know how to act around him. But one more ignorant question and she would get off and take the stairs.

You're a law student, in your last year? And before she could answer, he asked if she had taken Refugee Law in school.

The doors opened and they stepped aside so a woman at the back could squeeze between them.

I'm specializing in corporate, Priya said.

You didn't study IRPA? he asked.

IRPA. She tried to recall what the acronym stood for and came up with Immigration Refugee Something Act.

We did the Divorce Act.

Who's your principal? he asked.

Joyce Lau, she said. Mergers and acquisitions.

Joyce Lau wore her hair in a bun and drove an Audi. She was the youngest senior counsel in the firm's history and Priya had beaten out five people in her class for this job.

Gigovaz rubbed a hand under his chin. Joyce Lau, he said. Impressive, impressive.

When they reached her floor, Gigovaz got off too and veered toward Joyce's office. Pack your things, Miss Rajakaran, he said. You're moving to the seventh floor.

———

Priya stewed as they boarded the ferry, cursing her skin color and the whim that had caused her to glance Gigovaz's way in the meeting. When she'd asked Joyce Lau why he didn't want someone who understood immigration law, Joyce had just shrugged and said: Peter requested you. No one had signed up to intern with Gigovaz and now he'd found a sneaky way to rope Priya in.

The ferry juddered to life, all its mechanical parts humming and vibrating into action, as Gigovaz clasped his hands together, arms forming a triangle above the table. He was conducting a lecture on the importance of credibility. The truth is immaterial, he said. Do the claimants appear to be telling the truth? That is what matters.

He had put on his professor voice, erudite and condescending. You are not my mentor, Priya thought.

Gigovaz checked his watch. They're probably being interviewed by Immigration right now.

Wait. They're being interviewed without us? Priya asked. What about their right to counsel?

They're not being charged with anything, Gigovaz said. Technically, they have no rights.

A heating vent rattled overhead. The ferry was cutting through the water, forging straight ahead into flat, gray, foggy nothing. Tourists in raincoats shivered on the deck, snapping useless photos.

Ten years ago, five hundred refugees came from China, Gigovaz continued. Four boats in two months. My clients on the first ship were processed quickly and sent on their way with health care, housing supports, job applications, all those practical things. And then the Refugee Board hearings happened a couple of months later. Business as usual.

Priya wondered how quickly this case could be dispatched. A month, tops. Surely he didn't expect her to see the whole thing through.

Gigovaz was still lecturing: But as boat after boat showed up, what do you think happened? Suddenly the asylum seekers were branded criminals. And a prison in Prince George was reopened just to hold them. Now there were detention reviews, admissibility hearings. For months and months, the cases dragged on. We had to fight for every single thing. And that, by the way, was the same year we airlifted five thousand people out of Kosovo.

So refugee law is capricious, Priya thought. All the more reason to bring in an expert. Of course, then he'd have no one to lecture.

Here is what you have to understand, Gigovaz said, indicating the space between two hands. In immigration law, there can be a gap between policy and practice. And when it comes to refugees, this country has a split personality.

Three hundred people on board a ship rocking its way around the world on a collision course with Canada. They were tracked, Gigovaz said. Intelligence and satellite and reports of sightings from international ports. For weeks everyone waited. Now they were here.

What's going to happen to them? Priya asked. I mean, will they get to stay?

An overhead announcement reminded people to keep their pets in their cars. Gigovaz watched the speaker on the ceiling until the disembodied voice stopped.

My very first client was Rohingya. You know who they are?

When Priya shook her head, Gigovaz's index fingers rose, the steeple of a church, and he tapped them together.

They're a minority in Myanmar—Muslims in a country of Buddhists. Stateless and oppressed. Ibrahim Mosar. He was missing his right hand. Cigarette burns all over his chest.

Priya winced and Gigovaz said: I was like every other young refugee lawyer, full of piss and vinegar, and here was my client, calm as you like. Inshallah, Mr. Gigovaz, he used to say. Whatever God wills.

Que será será, she said. That's one way of accepting fate, I guess.

We do our level best, Gigovaz said. Our clients do their best. The rest is up to . . .

He lifted his palms as if balancing a platter.

Allah? she asked.

The adjudicator, Gigovaz said. He rooted blindly under the seat with one hand. They were approaching the harbor.

So what happened to Ibrahim? Priya asked.

Gigovaz stood, briefcase in hand. The claim was rejected, he said. They sent him back.

The authorities were giving out bananas and water in exchange for documents. Mahindan had everything in his suitcase, inside a sealed plastic bag—birth certificates, national identity cards, Sellian's vaccination record. He was waiting in the tangle of people for his turn, holding Sellian's hand, when a frenzied movement caught his eye, Ranga hobbling over at top speed, waving as if they were old friends. When the guard gestured for his paperwork, Ranga glanced at Mahindan for assurance before producing a battered identity card from his pocket. Mahindan turned away, irritated.

When it was his turn, Mahindan handed over his papers with pride, knowing how carefully he had prepared for this eventuality. This one thing was properly done. They took his suitcase too, but when Sellian began crying, the guard with the blue eyes allowed him to liberate the little statue of Ganesha and then patted Sellian's shoulder with a purple-gloved hand. Mahindan gazed at the battered old suitcase with regret. Hard-shelled and sturdy with brass locks and snaps, it and the meager trinkets inside—a wedding album, Chithra's death certificate, the keys to his house and garage—were all that remained of his worldly possessions. But he reminded himself he had something more precious. Safety. Here, it was possible to breathe.

The men and women were separated and forced into orderly queues. The adults had their wrists and ankles shackled. Mahindan understood by the way the guard fitted the two ends of the cuffs together, careful not to pinch skin, that the task was performed with regret.

Only for a little while, Mahindan assured Sellian. It is for our own safety.

There weren't enough Tamil translators and the masks the Canadians wore made it difficult to decipher expressions. Mahindan focused on eyes and was amazed by all the colors, the shades of blue, flecks of green, the different saturation points of brown. The only white people he'd seen before were United Nations workers, though he did not like to think of them now.

Mahindan had always thought of Canada as a country of whites, but now he saw dark eyes too, Chinese and Japanese and blacks and others who might have come from India or Bangladesh. Here was a place for all people.

Ranga sidled up. At last we are safe, he said, absently scratching at a long scar that ran down the length of one cheek.

Mahindan frowned and edged away. Every time he and Sellian turned around on the ship, there was Ranga and his gimpy leg. Behind them in the food ration line; unrolling his mat next to theirs at night.

A police officer barked into a radio. A Red Cross volunteer made emphatic gestures as he spoke. Mahindan heard the unfamiliar sounds, the harsh, guttural consonants falling flat, one after the other. In time this would be his language too. English. A new language for a new home.

His grandfather had spoken English. He had gone to London for his studies and worked as a civil servant in Colombo until the Sinhala Only Act ended his career. It was his grandfather's old suitcase that was now with the guards.

Officials and volunteers in scrubs and uniforms called to each other, their voices overwhelmed, their gestures and movements harried. Seagulls circled, screeching overhead. The disorder reminded Mahindan of being processed for detention in Sri Lanka, at the end of the war, when the Sri Lankan Army rounded up the Tamil prisoners. Except here there was nothing to be scared of, and even Sellian surveyed the unfamiliar landscape and the line of buses with more curiosity than fear.

Mahindan understood they would be boarding soon. He waited with the other men, trying and failing to inch away from Ranga. The queues lengthened as more people joined. Mahindan nodded to a family he knew from the detention camp, but they either did not notice him or purposely avoided his eyes. It had surprised him, when they boarded in Sri Lanka, how few of his customers were on the ship. All those days at sea and not once had they seen another boat. Maybe it was for the best they weren't here; it was good to make a clean break. Still, he wondered: Had they been left behind? Had their ship capsized? Were they drowned in the ocean? He felt his teeth rattle and focused his attention on Sellian for assurance. *We are safe.*

It had been hours since they'd disembarked, but he could still feel the sea in the sway of his legs. When he remembered the first rough days on board, the storm-churned waves, the low-grade nausea that dogged every day, he vowed to himself: never again.

He would have liked to squat, to take the pressure off his aching soles, but the shackles made it awkward. Everyone was quiet and even the children, pacified by food and drink, managed to behave. The mood was hopeful.

Sellian held up a juice box. Do you want some, Appa?

No, Baba, Mahindan said. You finish it.

Purple liquid shot through the straw. Sellian sucked in short, urgent bursts, his eyes flicking left and right. Mahindan watched him, overwhelmed with love and relief. He shuffled to the right, put his bound hands on his son's shoulder, and bent to kiss the top of his head. Sellian snuggled against him, and Mahindan felt emotion well up, joyous tears threaten. They had lost everyone and everything, but Sellian was alive and unharmed and now they were here. Sellian was here.

The bus at the front of the line opened its doors. A guard waved his arm and the women shambled forward, hands and feet fettered. Children held on to their mothers' shirts and trousers. The men looked sharp, straightening out their line in readiness, everyone restless to move on to the next stage of freedom.

The guard turned to scan the crowd and when he spotted Sellian, he beckoned.

Appa, what is he saying?

I don't know, Baba.

The guard held up a hand for each of them: stop for Mahindan and come for Sellian. Mahindan could not read his expression. The guard repeated the same short word over and over then strode toward them, impatient, and grasped the top of Sellian's arm.

Appa!

No! He's my son! The metal between his feet rattled and Mahindan felt his weight tip forward. The men on either side of him yelled as Ranga reached bound hands out to catch him. By the time Mahindan was upright, the guard had Sellian draped over his shoulder and was carrying him away. Some of the women in line had turned to watch. They shouted at the guard in Tamil to stop. Sellian was mutinous, kicking and beating his fists on the man's back. The juice box fell; purple liquid pooled in a puddle on the asphalt.

A loud voice cut through the racket. Mahindan saw the nurse who had taken his blood pressure hurrying to the guard. She spoke English with the voice of a Tamil mother, full of reprimand and authority. Her chin jutted forward. Her index finger jabbed. The guard rubbed his palm along the back of his head, finally setting Sellian down.

Mahindan struggled to crouch in his shackles as his son ran over. Sellian grabbed his arm with both hands and held tight, panting hard, his eyes large and teary. He pressed his face into his father's side. Mahindan felt the tightness of Sellian's grip, how easily it could be wrenched away.

Where are we being sent? he asked the nurse in Tamil.

He knew there was a very big country stretching out before him, but when he tried to imagine what it might be like, he had only a vague recollection of his grandfather's stories of England. Sheep and tall buildings, policemen who carried batons instead of guns.

The nurse did not wear a mask. At Mahindan's question, her eyes slid sideways and the corners of her mouth turned down. But when she spoke, she raised her voice so all the men in line could hear: Normally, there are some rooms close by where you would stay. But when this many come all at once . . . there is only one place with enough beds.

Mahindan felt foolish. Free men did not wear handcuffs.

The nurse turned back to Mahindan and softened her voice. Where the women are going, there are facilities for children.

Chithra had died in childbirth. For Sellian's whole life, Mahindan had been both his father and his mother. Not a day had passed when he hadn't seen his son, and the thought of letting him walk away, board a bus to an unknown place without him, made his insides twist.

Sellian began to cry. Appa! Don't leave me! Don't leave me!

Mahindan's throat constricted. What choice did he have? He must be brave for his son.

Baba, it is all right, he said. You want to play with other children, no? And see, all these Aunties will take care of you. It is only for a short time.

The nurse took Sellian's hand. See that small boy? Do you know him?

Sellian gulped and nodded. He wiped the back of his hand across his snotty nose. Mahindan's mettle faltered when he saw who it was— Kumuran's son. He said to Sellian, You know that child. Remember?

I will ask his mother to take care of you, the nurse said. I'm sorry, she said to Mahindan as his son's arms wrapped around his neck again. This is very rare. A ship and so many people . . . everyone is doing their best.

We're just happy to be here, Mahindan said, holding his son tighter. Ganesha's elephant trunk dug into the back of his head.

The guard called something out.

Come now, darling, the nurse said to Sellian.

Be a good boy, Mahindan said. Show Appa how you can be brave.

Sellian hiccupped, holding in his sobs, twisting his head to look over his shoulder as he was led away. Mahindan's chest closed up. Most of the women were in the bus now, staring out the windows. The men focused on their feet. Mahindan could feel Kumuran's wife studying him, her hard, unforgiving stare. He struggled to keep his face calm and encouraging. When he looked at Sellian, he saw Chithra's eyes, her front teeth jutting out.

Sellian disappeared into the bus and the doors wheezed to a close. Mahindan felt anguish like a tsunami surging to the shore. The wave crested up. He squinted at the back window as the bus pulled away, but all he saw was darkness.

Go Home Terorists!

Priya had been to the Canadian Forces Base at Esquimalt once before to visit the naval museum. She remembered her brother tugging her braids to annoy her but had no recollection of their parents being there with them. The memory was quite possibly a complete fabrication.

Gigovaz's car was waved through the security checkpoint and they headed for the processing facility, a gray slab set on a finger of land, hemmed in by forest and ocean. The sun had risen fully and here the sky was completely cloudless, the ground dry.

There were news vans in the parking lot. Cameramen shouldered equipment while reporters flipped through their notes. A podium was set up across from the building and a young man fussed with a sign that hung in front of the lectern.

Who's giving the news conference? Gigovaz asked.

Minister Blair, the man replied.

Public Safety, Gigovaz told Priya. Not Immigration. Interesting, don't you think?

Tarps lined the walkway to the entrance. A half-dozen people stood in a row holding homemade signs that they lifted up and down while chanting in unison. A man in a television news jacket panned his camera from right to left. Gigovaz walked past, oblivious. Priya read the signs. *Send the illegals back! Go home terorists!* She wanted to point out the misspelling.

Inside, the processing facility was deserted. At the front desk, Gigovaz spoke to a woman in a bowler hat, her hair in a bun. She gave them lanyards and Priya put hers around her neck. It had a blue *V* on one side and when she flipped it over, she saw her name and face on the other. It was her office ID photo, the one that had been taken a month earlier as she sat on a stool in the mailroom while a guy with a mullet instructed her not to blink. She looked startled and prim in the picture.

Where is everyone? Priya asked.

After you, Gigovaz said, making an exaggerated motion with his left hand and pulling open a heavy door with his right.

Outside was a commotion of voices and movement as helicopters droned overhead and ambulances idled. They were behind the facility now, facing another large parking lot, this one covered in white tents. Beyond was the ocean and the harbor, yellow cranes and wooden docks. Priya scanned the vessels until she spotted the cargo ship. It was huge—two hundred feet maybe—with a long white hull and a blue cabin toward the stern. Streaks of bubbling rust cut vertical lines down its side.

The sheer number of refugees was overwhelming, the queues that stretched out from every tent and table, winding and intertwining so that it was impossible to discern where one line ended and another began. Men, women, children, people of all ages, bedraggled and malnourished, shivering under blankets even though it was summer. Priya spotted a woman with an eye patch, a child hobbling along with the help of a stick, but for the most part there seemed to be little injury, which surprised her until she realized that of course these were the survivors. Arrival of the fittest.

People brushed by in all directions. A uniformed officer motioned for Gigovaz and Priya to step aside as two women in hospital scrubs hurried past. Volunteers in red shirts carried boxes labeled H_2O. Almost everyone wore masks over their mouths and noses. The bustle had an aura of chaos and bureaucracy. Priya deciphered the acronyms: Canada Border Services Agency, Canadian Forces, Victoria General Hospital, Royal Canadian Mounted Police.

Gigovaz attacked his BlackBerry with both thumbs as he walked. Keep an eye out for Sam, he said.

Person, place, or thing? she wanted to ask.

They passed a tent with a red cross printed on its side. A handmade sign read *Mask Required*. The door flap was pinned back and Priya caught sight of brown limbs, blood-pressure cuffs, and running shoes. A nurse ran out and bent over, her head down as if searching for a lost earring. She was covered from neck to shoes in translucent yellow plastic. A man in short-sleeved scrubs followed. He wore a surgical cap, latex gloves, and goggles. A stethoscope was draped over his shoulders. Deep breaths, he said, putting a hand on the nurse's back.

In the cacophony of voices, Priya listened for the Tamil, trying to gather up a word here and there. But the accents were long steeped and she was used to her parents' diluted version of the language.

A man in a wheelchair clutched a plastic bag in his lap. One of his legs ended in a stump. Behind him, a woman clasped hands with a pair of girls. One had two long braids. The other had a short, straggly cut, uneven, as if she had taken a knife to it. The pungent combination of chili powder, body odor, and urine that wafted ahead of them made Priya hold her breath. The shorn girl gazed over her shoulder unblinking as they passed by, and her stare was so accusatory it sent Priya stumbling back. Remembering Gigovaz and fearing she would reel into him, she spun around, but he was gone. Spotting him at the entrance to one of the larger tents, she hurried through the crowd, relieved for an excuse to move.

We can take five adults and linked minors, Gigovaz was saying to a dark-skinned man with a caterpillar mustache.

The mustached man had a clipboard and a fat yellow folder.

Sam Nadarajah, he said, introducing himself to Priya. I'm with the Tamil Alliance.

Gigovaz waved a hand in Priya's direction. This is my law student.

Priya Rajasekaran, she said quickly, before Gigovaz could butcher her name. She didn't like the way he'd said *my law student*.

An officer came out of the tent, herding a group of Sri Lankan men. Gigovaz, Sam, and Priya quickly stepped out of their way.

This can't be only three hundred people, Gigovaz said.

Sam put his clipboard between his legs and tried to open his folder. His pen fell down. He said, There are more than we expected.

Priya picked up his pen and handed it to him.

Romba nandri, he said, thanking her in Tamil, and Priya heard how soft his accent was at the edges.

No problem, she said in English.

Right now, it seems closer to four hundred, he told Gigovaz. Maybe five. We knew the size of the boat and we thought three hundred maximum. No one was prepared for this many.

Have you chosen my clients? Gigovaz said. Has Immigration taken their statements?

Medical checks, processing, statements, it is all in progress. No way to know . . . might take some time. Sam glanced at Priya, then added: There are not enough translators and it's holding everything up. Can you, maybe—

Gigovaz was already scrolling through his texts. That's fine, he said. I'll try to get a few things done in the meantime. Where do you need her?

The main medical tent, Sam said. There is only one nurse who speaks Tamil.

Priya opened her mouth.

It'll be hours before we meet our clients, Gigovaz said, still focused on his phone. You may as well be useful.

Priya's face felt hot. But I—

Come, Sam said. I'll introduce you. It'll be a huge relief for them.

Wait! Priya's voice came out high and strangled. I can't, she said. I don't speak Tamil.

Gigovaz looked up. What?

I'm sorry.

I thought you were Tamil, Gigovaz said.

I know a few phrases here and there, Priya said. But I can't translate. I can't carry on a conversation.

Both men stared at her.

You never asked, she said, wincing at the whine in her voice.

Gigovaz let out a breath of frustration. How are we supposed to communicate with our clients?

I thought there would be an interpreter, Priya said. This is not my fault, she thought.

Sam said, Okay. No problem. We have some people from the Tamil Alliance on their way. I'll assign one of them to you.

Someone called to Sam and he shook their hands quickly. I'll text you, he told Gigovaz. Nice to meet you, Priya.

I'm glad we're working together, she said in Tamil. She felt the unfamiliar sounds mangle up in her mouth and was embarrassed. She should have just said goodbye in English.

While her back was turned, Gigovaz had walked away and she had to race after him again.

A GOOD PLACE

There was a tall chain-link fence, barbed wire coiled on top. Two guards hauled back the doors to reveal a sprawling prison complex dominated by an eight-story building with blue-tinted windows. Mahindan was relieved when they drove around back and stopped at a smaller, friendlier-looking construction.

He shuffled off the bus with the others and waited as the cuffs around their wrists and ankles were removed. The man with the keys refused to meet his eyes. The building they were led into appeared inflated, a giant bubble that had ballooned out of the ground. Inside, it was all right angles and precise geometry. He blinked several times in the blinding whiteness. Everything gleamed, even the floor.

It reminded Mahindan of the space station in an old Stanley Kubrick film he had taken Chithra to see before they were married. They had watched, tense in the darkness, as the villainous computer on a spaceship came to life. At the crucial moment, when an astronaut was set adrift, a man sitting behind them thrashed his legs out, flinging Chithra forward in her seat, and she had screamed in shock. The man flailed and foamed, and they'd had to stop the film while someone shoved a set of keys into his mouth. Mahindan and Chithra had boarded the return bus home without seeing the ending.

Can this really be a jail? Ranga asked, and Mahindan did not reply. He walked a little closer to the newspaperman, who was ahead of him.

They were marched single file down a long hallway of doors. Through the rectangular window set in each one, Mahindan caught glimpses of bunk beds and sinks. Fluorescent lights hung suspended in elongated tubes, a series of horizontal lines passing above their heads.

He wondered what the women's prison was like and worried about how Sellian was coping on his own. For nine months they had been inseparable, ever since the United Nations trucks rolled out and everyone had fled Kilinochchi. Now, Mahindan's hand felt oddly empty at his side.

The men were taken to the bathroom, where they washed in groups. When it was Mahindan's turn, he stripped, unbuttoning his shirt and tugging at his waistband so that trousers and underpants both came off in a single yank. It had been months since he'd changed his clothes. Removing them felt like peeling away a filthy layer of skin. The stink wafted up, damp and fungal.

Standing naked, he felt exposed but also relieved. Now, in such close proximity to a bath, he was very aware of grime in all the creases of his body—lodged in his ears, under his fingernails, in the crack of his buttocks. When he rubbed his arms, tiny balls of grit formed on his fingertips, months of dried sweat and dust mingling up.

The guard pointed to a garbage bin. Mahindan threw his clothes in, shoes and all. The sandals sank down out of sight. He hoped they would be burned.

He was given a towel and a cube of soap and padded barefoot with eleven others into a tiled open room. The floor was wet. There were big dials at chest height and hooks for their towels, but when Mahindan squatted, he didn't see a bucket or a tap.

The water comes from the ceiling, the newspaperman called from the other side of the room. They were all facing the wall, bare backs to each other. Mahindan saw a spout high up, far above his head. He couldn't understand the mechanics of this Canadian bathroom.

Turn the dial, the newspaperman yelled. Mahindan heard rain and swiveled to see the newspaperman standing under a waterfall, rubbing the bar of soap briskly under his arms as if he had done this many times before.

Mahindan stood to the side and cautiously turned the dial. Water burst out of the tap. He put a hand under the spray and felt it was warm.

Stand underneath, the newspaperman urged them.

Mahindan saw the others following his advice and did the same, holding his breath as he stepped under the falling water. It pelted him hard. He swallowed back a yelp. All he could hear now was the loud gushing, hostile and unpleasant.

He rubbed the soap into his skin, working up a lather of small bubbles, months of blood and war all sloughing off in a black river running to the drain in the center of the room. Sri Lankan horrors washing away in Canadian waters, disappearing down Canadian drains.

He worked the soap into his hair, suds dripping off his beard. The guard called something out and the newspaperman's voice came to him watery, and far away.

Quickly, quickly, he said. There are others waiting.

Mahindan stood on one foot to clean between his toes. He rubbed the soap back and forth across his fingernails. It was difficult to maneuver all of this with his eyes closed, the water lashing him. He thought of the buckets on the boat, of the luxury of clean water that sprayed out effortless. Already he felt the superiority of this new country, with its disagreeable standing body wash.

They marched, towels around waists, into the change room. Mahindan exalted in the feeling of being inside his own skin, scrubbed smooth and several shades lighter. They took turns standing beside a ruler on the wall and putting their feet into a metal contraption. A uniformed guard passed them each a package through a window: gray trousers, a green sweater, and running shoes.

Mahindan marveled at the laces, at their clean white length, the clear tubes of plastic at each end. He pulled back the tongue and slid a foot in. It felt snug and warm. He laced up the sneakers, checked the label on the back, and was surprised to find they were not made by Bata.

He had never worn such shoes and wondered if Sellian was being given something similar, if he had taken this strange standing body wash too, if it had frightened him, if he had cried. He had misgivings about Kumuran's wife, about how she would treat the boy. The memory of Sellian hiccupping back tears formed a knot in his chest. But Sellian and her son were friendly, he told himself. And anyway, it was temporary. Like sending the boy to boarding school.

Boarding school, he repeated to himself. Did parents worry all day long when their children went to boarding school? No, they did not.

The guard signaled and they turned in unison, all of them seeing one another at the same time. Twelve men in identical uniforms, beards dripping, wet hair pasted to their foreheads.

The room erupted in laughter. Mahindan bent double, racked with the convulsions. After everything—the baby wailing at her dead mother's breast, the shredded tent, the days at sea—here they were. In a country with indoor rain and matching green sweaters. He straightened, clutching one side, and saw the guard staring at them, bewildered.

They returned to the long corridor, rubber soles squeaking against linoleum, pausing at every room while the guard motioned three people inside. Some of the men still chuckled to themselves. Mahindan rubbed the fabric of his sweater. He felt his arm inside the sleeve, the soft cotton against his skin. I am not an animal, he thought. And for the first time in a long time, it felt like the truth.

He was assigned to a cell with Ranga and the newspaperman. There were three narrow metal beds—one bunk bed and a single—with gray blankets and white pillows. The walls were concrete.

They chose beds wordlessly, Mahindan climbing to the upper bunk and falling in sideways. His legs hummed with relief and exhaustion. He felt the soreness in his feet. His whole body gave way, abandoning itself completely to the bed. The door suctioned closed.

The cell was open at the top like the stall in a public toilet. Mahindan gazed at the pneumatic tubes over his bed until his vision grew unfocused. He heard the muffled sounds of the line trooping on, his roommates moving in their beds, the rustle of sheets, the joints of the bunk creaking. It was the creak of the ship, the rustle of palm fronds overhead. A coconut fell to the ground, and Mahindan was asleep.

————

The tent shook. Mahindan trembled. He opened his eyes and a hand was on the ball of his shoulder.

Some lawyers have come, Ranga said.

Mahindan sat up quickly. Sellian! There would be news. He and his roommates followed the guard. They walked single file, Mahindan at the end, behind a limping Ranga.

Mahindan tried to recall his dreams. He saw images that were more like vague feelings and was surprised to recognize some as pleasant. He recalled embroidered blue silk, deep purple threads, the feminine scent of sandalwood.

There was a sign overhead, black with red lettering. Mahindan examined the exotic characters, all squared off and linear. This was Canada—clean with straight lines. A promising country to make a new start.

He was sorry to have been assigned to a room with Ranga, this barnacle who had latched on from the first and refused to be shaken off. But surely this was temporary. Only for a little while, the nurse had said. Good thing was, the newspaperman spoke English. Mahindan could pick up some words from him. Learn English, get a job, find a small place to live.

Sellian was a bright boy. They would teach him English in school, and in the evenings they could practice together. Mahindan reached out instinctively, but there was no small hand to hold.

They were approaching a trio—a big white man and two ladies with dark skin. The lawyers. Hope buoyed his spirits. They would know about Sellian.

One of the ladies spoke. Her Tamil was fluent and unaccented. She was the interpreter, a member of the Tamil Alliance. There were thousands of Tamils in Canada, she told them. Hundreds of thousands. So many Tamils, they had their own organization to represent them. What luck, Mahindan thought. He would have taken a one-way ticket to anywhere, anywhere at all, just to get out of that godforsaken country, but now, to find they had come to a place so full of their own, this was good fortune indeed.

The interpreter explained that Canada had known about the ship and had been expecting them for weeks. Their arrival had been foretold. To Mahindan, it felt auspicious. A deity paving the way, all these unknown Tamils coming to their aid in a foreign land.

The newspaperman introduced himself as Prasad. This was all planned? he asked. With the people in Sri Lanka who arranged our passage?

No, she said. The government had seen the ship with its satellite systems.

For what do we need lawyers? Ranga asked. He sat apart from the group, angled to the door as if ready to bolt.

This is the thing, the interpreter said. As far as the law is concerned, you have no status. To stay here, you must first become a refugee, and this is a little complicated.

But we're refugees, no? Ranga asked. Otherwise, what else?

What did these people think? Mahindan wondered. They had got on a rickety ship and nearly killed themselves crossing the ocean for a holiday?

The interpreter said it was all very complex, to do with legal definitions and bureaucracy. But not to worry, because the Tamil Alliance had hired lawyers to sort everything out. Mahindan saw Prasad nodding and this made him feel a little better. Of course there would be forms to fill. The Canadians must have their own special procedures. Good thing they had lawyers to help them navigate the formalities.

The big man was in charge. Mahindan could tell by the comfortable way he sat, legs spread out. He had uncombed, wispy gray hair that stuck out in all directions and two days of stubble.

The other lawyer was younger, in her late twenties, he guessed. She sat upright and at attention, as if at any moment she might be called on to perform some complicated action. When they had first sat down, she had written something at the top of her pad and then kept her pen in her hand, poised with the point leaking a stain of ink on the paper. Mahindan was disappointed not to see familiar Tamil script.

He asked about Sellian, then watched the two ladies confer with each other, saw how their hand gestures matched the big man's, heard the way their voices sounded like those of the guards, the officers who had boarded the ship. They had dark skin and hair. The interpreter had a gold stud in the side of her right nostril. The lawyer wore the pendant of a thali close against her throat. They looked Tamil but carried themselves like Canadians.

This would be Sellian, Mahindan thought, a Tamil and also a Canadian. He would wear clothes like these and move through this world with ease, and Canada would be his country.

The women's prison is not far, the interpreter said. I will arrange a visit.

He doesn't like to be away from me, Mahindan said. He gets very scared.

He thought of Kumuran's wife, the hatred in her eyes. All those weeks on the ship, their boys sometimes playing together, and not once had they spoken. Would she avenge herself on his son, would she mistreat him?

This woman who is taking care of him, Mahindan said. She is a stranger to him.

He's being watched by a Mrs. Savitri Kumuran? the interpreter said.

Mahindan blinked and sat back. No, her name . . .

The interpreter conferred with the lawyers while Mahindan, bewildered, tried to square what he knew with what had been said.

Yes, the interpreter said. It is Mrs. Kumuran. Good news is, you both have the same lawyers. We are going to meet her next. Listen. This is not Sri Lanka. I promise you, the boy is safe. Already, he will have been given food and a wash. About your son, she said, bobbling her head from side to side, there is nothing to worry.

Something about the way she said this and the certainty on her face made him believe her. This is Canada, he thought. Never mind about the woman. I can trust Canada.

How long are we to stay in jail? Ranga asked, and his hand briefly rose to touch the scar on his cheek.

When Mr. Gigovaz answered in English, he addressed them all equally, speaking with hands and mouth, both.

The first step was to prove their identity. The government would inspect their documents. There were many forms to fill. There would be a review to decide if they could leave jail, then a hearing to determine if they could ask for refugee status. And then another hearing to see if they would be *given* refugee status. It was a process, and the process would take time. No one could say how long.

Can my son not stay here? Mahindan asked. He's still small . . . only six.

You must be patient, Mr. Gigovaz said. Women and children will be given priority.

It all sounded convoluted and exhausting. Mahindan could not understand the difference between one hearing and the next. The whole time they were running in Sri Lanka, then later in the detention camp, all of his efforts had been focused on staying alive and getting out. He had not given much thought to what would happen after the boat docked, had only a vague notion that they would disembark and be free to go on their way. Now, it seemed, arriving was just the beginning. His optimism dimmed at the prospect of another long journey ahead.

The interpreter must have sensed the deflation in the room. Try not to worry, she said. You have come to a good place. There is room for you here.

Race! Chithra yelled, and they rose off their seats, speeding down the dusty red lane. Mahindan slowed to veer around a dog and Chithra overtook him, the bells on her anklets tinkling.

The April sky was cerulean, the paddy fields lush and green. Elephants plodded in the distance.

Mahindan caught up with her at the reservoir. A herd of water buffalo cooled themselves in the shallows, plunked down among the weeds, water lapping at their flanks.

Aiyo! she said, panting and laughing. Nearly ran down someone's Ammachi!

Poodi visari, he teased. Nothing but trouble.

Mahindan loved their lazy Saturday ritual. Slow mornings in the shade with a cup of milky tea. Idli if the rice and lentil mixture had fermented overnight. Then the weekly trip to the market. Later, they would go to his parents' house for a big family lunch, where the women would cook while the men talked politics and told bawdy jokes. Bellies full, they would return home to nap away the hottest part of the day. For the rest of his life, the memory of those heavy-lidded afternoons, the whirr of the ceiling fan and the gauzy view through the mosquito net, would remind Mahindan of happiness, perfect contentment.

They cut through the playground behind the Hindu Girls' College, where two women were hanging a Welcome Back banner. Near the side entrance, a man pulled up a sign that had been staked into the ground, red with a forbidding skull and crossbones. It had been four years since the Tamil Tigers chased the Sri Lankan Army garrison out

of Kilinochchi, but their parting gifts—land mines and booby traps—
were still being removed.

Mahindan and Chithra parked their cycles on a side street and
went to the market on foot. Trishaws idled. Motorcycles with their
kickstands down waited for their owners. People bustled by with
their shopping and children, everyone hailing each other with relaxed
weekend cheer.

How machan?

Come later to the house. Boys are arranging a cricket match.

Meenakshi! I told you not to climb that thing!

The woman who ran the Internet café leaned against the back door
of her shop. She was ancient, her face pockmarked and lined from
years of betel chewing. She gnawed the areca nut wrapped in a betel
leaf, one cheek bulging out and her jaw working hard. When she
opened her mouth, Mahindan caught sight of her red-stained teeth
and the gaps between them.

How Internet Auntie? he said.

She pressed a finger into Chithra's midsection. No babas yet? She
turned to Mahindan, leering. Two years married already. You don't
know what to do?

Older the spinster, longer the nose, Chithra muttered when they
were out of earshot.

Mahindan and Chithra were the first in their circle to settle down
and marry, and they hadn't been in a rush for children, especially with
the political situation being so unstable. But ever since the truces in
December, and now with the February ceasefire, the subject was up for
discussion again.

The girls all wanted to have their babies together, and he could
think of nothing better than his children growing up surrounded by
a gaggle of cousins, every auntie another mother, every uncle another
father. Chithra wanted at least four, three boys and a girl. Must have a
good number, she said. To replace everyone who died.

The market was a ramshackle construction, shops and stalls in close
quarters, customers vying for attention, vendors doing their best to
keep up. Children and dogs milled between legs. Over the hullabaloo
came the sound of men making kothu, the rhythmic clack-clack of
their cleavers. Sarongs tied at their waists, they stood chopping roti

over hot plates, bellies on display, smoke billowing to mix with the sweat and flies, the fragrance of fried vegetables and chili peppers.

Mahindan could recall how the market had been during the army occupation. Unmarried and still living at home, he had accompanied his mother on her visits, ostensibly to carry the bags. Most stalls sat empty in those days. The few residents who hadn't fled darted in and out with their eyes to the ground as uniformed soldiers patrolled with their weapons. His mother always gripped his arm a little tighter whenever they passed one.

Now, the market burst at the seams, action and commerce spilling out onto side streets. Chickens stuffed in cages awaited their fate. Garlands hung from shop rafters. Chithra made a beeline toward the fish stalls and Mahindan got stuck behind a delivery boy. Hundreds of ripe bananas hung, still on their branches, from the bicycle he laboriously pushed through the crowd.

Chithra was examining the mackerel, pressing with two fingers to feel the consistency. Fish were laid across the sturdy wooden table, a line of shiny scales and bright black eyes. There were plastic buckets for anchovies and sardines.

The fisherman wore a sarong. His wife was big-made in a blue polyester sari. They handled the fish with their bare hands, holding out each yellow fin and large eye for the customer to sniff. The wife had a tub of prawns cradled against her hip like a child. With her free hand, she made change for a customer.

It's my turn, Chithra said, putting her elbow out to prevent a man from cutting ahead of her.

The man turned to Mahindan with reproach and he shrugged as if to say, What to do? while smothering a grin.

The fisherman laid Chithra's mackerel across the scale. Three hundred rupees.

No?! she exclaimed, inflecting her tone so it became a half question. So much?

But just see how fresh. The fisherman poked his thumb into the pink gills and flicked one cupped hand to the sky. This fellow was happily swimming only a few hours ago.

Chithra cocked her head and put a hand on one hip. Ah, but he's only a small-small fellow, she said. Can you not take two hundred?

Brown paper was pulled out. The fish got wrapped.

Two hundred, the fisherman said. How can I sell for so little?

I'm only a poor woman on a budget, Chithra said.

All are on a budget, he said. Two hundred and fifty.

She handed over the money before he could change his mind and the fisherman shook his head in amusement. Your little woman is very clever, he told Mahindan.

At the produce stall, Chithra said she wanted to make kool, a seafood broth. They picked out long beans, spinach, and manioc as well as carrots, bitter gourd, and a white-skinned eggplant. Chithra didn't like the peppers.

These are not so fresh, she told the woman.

Two for one, the woman agreed. Have you seen my eggs?

Mahindan was about to point out that they were out of eggs, but Chithra said quickly: We don't need eggs.

Only twenty rupees, the woman said.

They left, weighed down with their purchases, Chithra grinning about her eggs.

So happy to have a discount, he teased.

What discount? The eggplant was overpriced.

All around them, people played the game, batting prices back and forth, pointing out imagined flaws as leverage.

How can you ask so much?

Can you not go down a little?

Last price, sir. Last price.

They browsed the sweetshops, the air scented with rosewater and sugary syrup, and bypassed the butchers. The man who sold idols and oil lamps was doing a brisk business. Everyone is getting married, Chithra said.

At the dry goods, Mahindan scooped red rice from a two-foot tub. Chithra weighed palmyra-root flour. At the counter, the woman doled out their cashews and raisins.

Can you not do something? Chithra asked, and an extra handful of nuts was added without comment.

Mahindan was always vaguely embarrassed by these interactions. When Chithra truly got going—over a big-ticket item, she was really in her element—he would leave and turn circles outside. Chithra couldn't understand his squeamishness.

One Saturday early in the marriage, when Chithra was sick with a stomachache, he had gone to do the marketing alone. She was appalled when he returned. Eighty rupees for a kilo of rice! Three hundred for a kilo of oranges? How much for eggs? She slapped her palm to her forehead and wailed: Aiyo! You'll be cheated all your life. These catchers must be so happy to see you. Here comes the fool who was born yesterday.

What would it be like to live with set prices? This was a premise Mahindan was testing at his garage. The first thing he had done after taking over the business from his father was to post a rate list and announce he wouldn't haggle. His father thought it was madness, but a year into the experiment, Mahindan's customers had got used to the new pricing scheme.

Their last stop was the potter who sold his wares behind the market.

What do you think of this one? Chithra held up a water jug with a bulbous bottom and a long thin neck. It was orange terra-cotta with a geometric red design.

They would take it home and season it, filling the jug with boiling water that they immediately dumped out, repeating the ritual three times before filling it again with water they would drink.

Anything you like, Mahindan said.

Chithra was particular about small household purchases. She liked to own things that were similar but didn't actually match. The novelty of being the mistress of her home was still fresh.

They waited their turn behind a young woman who was buying a similar jug. The shopkeeper named a figure and she paid without complaint. He wrapped her purchase in newspaper as she complimented his work. The young woman had an uncertain accent. She wore jean shorts and a red T-shirt. Her hair was tied back in a ponytail. Australia, Mahindan guessed. Though he knew people were also returning from England and America. Canada too.

For so long, the country had held its collective breath and now, finally, since the Norwegian-brokered ceasefire, it seemed as though everyone had exhaled. Farmers were returning to their paddy fields, families pulling padlocks off abandoned houses. People who had migrated decades ago were sending their grown children back, flooding the Tamil north with their Western money.

A new town center was emerging by the highway. The hospital had been rebuilt. The post office and bus station were fully operational. Reconstruction and repair, all the work that had begun when the Tigers chased the army out four years earlier, was now happening in a new spirit of optimism.

Very popular today, the shopkeeper said when it was their turn. He wound newspaper and added, Three hundred rupees.

Hundred and fifty, Chithra said firmly. I'm not one of these foreigners.

Someone hailed them as they left the shop.

It's the bride and bridegroom! Chithra said.

Ruksala arrived in a cloud of eau de cologne, Rama at her side. The girls sniffed at each other's cheeks, right first, then left.

How machan? Mahindan clapped his cousin brother on the back. Everything is ready for Friday?

Rama bobbed his head. Yes, yes. Everything ready. Just came from Kumuran's shop. You know he has taken over from his father?

I heard something, Mahindan said.

Garlands, food, all that is arranged? Chithra asked. Musicians?

Ruksala linked arms with Chithra and they set off as a foursome, the girls ahead of the boys. Now nothing to do but relax, Ruksala said.

And what of the oil lamp, have you taken a decision? Chithra asked.

So, Mahindan said, draping his arm over his cousin's shoulders. Last week as a bachelor.

Last week, Rama agreed, his feet turning out slightly as he walked. Rama was one of those young men who could only profit from matrimony, from the respect he would gain when introducing his wife. As he had this thought, Mahindan wondered if that was how other people saw his own marriage.

Mahindan and Chithra loaded their shopping into the baskets and pushed their cycles beside them. They left the crowds of the town center and crossed the open plot of land behind the Amman kovil. It was a Dravidian-style temple with a tower like a pyramid, its facade covered with detailed engravings and three-dimensional sculptures. Like much of Kilinochchi, the temple was obscured by bamboo scaffolding. During the week, painters were hard at work bringing luster back to its statues.

You heard Shangam is back? Rama said.

Ah? Tigers sent him home? Mahindan said.

He's coming to the lake tonight.

On Saturday evenings, all the young people gathered at the lake to watch the sunset, bottles of home-brewed toddy passing hand to hand. Chelva would play his guitar and they'd sing old Beatles songs. Or Jeyanthi would bring her portable CD player and blast Tamil rap. Emboldened by the liquor, they would dance like devils until one of them, inevitably Rama, would trip and fall into the water while the girls screeched in faux despair.

Must settle Shangam down with a nice girl, Ruksala said. Now there is peace.

Depends for how long, Chithra said.

The sun shone through the trees, casting diagonal shadows over the ground. Monkeys hung by their tails, purloined fruit in their paws. A dog nosed through a pile of garbage.

A couple roared by on a motorcycle, both wearing helmets, and Chithra made a dismissive sound through her teeth. She thought it was madness, expatriates returning to an uncertain homeland.

Why should we lose all our best people to other countries? Ruksala said.

Chithra is only worried about prices going up at the market, Mahindan teased, trying to head off talk of war and peace at the pass.

But Rama was already saying: Negotiations will succeed. See what the Europeans have done for Kosovo.

Mahindan and Chithra exchanged a glance. Neither of them had any idea what was happening in Kosovo, or where exactly it was on a map. Mahindan raised his eyebrows as if to say, Now see what you've gone and started.

Wait and see, Rama said. This ceasefire is only the beginning.

For the past decade, the LTTE—Liberation Tigers of Tamil Eelam—had been running the north, Tamil Eelam in the making with Kilinochchi as its capital. Here, everyone spoke the same language and worshipped the same gods. Tamils had their own police force, banks, and businesses. The Tigers had built a bubble where the government's quotas and language laws, all the rules designed to disenfranchise the Tamil minority, had no power. Now all that was needed was for the Sinhalese to make it official—section off the island and let the Tamils have their own country.

The Sinhalese will never leave us alone, Chithra said. That's what these ones with their helmets and sunshades don't realize.

But Rama had faith in a compromise: self-government without separation. Tamil Eelam as an autonomous province within a united Sri Lanka. He said, Who do you think funds the government? Norway. Biggest donor country.

And now that Norway has brought both sides together, Ruksala added, the Sinhalese will *have* to give us something.

It was always like this: Rama and Ruksala, their arguments buttressed by world news and international pundits, versus Chithra's instinctual cynicism. Mahindan tried not to get involved with their debates. What would happen would happen. What was the point of them arguing? What effect could they possibly have?

The Sinhalese are snakes, Chithra said. Norway or no, they will find a way to slither out of negotiations. She glanced around, then added quietly: Or Prabhakaran will. I don't trust our buggers either.

War is not good for business, Rama said. Bad economics. The Norwegians will find a solution.

Ruksala had a different opinion: The Sinhalese are finished with war, I think. Now they have seen what our boys can do, they know better than to fight us.

I t was as if no one had known she was coming. Grace was shown to a windowless room the size of a broom closet. The place looked as though it had been vacated in a hurry by the previous occupant. The drawers of the filing cabinet gaped open, immodest, a few desultory folders hanging inside. There was a computer monitor and a keyboard but no mouse, all the cords unplugged and strewn about.

Your new office, Kelly from Human Resources announced, before glancing at her watch and scurrying to a meeting.

The front pocket of Grace's handbag hummed. A text from Fred Blair. *Good luck today. You'll be gr8.* Grace sent a smiley face back. *Thx. So far, so good.*

She crouched under the desk, hunting for an electrical outlet. A shabby office was not an ill omen. She would make this work.

The computer demanded a password. A ten-digit number was taped to the phone on the desk.

It was lunchtime in Ottawa and the guy who answered her call sounded as if he was chewing. Sorry, he said. We have no record of your employment with the Immigration and Refugee Board.

Grace Nakamura, she said, then spelled out all the letters. I'm a new adjudicator in the Vancouver office. It's my first day.

You need to fill out an H46, he said. H46, not H46A. Can you access the intranet?

Grace stared at the blank computer screen and the rectangular password box. Not without a password, she said.

Fill out the form, have your HR rep fax it to us, and we'll get you up and running in five to seven business days.

What am I supposed to do without a computer for a week?

Grace tried to remember if it had been like this when she'd first started working for Fred. But that had been twenty years ago, before intranets and e-mail.

H46A, she said, picking up a pen. There wasn't any paper. She wrote on her hand.

H46, the IT guy said.

Eventually, Kelly from HR returned for the ten-cent tour and to introduce her to the other adjudicators. Grace shook hands, knowing she had no hope of remembering their names. There was a lot of chatter about someone called Mitchell Hurst who had just come back from a year-long sabbatical.

Paternity leave? Grace asked.

Mitchell's kids are in university, Kelly said. No, he took a year off to work with the UNHCR.

It was 10 a.m. and Kelly had already pelted her with a dozen acronyms. Grace didn't ask what this one stood for.

Mitchell's into the aid work, Kelly said. I swear one of these days the Red Cross is going to poach him. And then he'll be off digging wells in Kenya. It'll be a shame, though. He's one of the best adjudicators we have.

When they passed by his empty office, Grace lingered for a moment. A dollar-store garland was strung across the doorway, Welcome Home spelled out in shiny, multicolored bubble letters. A backpack was slouched on the desk chair, a bicycle helmet on top. Grace had an urge to grab the upright stapler off his desk. She clasped her hands behind her back and caught up with Kelly.

Grace spent the rest of the morning listening to collegial voices in the hallway. A few times she heard Mitchell's deep bass, hale and friendly, saying, *Thanks, yeah, it's great to be back.* She was starved for company and longed to skip ahead eight weeks to the point where she would know everyone's name and be able to swap stories from the weekend.

She had expected someone would take her to lunch for her first day, but when one thirty arrived and no one had stopped by her office, she went to the deli across the street for a sandwich to go.

Grace had a horror of first days, long moments clutching a plastic bento box in a cafeteria doorway, searching the tables of cliques for an anonymous space to occupy. But the lunchroom was almost empty— half a dozen round tables and a solitary figure she didn't recognize with the newspaper laid out in front of him. There was a color photo of a ship and people being led off its gangplank, their faces shielded by large umbrellas. The headline screamed in a thunderous font: PM TAKES HARD LINE ON MIGRANTS.

You must be the infamous Mitchell Hurst, Grace said, scraping out the chair across from him.

He had close-cropped red hair, graying at the temples, and a face browned with freckles. He was frowning as he glanced up, digging his thumbnail into the skin of a tangerine. Infamous?

I've just . . . I've heard a lot about you, Grace said. Why had she said such a stupid thing?

She tried again: You've just come back. Digging wells in Kenya?

Wells in Kenya? His eyebrows shot up. Who told you that?

Idiot, she thought. Two for two.

Mitchell shook his head and stripped away orange peel. Bangkok, he said. Nowhere near Kenya. And refugees, not wells.

Right. With the . . . Grace tried to recall the letters.

The Office of the UN High Commissioner for Refugees, Mitchell said. I was a resettlement consultant. Nargis kept us busy.

Grace didn't dare ask why there were refugees in Thailand or who Nargis was. But Mitchell sniffed out her ignorance.

Cyclone Nargis? he said. Worst natural disaster in all of Myanmar's history?

Sure, she said. We heard about that here.

His expression called bullshit on her lie. He split the tangerine down the center, set the two halves on a paper towel, and then the newspaper had his full attention.

Grace unwrapped her sandwich. The prosciutto and pear, so inviting behind the glass case at the deli, was unappetizing to her now. He hadn't even asked her name. This was the guy the whole office was fawning over?

I'm Grace Nakamura, she said.

When he finally lifted his head, she stared him straight in the eyes.

But his expression was passive, as if he didn't notice or care about his rudeness.

I started today, she said.

I know. Another government appointment. Where were you before this—Border Services? Department of Justice?

Ministry of Transportation and Infrastructure, she said. I was the operations director.

Of course you were. He turned the page of the newspaper and went back to ignoring her.

Grace had a bag of grapes she had brought from home. She ate one, swallowing the seed, and wished she had stayed at the deli.

The lunchroom had a sink and a microwave and a narrow strip of counter space in between. There was a sign-up sheet for the social committee tacked to the message board and a schematic illustrating proper lifting technique. For a fleeting moment, she missed her old job, the competence she felt wielding the laser pointer at meetings, advising ministers on policy.

But then she remembered the call from Fred, how flattered she'd been when her old mentor—now elected to the federal government and in a cabinet post—offered her a new opportunity. And anyway, it was only temporary. After her three-year term was up here, she'd be on to bigger and better.

Mitchell folded his paper and set it aside. He leaned back in his chair and ate a segment of the tangerine, watching her, impassive. He wore a suit but seemed like the kind of person who was more at home in hiking boots and a Tilley hat. There were fine lines around his eyes and mouth. She guessed he was nearing fifty, only a few years older than her. But he wore the condescending air of someone more senior. Smug bastard, she thought. Even though she wasn't sure what he had to be smug about.

Mitchell popped another orange segment into his mouth and chewed in slow, methodic bites. Grace broke eye contact and looked over his shoulder. Someone had brought soup for lunch; the aroma of chowder still lingered. A sign on the fridge warned people that it was emptied on Friday nights. There were footsteps in the hallway, but none of them came to her rescue.

What about you? she asked finally. Have you been at the Immigration and Refugee Board long?

Nine years, he said.

And before that? She grinned and extended a peace offering: Wells in Kenya?

Immigration law, he said. For a decade. And before that, law school.

What brought you here? she asked.

My clients, he said. I saw how arbitrary the process was, how much depended on adjudicators, and how many were totally unqualified and unprepared for the job. *In my opinion.*

He added the last line in a tone she couldn't read—was it sarcastic?—then balled up a piece of tinfoil, the orange peel inside, and threw it overhand toward the other end of the room. It sailed into the garbage can. Perfect two-point shot.

Well, good luck, Grace Nakamura, Mitchell said, standing up. Every decision is someone else's game changer. Frankly, I slept better when I was a lawyer.

Grace twisted the cap off her bottle of Fresca. It didn't matter that she hadn't gone to law school. This job is about having good instincts, Fred had said. The rest can be learned. She had taken the test, like everyone else. She had a right to be here, just as much as Mitchell Hurst.

———

There was an adjudicators' meeting later in the afternoon. The chair was a very tall woman with a gravity-defying bouffant. I called this meeting to brief you on the Sri Lankan cargo ship, she said.

Five hundred and three migrants: 297 men, 181 women, 25 minors. All of them claiming asylum. By now, the whole country knew about the ship. It had been the main news item the day before, on the TV in the background while she and the kids watched the neighbors' fireworks and Steve hunted for the sparklers. But Grace knew more than what was being reported.

Fred had called her with a heads-up. The government had received intelligence, he said. Half the people on board had ties to the LTTE, the separatist group better known as the Tamil Tigers, who had been waging war against the Sri Lankan government for more than twenty years. Terrorists. Losers in an overseas war who had fled to Canada to lick their wounds and regroup.

Canada has a reputation for being a soft touch, Fred had said. We must disabuse the world of that notion. I'm counting on you, Grace. The whole country is counting on you.

Grace wondered why the chair didn't mention any of this—the intelligence reports, the Tamil Tigers' long history of international arms dealing, the charity fronts they used to launder money overseas, Fred's suspicions that they planned to use Canada as a home base to resume their fight.

This will occupy all of our time, the chair said. These cases take priority.

Grace wondered if she should speak up. There were seven other adjudicators in the meeting and they would all have an equal hand in making decisions about who would be allowed to stay and who would be deported.

Detention reviews begin on Monday, the chair said. Clear your desks.

Grace thought she heard *clear the decks*. She scanned the room. Everyone had their gazes turned to the chair except Mitchell, who was jotting something down in his notebook. He glanced up and she looked away. They had all been here longer than her, but surely she had a duty to say something if . . .

Research has compiled these National Documentation Packages, the chair said. She stood between two piles of slim blue binders, palms pressed flat on top of each stack. These should get you up to speed.

Grace took a binder and passed the stack on, relieved.

———

Grace twisted the key out of the ignition and stepped onto the driveway in her bare feet, pumps dangling off her fingers. Kumi stood in the doorway, a hand shading her eyes, frowning at the sun. For an instant, Grace brightened, thinking her mother had been waiting for her, eager to hear about the new job. She raised a hand to chest height and waved in greeting. How are you, Mom?

But when she reached the door, Kumi greeted her with: The box with the deeds and bank statements. Where is it?

In the front hall was a big fruit bowl where Kumi's lost belongings collected: reading glasses, watch, her MedicAlert bracelet, a hairbrush left in the fridge. Today there was nothing inside. She was having a good day.

The box had red packing tape, Kumi continued, trailing Grace inside and closing the door. I've been searching in the attic for the past half hour.

One morning several years ago, Kumi had peered into the mirror and not recognized her own face. The diagnosis was swift: Alzheimer's, stage two. After setting the toaster on fire in April, she'd finally agreed to give up her apartment and move in with Grace. The attic had inherited Kumi's old boxes—milk crates full of photo albums and steamer trunks of file folders, things that had been preserved and ignored for decades. Her mother would have taken a cursory survey of the piles, then heard Grace's car in the driveway and come down hands on hips.

It must be up there, Grace said, bending to pick up a pair of Steve's brogues tumbled over each other on the rug.

And do you know what your daughters have been doing all this time? Kumi followed Grace down the hallway. Playing games!

The girls were seated on the floor in the den, two feet away from the wall-mounted flat screen, gazing up like supplicants at an altar. On the TV, a two-dimensional man drove haphazardly down the streets of New York while a police officer aimed a gun at the car's tires. Each girl clutched a controller, thumbs jabbing at the buttons.

Meg's left shoulder jerked. No, no, no! she yelped. Idiot!

The policeman slammed back into a brick wall and blew apart in an explosion of red.

Oh! Brianne flicked her index finger at the screen. You got ow-ned!

Grace rapped her knuckles on the kitchen counter. Is this what the two of you have been doing all day?

Meg waggled the backs of her fingers in response. Brianne grunted. Neither turned around.

Grace could see the girls' ponytails and the bony knobs of vertebrae running identical lines down their backs. She draped her suit jacket over a chair. Come help me with dinner, she said.

Brianne hunched over and flicked the joystick with her left thumb. After, she said.

Which either meant after we're done with this game or five minutes after never.

They have nothing better to do? Kumi buzzed around Grace like an insistent fly.

On the island counter, a box of Cheerios had been left on its side. An empty milk carton stood beside it, spout open.

The cleaning service is coming tomorrow, Grace called into the den. Is your room tidy?

Meg screamed, YES!

Brianne said, Sweet.

Grace tied an apron around her back and wiped down the counter. She wasn't sure if either of those responses was meant for her.

Children need boundaries, Kumi said. And responsibility. You have to give them a useful—

What do you want with those old boxes? Grace asked, opening the fridge.

The ledgers and account books, Kumi said. I want to know what the business was worth.

Grace rummaged in the vegetable drawer. What business?

What do you mean, what business? The family business! Your grandparents' business!

Grace's grandparents had owned a laundromat before the war. Growing up, Grace took piano lessons from a woman in Gastown. Whenever they drove down Powell to get to her class, Kumi would point to a nondescript building and say, That was ours, before the government stole it. And Aiko, Grace's grandmother, would quietly tut, No, no. How good this country has been to us.

Crouched at the fridge, Grace peered up at her mother, half-hidden by the door. Gently, she said, The business is gone, Mom. Long ago.

Yes, yes, Kumi said. But the account books. We still have those.

We do?

Yes, of course, Kumi said. Big ledgers to record every transaction. We always had steady customers, not just Japanese, either. She paced as she spoke, crisscrossing the confined space so that Grace had to dance-step around her to reach the sink. Think what it could be worth if we sold the business today, Kumi said, touching her index finger to her thumb. And the value of the land! We owned that land. There are deeds to prove it.

Mom. Grace put her hands on her mother's shoulders. Be careful.

It was risky for Kumi to walk and talk at the same time, but often,

when she got worked up over something, she forgot to be careful.
Kumi frowned but came to a stop. She held the counter with one hand
and said, Happy?

Thank you. Grace turned to the sink. She wondered where this
sudden interest had sprung from. Her grandmother, when she was
alive, had never talked about the war or her life before it. And apart
from the occasional grumble on Powell Street, neither had her mother.

Grace spoke over the running water. What's the point? The land
belongs to someone else now.

There were craft breweries and coffee roasters on Powell Street,
trendy lofts and affordable-housing co-ops. No trace of the Japanese
community that had once thrived there.

It's the principle, Kumi said.

The TV powered down and the girls stomped in. Grace pointed to
the dishwasher and said, Unload, please. To her mother, she said, Leave
it alone. There's nothing to be gained.

She wondered if this was boredom. Alzheimer's had stolen all of
Kumi's favorite hobbies—crosswords, sudoku, knitting—and these
days the only plots she could follow were undemanding ones in
middle-grade novels.

Meg yanked down the door and the dishwasher released a gust
of hot, lemon-scented air. The twins had always been tiny things,
barely six pounds at birth and the smallest in their classes all through
elementary school. But the past six months had stretched them out.
They were tall now, with long white limbs that flailed about, newly
in possession of five extra inches they didn't yet know how to control.
They moved with infinite slowness between the dishwasher and the
cupboards, transferring one plate at a time, working their way through
the two racks as inefficiently as possible.

How was your day? Grace asked.

Fine.

Did you do anything? she asked. Or just sit in front of the TV?

We went out, Brianne said.

Where did you go?

I dunno, Brianne said. The park. Around the block. We went places.

What else did you get up to today?

Nothing, Meg said.

The conversation ground out and Grace wished she had just let the girls play their video game. This was how they were punishing her for forcing them to help.

Stand up straight, Grace said.

The girls were perpetually hunched. Over a computer, over a video game, over their own chests, as if protective of their organs.

Do you want to end up hunchbacks? Grace asked.

The girls bent double and began golomping around, their arms swinging low, purposely hitting each other. They made unintelligible grunting noises, moving around the small kitchen, kicking out their legs in exaggerated motions.

Stop fooling around! Grace snapped. Or we'll never eat.

Whatevskis. Meg straightened up and flipped back her hair.

Brianne let the cupboard door slam shut and Grace winced.

Kumi had been forced out of the kitchen proper and was now pacing by the dining table, traversing its length in quick strides then turning to retrace her steps, one hand skimming the chair backs.

Everything was kept quiet, Kumi said. They thought they were protecting us.

Can we talk about this later? Grace asked.

Kumi paused midstride. Later? There is no later. *Now* is the time to take stock of what was done to us.

Grace flinched at the word choice. *Done to us.*

Think of Obaachan, Grace said, invoking her grandmother's memory. She would not have wanted it.

They took everything from us. Our homes, our jobs, our dignity. Kumi pulled out a chair and sat on it sideways, shoulders slumping. Our childhoods.

Who took everything? Meg asked.

That's right, Kumi said. You girls should be a part of this too.

I don't think—

Part of what? Brianne asked, shutting the dishwasher.

Girls, Kumi said, standing. Come help me in the attic.

SIDESHOW

A young woman hailed Priya and Gigovaz as they entered the offices of the Immigration and Refugee Board. It was Charlika Jones, the Tamil Alliance interpreter whom they had met the week before at Esquimalt. She had shoulder-length hair and a gold stud pierced through her nose. Compact and plump with a forthright manner, she'd told them to call her Charlie, then announced: I kept my ex's name. That's about all he was good for.

Priya guessed they were the same age, give or take a few years. She recognized Charlie as someone both fluently Canadian and authentically Sri Lankan, one of those third-culture people who slipped in and out of identities like shoes. If Charlie went to Sri Lanka, people wouldn't greet her in English as they did Priya.

The building's lobby was an extravagant art deco affair with etched glass doors, marble walls, and polychrome terrazzo flooring in a sunburst pattern. It was the kind of place that had blown the budget on first impressions. The rooms where they conducted the detention hearings were sure to be claustrophobic and nondescript.

It was a quarter to ten and their clients were scheduled for their first detention reviews. The Tamil Alliance had given Gigovaz nine names at Esquimalt: five adults and four linked minors, their randomly assigned clients. Nine of the 503 asylum seekers who had the misfortune to arrive when the country was in a sour mood. Priya had listened to the morning news with her toast and coffee. Canada is a sovereign nation, Minister Blair had said. We will protect our borders from thugs and foreign criminals and those who seek to abuse our generosity.

They waited for the Correctional Services bus that was en route with their clients, Gigovaz with the *Globe and Mail* held to his face, Charlie sipping on a take-away coffee. Priya had nothing to occupy her hands and tried not to fidget while she brainstormed small talk.

Nice weekend? she said.

We had our annual general meeting on Saturday. Charlie rolled her eyes. Bunch of Lankans this-and-that-ing for five hours. But there was a good booze-up afterward.

Are you with the Tamil Alliance full-time?

No, no. I'm a free agent. I do jobs for them when they need it, sometimes for money, mostly not. My ASL work is what really pays the bills.

Sign language?

You know those conference interpreters? Charlie nodded proudly as if to say, Yeah, that's me. Then she added: The Tamil Alliance is a good group. You should come to the socials.

Priya demurred. Maybe. Work is pretty all-consuming right now.

In Priya's family, there had always been a tacit discouragement from fraternizing with other Sri Lankans. When Priya had mentioned her university's Tamil Students' Association in passing, her father had said, Don't get mixed up in all of that.

All of what? she asked.

Politics, he said darkly. We're here now. Stay out of it.

On the few occasions when the family went to temple, they left straight after puja and never lingered for the potluck. Priya's mother used to say Sri Lankans were petty. Everything is always a competition with those people, Ma complained. Whose husband makes more money. Whose child is a doctor. If you are happy, what do I care?

Instead, her parents had made friends with other immigrants—the Nowaks, the Dhaliwals, and the Wangs next door. And Priya was left with a vague distrust of other Sri Lankans. For years, they'd paid for an unlisted number. Her father's mysterious explanation: I don't want any trouble.

Priya and Charlie watched the main door, where a security guard stood checking IDs and riffling through bags. She saw a familiar face and realized it was a reporter from one of the local newscasts. He was shorter in person.

Charlie grumbled: The gutter press has access, but they won't let a not-for-profit community group bear witness.

Detention hearings were closed to the public. Charlie would have to wait in the lounge while Priya and Gigovaz took their clients in one by one. They'd have a different interpreter inside, a neutral third party appointed by the Immigration and Refugee Board.

Is this normal? Charlie asked. Imprisoning refugees?

Priya expected Gigovaz to reply. This was his specialty; she was just a tourist. But when he said nothing, pretending not to hear, she was forced to answer: This isn't really my area of expertise, but from what I understand, detention isn't the norm.

Then what are they playing at? Charlie asked. These people have literally fled a prison camp to come here. The men, at least, okay, are in a separate jail, but locking the women and children up with actual criminals! It's inhumane! How soon can you get them out?

Gigovaz got cagey whenever anyone asked for a timeline. You must be patient, he'd counseled their clients the week before. And to Priya: Usually, my cases are wrapped up in a few months. But when this many people come all at once? And the political will is against them?

How long? Priya had pressed.

Years, he'd admitted. It could be years. To which she'd thought, relieved, there was no way he expected her to stick it out for the rest of her internship. Surely, once their clients were released from detention, she'd be free too.

Now Priya told Charlie: If today's detention reviews go in our favor, they could be out by the end of the week.

Don't get your hopes up, Gigovaz said darkly, folding his newspaper and slapping it on his thigh.

Priya scowled before she remembered Charlie was watching. It was just like Gigovaz to give her an impossible test, then discredit her when she failed.

Here's how the process typically works, Gigovaz told Charlie, turning his back on Priya. Let's say you arrive at the airport as a refugee. First you need permission to make an asylum claim. That's called admissibility, and it's usually a rubber stamp. Usually. Unless you're a known criminal or you've been deported before, someone at the border—Immigration or Border Services—determines that, yes, you're eligible to seek asylum. That takes a few hours, maybe a few weeks, during which time people are usually given the benefit of the doubt and allowed to go free while their admissibility is reviewed.

The real hurdle, Gigovaz said, came months later, at the Refugee Board hearing. Two or three adjudicators grilling the claimant on every detail of their story. The Board made the final call.

On permanent residency, Charlie said, nodding her understanding.

Permanent residency. Gigovaz reached up and grasped the air tight in his hand. That's the brass ring.

Were you born here? Charlie asked, and when Priya nodded, Charlie said: We came when I was three. As immigrants. We were lucky. She addressed Gigovaz: You keep saying *usually*.

Gigovaz tugged on his ear and exhaled a long breath. Five hundred plus claimants and the government is hell-bent on deportation. We'll have to argue for admissibility, which is *not* the norm, no. And with so many detention reviews to get through, like the ones we have today, it'll be months before hearings on admissibility are even scheduled.

Does get-out-of-jail come first? Charlie asked.

Not necessarily, Gigovaz said. They could still be held in custody when admissibility hearings begin. It's not unheard of.

Detention reviews, the admissibility hearing, then the Refugee Board hearing: a long series of judgments, each an opportunity for failure and deportation. Priya was thinking of what Charlie had said. *We were lucky.* She felt an upswell of melancholy and for a split second was sorry for Gigovaz too, that wading through this legal morass was his job.

Gigovaz indicated the newspaper he'd been reading—Priya caught the words *illegal* and *ship* in the headline—and said: Pay attention to how this plays out in the press. Sovereignty? Blair will have instructed Border Services to press the issue of public safety and throw every specious argument in the book at us.

Gigovaz had Priya clipping all the news coverage, a task she hated. Beat reporters who knew nothing of the law, and worse was the online peanut gallery. Already, the sight of Fred Blair, the way he screwed up his eyes and glowered when he proclaimed *the line must be drawn somewhere,* made her fists clench. Two decades overseeing toll booths and now he fancied himself the authority on public safety.

But the Immigration and Refugee Board was independent. It was not the government. The IRB acted within the framework of the law, and its adjudicators were the ones who made the decisions. She wasn't ready to adopt Gigovaz's cynicism.

This whole thing has become a sideshow, Gigovaz said. Blair is going to drag it out for as long as possible.

Don't they realize how traumatic prison is? PTSD, depression . . . Charlie trailed off.

We'll put forward the psychological assessments as mitigating factors, Gigovaz said. But whether compassion plays any role in the adjudicators' judgments . . . that's anybody's guess.

Where will they stay when they get out? Priya asked.

Some have family here, mostly in Toronto, Charlie said, still frowning. We're trying to get in line for spots in boardinghouses. And there are volunteers who have offered their spare rooms and basement apartments. Refugees are eligible for a small stipend as well, but really, it's not enough to get by on, not in Vancouver.

Priya felt chastened by this, the goodwill and camaraderie of so many people willing to take strangers in, all because of a shared sense of, what . . . ethnicity? . . . diaspora?

Charlie motioned to the revolving glass door. Here they come.

The two women arrived first, in their matching outfits and numbered running shoes. Priya had met them at the prison in Burnaby the week before.

Savitri Kumuran was thirty-one, a widow with two dead children left behind in Sri Lanka and a six-year-old son. During her interview with Gigovaz, she had been calm and well-spoken, candid in her answers. She and her husband had run a jewelry store in Sri Lanka. At home, she'd said in a dreamy way. Back home.

But later, Gigovaz told Priya: That one's a depressive. If we don't get her out of there fast, she'll crack.

Today, Savitri's thick hair was gathered in a scrunchy at the nape of her neck and hung down her back in heavy, undulating waves. She was surprisingly light-skinned for a Tamil, with high cheekbones and a cleft chin, a natural stunner. Her hand rested at the base of her throat. Priya saw her blank, despondent expression and thought: This woman is two years older than me.

The second woman was Hema Sokolingham, who was thirty-eight and also a widow. Jittery and nervous during her interview, she'd avoided Gigovaz's eyes and addressed herself exclusively to Priya and Charlie. She had made the journey with her two teenaged daughters, who, as minors, were mercifully spared the reviews and hearings.

What about Hema? Priya had asked Gigovaz. What are her chances?

But Gigovaz had only shrugged and said, There's something she's not telling us.

Charlie leaned over and whispered: Do you see this? They're being led in chains like slaves!

Are the cuffs necessary? Gigovaz asked the guard.

Hema massaged her wrists as the restraints were removed. Thank you, she said very softly in English. Her hair hung in a long braid down her back; she had crooked teeth.

Charlie rubbed Hema's arm and asked in Tamil: Nalamaa? How are you?

The men followed: Prasad, Mahindan, and Ranga, all clean-shaven on Gigovaz's orders. A brown man with a beard begging for asylum? he'd said to Priya. Not on my watch.

All five refugees seemed slightly altered since the week before. Fresher and well rested, with clear eyes and trimmed, clean nails. Priya wondered if this wasn't a mistake. Would the adjudicators be more sympathetic if they saw the refugees as she had, filthy and shattered, disembarking at Esquimalt?

Prasad pumped their hands and spoke in English. Good morning, good morning. Very nice to see you.

The others hung back, craning their necks to peer at the soaring ceiling, scuffing the floor as if testing its quality.

Prasad was the only one unaffected by his surroundings. A journalist in Colombo, he had a degree and spoke fluent English. Gigovaz had already told Priya: He's our best bet. Our model migrant.

Office workers, absorbed in their smartphones and newspapers, skirted around them. Priya had a vision of them as a tour group with Gigovaz as their guide. Prasad bombarded him with questions. For how long had Canada known about the ship? Why hadn't they come out to meet them, sent help sooner?

Mahindan and Savitri broke off from the group, their heads close together. Mahindan appeared agitated, one restless hand twitching at his side, but Savitri only shrugged her shoulders and twisted her hopeless palms up. What was this about? Priya wondered. But then she remembered Savitri was taking care of Mahindan's son. Had a visit been arranged yet? She felt guilty for not keeping tabs on the situation, then immediately annoyed. It wasn't her job to be a social worker.

Ranga hobbled over and tapped Savitri on the shoulder, massaging his leg as he spoke. A greengrocer from a village in Mannar, he'd lost his livelihood after a midnight shell attack blasted his vegetable stand to smithereens. I came in the morning to find the place flattened, he'd told them. After that, what to do? My life was finished.

He's asking about what Mr. Gigovaz said the other day, Charlie said. About their identity documents.

We're not releasing your names to the Sri Lankan government, Priya said quickly. If you still have family at home, you don't need to worry about reprisals.

Ranga started to say something, but Gigovaz checked his watch and announced it was time to go. Mr. Mahindan, you're first. Ms. Jones will keep the rest of you company here.

As expected, the hearings room was dreary, a windowless box with fluorescent squares of light embedded into the polystyrene ceiling tiles. Four long tables had been arranged in a square, microphones affixed to each seat. It felt claustrophobic and subterranean, like the interior of someone's cramped basement.

As they entered, a gaggle of reporters turned to stare. It was a full house: the reporters, a stenographer, a sketch artist, and a white-blond man with a transparent mustache whom Gigovaz introduced as the interpreter. He sat adjacent to Mahindan with two hardcover dictionaries, a notebook, and a pen laid out in front of him, all set at right angles to the edges of the desk.

Gigovaz pointed out their adversary: That's Amarjit Singh, representing Border Services.

Border Services, the agency responsible for patrolling the perimeter, the country's official bouncers. Priya had buckled down the night before and committed all the players to memory.

A clock ticked lazily on the wall. They were just waiting for the adjudicator. There were eight in total, and who a claimant saw on any given day was the luck of the draw.

We've got a new one, Gigovaz said. Grace Nakamura.

Is that good or bad? Priya asked.

He frowned and muttered: Government appointment. Handpicked by Blair.

The reporters had surrendered their smartphones to a box beside the guard. All eyes were on Mahindan as they scribbled in their notepads. There was a publication ban on the claimants' names. In their articles, the reporters would have to be circumspect. *Dressed in a prison-issued green sweater and gray sweatpants, the migrant sat with his fists clenched in his lap.*

A door on the far side of the room opened and the adjudicator strode in. She wore a crisp pantsuit, her hair slicked back in a chignon. A guard followed in her wake, closed the door, and stood in front of it with his hands in his pockets.

Nakamura had the best seat in the house—a high-backed chair with padded armrests. She was small but commanded the room with the air of someone much larger. Even without an elevated bench, robes, or a gavel, there was a stern aura of judgment in her demeanor. But she was not a judge and this was not a court, Priya reminded herself. This was an administrative hearing. It existed in the fuzzy boundary between bureaucracy and the law.

Nakamura spoke into her microphone. This is a detention review for Mr. . . . She consulted her notes and with a small frown of concentration struggled out, Mr. Poon . . . am . . . ba . . . lam Ma . . . hindan. Let's begin with attendance.

The interpreter's name was Nigel Blacker. Nakamura asked him and Mahindan to confirm they understood each other and they exchanged a few words. When Blacker spoke, Priya was struck by the incongruity—the flawless Tamil coming out of this blond man's mouth. It was impossible to know what he and Mahindan were saying.

Back at Elliot, McFadden, and Lo, Joyce Lau would be shepherding the merger of Henley and SunEx. A week and a half earlier, Priya had been checking off the boxes for the regulatory approvals. Why was she here? Charlie had more right to be in this room than she did.

Nakamura said: We will begin with Ms. Singh, who is representing the Canada Border Services Agency.

Singh leaned forward and depressed the red button on her

microphone: The Minister of Public Safety is of the opinion that the claimant's identity has not been established.

Gigovaz waited until Blacker had translated, then said: My client has provided ample evidence of his identity—

Singh cut him off, addressing her rebuttal to Nakamura: Additionally, the Minister is concerned the migrant is a flight risk.

On what grounds? Gigovaz asked.

We have reason to believe the ship was part of a smuggling operation. If that's the case, everyone on board is in danger of being coerced to avoid future hearings.

Mahindan's eyes swiveled back and forth between Singh and Gigovaz, watching their body language and expressions, and then he listened carefully to Blacker's translations. His expression was by turns terrified, expectant, hopeful, and helpless.

Priya wanted to reach out and pat his arm as Charlie had done to Hema, but she didn't have the nerve. She watched the interpreter at work instead. Blacker indicated the person who had spoken, then altered his tone and mannerisms to reflect theirs. What was his story? This Viking of a man with his unaccented Tamil, his perfectly vibrating r's?

Gigovaz said: I request the Minister provide evidence of this smuggling claim. Otherwise, it is hearsay.

Photos taken on board have been submitted, Singh said. It's clear the vessel underwent extensive refurbishments. For example, it was equipped with sanitation systems to accommodate a long trip. All of this suggests a broader criminal enterprise.

Priya had reviewed the photos of the boat in the Evidentiary Package. She had seen the rusty toilet, an aluminum funnel elevated on a platform with a plastic footrest on either side, the whole crude contraption ringed in orange-brown rust and enclosed in a tiny closet.

Nakamura cut in. Five hundred people arrived on a retrofitted cargo ship. Who arranged for all of this, if not a smuggling ring?

With respect, Gigovaz said, that is all circumstantial. We must follow the best-evidence rule.

Nakamura scowled briefly and Priya squeezed her fingers together. What Gigovaz was saying made sense. Singh should not have introduced conjecture into the proceedings. There was something so informal and unseemly about this whole review.

Gigovaz cleared his throat and tried again. Instead of guessing what *might* be, let's consider the direct evidence. Mr. Mahindan has provided a birth certificate, a national Sri Lankan identity card, school certificates, and a marriage license, as well as the death certificate for his late wife. He is cooperating fully with the government's efforts to establish his identity.

Nakamura turned to Singh, neutral again. Have the migrant's documents been verified?

The legal back-and-forth progressed with infinite slowness, each person speaking only a couple of sentences at a time to allow for translation. While Blacker interpreted, everyone else murmured. The reporters, without the benefit of their recorders, scribbled in their notebooks. Clumped together on one side of the room, they reminded Priya of a jury.

The room was dry. The air conditioner hummed in the background. Priya watched Mahindan swallow. He opened and closed his mouth without speaking. She scrawled a quick note and pushed her legal pad toward Gigovaz. H_2O? Gigovaz wrote: *Water cooler, lobby.*

How's it going? Charlie asked when she saw Priya emerge.

She and the others had found seats in a little lounge area and were chatting amiably in Tamil. Priya was surprised to see them looking relaxed, almost happy. A bored prison guard stood nearby. I don't know, Priya said. Slow.

Watching opposing lawyers litigate, Priya usually had a sense of who was on top. But she had no barometer for reading these quasi-judicial meetings. What I know is mergers and acquisitions, she thought. What I don't know is any of this.

It was nearly eleven. Joyce would be ushering the executives into a conference room. There would be jugs of water, a coffee service brought in. Priya would have been there too, if she hadn't stared at Gigovaz at that stupid meeting. She'd be passing out booklets, sitting cross-legged at the edge of her seat, taking notes as Joyce presided over the marriage of the country's two largest pharmaceutical companies.

Are there many judges inside? Prasad asked.

Only one adjudicator, Priya said. It's not really a courtroom, just everyone sitting in a kind of square. It's a bit less intimidating.

Charlie reported all of this to the others while Priya bent over the water cooler. She filled two paper cups and held them up as she passed. Bring water, she said. It's really dry in there.

When she returned, Singh was speaking: We're investigating hundreds of cases. Naturally, the process of verifying identity is slower than usual.

Priya placed both cups in front of Mahindan. He gave her a grateful smile. She tried to pull back her chair as quietly as possible.

Mr. Mahindan is being held in a prison with restricted privileges, Gigovaz said. His six-year-old son is living among strangers. It is important to consider the psychological toll, on the child in particular, of separation and detention.

The claimant is a foreign national from a country where known terrorists have spent the past three decades waging a civil war, Singh said. The Minister is anxious we conduct our due diligence to protect the nation's sovereignty.

Sovereignty. That word again. Pitched high, like a dog whistle.

Nakamura held up a hand. Very well, I have made my decision. Mr. Gigovaz, I find your concerns premature. This man and his group only arrived last week. Some delay is to be expected. The migrant will remain in custody and we will review the case again in a week. Please bring in the next claimant.

Rama's Song

Chithra and Ruksala scheduled their ultrasounds on the same day so they could all take the morning off and have lunch together. Leftover string hoppers with egg curry and extra hot pol sambol, which they ate with their hands at Mahindan and Chithra's table, the ceiling fan ruffling their hair.

The LTTE have had it with the government, Ruksala said, coaxing an egg out of the curry pot.

The ceasefire had ended. The Tigers had left the negotiating table and even Rama thought it was for good. Their cousin Shangam had put his uniform back on and returned to service, but Prabhakaran, the LTTE's leader, said it wasn't enough. More fighters were needed. Every patriotic family was encouraged to send at least one.

They're building up to something, Rama said.

What? Chithra asked, pausing with the sambol bowl lifted.

But Mahindan gave a twitch of his head and Rama didn't answer. Instead, he complained about the replacement teachers at school. Untrained clowns who can barely add, fumbling their way through an algebra lesson, Rama said, tapping the tips of his gathered fingers on his empty plate.

Ruksala leaned over and tossed him another string hopper— a cobweb-shaped nest of rice-flour noodles. What use is education to the LTTE? she said. Sooner boys and girls leave school, sooner they can fight. Sin, no?

Half the science equipment is broken and cannot be repaired, Rama said.

As a reprisal for the Tigers leaving the negotiations, the government had enacted embargoes on LTTE-controlled areas, halting shipments at ports and vehicles at checkpoints to inspect every crate and car trunk. As a result, everything from milk to extension cords was in short supply.

Can't get anything down for the garage, Mahindan said, rotating the cupped palm of his left hand upward. Brake fluid, motor oil . . . nearly impossible!

Mahindan was benefiting from the diesel embargo, though. The price had doubled overnight and everyone wanted their engines converted to kerosene. Drivers blew a few drops of petrol in through a tube and, once ignited, their engines ran on the cheaper fuel. It was a foul-smelling operation for Mahindan but necessary money, especially with the baby coming.

And see the state of the hospital, Ruksala said, frowning. I'm thinking of calling a midwife to the house.

Chithra slapped the heel of her palm against her forehead. Don't tell me! Think what could happen.

Privately, Mahindan felt this wasn't a bad idea. Their appointment that morning had not inspired much confidence. Patients on stretchers left idling in corridors, half the maternity ward cordoned off with plastic sheeting. The renovations—funded by UNICEF and begun during the ceasefire—had been put on hold indefinitely when cement embargoes drove the price of a bag from 600 to 6,000 rupees.

They'd waited two hours for their appointment, only to be seen by a trainee nurse instead of the doctor. Last month, two obstetricians left, the nurse told them, tapping a weight across the scale with her finger. People—especially doctors who were paid by the government—had been defecting to Trincomalee and Batticaloa, Tamil-majority areas in the east where the LTTE's foothold was weaker and the army's MiGs didn't fly overhead.

Even after making it into the examination room, they'd had to wait for the ultrasound equipment. Chithra had sat shivering in her paper gown and Mahindan had seen the half-empty medicine cabinet behind her.

How many women before us just had their children at home? Ruksala asked, ripping a string hopper between her fingers and mixing in the curry. I am seriously considering.

Mahindan raised his brows at Rama, who just shrugged. He said:

Twenty doctors for a population of what? Hundred and fifty thousand? It's not enough.

Can't blame them for leaving, Chithra said, picking cardamom pods out of her curry. Sometimes I too think of going.

Where? Ruksala asked, a handful of food paused at her mouth.

I don't know, Chithra said. She rubbed her midsection absently with her free hand. She was barely three months pregnant but already had a habit of stroking her belly when she spoke of difficult things. With the baby . . . I don't . . . If only there was a safe place.

India? Rama said. You'll only get stuck in one of those camps.

Mahindan squeezed Chithra's shoulder. Her talk of leaving had begun around the time they learned she was pregnant.

No sense in going anywhere, Mahindan said. Here we have a house and jobs and our parents.

We'll bring our parents, Chithra said. She set her hand on her plate and leaned back in her chair.

Mahindan had his fingers tented over a little ball of string hopper and curry. We'll only become like these displaced people going here and there. Is this how you want to bring up our baby?

Trinco and Batti. Those are still Tamil areas, Chithra said.

Ruksala lifted the lid off the water jug and, holding its fragile neck, refilled their tin cups. Embargoes and shelling, she said. We've lived through the troubles before.

Difference is, there are children coming, Chithra said. With the ceasefire, I fooled myself into thinking . . . but now—

Now we have become our parents, Ruksala said. And in another twenty-five years, who knows? Our children may be having this same discussion.

Don't speak like that! Chithra slapped the table. Her lip trembled and she covered her eyes with one hand.

Hormones, Mahindan thought. Chithra, normally so stalwart, was fretful and teary in her pregnancy.

It's not so bad, Rama said quietly. Only one bomb, and no one has been hurt.

We are used to this, no? Mahindan added, rubbing Chithra's back. As long as the Tigers hold the area, there is nothing to worry.

Aiyo, sorry-men. Ruksala reached across the table.

Chithra sniffed and waved Ruksala's hand away. Mrs. Ramamoorthy at the office is saying they are recruiting men.

Construction workers, Mahindan reminded her. Jobless fellows who have nothing else to do.

Mahindan was annoyed at Chithra's boss. The silly woman was filling her head with unnecessary worries. All through the occupation, when the army's garrison held the town and Sinhalese soldiers patrolled the streets, Chithra used to walk past their leering gazes with her head held high, long plait swishing at her hips. Mahindan would cringe at her stories, how she'd once mouthed off to a soldier who was giving an old man a hard time, but Chithra always said: Can't live in fear.

He echoed her words back to her now. No use in fear, Chithra.

Better to stay here than live in the east, Ruksala added. One thing about the LTTE, they keep us safe. In Kilinochchi, you can go here and there, even alone at night, and not worry. But in the east, in government-controlled areas? She shuddered. Even in their own homes, women are getting attacked.

I don't know. Chithra's gaze wandered to a gecko upside-down on the ceiling. She pushed her chair back but didn't move her hand, lying flat, fingers together, on her empty plate.

Mahindan knew she was thinking back to their appointment, to the moment when the trainee nurse finally wheeled the ultrasound machine into the room only to have the power flicker off because there was no diesel for the generator.

These embargoes will kill us, Chithra said.

They rose from the table and went behind the house to wash their hands and rinse their mouths under the pump.

We've lived with embargoes before, Mahindan said. We'll survive them now. He shook his hands, flinging water droplets, and squinted at the sun.

Funny story about embargoes, Rama said, pushing his glasses up his nose as they returned to the table. I nearly got stuck on the Sinhalese side on the way back from Anuradhapura last week.

Mobility was another thing they'd lost when the ceasefire ended. Government land and LTTE-controlled territory were now divided by razor wire, a mile of no-man's-land in between. Anyone crossing from one side to the other had to clear both army and Tiger checkpoints.

And don't you know, Rama said, at six, fellows shut everything down and go home for the night. Had to speed on the A9, sweating the whole way. And not only time, petrol tank was nearly empty too. He gave a quick side-to-side nod of his head and continued: But managed to arrive at the barricade and naturally soldiers want to inspect the motorcycle, make sure I'm not sneaking in some embargoed this or that.

Chithra snorted.

Fellow put a gull look on me and took the batteries in my torch.

Mahindan choked on a bit of toffee. Don't tell me!

Rama wagged a finger, imitating the soldier: Don't want this falling into rebel hands.

What nonsense, Ruksala said. The Tigers are bringing in ammunitions and multibarrel rocket launchers from North Korea, never mind this meaningless embargo. Meanwhile these fools are worried about double-A batteries.

Rama chuckled. Fellow spoke half-decent Tamil, at least. First time I've heard a soldier even try.

Mahindan noticed the clock and said, Ah! Are we going to temple?

There was just enough time for a quick puja before Mahindan and Rama had to return to work. The girls, who had taken the full day off, said they wanted to stay in and nap. Later, they would have tea and devour old romance novels, reading the bawdy parts aloud for a laugh. Mahindan hoped an afternoon with her best friend would cheer Chithra up.

As they were cycling down the lane, Rama said: I didn't want to tell Ruksala, but a funny thing happened on our side also. The fellow saw my identification card and asked my profession. What subject did I teach, since how many years, in what school?

Mahindan frowned. He sometimes went through the checkpoints too, on the rare trips he made to meet distributors in the south. Are you worried? he asked.

Usually the Sinhalese ask the questions, but our people, once they see I'm Tamil, they just wave their hands and say, Go.

But they let you pass, no?

Yes, yes. I'm sure it is nothing. Don't tell Ruksala.

The Murugan kovil was a modest building with a covered

colonnade and a lovely sandstone tower, every inch of which was decorated with carvings and sculptures. To the left was a stand-alone bell tower under which the temple boy was braced with the rope. The huge brass bell was tolling as they cycled up, and they hurried to kick aside their shoes, strip off their shirts, and run their feet under the taps.

The interior was dim, heady with camphor smoke and sandalwood. Mahindan and Rama sat cross-legged on the floor in a circle with a dozen other bare-chested men around brass platters of fruit and flower garlands. The inner sanctum was devoted to Murugan, the temple's main deity. Enthroned, the god presided, beholding the devotees, while the priest intoned in Sanskrit. Mahindan folded his hands, closed his eyes, and settled in, letting the smoke and incense, the familiar rhythmic invocations, wash over him.

Ever since their wives had got pregnant, he and Rama had taken to coming to temple once or twice a week during their lunch breaks. Mahindan's prayers were always the same: a healthy pregnancy, easy delivery, a clever child. At night, before they fell asleep, Chithra would pull up her nightdress and Mahindan would put his mouth to her stomach and sing a silly made-up song. When Chithra laughed, he felt the vibrations through her belly and imagined their baby floating inside, hearing Amma's laugh from within and Appa's off-key crooning from without. You are loved, he told the baby each night. You are so loved.

It was incredible to think of the miracle Chithra's body was performing. Every day, hands and feet lengthening. Eyelashes, fingernails, all the tiny details blossoming into being.

Whom would the baby take after? Would it have its Ammachi's exuberant laugh? Nila Auntie's photographic memory? Whole evenings passed in happy speculation, hours at a time when they were so focused on their nascent family it was almost possible to forget the turmoil outside.

The priest was shaped like a barrel. His forehead was marked by three lines of white ash, a dot of yellow sandalwood, and red kumkum in the center, white stripes across his arms and wide chest. He balanced an oil lamp on a platter and moved the flame back and forth in front of Murugan, chanting mantras to coax the god to bring his holy power down and dwell in his statue. To his left, a temple boy banged a gong.

Mahindan was lulled into a trance. His lips barely moved, the verses so ingrained they intoned of their own volition. How many expectant fathers had come before him to recite these same prayers? He was filled with a deep sense of peace, taking his place in the ancient fraternity.

A safe delivery. A healthy baby. Requests his father too must have made, and his grandfather before him, at temples in Colombo. Places where his own child, if there was freedom, might also choose to worship one day. His greatest hope for the baby: a life uncircumscribed by war.

There was an old photograph of Mahindan's grandfather from when he was deputy head of the irrigation department. In the photograph, Appappa wore Western dress: a suit jacket and tie with heavy black-framed spectacles and slicked-back hair. In his day, the family had owned a bungalow in Colombo 7, had servants and matching cutlery. If not for the terror of '83, they might still be in the capital.

It wasn't that Mahindan wanted servants or a house in Colombo. Food tasted better when he ate with his hands. He loved his work, the simple way he and Chithra lived, the family they were creating. But he wanted their children to have more choices. Choices his grandfather had enjoyed before the Sinhalese got jealous and instituted quotas that stripped away Tamil rights.

The priest lowered his lamp and everyone, on their knees, bowed to the divine. Mahindan, face to the floor, prayed: Let these troubles end. Rising as the sacred fire was offered, he put his hands to the oil lamp, scooping the holy smoke in a swift motion and bringing it to his face and head. Inarticulate pleas circled in his mind. For my child. For my child.

The sacrament platter came around and Mahindan dipped his middle finger into the red kumkum paste, applied a dot to the center of his forehead, and smeared the rest against the side of his neck. After puja ended, the priest invited everyone to the back room for lunch.

Want to stay? Rama was always up for another meal. He checked his wristwatch and said, Still have a little time.

Mahindan touched the kumkum on his forehead absently. He felt restless, not fit for company.

Come, Rama said. Empty your mind.

They made a circle of the temple, palms pressed together and raised to their foreheads, bowing to each deity in its alcove. When they reached Ganesha, Rama stopped. He dropped his hands to his chest.

Ooooooommmmmm.

Rama had a beautiful voice. Deep and sonorous, it seemed to rise from the center of his being. Mahindan joined in and together they held the sacred syllable until it swelled to fill the space, mingling with the camphor and incense.

Ooooooommmmmm.

Mahindan's heart beat strong and steady. His body tingled, every chakra awakened, alert to the call.

Ooooooommmmmm.

Om. Oneness. Perfection. Everything. They held on to the note until their breath gave out and Mahindan felt the sound resonate, reaching the ears of each deity around the room, Lord Murugan in the inner sanctum.

Then Rama began to chant. Om Gam Ganapataye Namaha. His voice was steady, rich with certainty. The *gan* sound vibrated in the back of his throat. In another life, he might have been a Brahmin. Om Gam Ganapataye Namaha. Mahindan joined in and they traded off a call and answer, keeping time with their feet, every new om a slow exhalation that calmed his nerves.

Om Gam Ganapataye Namaha. As they chanted, Mahindan heard his voice expand, strengthen into certainty. Agitation dissipated. His mind was a still, clear pool. His body empty, a vessel for the holy sound. Om Gam Ganapataye Namaha. He was one with Rama, one with all creatures. The Divine.

They ended with three final oms. And when they were finished, Mahindan turned to his cousin and beamed.

Better? Rama asked.

You know, machan, Mahindan said, I always think of that as Rama's song.

Lord Ganesha's song, not mine, Rama said. Now stop your foolish talk. Must get back to work.

They took their time leaving, dallying in the sanctuary of the temple, all the gods watching over them. Rama sang a hymn from the Thiruvasagam under his breath. Mahindan felt a dreamy contentment as he pulled his shirt from his back pocket and slid his arms into the sleeves.

A long colonnade led out from the temple, the underside of its roof garlanded with orange blossoms that swung and released their scent in the breeze. Rama was singing the upbeat verses now, drumming out the rhythm on his trouser legs.

Come on, turtle, he called, sauntering down the colonnade with his feet turned out.

The temple bell clanged and Mahindan, still fiddling with his shirt buttons, glanced up. Rama stopped in his tracks. Parked opposite the temple was a tractor, a group of somber boys seated on the flatbed and two cadres in camouflage waiting with their guns.

Mahindan remained very still. The dark gloom of the temple was at his elbow. He thought how easy it would be to slink back inside. The cadres raised their hands as if in a friendly wave and Mahindan felt a sickening lurch when he recognized Arun. Mahindan could see they wouldn't come forward into the colonnade. But Rama could not remain a statue either.

The bell tolled again and he saw a teenager yanking the rope with both hands. He was not one of the ascetic, thin-limbed temple boys. His trousers were rolled up at the ankles; his shirt, unbuttoned, flapped open.

Rama, as if hypnotized, moved forward to the cadres. Guilt compelled Mahindan to follow, sharp pebbles digging into his bare heels. He and Rama had been in school with Arun, who even as a child had been an infamous bully, the kind of person war was made for. When the recruiters came, he was the first to sign up, hadn't even waited for school to finish.

Mr. Ramachandran, Sri Teacher, Arun called over the tolling bell. It had been years since they'd last seen him and in the interim he'd lost his left ear. We have brought an invitation, he said. On behalf of the Leader.

The boy under the bell tower giggled. Mahindan, halfway down the colonnade now, steps behind Rama, turned and saw his glassy eyes, his unsteady stance. He had relinquished the bell pull and had a cricket bat in his hands, pressed into the ground like a crutch.

Me? Rama's voice betrayed him, rising to a shrill. Mahindan could see the tremor in his back, the fragile, unprotected nape of his neck. But I am a . . . a . . . teacher . . . my students . . .

Any fool can teach math, Arun said. Tamil Eelam needs you for a higher cause.

A higher cause, the drunk boy cackled. He began walking toward Mahindan, swinging the bat.

In the back of the lorry, the captured boys stared straight ahead. Mahindan's vision blurred. His center of gravity wavered and he had to brace himself, feet planted. They were now out from under the colonnade, at the mercy of the unforgiving sun, the burning earth scorching their soles.

What is the matter with you, machan? Arun came forward and clapped Rama on the back. You're a teacher, no? Help us teach these Sinhalese buggers a lesson.

Mahindan watched, helpless, as his cousin was led away past their cycles, cast aside with their slippers under the cool shade of a palmyra tree.

The other cadre had been holding the rifle that was strapped around his neck. He dropped the gun and took Mahindan's arm.

You're a teacher also? he asked in a friendly way. He was older than Arun but didn't seem to resent not being in charge.

Mahindan felt himself being led forward. Rama's chanting still rang in his ears. *Om. Gam. Ganapataya. Namaha.*

Mahindan's legs began to shake. He could barely stammer out the word *No*. Then an idea came to him like a gift from God. A mechanic, he said. I . . . am a . . . Cars, buses, lorries . . . I . . .

His mouth was parched. He thought he might choke on his own words, and coughed instead.

I repair them . . . in my . . . my . . . (cough) . . . shop.

You know to convert an engine? Arun asked.

From diesel to kerosene? Relief flooded in, and with it came courage. Yes. I'm doing this for everyone these days. Engine, brakes, new tires . . . all, I can do.

He heard the words spilling from his mouth and hated himself.

Arun waved his accomplice away and Mahindan's arm dropped free. Praise God! He wanted to fall to his knees.

Let the mechanic fellow be, Arun said. He flung Rama so he stumbled toward the lorry. Get in! Get in!

Rama struggled to hoist himself onto the flatbed, pulling up halfway before his feet crashed to the ground. His legs buckled. Mahindan turned away, ashamed, and from the corner of his eye saw Arun give Rama a rough push up.

Tell Ruksala, Rama called, his voice breaking.

Mahindan couldn't meet his eyes. I will.

Where is your place? Arun asked, and Mahindan gave the directions, eager to be helpful. He tried not to stare at the puckered skin where Arun's ear should have been.

Useful to have a mechanic, Arun said, getting into the driver's seat. Reaching his hand out the window, he slapped the side of the door twice and called to the boy. Hurry up, idiot!

He started the engine. The boy leaned heavily on the bat and contemplated his feet.

Catch up on your own, then, Arun shouted.

The passenger door slammed shut and Rama raised a hand. Mahindan did the same and for a moment they held each other's gaze. Then the lorry drove off.

The drunk boy swayed and staggered forward. He looked young and terrified. Mahindan felt only his heart thumping relief. Their eyes met just as the boy opened his mouth and vomited.

The Nature of Things

Priya let herself into the family home, left her flip-flops on the mat, and cranked open a window. The house smelled like burned garlic and frying onions. Her father and Rat were in the living room, playing chess. Appa held the black bishop, squinting through his specs at the battered old game board as he considered his next move. A paper clip stood in for the white queen. Rat had laid it midboard to stare down a black knight.

Priya's father was a small man, five foot six with slender limbs and a basketball for a belly. When Ma was alive, she used to tease him about being five months pregnant. Twin tufts of wiry gray hair sprouted up around his bald spot. Priya pecked his cheek and said, Hello, Appa. She didn't know why, but she had started calling him this after Ma died. Before, he'd always been Dad.

Her elder brother was taller by several inches, darker skinned with close-cropped hair and a lanky, lazy frame. He had come straight from work and sat slouched in a recliner, tie slung across the armrest, legs spread apart.

Priyanke, he said.

She saluted him military-style. Linga*rat*nam.

At eleven, Rat had announced he wanted to be called Michael. I hate my name! Do you have any idea what they call me at school?

Ma had cried and Appa had grown sullen. But for his eighteenth birthday, they'd brought the paperwork home and made it official, though Priya still refused to call him anything but Rat.

A documentary played in the background on the TV: two monkeys in side-by-side cages interacted with an unseen experimenter whose blue-gloved hands moved in and out of the frame.

The Nature of Things? Priya asked.

Rat put a finger to his lips and scrutinized the chessboard.

The familiar voice of David Suzuki narrated: The capuchin monkeys trade a stone for a slice of cucumber. As long as they both get the same reward, they will happily make this trade over and over.

I saw your firm is involved with this illegal ship, Rat said.

Appa made an incoherent grumble, but when Priya glanced over, she saw Rat's castle take his bishop. Not illegal, Priya corrected. Arriving at the border and requesting asylum is completely legal. The government is throwing around a lot of false accusations to obfuscate the issue. She heard Gigovaz's words in her mouth—*obfuscate*—and stopped.

Rat raised his hands in mock surrender. Hey, I'm just repeating what they said on the news.

Yeah, and reporters just parrot every false claim the government makes, Priya said.

So what's the story, then, with these boat people? Rat asked. What's your firm doing?

Priya, her father said, without raising his head. Go help your uncle.

Uncle Romesh had lived with them for years—ever since he'd moved to Canada—an indulgent third parent, more affectionate than stern. Growing up, Priya had always felt a distance between her father and uncle, a coldness she couldn't understand. Once, after witnessing a sharp interaction, she'd asked, Don't you like Uncle? Appa had only said: Of course, of course. He's my brother.

But when Ma got sick, she had told Priya: Romesh must not leave.

Leave? Priya had asked, wondering if chemo was fogging her mother's mind. Where would Uncle possibly want to go?

Don't let your father send him away, Ma had said, pressing Priya's wrist. This is Romesh's home too.

But whatever clash Ma feared never came to pass. It was Uncle who kept the household running when she was sick. Afterward, he had allowed for a six-month mourning period and then instituted a schedule of activities. On Mondays, he and Appa played euchre at the Vietnamese community center. On Wednesdays, it was cricket with some Bangladeshi friends. They had become addicted to *The Young and the Restless,* which they taped on the TiVo and watched before bed every night. Loss had bound the brothers in a way that Ma, during her life, never could, and the distance Priya had intuited seemed to disappear.

Uncle Romesh was in the kitchen, wearing a sarong and a checked shirt, sleeves rolled up to his elbows. The counter was dusty with flour. There was an open bottle of coconut oil and a Pyrex measuring cup of water beside it. He was wrestling a hardened ball of dough, trying to roll it out flat, and listening to a call-in radio show.

Ma's cookery book lay open. Priya turned a page, timeworn and almost see-through, like onion skin. Her mother's precise writing decorated the margins. Her notes were in English, but the letters retained the rounded swirls of Tamil, more art than writing. Priya touched her fingers to the faded lead.

Gothamba roti? she said. Ambitious.

Uncle knocked the dough against the butcher-block cutting board. Impossible!

The radio host was opining on the G8 summit. Priya tried to ignore his grating voice as she came around to Uncle's side of the counter. Just buy it next time.

He put an arm around her shoulders and squeezed. How are you, darling? How is work?

My boss is a drunk, Priya said.

If Ma had been alive, she would have said, Chi, chi . . . don't speak like this. But Ma was gone and there was no one left to admonish her.

I thought you liked the boss. Uncle opened the cupboard door under the sink and threw the dough into the compost bin.

Priya took out the rice cooker and explained about Gigovaz and her new assignment. She measured basmati and poured the water from the measuring cup. Uncle spooned in a bit of turmeric and rolled a handful of cardamom, cloves, and curry leaves into a cheesecloth. Priya had taught him this trick. Ma used to throw all the spices straight into the rice and they would have to pick out the debris while they ate. Priya and Rat would whine over the effort, the unexpected bitterness of a cardamom pod when accidentally bitten. And Ma would scold them for complaining. Didn't they know there were children starving in Ethiopia?

Uncle had heard about the ship. Five hundred people! he said. Shook! And now they've put all the fellows in jail, isn't it? He lowered his voice and added, It's good they have you.

Why are we whispering? Priya asked, amused. Sometimes Uncle could be as superstitious as an old woman. The whole time Ma was sick, he'd refused to say the word *cancer*.

Just, he said, and nodded in the direction of the living room. Let them listen to their program.

My clients would be better off with someone who knew what they were doing, she said.

Gigovaz had lent her a copy of the refugee-law textbook and she'd been making slow, grudging progress. The unfairness of her new assignment gnawed away at her. The entire trajectory of her career blindsided by skin color.

All I've done so far is fill out forms, she said. Monkey work.

More and more, Priya got the feeling she was there for Gigovaz's benefit. He fancied himself a professor and liked to hear his own lectures. Priya noticed the pride he took in introducing her as *my law student*. The way he turned his impatient, fleshy hand was maddening. He still didn't know how to pronounce her name.

A caller on the radio was philosophizing. His accent had a buried South Asian undertone, all the *w*'s pronounced like *v*'s. Uncle turned on the tap and, in the conversation's pause, they heard the caller say: There are two ways of immigrating. There is the hard way that I took of getting higher education, learning English, and gaining work experience. And there is the easy way of becoming a terrorist and claiming refugee status.

Ah! Uncle flinched and pulled his hand out from under the water.

Lock and load would be my approach, the host agreed.

Priya turned the radio off. Why do you listen to this station?

From the living room, they heard Rat roar, gleeful.

Priya poked her head in, glad for a distraction. She didn't want to think about work anymore. On the screen, a monkey flung a slice of cucumber at the researcher, smacking the cage and rattling the bars in a fit of pique.

David Suzuki explained: Capuchin monkeys act out when they sense an unfair advantage. They're content with the cucumber until they see another monkey receive grapes.

Rat, still sniggering, paused the program and stood. What's for chups? he asked, rubbing his midsection and walking into the kitchen.

Priya punched him in the stomach. You got a little bun growing in there too?

The ceiling in the attic had sprung a leak. Grace held the ladder as Steve descended. He wore his tennis whites and a baseball cap.

It's the flashing again, he said, hopping off the last step. I knew those guys from Burnaby did a hack job.

Roofers are impossible, Grace said.

They carried the ladder to the garage and hung it horizontally across two nails.

We really need to get it fixed, Steve said. Some of the beams in the attic have begun to rot.

They returned to the house through the back door. The big family calendar was spread open on the kitchen counter. Grace flipped forward a couple of pages and said, Okay, I can't do this coming week, but the one after isn't bad. I could probably find an hour to duck out of the office.

Great. Steve took a glass from the cabinet.

And this week? she asked. If I find a roofer, could you make it work?

I can't do this week. Opening the freezer, he scooped a couple of ice cubes with his bare hand.

Grace noticed an appointment she had forgotten. The girls have their violin exams on Thursday afternoon, she said. And before Steve could reply, she added: It's your turn.

I'm in back-to-back meetings, he said. You know how these music things are. You have to get there early, even though they're always running late, and inevitably there's traffic. When it's all said and done, you've lost half the day.

I started this job a month ago, Grace said. How would it look, already asking for time off?

I've used all my personal days, Steve said, and poured lemonade into his glass.

Grace felt guilty. It was true she had been out of commission for the past few months arranging Kumi's move, and it had fallen to Steve to pick up the slack. But then he walked out of the kitchen as if the matter was settled and Grace was annoyed. What about the rest of it, she wanted to say. What about the away games when he was gone and she flew solo, all the times she had to leave work early or refused to stay late because even with Kumi on call, a substitute parent, the twins still needed their mother.

The doorbell rang and Grace closed the calendar. The girls could take the bus to their music exam and the roofer would have to wait. Let Steve put the buckets out the next time it rained.

Fred had his hand cupped to his ear when Grace opened the door. Courier them to my house, he said. I'll be there later.

Grace waved him in and signaled toward the back of the house. He followed, still talking on his phone.

The wiretaps and the warrant, he said. Yes, both.

They went out through the French doors, the stonework on the patio hot under Grace's bare feet. The afternoon sun was still high in the sky, casting a beneficent light over the expanse of green lawn with its neat riding-mower tracks. She opened the umbrella over the patio table for shade. Over the privet hedge, Grace could see the sloped roofs of neighboring houses, their brick chimneys and conical evergreens. In her own garden, the peonies in full bloom hung heavy from their stems.

A jug of lemonade stood sweating on the patio table. Grace poured out two glasses while Fred wrapped up his call. She was sorry her mother wasn't here, that she'd gone to the pool with the twins.

Kumi had been disappointed when Grace went to work for Fred. Administrative assistant, she'd said, making a face of distaste, when Grace came home, excited, with the job offer. You're going to bring this man his coffee and answer the phones? That's what you went to university for?

For all Grace's success, the promotions and raises, Kumi remained unimpressed. In her eyes, Grace had never risen past secretary. But if she saw Fred now, a cabinet minister here in her house, maybe then Kumi would understand the prestige of Grace's work.

Fred had last visited just after Christmas, before returning to Ottawa for the next session of Parliament. For weeks, Grace had caught him only in glimpses—commanding behind a podium or haranguing the Opposition in the House of Commons. In person, without his pinstripe armor and bow tie, he was shrunken, awkward in khakis and short sleeves.

Fred turned off his BlackBerry and laid it on the table. Sorry about that. He leaned over to peck Grace once on each cheek. She had always found this old-fashioned habit charming.

Still battling the godfather? Grace asked.

Eight people dead at the Prince Regent Hotel and he's filing a Charter challenge against extradition!

There had been a shootout in front of the city's premier hotel the weekend before. Rival drug gangs, and three tourists caught in the crossfire. The twins were at the beach when it happened, and Grace had spent a frightening couple of hours waiting by the phone. Steve, of course, thought she was overreacting.

They're at English Bay, he said. Nowhere near the shooting.

They could have changed their minds, Grace said. Who knows where our children are?

She'd perched on the edge of the coffee table, inches from the TV screen, trying to spot the girls in the flurry of activity.

They have no reason to be downtown, Steve had said, switching off the TV. Don't jump to conclusions.

Fred didn't think Grace was overreacting. Snakeheads, Triads, bikers, the Sikh gangs . . . if you only knew half of what I see in this job.

When we were kids, we'd play outside until the streetlights came on, she said.

This began when we started letting people in willy-nilly, Fred continued. Skilled workers and immigrants, that's one thing. But look at this menace, the *godfather*. Bastard ordered six executions and got a couple of innocents killed, Fred said. Now he wants to play the victim. Some bleeding heart at Immigration bought his story twenty years ago and we're left to pick up the pieces.

Fred squinted against the sun, pulled off his glasses, and dug in his breast pocket for a pair of aviators. Speaking of, how are things at the new job? Have you whipped them all into shape yet?

It's going well.

He shook his head. They're making a mockery of public safety over there. Things have to change. I expect you to set a new tone.

Grace saw her face reflected in Fred's sunglasses. Well, there's a learning curve. . . .

You always had a sharp mind.

But I'm cresting it. Grace pulled her shades off her head and down over her eyes. A month in and she still felt like an imposter. Team meetings were about information dissemination, not discussion. Requirement of nexus, real versus speculative risk—she was unequal to the legalese. But all her colleagues were so confident and independent, to ask for help would be to admit defeat.

I'm reading a law book, she said. It's been helpful.

Several of the adjudicators had the same text on refugee law on their shelves, so Grace had bought a copy too, but she was finding the reading hard going.

Fred waved his hand. You don't need any of that, he said. Trust your instincts. Precedent and case law—where has it got us? Smuggled-in convicts who are a continual headache for Public Safety.

Grace thought about the Prince Regent Hotel shooting, how the terror hadn't left her until the girls walked safely in the door.

Fred said: These people get a foot in the door, put down some roots, and then they're impossible to turf. Informants, wiretaps—if you only knew how much this Russian mobster is costing the taxpayer. But the police and Border Services—those are the true heroes. They are on the front lines every day.

The automatic sprinklers came on and Grace tuned out briefly to watch them under cover of her shades. Fred sometimes forgot he wasn't behind a microphone.

Fred had given Grace her first job. Twenty years earlier, before Steve, before the twins, there had been Fred trusting her with his calendar and his voice mail and then asking her opinion on white papers. When a position opened up for a policy analyst, he'd nudged her into the promotion. There were other, better candidates, Grace thought. But Fred told her: You don't need a master's to do this job. By the time Fred made the move from provincial to federal politics, Grace was the director of operations and his right hand.

And when she'd confessed boredom at Christmas, Fred offered a reprieve: a three-year term with the Immigration and Refugee Board. Think of it as a secondment, he said. A stepping stone to better things. There's an opening to fill and a backlog of cases. I can't think of anyone more suited.

Grace thought of Mitchell and what he'd have to say about her qualifications.

Do you know a Mitchell Hurst? she asked.

King of the bleeding hearts, Fred said. Has he given you trouble?

No, Grace said reflexively, and then wondered where the impulse to protect Mitchell had sprung from. He's been . . . fine. Everyone's very welcoming.

Hurst is one of the old guard, Fred said. The Liberals stuffed the place with his ilk, left-wingers who let *feelings* undermine common sense.

Fred wanted to talk about the ship. Trial by fire, he said. What did the *Vancouver Sun* call it?

Grace rolled her eyes. The "ship of dreams"?

Oh yes, those terrorists dream big.

On the other side of the hedge, someone cannonballed into a swimming pool. Two children shrieked, gleeful. On Friday, Grace had conducted a detention review for a man whose child was being held at the women's facility. His lawyer called the separation an undue hardship and Grace had felt a small twinge. But then she thought of all the times she had spent working late or away at conferences when the girls were small. These little absences were only short chapters in long parent-child histories. The man and his son had the rest of their lives together, and if their case was legitimate, they would spend it in Canada. Though when Grace contemplated the mechanics of the decision—how would she separate sincere testimony from tall tales? what were the criteria, apart from intuition?—her thoughts fragmented, flustered strands unfurling in all directions.

Fred tapped his index finger against the side of his glass in an allegro. The whole world is watching our every move, he said. This is just the tip of the iceberg.

What do you mean?

It's difficult to get good information out of these countries, but from what we can gather, it is certain there are more ships. Who knows how many more illegals. This is a test, Fred said. One false move on our part and we'll be inundated with freeloaders.

Grace imagined a fleet of rusting cargo ships floating in the Indian Ocean, all of them waiting on a signal. Five hundred and three people on a sixty-foot boat. Nothing was too outlandish. Alarm flooded her stomach and she willed it away by reminding herself that she hadn't made any mistakes. Not yet.

Fred said the real problem with the system was its porousness and Grace could identify with this. It's one big gray area, she said. The lack of IDs, for example. These people come without any papers and we're supposed to take them at their word? They could be anyone.

And you can't trust the ones with documents either, he said. There are good reasons to believe half the people on board are LTTE.

What do you mean?

There were things recovered from the ship. Identification documents. I'm sure Border Services will raise it at the hearings.

Really? Grace thought of the migrant with the young son. He had arrived with a raft of paperwork. She hadn't even considered it might all be fake.

These people are not who they say they are, Fred said. The LTTE are using civilians as cover to sneak in. Don't forget, these are the terrorists who invented suicide bombing. India tried to mediate a truce and how did the Tigers thank them? By blowing up Rajiv Gandhi. You can't put anything past them. If even one of them gets in . . .

Grace's mouth went dry. This was what she hadn't fully appreciated when she accepted the job. It wasn't just about sifting legitimate from illegitimate; the real and present danger was inadvertently letting a dangerous offender in.

Fred said, Bottom line: legitimate refugees should apply for status before they arrive, at the High Commission in their own country. Our families took the slow, legal route in. Why should others be allowed to skip the paperwork and cut to the front of the line?

New World

The television was a riot of noise and color—the announcer's voice sonorous over the hysteria, words spinning and flashing across the screen. The camera panned overhead like a drone as people in the seats screamed and clapped their hands.

Those who were chosen ran down the aisle, slapping outstretched palms, crying, hands on their heads or covering their faces. There were old women and young boys, black men, Asian girls, a man leaning on a cane, a young woman with a tie printed on her T-shirt. All of them wanting to win, each one hoping to beat the odds.

In the prison's recreation room, the dilapidated folding chairs were arranged in two banks in front of the television and every wobbly seat was taken. Sometimes there were arguments over what program to watch (Mahindan could never understand why; comedy show or tele-drama, it was all incomprehensible to most of them anyway, and half the time the television broke down midprogram), but this prize show was the uncontested favorite. Everyone hummed along with the familiar, synthesized tune.

Mahindan did not join them. He was hunched at a table in the back of the room, laboring over a series of hieroglyphics in an exercise book. The symbols were arranged left to right with space underneath where Mahindan was meant to re-create them. He was making slow and plodding progress.

What he was good at was taking apart the innards of vehicles, reducing a trishaw or motorcycle to its component parts before putting all the pieces back together. He stared at the enigmatic figure in front of him, separating and reassembling. Two identical semicircles joined to a vertical line. It was full of portent and meaning, all of it inaccessible.

He had taught Sellian to write just like this, the fat red pencil clutched between his small, clumsy fingers. Sellian was forever distracted. Mahindan would go away to answer the door or check on the rice and when he came back, Sellian would be doodling pictures in the margins.

Ai! Mahindan would yell, smacking the back of Sellian's head. Useless child!

Mahindan drew a shaky semicircle and tried to set thoughts of Sellian aside. It had been six long weeks since their separation and he found it unbearable to dwell on just how much he missed his son. This was nothing like sending the boy to school or packing him off to stay with relations for the night. In Kilinochchi, Mahindan had never worried about Sellian when they were apart. At home, he'd been grateful, relieved to have a break. But here, his inability to leave, to walk out the doors and go collect his son, stirred up every apprehension. Was the child well? Was he eating? How frequent were the nightmares? Had he wet the bed again?

Standing on the gangplank the month before, breathing the crisp, free air, he'd seen a new land stretched out at their feet, every opportunity theirs to earn. Now, Mahindan summoned that optimism once again. Sellian was not in any danger. And the best thing Mahindan could do was learn English.

The Tamil Alliance came regularly with supplies: exercise books, CDs, pencils, maps of the country. Mahindan and his roommates were learning the geography of Canada. They quizzed each other on the provinces, Mahindan closing his eyes and reciting while Prasad checked his progress. He could get as far east as Ontario. After that, all the names mushed up together. Nova Brunswick. New Prince Island.

They had a portable CD player on loan from the Tamil Alliance that they shared with the men in five other cells. Mahindan had fallen into a grudging coexistence with Ranga (what choice did he have?), and when it was their turn with the CD player, they sat on the bed, each with an earbud, sounding out the syllables of unfamiliar words.

At meals, they practiced their English by pointing to various compartments on the divided tray and stating what was inside. Bread, chicken, carrots. There were things that had no Tamil equivalent. Prasad said lasagna was Italian. *Lasagna*. Mahindan took it out for a test run, feeling the foreign sounds rattle against his teeth, working his tongue around the vowels.

Make your tongue flat, Prasad coached him. Lah. Lah. Lah.

One good thing about this place: it kept them well fed. Chicken and pork and eggs, more meat in a week than Mahindan was used to having in a month. He was bloated with constipation. He had asked for kadukkay powder and coconut water, but Prasad said they didn't have all those things here. He'd been given some tablets instead, but they weren't helpful.

The symbols had to be drawn between the lines. Mahindan placed the tip of the pencil on the blue rule and drew a straight edge up to the red, keeping his eye on the original the whole time, taking care not to press down on the lead too hard. After he was finished, he would rub out his work and give the book to Ranga.

On the television, a woman in an orange shirt came racing to the stage, arms flailing. Two doors slid back to reveal a silver car. A glamorous lady in a short blue dress walked around it, trailing her fingers against the sleek chrome and metal. The announcer said words Mahindan could not understand. The audience shrieked its approval. Rainbow chevrons lit up in a pattern of arrows. Mahindan blinked against the flashing lights. He could not take his eyes off the car.

How to work with this racket? Ranga stuck his fingers into his ears and closed his eyes, reciting numbers under his breath in English.

Beside him, Prasad, unfazed, set his novel on the table like a tent and reached for the Tamil–English dictionary.

A guard came to the doorway and called out something in English. Mahindan picked out three words. *Bus. Here. Now.* Every day, his store of vocabulary expanded.

The guard read five names from a list, dropping vowels and mangling up consonants. The men he called stood and picked their way to the aisle. Mahindan watched them leave, the combination of hope and fear on their faces. Even though it had been more than a month since they arrived, no one had left detention.

Best of luck, machan! a few people said.

Don't come back, someone called out.

No need for us to see your ugly faces again.

Every day, the same routine: breakfast, television, detention reviews. Later, when the men returned, shoulders hunched, there would be conciliatory murmurs, pats on the back. *What to do? Only try again next time.*

Some, like Ranga, were growing frustrated, but Mahindan had adopted the stoicism of his lawyers, confident all would work out in the end. Mr. Gigovaz had warned them—had he not?—from the very first day that they must be patient. What use was it to harp on about what had been lost in Sri Lanka, to pout and mutter about what little they had gained here? Mahindan was contemptuous of such lazy cynicism and prided himself on his positive attitude.

Whenever Ranga hissed derisively through his teeth and made some ungrateful complaint about *this country and their rules,* whenever he brooded on his old life in Mannar, the lost prosperity of his vegetable stand, Mahindan turned and walked away. He was forced to share a cell, even workbooks, with this man, but he refused to indulge his sulking.

Mahindan had already faced three different judges and failed all three detention reviews. From now on, there would be reviews only every thirty days, one bid for freedom per month. The first failure had come as a shock, the allegation that his identity was suspect. He had all his papers in order; what was the confusion? But Mr. Gigovaz had said not to worry. The government was being overly cautious. There were too many Tamils and not enough government workers to process them quickly.

You see? Mahindan had said to Ranga the day before, when another busload of men returned shaking their heads. No one is allowed to go. You aren't the only one.

Not that it helped. Ranga's expression only darkened. They'll keep us here forever, he said. They're no better than the Sinhalese.

How can you say such things? Mahindan had thrown up his hands. Have you forgotten how those devils made us suffer?

What was most difficult for Mahindan was feeling stalled. Every day he passed in this jail was another day he wasted fretting about Sellian instead of searching for a job.

Outside, a dismal rain spat halfheartedly against the window. In the exercise book, the next character was a single curve, like a crescent moon.

Mahindan missed working with his hands, letting his mind run free as he lay under a bus, fingers slippery with grease, inhaling the kerosene and rust. He missed doing the work he was good at— repairing brake lines, diagnosing faulty transmissions.

Hidden between the pages of the exercise book was a drawing Sellian had made in blue crayon—a cement block house with a palmyra tree in front and two stick figures, under which he had carefully spelled out in Tamil *Appa* and *Sellian*. He had labeled the picture *Home*.

Sellian would have taken over the garage if they had stayed in Kilinochchi. But now they were here, and when Mahindan saw professionals like Prasad and Charlika, people who wore suits and spoke in English, who were not frightened by the shower, he was proud to give his son a better legacy.

———

Sellian always ran to his father when he came for Saturday visits. Mahindan bent down and reached out as his son barreled into his arms. Each time was a relief, like exhaling a long-held breath, the moment when the small, familiar body made contact, Sellian sweet-smelling in his arms, holding on as if for dear life and panting hard into his chest.

Don't go, Sellian whispered. Don't go.

Where to go? Mahindan would say. Always, I am here.

Mahindan was happy to remain in the hug for as long as Sellian wanted, marveling at every change he noticed, every ounce of added weight, storing it up for later as a balm for his nerves when, alone, anxiety snuck in.

But Saturdays were also when Mahindan assigned Sellian his studies and checked his work from the week before.

You need to read and write in English if you are going to succeed in this country, Mahindan told him.

They sat across from each other at a square table in the visiting room. There were guards at the doors and a machine that belched out Coca-Cola in a plastic bottle when you fed it a coin. Sellian's eyes flicked to its polished red surface every few minutes as he swung his legs back and forth under the table.

It is easier to learn when you are young, Mahindan said.

Yes, Appa. Sellian stuck his hands under his thighs.

On the opposite side of the room, Prasad was deep in conversation with that man from the Tamil Alliance, Sam Nadarajah. They spoke English, a newspaper on the table between them. Nearby, Charlika was clumped with Ranga and a group of men, engaged in an earnest debate about cricket. She made a joke and Sellian smiled faintly.

Don't you want to be like Charlika Auntie one day? Mahindan asked. Successful professional with a Canadian passport?

Charlika Auntie has a car, Sellian said, perking up. A sports car.

And so? Don't you want a sports car one day?

It's red.

Come now, Mahindan said. Tell me your letters.

Sellian dutifully recited: A-B-C-D. Halfway through the list, he faltered. What is after *L*, Appa?

Mahindan didn't know. The unfamiliar sounds were a puzzle he could not assemble. Ah, so you've been playing the fool all week instead of studying, he said.

Mahindan wished he could supervise his son's work directly. He worried that Kumuran's wife was no use. Women were too soft, and anyway, Sellian was not her son. She wasn't mistreating him, at least. Whenever he asked, Does Auntie take care of you? Sellian only shrugged and said, She sleeps all the time.

Q, Sellian said. *L* . . . then *P* or *T*?

Mahindan folded his arms across his chest. I can't be telling you a hundred and one times. Revise properly this week.

Yes, Appa. Sellian slouched in his chair. His gaze traveled to the group with Charlika.

Six runs! Charlika said, slap-brushing her hands together at the punch line. Match over!

The group cracked up, heads thrown back, hands banging the table. Mahindan thought: Sellian would rather be with them. He tried to be kinder.

Okay, pillai. Tell me about this car.

I had to sit in a special seat in the back.

Like a big man with a driver?

Sellian grinned. Like Prabhakaran.

Mahindan startled at the mention of the LTTE leader's name. He scanned the area quickly. The guards were placid. The visiting room was full and their table was surrounded by groups of others, everyone talking loudly and gesturing.

Mahindan leaned closer and spoke quietly. Sellian, don't say this.

Why, Appa?

The Canadians, they don't like this kind of talk here.

Sellian's brow wrinkled in confusion. What kind of—

And no more Lions and Tigers, okay? You must not play this game with the other children.

But, Appa—

No, pillai. This is important. Listen, all of that . . . Tamil Eelam, the Tigers, Prabhakaran . . . that is all in the past now. We have left Sri Lanka and we must leave all of this behind. Put it out of your mind.

But how to do that?

Just don't think about it. Don't speak about it. And it will go. He twisted his wrist in the air to suggest things disappearing with ease.

Ganesha too?

Ganesha is okay. The gods brought us here. We cannot forget them.

But—

No. Sellian. A guard was staring at them now. His expression was grim. Mahindan grasped his son's arms. Now listen to me. We must make the Canadians happy or they will not let us stay here. Do you want to go back?

No, Appa. Sellian's lip trembled and Mahindan felt a piercing guilt. I don't want to go back, Sellian whimpered. Please, Appa . . .

Charlika and Ranga glanced over.

Mahindan quickly patted his son's head. Okay, okay. Don't cry. Be a good boy and no one will send you back.

⸻

In the recreation room, the television screen flickered, the image pleating like a sari and quivering for a moment before straightening out. The woman in the orange shirt ran on the spot and clapped her hands when she saw the car. She was wide on top and small on the bottom, a generous chest and stomach balanced on a paltry pair of legs. Mahindan did not understand what was being said, but the trajectory of the game was easy to follow. The man in charge carried a microphone. He had a big face and short-cropped hair. His eyes squinted out from behind thick glasses. Mahindan knew he was the boss because he was the only one in a suit. He presided over the competition with a detached boredom.

The boss thrust the microphone at the woman's mouth. She could have the car, but first she must say the correct combination of words. In the audience, everyone was screaming, on their feet holding up two fingers or four. The woman in the orange shirt wore a plaintive expression. When the camera came close, Mahindan saw she was breathing hard, chest and shoulders heaving with exertion. She looked confused and scared, overcome by the good fortune within her grasp and the bad luck hovering just behind it.

Prasad moved his lips silently as he read. Occasionally he would chuckle and raise his head, as if wanting to share a joke, but when Mahindan or Ranga raised expectant eyebrows, he shook his head and returned to his book. Mahindan watched him read, eyes narrowed with attention, while the woman in the orange shirt bit her lip and spoke into the microphone.

Prasad must have been very clever to have earned a spot at the university. And those fools had forced him to leave. Sometimes, when he thought of home, Mahindan was overcome with rage.

He had quizzed Sam Nadarajah, so he knew how schooling worked in Canada. Our people work hard, Sam had told him. And in this country they reward you. Tamil or Sinhalese, brown or white, only thing that matters is the grades. It is not like back home. One Tamil for every seven Sinhalese admitted into the university—it is not like that here.

Twenty years ago, Sam had come to Canada just like them, a refugee on a ship. And today, he owned a sari shop, sent his daughters to university, had even married again. I was a widower too, Sam confided. With two small girls. There were times I did not think I could survive.

Mahindan was astonished to learn his second wife was a white woman, but Sam had just chuckled and said, I told you, here we are all the same. I teach her to speak Tamil. She shows me how to roast turkey. Best of both worlds.

Mahindan held this image of Sam and his sari shop close, a vision of his own future. Once he and Sellian got out of detention, Mahindan would get a job. Cars were the same from one country to another. He could work changing tires or even pumping petrol. It did not matter what he did once he got out. His motto: Learn English, get a job, find a small place to live.

Mahindan compared the two letters on the page—the one in printed ink, bold and sure, and his shaky facsimile beneath. There were a lot of straight lines in English. The language looked the way it sounded, harsh and utilitarian. Mahindan tried to draw a letter without lifting his pencil off the paper. Letters were the first step, then words, then sentences. A-B-C. *Child, car, carrot.* Hello, my name is Mahindan. It is a nice day. It is a very nice day. *Good* was another word for *nice.* The opposite of *good* was *bad.* This was a *table* and that was a *chair* and they were now inside a *jail.* Some English words they already knew—*Internet, cellphone, television.*

On the television, the woman struggled with her answer. She bounced on the balls of her feet. The crowd in the audience cheered. They were on her side. They wanted her to win. Hundreds of people sitting and watching, all of them hoping for their names to be called, for a chance to run screaming to the stage, to make numbers materialize on a board, to have the boss pat their back and declare them the winner. Hundreds of people who wanted to stand where the woman in the orange shirt stood. Hundreds of contestants, but only one winner. It all came down to this. The woman in the orange shirt squeezed her fists at her side. The boss waved the microphone under her chin. She tugged on her shirt and licked her lips.

When I get out, I'm going to buy that car, someone said.

And that beauty to drive it, someone else added.

Everyone snickered.

Everything on Canadian television was like this car—polished and shiny. It made Mahindan wonder if he had ever owned a single new thing in his life. Whenever he thought of his house in Kilinochchi, he recalled the sand between his toes, the damp floors in the toilet, the tilted old commode. It was impossible to imagine the silver car onstage parked in front. These glossy, gleaming things belonged here, in this new world.

The woman in the orange shirt took a deep breath. Her arms shook with trepidation, with hope—how closely those things were connected. The host pointed to the car and said something. The audience chanted. The microphone was a black egg. The woman leaned toward it. Her voice turned up at the end—her answer a question. She spoke with her eyes closed. She could not bear to know. The camera jumped to the game board, to the last blank square. A number appeared. Bells, cheers, the woman running on the spot, then down on her knees, in thanks, a close-up of the car, the blue-dress lady waving serenely because none of this, the lights, the screams, the hopes dashed and realized, the up-swelling music, none of it had any power over her. She was not part of the competition. Or she had already won. And this was the ultimate prize, being onstage among all the beautiful things.

Don't Rock the Boat

T he twins were preening in front of the mirror in the foyer, each of them jostling for a better view. Brianne had on a pair of tiny white shorts that inched a little higher up the backs of her thighs every time she leaned forward. A tank top drooped off her shoulders, sagging over her flat chest. Meg was no better, in skintight leggings and a hot-pink T-shirt with a stretched-out neck that exposed the ball of one shoulder and a thin bra strap. They saw Grace's reflection, standing behind them, and turned.

Mumsie, Brianne said. I need new sandals.

You *want* new sandals, Grace corrected, moving to the console table to switch on the radio and peek into the fruit bowl. Inside was Kumi's MedicAlert bracelet, a single earring, and a manila envelope.

Grace shook out the envelope, sending a clutch of black-and-white photographs and faded documents showering into the fruit bowl. What's wrong with the shoes I bought you a couple of months ago? she asked.

These ones are different. Brianne held out a magazine. The top corner of a page had been folded down. Can I have a pair of Jesus sandals? Please?

The radio program broke for local news and weather and Grace turned up the volume. Today the big story was the turf war in the suburbs between the Somalis and Sikhs. One crime lord had kidnapped another one's daughter and was demanding a ransom. The girl was fifteen. Grace shuddered to think what was being done to her.

See? Grace told the girls. This is why I worry about you.

You and Dad aren't billionaires, Meg said, switching off the radio. No one cares about us.

Mumsie, the sandals, Brianne said.

Come and look at this. Grace plucked a photo from the fruit bowl and held it out to Meg.

Brianne paused for a moment, as if judging her odds, then came to join them, still holding the magazine.

The young men in the photo were arranged in two rows, the front group seated on a wooden bench, the others standing behind them. Bats, mitts, and balls lay on the grass at their feet. The word *Asahi* was scripted in black across their shirts.

Grace pointed to a player seated forward with his palms on his knees. Have I ever told you about my grandfather Hiro? He came here in 1924, the first one in our family.

She didn't tell them the rest. That Hiro had come from Hiroshima, that the family he'd left behind—parents, uncles, aunts, cousins, loved ones he had always planned to see again someday—later died or vanished in the wake of the bomb.

Instead, she said: Issei. It means first generation.

We know Issei, Brianne said, scornful.

Issei, Nisei, Sansei, Meg said. And we are Yonsei. Gran taught us.

Our great-grandfather was a baseball player? Brianne said. For reals?

For reals, Grace said. He used to pitch entire games without giving away a hit. Huge crowds would come to watch. Not just the Japanese—they had white fans too.

Meg, rummaging through the documents, had found her great-grandparents' marriage certificate. How come it says his first name was Matsumoto?

In Japan, family names are traditionally listed before given names, Grace said. When she got very old, your great-grandmother Aiko would sometimes forget and write her name in the wrong order.

Brianne found Hiro's ticket to Vancouver.

I didn't know this still existed, Grace said, running a finger over the embossed logo of the steamer company, the third-class ticket. If your great-grandfather hadn't gotten on that ship a century ago, none of us would be here.

She thought briefly of the Tamil ship, then pushed it away. This was different.

Who's she? Brianne held up a sepia photo of a teenager in a kimono, posed on a cushion, knees pointing one way, chin turned the other.

That's your great-grandmother Aiko, Grace said. See, you got her mouth. And the same face shape. You know, I think this might be the photo the matchmaker sent to Hiro.

Matchmaker!

When Canada opened up immigration to women, girls in Japan and boys in Canada exchanged photos through matchmakers.

What? That's so random, Meg said.

I dunno, Brianne said. I think it sounds exciting. A ship with a bunch of—how old was she? sixteen?—a bunch of girls all going on this big adventure.

Yup, that's how Aiko felt.

Grace could still remember the conversation she'd had with her grandmother, when she was Meg and Brianne's age.

I was eighteen, Aiko had said. I was ready for adventure! To go to Amerika!

America? Grace asked, thinking her grandmother had got on the wrong ship.

Amerika, Canada, Aiko said with a shrug. Same, same.

Meg was still skeptical. What if, like . . . the guy doesn't send his own picture?

Oh, there was some of that, Grace said. A girl on Aiko's ship refused to get off when she saw her fiancé.

The twins guffawed. Meg said, She peeped the dude and said no thanks?

But Hiro was an athlete, Brianne said, straightening her spine.

Oh, your great-grandfather was a catch, Grace said. But he wasn't an innocent. He had his picture taken in front of the Prince Regent Hotel.

Just imagine, Aiko had said, relaying the story to Grace. Me, a girl from Wakayama, expecting to be the mistress of a palace!

Instead, Hiro brought his new bride to the boardinghouse on Powell where he was renting a room. Aiko started her new job the next day, cleaning floors and washing chamber pots for the landlord.

Bait and switch, Brianne said. Lame!

That was how life was back then, Grace said. It was the same for all the Japanese. They were new and had to start from scratch and prove themselves. Hard work. There was nothing else for it.

It's almost one, Brianne said. We gotta bounce. When she stood, one strap of her tank top slid off her shoulder. Mom, what about the sandals?

Since we're discussing clothes, Grace said. Perhaps the pair of you would like to put some on. Leggings are not pants, she told Meg, then turned to Brianne and said: And if you think I'm letting you leave the house in that shirt . . . She raised the straps and folded them, lifting the neckline two inches. We can take this to the tailor if you like.

Mom! It's supposed to hang like this.

Then put something on over it.

Moooom!

Do you want these Jesus sandals or not?

I need a pair too, Meg said as the girls ran up the stairs.

Grace was left with the photo of her grandfather and the niggling feeling of having been tricked. She pondered the proud young man in his baseball uniform. What was he thinking as he awaited the flash? What future did he imagine?

The photo was dated: 1934. The same year Hiro and Aiko opened their laundromat. By 1937, they would have a daughter and a house; four years later, twin sons. And then came the internment in 1942, when the family was separated and Hiro was forced to haul rocks at a labor camp. Would they have taken it back if they could, returned to Japan, if they'd known what they would lose? The business, their dignity, home, and the place where they had built it?

They weren't released until war's end in 1945. And then given an impossible choice: move east of the Rockies or be repatriated to Japan. Grace's grandparents chose Ontario. Aiko went back to being a cleaning lady, working six to six at a Howard Johnson close to their one-bedroom apartment, while Hiro got a job at a gas station. He would stand at the bus stop at the end of every graveyard shift, fighting sleep and watching dawn break.

One winter night, a passing driver swerved on black ice. When Kumi told the story, she lingered on the sound of the phone, a shrill siren in the dark, waking up the household. Kumi remembered being left in charge of her younger brothers, having to pour their cereal and make up stories to distract them, while Aiko took a bus to the hospital. There was no money for taxis and she was too afraid of their white neighbors to ask for favors.

Grace heard her mother's tread on the stair and glanced up, half expecting to see a teenaged girl, groggy in her high-collared nightgown. Instead, she saw a woman in her seventies, wearing wide-legged pants patterned with bright yellow bumblebees. Kumi had always had an eccentric sense of style.

Are these pants mine? she asked. I found them in my closet.

You've had them for years, Grace said. But if you think they're . . . gaudy—

No, no, what do I care about fashion?

And just like that, Kumi was herself again, prickly and self-assured, negotiating the descent a step at a time, a cardboard box in her hands. More relics from the attic, Grace thought. Things best left alone.

I want to get a copy of the order-in-council, Kumi declared when she reached the bottom. She looked uncertainly at the box she was holding, as if seeing it for the first time.

Thanks. I'll take that, Grace said.

Kumi seemed relieved to pass over the load. She drew herself up, hand on the banister, and repeated: I want to read it for myself. The order that made us lose everything.

Speak to the government. Grace set down the box and dusted off her hands. Or the university archives.

I *am* speaking to the government, Kumi said. I'm speaking to you.

I don't work there anymore, Mom. I have a new job, remember?

Grace had never seen her mother like this. Kumi was on the warpath, writing to her cousins, combing through old political debates, ranting about evacuation orders and the War Measures Act. She'd fallen in with a group of Nisei, seventy-something pensioners with vague memories of the internment and strong opinions about redress, who met regularly to complain and agitate. Lately, Grace would come home to find her mother on her knees in the attic, headfirst in an old trunk, her wide behind torqued in midair. More often than not, the twins would be up there too, labeling boxes or studiously sorting through papers and photo albums. Grace was glad Kumi had the girls to watch out for her, but she didn't like them getting entangled with all these old ghosts. Aiko used to tell her: Focus on tomorrow. No point regretting yesterday.

We need to go to Slocan, Kumi said. Steve too. Let him see what was done to us.

There was a rancor in her mother's voice Grace had never heard before.

I thought you loved Slocan, Grace said. You told me it was like camp, being on an adventure.

Kumi sucked her teeth in. I was five, she said. What did I know?

We're ready! Brianne called.

The twins galloped down the stairs, taking the last step at a jump, one after the other. Meg wore a short jean skirt over her leggings. Brianne had put on a T-shirt. Grace decided to let the microshorts go.

Sunblock, she said, holding out the tube.

SPF 45! Meg said. Totes overkill.

You'll thank me when you don't get skin cancer.

The sunblock made an obscene noise when Meg squirted it out of the tube.

Where are you two lovelies off to? Steve appeared on the stairs, blond hair flopping in his face. Steve at forty-five still looked like a high school hockey star.

Main Street, Ambleside Park, Meg said.

Mind your old pa tagging along? He ran a hand through his hair. I need to pop in for a cut.

The twins lit up. Steve was the friendly golden retriever everyone loved unreservedly. Kumi watched the exchange, eyes flitting back and forth between the speakers, bewildered.

I can't just pick up and go on holiday with you, Grace told her mother. They really need me at work . . . it's just not a good time.

Holiday? Kumi said.

To Slocan, Grace said. I can't go to Slocan. And you know Steve's schedule.

Slocan, Kumi repeated, wondering. Everyone stopped what they were doing and remained silent while she mouthed to herself. Then she rallied and said: I'll take the girls, then. We'll go before school begins.

On your own? Grace hoped her mother wasn't going to start in on the driving again.

Yuki will take us, Kumi said, naming who Grace assumed must be one of her new friends.

Where are we going? Brianne asked.

No one's going anywhere, Grace said. She held out the MedicAlert bracelet to her mother and added, Please wear this.

Slocan, Kumi said, slipping the bracelet into her pocket. And New Denver. I've always wanted to see the Nikkei Memorial Center.

Cool beans, Meg said.

Grace eyed Steve, but he just shrugged. It's nice you girls are taking an interest in your family history.

The twins walked out with Kumi, each of them taking one of her arms so she'd be able to join in their chatter. Yuki was born in Slocan, Kumi said. Imagine, girls, what would it feel like to be born in an internment camp?

Mom! Grace called from the door. Put the bracelet on!

Steve slid his feet into a pair of boat shoes and slipped his wallet into his back pocket.

I don't understand, Grace said, returning the photos to their envelope. All these years, barely a peep about the past. And now, suddenly, this is her mission in life.

Grace had learned about the war in school. Among the glorious tales of Allied victory were oblique references to the distrust of the Japanese, their marginalization in the military. But when she had questioned Kumi, she said the topic was off-limits: It was a difficult time for your grandmother. Don't bother her about it now. Don't rock the boat.

Steve opened the closet and jiggled the pockets of a blazer in search of his keys. Your grandmother really never talked about any of it? Her life before the internment?

Once my grandparents got to Ontario, I think they just put their old life behind them and moved on. Mom talked about reparations a few years ago, when my grandmother was still alive, but Obaachan wasn't interested. Wergild—who wants that? Here's some blood money for your misery, now please stop whining. It's so easy to cut a check. But what does it solve?

There was a quiet dignity in the path her grandparents had chosen. The years Aiko had toiled cleaning other people's toilets, the overnights her grandfather had spent making change at a dimly lit gas station in Ontario. Grace was proud of their stoicism. They got on with the business of living.

Daaaaaaad!

Steve kissed her. I'm being summoned.

Grace said, I told the girls they could have new sandals.

Didn't they just—

I was brokering a peace agreement, Grace said. She pressed the
sunscreen to his chest.

All right, Mumsie.

Priya was at work for the third Saturday in a row. There was new evidence that Border Services had been hoarding. All week long, Priya had been leaving messages on Singh's voice mail. Finally, a CD marked Confidential had arrived by messenger, predictably at 5 p.m. on Friday.

This is the game, Gigovaz told her. We just have to play it.

Now he was sequestered in his office with the blinds down, poring over the CD's contents.

Five floors above them, Joyce Lau was putting in billable hours on a class-action lawsuit. Priya knew this because she'd run into Joyce while waiting for the elevator.

You're doing good work with Peter, Joyce had said. The round button for the twelfth floor lit up under her French-manicured nail. I told him he owes me.

What about me? Priya wondered. She reached for the seventh-floor button and said, The work is interesting.

This was the first time Priya had seen Joyce in weeks and she was conscious of the numbers above the door lighting up like an impatient countdown.

Refugee law is tougher than corporate, Joyce said. No question.

There was no elegant way to say it, and they were speeding toward the seventh floor. Priya made a running leap.

The thing is, she said, I'm still interested in corporate.

The elevator opened on a deserted expanse of gray desks and blank computer screens. Joyce reached out a hand to hold the doors back. Peter is smart and experienced, she said. Try to soak up as much as you can.

Priya spoke quickly: Corporate law has always been my end goal.

I haven't forgotten about you, Priya, Joyce said.

But Priya didn't buy it. Her internship was only nine months long and she'd already spent more than a third of it in the refugee wasteland. It was October and time was ticking on.

A text lit up on Priya's phone. Rat asking: *where r u?*

Today would have been her mother's sixtieth birthday and Priya was holding everyone up from going to temple. She could just imagine the sour expression on her father's face when Rat reported back that she was still at the office.

Since the summer, Priya had been avoiding direct mention of the boat in Appa's presence. Uncle often asked about her clients and how their cases were progressing, but in an unspoken pact they changed the subject whenever her father entered the room.

Priya had once tried to do a school project on Sri Lanka. It must have been in grade ten or eleven. Uncle was newly arrived and she had only the vaguest notion of the situation over there. But when she mentioned the idea of interviewing Uncle about the war, excited at the prospect of embarking on a genuinely interesting assignment, the certainty of an A, her father had said sharply: Why do you want to ask about all of that? Leave it alone. Stung, Priya had recoiled and her mother had said: Darling, there's a woman in my office from Yugoslavia. Why don't you speak with her? So Priya had done her project on Bosnia instead.

Now Priya sat spinning in her desk chair, trying to recall if Uncle had been present when she'd first brought it up. She was alone in the cube farm, waiting on Gigovaz. When it came to him, she was stuck in a perpetual game of hurry up and wait. What was he doing in there, knocking back a mickey?

Sometimes, on an afternoon when they didn't have hearings, he'd emerge from his office and Priya would see his eyes were squinty, unfocused. Once, she had walked in on him clipping his toenails, heel balanced on the lip of his garbage can. He wore a wedding band but had the uncared-for air of a man who lived alone. People told her things—clerks, admins, other interns. Usually in the bathroom or the copy room. No one of consequence was ever in the copy room.

Gigovaz's door opened and he waved her into his office. He was holding his Elliot, McFadden, and Lo LLP mug. There were rumors about that mug too.

What have you got? she asked. Priya hoped it was nothing so she could go.

Gigovaz lumbered to his desk and set the mug down like a paperweight on a stack of folders. He turned the monitor to face her. Tell me what you see.

There was an image on the computer screen, a rectangular yellow card with a black-and-white headshot in the middle and Tamil and Sinhalese script above it. A national identity card, jagged lines indicating it had been torn into quarters and reconstructed. The man in the photo was old and balding, with a broad nose and hooded eyes.

Who is this? she asked.

Gigovaz sat at the edge of his desk and moved the mouse. Another ID card popped, an old woman this time. He summoned a couple more images: birth certificates and marriage licenses, all with the same domed Sri Lankan crest crowned on top.

These were found on the ship, Gigovaz said. Documents for five people, none of them on board.

Priya peered at the screen. Are they forgeries?

Don't appear to be. And as far as we know, there were no casualties en route. It's funny, though. Someone went to the trouble of destroying these papers. Why leave them behind?

You're assuming it's nefarious, Priya said with a laugh. I once saw a woman toss a mango stone over her shoulder and bean the man walking behind her. Thwack! Right in the forehead. *Litterbug* takes on a new meaning in Sri Lanka.

She tapped her fingers one by one against her thumb, thinking. Singh was pushing the question of identity hard, and yet so many claimants—like Hema and Savitri—had arrived without a scrap of documentation. And now these mystery papers. What conclusion would Border Services jump to?

Singh is going to say these are LTTE members, Priya said. And that people have trashed the evidence of their old lives and adopted fake names to get in.

That was my first thought too, Gigovaz said as he positioned two image files side by side. And unfortunately, the woman here and this young boy . . . on a cursory glance, they could be Mrs. Kumuran and her son.

Savitri's eyes are totally different, and her kid's ears are not as droopy, Priya said. But sure, if you don't pay close attention. She put on a simpering voice: The Minister is of the opinion that all these brown people look exactly the same, which is to say, like terrorists.

We will protect the nation's sovereignty, Gigovaz added, squinting and glowering like Blair. We will not allow our refugee system to be hijacked by an army of terrorist clones.

His impression was spot-on and Priya laughed, delighted. But Gigovaz's grin, top teeth biting down on his lip, was so awkward and self-conscious that she quickly cleared her throat and gestured back to the computer screen.

There's another possibility, she said. These could be dead relatives, maybe with LTTE connections, and now people are scared to speak up.

Speaking of relatives. He opened another two image files side by side and said, These two gents have the same last name. Brothers maybe, or cousins.

Priya shook her head. Names are reversed in Tamil. Last names don't mean anything. Tamil boys get their fathers' last names as their first names.

So you and your brother have different last names?

No. But *we* are Canadian. Tamil men go by their second names like we go by our first ones. Here, I'll show you. She plucked an envelope from the recycling bin, took a pen from Gigovaz's desk, and wrote:

Poonambalam Mahindan
Mahindan Sellian

She pointed and said: Poonambalam was Mahindan's father's second name. Mahindan was just a name his parents liked. Like Peter or Priya. Mahindan's son is Mahindan Sellian.

All this time I've been calling him Mr. Mahindan, Gigovaz said.

Sorry. I thought you were being polite. Anyway, that's how people would refer to him. Many men abbreviate their first names. P. Mahindan. M. Sellian. In any case, names won't tell you much. You can't use them to trace family trees.

Do me a favor and give Amy Singh a call, Gigovaz said. No. Second thought. Write her an e-mail and explain all of this. Copy me.

Priya tossed the envelope back into the recycling bin. If there was even the slightest hint that one of their clients had faked his or her identity or helped someone else do the same, it would be game over. Even if their clients weren't involved, Singh would still use the uncertainty created by these ripped-up documents against them. To argue for extended detention if nothing else.

Border Services is working to track down these mystery people, Gigovaz said. In the meantime, we'll have to speak with our clients. And hope they're not lying if they claim ignorance.

Priya didn't relish the thought of putting this question to their clients. Already, they were restless, wondering why, after three and a half months, they were still stuck in jail.

But what is the problem? Mahindan had asked after failing yet another detention hearing. I gave all my papers. Why does the judge still keep me in this place?

Try to be patient, she had replied through Charlie, regurgitating Gigovaz's words. Your documents are legitimate. Eventually you'll be free.

Now, she asked Gigovaz: Why *is* it taking so long to verify everyone's paperwork?

I'm sure they're sending it all to Sri Lanka for corroboration, Gigovaz said. Each document one at a time. Nice and slow.

She imagined Singh in a basement mailroom sealing each birth certificate and marriage license in its own envelope. A thought jarred her.

But there's a ban on sharing our clients' names with the Sri Lankan government, she said.

Singh swears up and down they are honoring the embargo. He shrugged and shook his head. Frankly, I don't believe it, but suspicions aren't proof.

Priya puzzled over this injustice, overwhelmed by the odds their clients had already overcome, the hurdles still in their future. It irked her, the gulf between the letter of the law and how it was executed. How could a process so influenced by public opinion and politicking have the audacity to call itself law? You had to hand it to Gigovaz, though. His determination was heroic.

I've seen it all, Gigovaz said. Maybe you're too young to remember this. In the eighties, a group of Tamils washed up on the east coast. In lifeboats, if you can believe it, a hundred and fifty of them shivering in the Atlantic. Gigovaz waved his hands at his ears and said: Up went the hue and cry, all the usual nonsense about Canada being a soft touch and an *armada* of criminals just waiting to set sail. But guess what? Every single one was allowed to stay. As it happens, you've met one of them.

Sam?

Gigovaz nodded. Mulroney was prime minister, he said. And make no mistake, there was public pressure to send them all back, but I'll never forget what Mulroney said. *Canada is not in the business of turning refugees away. If we err, let it be on the side of compassion.* The crowd we have in power now, to them this boat is an opportunity. My clients from Eritrea, Iraq, Afghanistan, even—they aren't subject to such intense scrutiny or government intervention. But with our Tamils, well, you can bet Singh has been instructed to be as punitive as possible and delay every step.

Gigovaz paced, on a roll now. Look at Mahindan's file. Look at Prasad's. Proof of identity is ironclad, and Border Services knows it. But they also know that by killing time, letting people rot in jail for as long as possible, they are sending a message. Joe Public is tricked into thinking he's being protected. Eventually, Border Services will have to concede that, yes, these men are who they say they are. And then they'll harp on some other baseless reason to reject their claims.

Okay, that's Border Services, she said. But the Immigration and Refugee Board has no excuse. They're supposed to be neutral. I don't understand why they don't cut through the games.

What have I been telling you? Gigovaz yelled.

Priya flinched.

Gigovaz threw up his hands. His face flamed red. Half those adjudicators are patronage appointments. Do you think they've studied the Act? Done their due diligence? Or do you think they just let Blair drip his poison in their ears? *Illegals. Snakeheads. Terrorists.* You scare people stupid and then you pull their strings.

Gigovaz danced around like a marionette, lifting his knees and dangling his arms at the elbows. It would have been funny if his face wasn't deadly serious.

Meanwhile, innocent people rot in jail, he said. And what is this doing to their psyches? But never mind that. Blair and the prime minister have to court the law-and-order vote.

He stormed out of his office muttering, leaving Priya alone. And then she was outraged too. She started to follow him but stopped in the doorway, watching as Gigovaz wound between the cubicles, now halfway to the kitchenette. She wanted to scream at his back: This is not my area of expertise!

What he needed was someone who understood refugee law inside out and could intuit the political machinations buried between the lines. So what was she doing here?

What Do They Know?

When they asked about the documents, Mahindan said he knew nothing. The clock on the wall ticked. The ceiling vent exhaled an ambient hum. Mahindan sifted through the photographs they had spread out in front of him—four full-color eight-by-tens with glossy white borders. He kept his eyes trained on the table, focusing on the margins between the photos. He saw the flecks of dust, the smudged fingerprints of all the people who had gathered here before them.

He faced Charlika and Priya and said, I don't know anything about this.

They had come without Mr. Gigovaz. Maybe he had more important things to do and had sent them to take care of the small details. Or maybe they thought Mahindan would speak more freely without him in the room.

Listen, Priya said. This business about identity is serious. Border Services is looking for any excuse to deport you.

Deport me? Mahindan repeated when Charlika translated.

Priya waved her hands. Any of you. *All* of you. They just need *one* excuse, she said, holding up her index finger. If any of these documents they've found can bring your identity, or anyone else's, into question, you have to let us know.

Mahindan had known deportation was a possibility, but he'd been led to believe—or had he allowed himself to believe?—it was a risk so remote it was safe to ignore. He cast around for assurance and his identification papers came back to him. School certificates, driving license, birth certificates—the neat bundle he had handed over at the dock. He breathed a little easier, knowing there was no reason for anyone to doubt who he was.

Mahindan, Charlika said. Your lawyers are on your side. Whatever you tell them, they have to keep secret. It is the law.

Priya picked up one photograph and held it under his nose. He could not avert his eyes.

Do you know this woman? Charlika asked.

The woman pictured on the identity card was elderly, with a dimpled face—a grandmother, someone's Ammachi. In the photograph, she wore a dramatic red pottu, like a third eye, in the middle of her forehead. *Ramanan Mahadevi.* He had not known her name.

Sri Lanka came back to him: shell-shocked cows on the side of the road, their ribs prominent under emaciated flanks; clouds of dust that puffed up underfoot; the bodies they passed without looking.

Sweat trickled down Mahindan's temple. The sun, unrepentant, roasted his head. Sellian hung heavy on his back, heels digging into Mahindan's waist, thin arms clasped tight around his neck. A slow procession of vehicles and livestock and people, all of them limping east on the A35.

People pushed barrows, children and the elderly seated inside, surrounded by clothes and cooking pots and burlap sacks of rice. A toothless man, his palms lifted in prayer at the center of his forehead. *Why has God done this to us?*

Outside the meeting room, two guards with loud voices walked by. Their words floated in and Mahindan caught two of them. *Weak, yes.* Priya and Charlika watched him, waiting patiently for an answer, expectation etched in the rise of their brows.

Priya put another photo in front of him: the driving license that should have belonged to Kumuran's wife. What had that silly woman been thinking?

Charlika said: Just tell us the truth.

Mahindan stared at a spot in the middle of the room until everything receded into a blur. A sapling pushed out through the latticed window of an abandoned building, its bushy leaves impervious to the crumbling plaster, the facade pockmarked by bullet holes. The war still raging and nature already reclaiming her landscape.

We knew when the bombs were coming, Mahindan said. He raised a hand and brought it down from overhead, doing a pitch-perfect imitation of the high whine of incoming artillery. Both Priya and Charlika winced. When we heard the noise, he said, everyone took cover. There were ditches along the side of the road and we jumped in. Or just stayed in a doorway. Sometimes there was nowhere to go and people waited under trees like animals.

He remembered the couple on the road, two men with their arms around each other. A bicycle on its side, handlebars mangled. Their duffle bag had been blasted open, all its contents entrailing out in a tangle, a wild dog nosing around. Close your eyes, Mahindan told Sellian, then shooed the dog away with a stick. It was better to come upon a place where the bombs had already fallen. Death had taken its due and moved on.

All the time, we were passing bodies, Mahindan told Charlika and Priya. I tried not to get close, to just go around. But there was one woman, old, under a tree.

She lay fetal in the shade, ending life in the same position she had begun it. The blast had blown up her sari, exposing her bare legs, brown skin wrinkled and puckered, the knobs of her dusty knees, a change purse tucked into the waistband of her underskirt. Her eyes were still open. A better man would have closed them.

It was indecent, Mahindan said in Tamil, and when Priya looked away, he could see she had understood.

Mahindan collected the photographs into a pile and turned them all facedown. I do not know these people, he said. That is the truth.

A guard took him back to his cell. It was late morning and the hallway was a line of open doors. Mahindan, walking a little ahead of the guard, caught glimpses of men inside their cells dealing cards, speaking quietly, or lying on their bunks and staring blindly at the ceiling. They had been in this country nearly four months. As time went on, more men were growing lethargic, giving in to despair.

The night terrors—which had died down on the boat as they sailed farther away from Sri Lanka—had recently revived, so commonplace again they no longer sent the guards sprinting. Men screamed in their sleep, reliving old horrors. Names were shouted, or just the word *No*, indecipherable lamentations. It was a terrifying alarm to wake up to, and every time it happened in their wing, he sat up straight in the darkness, blood pounding in his ears.

Mahindan heard the tap-tap of the guard's shoes, the squeak of his own rubber soles against the linoleum. They passed under a flickering fluorescent tube and he rubbed his eyes. He was still thinking of the A35, of coconut fronds that hung exhausted in arid fields, bus tires puffing up dust in their wake. How his mouth was always dry, teeth mossy, tongue gritty. What he had not told them: dogs were not the only scavengers.

In their cell, Prasad sat on his bed, a running shoe between his knees. He had the tongue pressed in and was threading the lace, pulling it through the holes like a woman darning a shirt. He paused, lace held in the air, when Mahindan came in.

There are some documents, Mahindan said in Tamil. The lawyers are asking questions.

Documents? Ranga asked, his voice rising. He was at the sink with his back to them, facing the mirror and rubbing his wet hair with a towel.

It was nearly the lunch hour, but Ranga no longer woke up to take breakfast with them. Increasingly, he spent more of his time sleeping, lingering in bed in the mornings and always the first one back to their cell at night. Hope was a dangerous thing to lose.

Mahindan turned toward Prasad and said, Identity cards, driving licenses, and things like this. They were found on the boat.

The guard loitered in the doorway, waiting to escort Prasad to the lawyers.

One minute, please, Prasad told him in English.

I don't know about any documents, Prasad said, returning to his shoe and working the lace through quickly.

That's what I told them, Mahindan said.

Savitri and the others, those fools! Still, Mahindan would not worry. It was in everyone's interests to keep quiet. A few meaningless pieces of paper—what harm could they bring?

There was a metal shelf, attached to the wall, where they stored their small collection of borrowed possessions. Mahindan moved to the shelf and picked up the portable CD player. Ranga was in the periphery of his vision, still drying his hair. Anyone could see the guilty sag of his posture. Prasad yanked on the two ends of a lace and crossed them over each other.

Ranga folded the towel in half, slowly, addressing it as he spoke. They want to speak to me also?

Just tell the truth, Mahindan said. You don't know anything, do you?

Ranga hung the towel over the rack, lining up the two bottom edges. No, he said. I don't know anything.

Prasad was bent over, making bows with the lace and wrapping them around each other. Mahindan set the CD player down and picked up an exercise book. He flipped it open and saw his own writing. His letters were improving, less shaky, more sure. He repeated the alphabet silently to himself, practicing. A-B-C-D-E.

The springs under the mattress creaked when Prasad stood. He brushed the seat of his trousers and thanked the guard for something Mahindan could not fully interpret. English, the dull, tone-deaf quality of its consonants and vowels, was growing more familiar even if he still couldn't understand much.

Prasad left with the guard, pulling the door shut behind them.

Ranga said, Mahindan—

What is after *R*? Mahindan asked without turning around.

What do they know?

This bloody alphabet, Mahindan said, putting the exercise book down and picking up the CD player again. I can never recite the full thing. *P* then *Q* then *R* then . . . what?

I don't know.

Mahindan stared Ranga down, saw the long scar on his cheek. That's right. You don't know. I don't know either. Neither of us knows.

Thali

There was something suspicious about the way the woman answered the questions. Grace watched her steadily, waiting for her composure to crack. But the woman just sat there and gave straightforward responses as if being asked about the weather and not her connections to a terrorist organization. Her only tell was the unconscious way she kept touching her neck.

We have reason to believe Savitri Kumuran is a Tamil Tiger, Singh said. As a member of a known terrorist organization, she doesn't have the right to claim asylum.

This is a detention review, not an admissibility hearing, Grace reminded Singh.

One day, Grace knew, she would have to make decisions on asylum and deportation. But this was not that day. Today, she had to decide if it was safe to set this woman free.

I ask that my client's mental health be taken into account, Gigovaz said. I refer to Exhibit B-3, the psychiatrist's report. Mrs. Kumuran has been diagnosed with PTSD and depression, and it is her doctor's opinion that the strain of living in a prison is causing irreparable harm to her mental health. With a small child, and family in Toronto who have agreed to put up a bond, surely there is no reason to continue detention.

This was a recycled argument, raised at every hearing: *my client's mental health*. So common a refrain, Grace's instinct was to dismiss it. Of course detention was depressing, but that had no bearing on the question at hand: Was it safe to let this woman loose on the public?

The thing to focus on was what the Mounties had found on the ship: identity documents supposedly belonging to no one, which someone, nonetheless, had attempted to destroy. Here it was, then— proof to back up Fred's suspicions. He'd told her half the migrants were LTTE. She considered the woman and remembered his warning: *These people are not who they say they are.*

Singh said: The migrant has gone on record listing her profession as a teacher in Kilinochchi, a known Tiger stronghold.

Grace recognized Kilinochchi, the name of the Tigers' de facto capital. In a day filled with exclusionary evidence and suspicious affidavits, it was a relief to grasp on to this nugget of knowledge.

Teachers were instrumental in training future recruits, Singh continued. On that basis alone, we ask that she remain in detention until her admissibility hearing.

Gigovaz spoke up: And where, may I ask, is the proof of this claim?

Singh said: It is well-documented that the Tigers recruited child soldiers, and your client has admitted she taught children aged eleven and older.

Grace thought Singh was reaching. If this woman was a danger, it wouldn't be because she'd taught kids to read. Grace was learning that sometimes lawyers threw spurious arguments at each other for the sake of being adversarial, rather than making a real case. It was up to her, as the adjudicator, to rise above the petty sparring, to keep her focus on the migrants, vigilant for any hint that betrayed their true motives.

Grace interjected to address the woman directly. What do you know about these documents from the ship?

The migrant kept her poker face when she said she knew nothing, but Grace had scrutinized the image files and spotted a photo on a driver's license that bore a resemblance to this woman.

And what about your children? Grace asked, remembering that one of the identification cards pictured a young boy.

I had three sons, madam, the woman said through the interpreter. Two died in Sri Lanka. The smallest one is here, with me. She touched her neck and said, He is six.

And your husband? Grace prodded.

He is also dead. She flicked her hand in a dismissive way.

Singh raised her eyebrows and Grace wondered what kind of mother would send her children into battle.

Gigovaz spoke up. Mrs. Kumuran, tell us how your family died.

The woman spoke robotically, and when he repeated her response in English, the blond interpreter channeled her stilted tone.

We ran in the jungle. Bombs were always falling. My husband was hit. We had to leave him. No choice.

Grace thought of the way Steve slept with his mouth slightly open and decided fiercely: I would never leave him behind.

And your children? Gigovaz asked.

My elder sons died of dysentery in the prison camp. I heard about the boat. I had one son left. And I thought we would die if we stayed. So when the agent came and offered us two places, we took our chance.

Grace decided this was a lie. Her sons must have been killed fighting with the Tigers. Her self-possession was too complete, her answers too perfect. She didn't fidget or avert her gaze. A chilling thought came to her: This woman has been trained.

Singh pounced. You said you heard about the ship while you were in the refugee camp. What did you hear exactly?

Just that there was a boat and a man was arranging passage.

A long journey. Were you not worried?

Better to die in the ocean than in that godforsaken camp.

A young reporter gasped. Grace remembered the documents. Had the five mystery people died midvoyage? There were so many unknowns, and yet the responsibility for making a decision, one that would affect the entire country's safety, lay solely on her shoulders.

And how much did you pay this smuggler? Singh asked.

I had twenty thousand rupees, which I gave her and also my jewelry, the woman said. Fleetingly, her fingers grazed her neck.

Her. Was the agent a man or a woman? These people couldn't even keep their stories straight.

What did you give him exactly? Singh asked

And as the woman itemized the pendants and earrings, Grace wondered: What kind of a refugee is laden down with gold? No medicine for her children and yet she had sapphires.

Singh said: But you kept your necklace.

Savitri said: Yes, I kept that only.

Grace saw the way Singh's lips pressed together, the barely

perceptible tremor of excitement in her hands when she folded them on the desk. Singh had set a trap and the woman had walked straight into it.

The necklace has been confiscated, Singh said. We have now confirmed it is a Tamil tah-li, an item of jewelry only given to LTTE wives.

The reporters perked up. The migrant put her hands on top of her head and stared at the table in shock, appalled that the secret was out. She pressed them over her face. Finally, a crack. The jig was up, and Grace felt vindicated, relieved.

The woman's lawyers were on high alert, scrawling back and forth on a legal pad between them.

Gigovaz said, It's been nearly five months. Why is this the first time we're hearing about this supposedly incriminating evidence?

Singh said, The Minister has been as forthcoming as necessary, but we aren't required to disclose every scrap of evidence we have.

This is a rather significant scrap, wouldn't you say?

Grace privately felt Gigovaz had a point. On the other hand, Singh must have had a strategic reason for only bringing this information forward now. Fred's caution returned to her. *One toe across the threshold and these criminals are impossible to turf.*

Poise broken, the migrant's expression now was hopeless. Grace tried to imagine her biting off the end of a grenade. There were women in the LTTE. Grace had seen the photos, young girls with apple-round cheeks and bowl-cut hair, in fatigues with M-16s slung across their backs.

The migrant had her hair tied in a scrunchy. There were bags under her eyes. She looked like a schoolteacher.

Gigovaz was still talking, reading from the legal pad, even as his colleague continued to scribble on it at top speed. In Tamil culture, this necklace is the equivalent of a wedding ring, he said. All wives receive one.

These are particular tah-lis, only given to wives of LTTE fighters, Singh said. This woman is a risk to the nation's security.

Grace had had enough of the back-and-forth, the lawyers running the show. This was her courtroom. She would take back control.

She asked, Why are you here, Mr. Gigovaz?

Excuse me?

Most of the migrants I see have been assigned public defenders, Grace said. And yet here you are, from a top-tier firm. So I'm just wondering who's paying you.

As part of my firm's commitment to public service, we have taken five cases partially pro bono.

I see. And who pays the rest?

The Tamil Alliance, a not-for-profit community group, has hired us, Gigovaz said.

And two lawyers, Grace said.

Gigovaz always arrived with a young woman in tow. She took notes but said nothing. Grace had never given her much thought, just assumed she was some kind of secretary. Now the girl spoke up: I'm a law student.

I see. A law student.

She squinted at Grace. I'm also Sri Lankan, she said. And as a Sri Lankan, I can tell Ms. Singh that it is pronounced *thali,* not *tah-li.*

The student put her hands under the table quickly.

Singh said: Our expert—

The student cut her off: Well, where is it? She pulled an amulet from under her shirt. This was my mother's thali. My mother was a citizen, not a terrorist. Show us our client's thali and let's compare.

The words tumbled out in a trembling rush and Grace was bolstered by the knowledge that there was someone else in this room who felt out of her depth.

Singh spoke directly to Grace: Our intelligence suggests this is a specific tah-li, not the generic one that formalizes all marriages. As I said, this one is only given to LTTE members. To signify the husband's bravery, it has two tiger teeth with a tiger symbol in the middle.

The student spoke a little louder: I'm Tamil and I'm telling you there is no such thing as a Tiger thali.

Singh turned to her: Do you know that for sure? When was the last time you were in Sri Lanka?

The student banged her fist on the table and the sketch artist startled.

You can't even pronounce it right, she yelled. So how would *you* know?

The reporters were thrilled. This was the most exciting thing to happen all week. Grace could just imagine them returning to their newsrooms, fizzing with the drama.

Okay, let's all take a deep breath, Grace said. She let the interpreter finish speaking, then added: I'm going to count to three silently and I don't want anyone to say a word.

Grace flipped through her case file, feeling competent and finally in charge. Ms. Singh, she said. Is there a photograph of the jewelry in question?

It was sent to an expert overseas for authentication.

Who is this so-called expert? Gigovaz asked. I find this all rather curious. As Border Services has pointed out many times in this very room, there are 200,000 members of the Tamil diaspora already in Canada. Surely the Minister could have found a local expert.

Grace felt a spark of irritation. What was Gigovaz playing at, bringing Fred into this?

Ms. Singh, when do you expect to hear back from your expert? Grace asked. She didn't know what to make of the necklace, but the documents they had found on the boat troubled her. Whom did they belong to and where did they fit into all of this?

Singh said, It could be months before his report is completed.

Nothing that has been said today by Ms. Singh sheds any light on why Mrs. Kumuran is believed to be a security risk, Gigovaz said.

Grace swallowed. Decision time. What to make of this conflicting soup of information? An iffy necklace and suspicious documents no one wanted to claim. A mother who spoke so callously about her own children's deaths—what was such a woman capable of?

The Tigers were an equal-opportunity employer. Women from the Black Tiger division planned and executed suicide bombings. What it came down to was safety. Grace thought of her daughters and decided she didn't know enough about any of this to take a chance.

She pinched the bridge of her nose and shook her head. Given the elite role of women in the LTTE, there are sufficient grounds for doubt, she said. I feel it prudent to exercise caution and am ordering the migrant to remain in detention for another thirty days. Perhaps by then we will have heard from Ms. Singh's expert.

Gigovaz was on the verge of cutting in and Grace addressed him directly when she added: I am satisfied Minister Blair is doing what is necessary to ensure the nation's security.

The interpreter repeated her judgment in Tamil, and Grace marveled at his ability to perfectly emulate her tone and pitch. The woman bunched her fists against her eyes and gave a low, keening wail. The sound startled Grace, regurgitating an unpleasant surge of sympathy. It was the last hearing for the morning. Pushing back her chair, Grace moderated her pace as she exited the room.

PEACE AND QUIET

Appa wanted to know what was happening at the office. He laid his tiles down one at a time then turned the lazy Susan so the game board faced Priya. She had been feeling sluggish after two helpings of prawn curry, but now she was alert and full of prickly foreboding as she moved her letters around the little wooden pew. The dishwasher rumbled contentedly in the background, the smell of fenugreek and ginger still lingering over the kitchen. Outside, the wind whipped up piles of dried leaves, sending them somersaulting down the sidewalk.

I'm still working with Gigovaz, Priya said, setting down her letters.

Furtive, Uncle read. He tallied the points under his breath in Tamil then said, in English: Twenty-one points. Very good, pillai.

You took my spot, Rat said, and Priya stuck her tongue out at him.

Growing up, Scrabble had been a parentally mandated family ritual in which Priya and Rat had participated, sulky at certain ages and jocular at others. The weekly games were resurrected after Ma's lymphoma diagnosis, when they found themselves spending more time in their childhood home than in their adult ones. They'd pull in an armchair from the living room so she could watch, but the bag would still be half full of tiles when Ma fell asleep, her cheek against the headrest, mouth slightly open.

For how much longer will you have to work with this Gigovaz? Appa asked.

Priya swiveled the board to Uncle. Forever, she said. Now that he's caught his happy little worker bee, he'll never let me go.

Aiyo! Uncle exclaimed, startling everyone with his outburst. He threw his hands out and said, You should see these tiles. Useless! Useless!

Uh . . . I'm sure you'll think of something, Uncle, Rat said.

You must assert yourself. Appa pressed his index finger hard on the table. Tell them you want to work in this, this, this . . . what is it called . . .

Corporate law, Priya said.

She could feel her father's stern gaze, the way he stared and scowled as if by force of will alone he could change her actions and by extension her future. Priya kept her eyes on her tiles, swapping them around haphazardly, forming gibberish nonwords. It was so typical of her father to dictate solutions when what she needed was commiseration.

Corporate law, Appa said, at the same moment Uncle asked: Ahney! Michael, can you turn on the light?

They had been playing by lamplight supplemented by the pendants in the kitchen and Priya thought the dining nook was sufficiently lit, but Rat leaned back without complaint, his chair balanced on its hind legs, to reach the switch.

Corporate law, her father repeated, tapping the same spot on the table. If you want something, you must ask for it. He flicked his cupped palm in the air. Otherwise, how?

Appa, what do you think I've been doing? Priya said. But I'm hardly in a position to make demands.

Now see here, Uncle said in a false jolly way. I have a very nice word. P-R-O-T-E-C-T. Double-word score. Eleven and two is twenty-two.

Good one, Rat said.

When are you finished at that company? Appa asked.

The board exam is in May, she said. And there's a ten-week prep course before that. So basically, I have until March to get enough experience under my belt to land a job after I qualify. These cases won't be wrapped up by then, so my only hope is Gigovaz lets me return to corporate.

Priya's instinct was to remain on the neutral ground of her career, but Rat was plunging his hand into the bag of tiles and asking, What's the holdup, anyway? Why haven't they released anyone yet?

The government is taking a hard line. I mean, yeah, there are hundreds of cases to process, but Blair's directing Border Services to drag their feet and play out the fiction that they're hunting terrorists.

Of course there are former fighters on board, Appa said. He cut his hand through the air, palm down, as if announcing a verdict. A thirty-year war and these are the survivors? Naturally, some must have been involved.

Uncle stood abruptly, clattering his chair back so suddenly it nearly toppled over.

Whoa, Rat said.

Going to toilet, Uncle said, already halfway to the stairs. Keep playing, keep playing.

Appa's mouth pressed into a line and angled down slightly.

Is that really what you think? Priya asked.

Yes, yes. Use your brain, pillai. In the end, all these poor buggers must have been made to take part whether they wanted to or not. But have they come here to make trouble? He shrugged. That, I have my doubts. Ninety-nine point nine only want peace and quiet.

Yeah, you know, Rat said, if I was a Tiger, hell-bent on relaunching the war, Canada wouldn't be my first choice as a base of attack.

Appa played his signature move, adding an *s* to Uncle's *protect*, and the tension dissipated. Or maybe it had never existed. Had she dreamed it, the taboo about the ship?

South India, Priya agreed. That's what Gigovaz thinks too. Common sense and geography.

For real, Rat said. What kind of low-rent terrorist gets on a boat when he could just take a plane?

Never mind all that, Appa said. Why does this Gigovaz not find someone who is actually working in refugee law?

Maybe he thinks a Tamil is the best person, Rat said. To another lawyer, it would be only a job. Maybe he wants someone who is invested in the clients.

Anyone would become invested, Priya said, thinking of Mahindan and the yearning in his voice whenever he asked about his son. She gave up on her letters and laid down Z-E-A-L, wasting a ten-point letter on a nondescript square.

He's not thinking of the consequences for you, her father said. *Because* we are Tamil . . . the position he's put you in.

What consequences? Rat asked.

Okay, okay, Uncle cut in loudly, returning to the kitchen. He pushed his glasses up on his nose, index finger to bridge, and peered at the board. Ah! Very nice words. Whose turn now?

Rat shook the cloth bag at Priya and she dove her hand in unseeing, attention wheeling from her father to her uncle, each, it seemed to her, determined not to acknowledge the other.

It's your turn, she told Uncle.

What position is he putting Priya in? Rat asked again.

He and Priya stared at their father, but Appa was fixated on his tiles and did not answer.

HOMELAND

Mahindan closed the hood of the car and straightened, then raised his arms like a cactus and stretched his shoulders back with a loud, indulgent groan.

The car was a gemstone. Bottle green and snub-nosed, a '53 Morris Minor with an Austin-made engine that still ran as well as the day it was first driven. Weathered and rusted, with one back wing inexplicably painted orange, it was Mr. Chanakayam's pride and joy. A solid British car.

The old man had finally consented to bring it in for servicing, and Mahindan had spent a happy afternoon examining the undercarriage and rooting around beneath the hood, delighting in the custom-made engine cover. You had to admire the brash showiness of the thing. Green to match the car and shaped like a steam train, with a brass nameplate on top. *Morris* in black letters. An unnecessary indulgence, like the hood ornament. Even the Japanese, for all their skill, didn't make vehicles like this.

Mahindan wore slippers and a white sleeveless banian. He turned his shoulders in circles and pressed his chin to his chest to stretch out his neck. Wiping his hands on a rag and slinging it over one shoulder, he calculated sums in his head. He couldn't find the receipt pad—he could never find anything in this place—and jotted down the bill on the wall with a marker. The cement walls were graffitied with decades of grease and spray paint, old notes scrawled out in his father's hand. *Motorcycle—chain tension. Hundred rupees owing. Order filters.*

The garage was a three-sided block, open to a quiet, dusty road. The sun slanted through the thin, hairy roots that grew down from the branches of a massive banyan tree, throwing friendly shadows across the rust-colored earth.

Mahindan was searching for his keys and the padlock when he heard the commotion. Outside, a lorry rolled toward him, dragging a Toyota Corona in its wake. In the cab of the Isuzu, the driver wore green-and-brown camouflage and a matching cap with a visor. As the lorry eased to a stop, two boys jumped off the flatbed. Mahindan's stomach sank when he saw the driver was Arun.

Ah, good. You're still here.

Arun slung an arm around Mahindan's neck, as if to embrace him, then brought the other arm across his throat to form a vise instead. Mahindan found himself bent over and gasping, his head caught in the lock of Arun's forearms. Their scuffling feet kicked up clouds of red dust.

I could break your neck, Arun said. That's the first lesson the Tigers taught us.

Behind them, the boys called instructions to each other as they loosened the chains on the car and released it from the lorry. Mahindan's head was twisted painfully. From this angle, he saw his garage upside down. The untidy confusion of fenders and headlights and other body parts. Paint cans jumbled with cinder blocks and jugs of petrol. A funnel he had searched for in vain earlier that day hung in plain sight off the handlebar of a broken bicycle.

You don't think of joining us? Arun asked. He pressed Mahindan's head down with one arm while tightening the stranglehold with the other. We can make you into a man.

And then who would repair your vehicles? Mahindan strained to get the words out. His throat was painfully constricted, but he didn't want to give Arun the satisfaction of hearing him cough.

Arun laughed and let go. Yes, yes. A good point!

Mahindan stumbled to stand straight, resisting the urge to rub his throat as he inspected the Corona's flabby back tire. A nail was wedged between the treads. It couldn't be salvaged.

The boys drove off in the lorry and he was left with Arun, who wandered into the garage while Mahindan crouched beside the Corona.

Choose a good replacement, Arun called over his shoulder. Not one of these wasted ones. He pulled out a tire that was leaning against a tower of others and sent it rolling out of the garage and across the lane.

Mahindan hadn't seen Arun for some time. He'd lost weight. His eyes were jaundiced, the remaining ear prominent against his gaunt and shrunken face.

Some people joined the Tigers because they believed war was the only path to peace. Others, without jobs or family, had nothing to lose and saw the LTTE as their last hope. Arun had joined to terrorize. Even during the short-lived ceasefire the year before, when others returned, relieved, to civilian life, he had found a way to stay on.

Not all the cadres were like Arun. Mahindan liked many of them. Old classmates who hung around while he topped up the brake oil or diagnosed a faulty transmission, reminiscing about school pageants and game days, lime-and-spoon races, and the time Rama nearly choked on the spoon and dropped the lime, only to trip on it and break his glasses when his face hit the ground. There was something about joining the LTTE that made these men nostalgic.

Mahindan wedged a block of wood under the Corona's front tire and secured the parking brake. Arun inspected the wrenches and pliers hanging on the wall. He stepped on the buzz box of a hand welder, balancing on one foot then the other before jumping up and down twice. Mahindan cringed. He only had one buzz box and if Arun broke it, he wouldn't be able to get another. Mahindan glanced at the calendar and its picture of Lord Krishna, blue-skinned and serene, presiding over the business from his lotus position in the sky, and prayed Arun wouldn't go searching for the cash box. Mahindan had tucked it under some dirty rags when he'd heard the lorry approaching.

Arun kicked an extension cord out of the way as he continued his tour of the garage. You must see how they treat us, he said. All these small-small villages, everyone cheers when we arrive.

Arun sang the same song every time, but Mahindan knew this wasn't the case. They want nothing to do with us, Rama had said on one of his rare leaves. And when Chithra's younger sister joined the Tigers, she brought home the same stories.

Mahindan stood on one foot, braced himself against the car, then brought the other foot down hard with all his weight on the arm of the spider wrench. He felt the lug nut crack free.

Wives are taken care of, Arun added. You might think about it.

The carcass of a three-wheeler lay in pieces on the floor, awaiting resurrection. Mahindan was relieved to see Arun crouched beside it, far from the money box.

Where is that pretty wife of yours? Arun called. When does she come from office?

Chithra would be slinging her handbag over her shoulder and waving goodbye to the ladies at work.

She's always going here and there, Mahindan said. These women. Who knows what they are doing? He cranked the handle of the jack a little quicker, but speed made his hands clumsy. Taking a deep breath, he tried to focus. And now that she is pregnant, he added, I can't say anything.

Is she really? Arun stuck his head through the open window of Mr. Chanakayam's car and pocketed something he found inside. Well, well. So you are a man after all.

She has put on a lot of weight, Mahindan said, rolling the flat tire away. He didn't dare check the clock. Chithra would normally have arrived to collect him by now. Maybe she would take the back lane and bypass the garage. He wished he could send her a message: Go straight home.

Mahindan sweated with the spider bar, using both his hands and all his strength to tighten the nuts on the new tire.

Arun wandered over to watch. We're bringing a bus on Wednesday night, he said. For special servicing.

Mahindan cranked down the jack. Wednesday night. He'd send Chithra to her parents' or to Ruksala's.

That pariah dog, she'd said the last time Arun's name had come up. It'll be a blessing if he gets caught to a bomb.

When Mahindan had hushed her and begged her not to say such things (One of these days your big mouth is going to land us in trouble), she'd shrugged and said, Well, there is always malaria.

He remembered malaria now as he noticed Arun's legs. Even his knees were emaciated. Sick or not, the devil remained strong. Mahindan could still feel the constriction in his windpipe.

Finished, he said, standing and rubbing his hands on his trousers.

Wednesday evening, Arun said. Be prepared.

He left without paying and Mahindan watched with relief as the Corona sped off. Still no sign of Chithra.

He retrieved the tire, checked the buzz box, rolled down the corrugated door, and, after affixing the padlock, walked home. Behind the house, he pumped water then squatted at the bucket to wash his hands and face. He scrubbed at his arms with a cake of soap. All the new nicks and scratches he had acquired that day stung.

There were sounds from inside. Drawers rolled on casters, the beaded partitions rustled between rooms. Chithra had changed into a housedress. She waddled out with a king coconut in two hands, sucking on a straw. A thumbprint of red kumkum was smudged across her neck. She was barefoot. The little bells on her anklets jingled.

You went to temple, Mahindan said.

She gave him the coconut to hold while she struggled down into the chair beside him. Went to say a prayer for the elephant baby, she said.

Chithra was in the eighth month of her pregnancy, but she was so big she said it felt like longer. *Wait and see when this child comes if he is not an elephant.*

We'll call him Ganesh, Mahindan said.

Just go-men! She gave his arm a light slap.

Chithra was superstitious about names. She balanced the coconut on her belly and dropped her head to the straw. Her thali gleamed in the mellow evening sun.

This was Mahindan's favorite time of day—sharing a king coconut, gazing over the lantana bushes, and listening to birdsong as evening closed in. The sweet water was the perfect antidote to rusty undercarriages, angry sparks spitting from the welder.

Anyway, it will be a girl, Mahindan said, taking the coconut.

Chithra pressed at her belly, trying to coax the baby to kick. Amma says, the way I'm carrying, it must be a boy. She leaned over and pinched his nose. Just hope he doesn't inherit his father's elephant trunk.

She levered herself out of the chair and went inside. He heard pans clanging, the high squeal of a knife being sharpened. Then Chithra came out with a bag of onions.

Come and help me with this, she called. Jobless fellow!

They cooked under a lean-to at the side of the house. Mahindan took over the chopping while Chithra measured red rice into the chatti pot.

Finer, finer, she said, hovering at his shoulder.

You modern women, he said. Too many demands.

Watch your mouth, she said. Or I'll leave you with the elephant and join the LTTE. She dropped her voice a little as she said this, even though there was no one to hear.

And what do you think those girls are doing? he teased. Washing the men's jungis and frying their vadai.

She bobbed her head from side to side. Mr. Funny Man. And you know everything.

Ask your thangachi next time she comes.

They were joking, of course. Everyone knew the truth was another story. The female cadres were as fearsome as the men and were being chosen for the most dangerous assignments. The girls put their names in a lottery to be sent on suicide missions. They took their last meals with Prabhakaran himself. No one is made to do it, Chithra's sister had told them. There are more than enough mad fools who very happily volunteer.

Mahindan worried this could change. Nila had only joined out of a sense of inevitability. One day they would have come for me, she'd said. No boys in the family, and I am unmarried. If I volunteer early, go on my own, they might take care of Amma and Appa. The money had yet to materialize, but it was true that when the recruiters came around, they always let her parents be.

Strapping bombs to girls and nicely sending them to do men's dirty work, Chithra said. Trust our people to invent this idea.

Reminds me, Mahindan said. Will you go and stay with Ruksala on Wednesday night?

Another job for the Tigers?

What to do, Chithra? Can't say no.

No, no. I know. She rubbed his shoulder then moved her hand to her belly, absently. Anyway, Ruksala will be glad. Now that her time is close, she misses Rama more.

Mahindan thought of the job on Wednesday night. The Tigers didn't tell him what they wanted until they arrived, and he never found out what happened after the vehicles left his garage. But if explosives were involved, they came wrapped in Velcro. He handled them gingerly, terrified the whole time. The weight of the canisters, their heft in his hands remaining long after the job was done.

Every time he was made to rig up the brakes on a car or strap bombs to the underside of a truck, he thought of how he was bound to these weapons, one link in a chain of events that would end a life. It gave him nightmares, the possibility that one day he'd work on a vehicle that Rama or Nila would be made to drive. But what choice did he have?

Was he worse than the engineers who built these explosives? The man who invented gunpowder or the companies that profited from its sale? The secretary who worked for the head of the company, who answered his telephone then took her salary to the market and bought food for her family? Was Mahindan any worse than this woman?

The Tigers claimed it was all in service of the greater good. Short-term sacrifices for long-term gain. Mahindan hated the Sinhalese and wished to be free of them, but blowing up this or that minister, sending a woman strapped with explosives into a market in Colombo, how would this bring them closer to Eelam? All it did was set the Sinhalese more firmly against them.

He didn't mind so much when they targeted the army. When they attacked the garrison at Elephant Pass or liberated a Tamil village. But watching Prabhakaran on the news proclaiming the Black Tigers as heroines, triumphing over a civilian target blown to smithereens, Mahindan wondered: And so what? More dead bodies, but still no homeland.

It began to rain a little, so they ate inside. Chithra complained about a coworker: He's one of these last-minute cases, utterly useless!

Mahindan told her about Mr. Chanakayam's car, how he'd popped open the hood and found the old man's handiwork—a Pringles chip can duct-taped to a cracked exhaust pipe, holding the two parts together. Chithra was midlaugh when the lightbulb flickered off. The radio fell silent.

All hail the Liberation Tigers of Tamil Eelam, Chithra said. These buggers think they can run a country? They can't even manage to keep the lights on.

BACK TO HELL

The woman said her husband had been killed by a bomb. He was plowing the paddy field when it happened, coaxing the bulls through the sodden ground, the straw hat she had woven shielding him from the sun. He was barefoot and shirtless when the bomb came, and his sarong had been ripped off by the blast so that when they found him, he was naked and in pieces among his dead animals.

All eyes were on the woman as she spoke—the lawyers, the interpreter, the reporters shaking out pens and furiously scrawling in notebooks. She had a prominent mouth that jutted out distractingly, overcrowded with big white teeth. There was a script, carefully fabricated to strike a balance between detail and emotion, and the woman relayed it in a practiced, vacant tone, staring at a point on the far wall. She would not look at Grace.

Although no one had been released from detention, at the beginning of November the chair had announced it was time to move on to admissibility hearings. They would begin with the women and unaccompanied minors, but in the new year they'd add men to the schedule too.

Now, in addition to detention reviews, Grace had to listen to all the gory details of people's alleged life stories and decide whether or not they could apply for asylum. Before each hearing, she braced herself for the onslaught.

This was Grace's third straight week of admissibility hearings and her last one for the day. If she left within the hour, she would avoid the Friday rush. But they were already four hours and nine minutes in, and the end was nowhere in sight. Warm air gusted from the vent above Grace's head. Heat spread outward from her chest, rising up her neck.

Her mouth was dry, but she had left her office in a hurry and forgotten her water glass.

Grace stifled a yawn. It had been a bad night. She'd been standing at the front window watching a group of men coming at the house, running as though they were being chased, Steve in the lead. She'd had her hand on the deadbolt when Meg screamed in terror, waking Grace up, her stomach riotous with panic. Steve, his back to her, was snoring. The red digits on the nightstand shone 2:48. Grace lay there, in confusion, while the house slumbered.

Meg's scream had been real. Even now, Grace could recall its verisimilitude, its pitch-perfect texture. Meg, her firstborn by minutes. How closely our nightmares can mimic reality.

The woman claimed her name was Hema. She and her two teenaged daughters had arrived without so much as a library card and, in lieu of documentation, had signed a meaningless piece of paper affirming their names and ages.

The husband was only the first casualty. My sisters and mother, the woman said. All dead. My nephews and cousin brothers also gone, stolen by the LTTE. They would come with their tractors and stop opposite the house, all the boys they'd already caught crammed onto the flatbed trailer hitched at the back, chins on knees, staring out, dejected.

She used the word *caught* instead of *recruited*. Or the interpreter did. It was impossible to decipher who was saying what.

The interpreter jotted notes as the woman meandered through her tangents, flicking the pen up from the pad as he dotted each sentence with a finishing flourish. He strolled in every day with his things under his arm—a notepad, a legal reference guide, a Tamil–English dictionary, and two ballpoint pens—and lined them all up at punctilious right angles. Grace was irritated by this fair-haired man and his obsessive compulsions, this interloper who had no real role at these proceedings, no tangible responsibility, yet was the only one who understood every word.

The woman said she had two younger brothers. They were clever boys, good with their heads but useless with their hands. In her retelling, the brothers became sanctified. They were transformed into a single entity.

The brothers had never held a gun in their lives, didn't even have the stomach to slash a knife across a chicken's neck. The brothers were sensitive and squeamish. They had flat feet. The woman reported all of these details in a deadpan voice, like a truculent child repeating a history lesson.

Grace watched her speak, not understanding a word, scrutinizing her body language for a hint of what she was saying. The whole room held in suspense, at the interpreter's mercy until he translated whatever he thought fit to repeat, with whatever commentary he chose to add or delete. Grace had the urge to knock his sanctimonious little stack of books and pens right off the table.

The brothers had hidden in the chicken coop when the recruiters came with their tractor. At first, their mother said she didn't have any sons. But the LTTE had their own ways of ferreting out the unwilling. The woman's mother was beaten. Palmyra fronds have dry, serrated edges. They can slice through skin.

A startled gasp threatened, but Grace swallowed it down, reproaching herself for getting emotional. *Focus on the job.*

The mother begged the Tigers not to take her sons. They were needed in the paddy field, and, anyway, they did not know how to use a gun. Please, please, don't take away my boys. What do you want them for? They will be of no use. The woman said she never saw her brothers again. Her mother had died from the beating. Grace was skeptical. Was it possible to die from a beating? Squirming inside her clothes, she longed for air-conditioning, to remove her suit jacket, undo her buttons, and air herself out in front of an open freezer.

In the last days of the war, the woman and her daughters had deserted to the Sri Lankan side.

Grace wanted to know when, but the woman would not say. April? Grace asked. Or May? Early or late? The woman said she did not know; she did not have a calendar. Every day and night, it was the same—bombs and shelling and people dying.

The time of day, then, Grace said, glancing at the clock. Ten past four. So much for avoiding rush hour.

I don't know, the woman said. I didn't have a watch.

She sat there, stubborn and unyielding as a rock. She had arrived in Canada and now that she was here, she would not be moved.

Grace fanned herself with an empty file folder. It must have been eighty-six degrees in the room, but no one else seemed bothered.

What was the position of the sun in the sky? Grace asked. Surely you recall. Was it high? Was it setting?

The woman glanced at her lawyers. No, Grace thought. They can't help you.

The woman twisted her hands together, finally shaken out of her stupor. She fumbled for the answer. It was . . . it was . . . we had not had time for lunch . . . no . . . oh . . . that day there were clouds.

Tell us how you did it, Hema, Gigovaz said. Tell us how you crossed to the Sri Lankan Army side.

The young lawyer—the student—pushed a little cup of water toward the woman and said: Have a drink.

Stalling tactic, Grace thought. She could picture the circle of water in the cup, the tiny bubbles on its surface. The woman put the paper cup to her lips and drank. Her microphone was still on and the whole room heard the small gulps. Grace's tongue was like sandpaper. She could grant this woman's admissibility or she could do the safe thing and ship the three of them back to where they came from. She longed to go home and make this decision in peace.

The woman said, There was a lagoon.

Immediately, Gigovaz interjected. He wanted Grace to know this was the Nandikadal Lagoon. Here was the LTTE's last stand—Tigers and civilians all trapped together on a narrow strip of land between lagoon and ocean. It was all well-documented. Exhibit L in the Evidentiary Package.

She was galled by his presumption of her ignorance, the unnecessary interruption in this already drawn-out saga. Mr. Gigovaz, Grace said. Are you giving testimony or is your client?

The woman said there were Tiger cadres guarding the lagoon, shooting at deserters. But people were streaming across anyway. When he translated, the interpreter waved his arms out in front of him as the woman had done to indicate waves of people.

The army was on the verge of victory and everyone was terrified. The lagoon was a murky brown, heavy with blood and the bodies of the fallen. It appeared impassable, but there were shallow areas. The Tigers were pointing out the paths, turning their backs as people waded across.

Grace cut in: I thought they were shooting at you. Now you're telling me they were helping you to escape?

The woman grew flustered. Just when Grace thought she might finally catch her eye, she turned away. She shook her head yes, then no.

These people, Grace thought. They want to have it both ways. Well, she said, which one was it?

The woman said: The cadres had orders to shoot, but not everyone was following. Some might have been like my brothers—forced to fight. Anyway, they had joined to shoot at the army, not their own people.

The woman had recovered her nerve. She was on a roll now, intoning again in that dull, flat voice. The interpreter matched her tenor, belaboring every word and stringing out the sentences. Grace thought he was probably paid by the hour.

The woman said the whole lagoon was being bombarded. Shells spiraling at them, blasting into the water. People were falling back, shot by Tiger cadres or felled by bombs. The woman and her daughters pressed on. The water was up to their waists. It was slow going. Up ahead, they saw a cadre. He was just a boy, maybe sixteen or seventeen. His gun was pointed right at them.

The woman put both hands over her face as the interpreter relayed her story. Gigovaz pushed a tissue box toward her and she blew her nose.

Singh was writing in her notebook. The excitement in the reporters' corner was palpable. They stared out like a single hungry entity, recording everything Grace said word for word so she could relive it all in the newspaper the next day and Fred could scrutinize her performance.

I was so frightened, the woman said. I did not want to die. But then one of the other cadres, a girl, shot her gun. But not at us—at the one who was going to kill us. She shot him and he fell down and she threw her gun into the water and took my hand and we all ran together.

Was she telling the truth? Grace peered at the woman, hunched across the room, refusing to meet anyone's eyes. Why was she really here?

Grace was sweating freely now, the blouse beneath her suit jacket staining. She said: Please explain to me, madam, what the Tigers were doing. Were they helping you to cross the lagoon or were they trying to prevent you?

The woman trembled. She pulled her sleeves down further over her hands, as if she was trying to disappear into the sweater. It was . . . they were . . . My daughters and I were not the only ones . . . there were many others with us who also ran.

That doesn't answer my question.

Grace was weary of this woman's stuttering. If the story was true, if it was hers, surely she would be able to recount it in a straightforward way.

It was nearly five now and Grace had a dull pain in her shoulders, crawling up the base of her neck, the prelude to a headache. Her thirst demanded quenching.

The interpreter was speaking. Grace raised a hand to silence him.

Okay. Fine, she said. Let's talk about what happened after you allegedly crossed the lagoon.

The Sri Lankan Army was there. They saw us coming and they saw that we did not have weapons, that we were not Tigers.

Singh spoke up. But wasn't there a Tiger cadre with you, holding your hand?

Yes, but she was not wearing a uniform, so after she threw away her gun, she was like the rest of us.

I see, Singh said. And in your interview with the immigration official at Esquimalt you said the army was kind to you.

The woman flared up. Kind? They were monsters. We were made to live in a cage, a high fence all around. People dying everywhere.

Exhibit F, Singh said. After the war, the Sri Lankan government set up temporary IDP camps. A UN report found the conditions to be satisfactory. In fact, there was no reason for this woman and her daughters to leave. Eventually, they would have been relocated back to their homes.

In her notebook, Grace scrawled out the letters *IDP* followed by a question mark.

No, the woman said. We would have died. There was not enough food or water. Every day people going missing.

I thought you said there was a fence, Grace said.

The army men. They took people. The woman dropped her head as she said this. Grace knew there was something she wasn't saying.

Where were these people taken? Grace asked. Her shirt was soaked through now. She did up the buttons on her suit jacket, hoping no one would notice.

I don't know. Men and boys were being disappeared.

Singh started to say something, but Grace cut her off. Let's go back, Grace said. You crossed the lagoon and were met by the Sri Lankan Army. In your interview with Immigration, you said they gave you tea and medicine. Is this true?

Yes, the woman said. That is true.

And this was the Sinhalese. The people you called monsters.

They were kind to us then, yes. Those people were good.

Singh said: Naturally, in the midst of a war, the state's efforts to safeguard its citizens are hamstrung. But the war has ended and the reasons for which the migrant sought protection have ceased to exist.

Gigovaz spoke up: People were going missing from a government-run refugee camp. Not only did the state fail to perform its duty, it in fact participated in the persecution of its own nationals.

The lawyers liked to hear themselves speak. They had been sidelined for the past two hours, and now, seeing their opportunity, they jumped on the chance to hold forth with their legalese.

Singh said: Sri Lanka is a democratic country with a rule of law. We're not talking about a totalitarian state here.

A democratic country with a long history of human-rights violations against its Tamil minority, Gigovaz said. In Mrs. Sokolingham's case, there is a risk of persecution. Gigovaz was emphatic, punctuating his arguments with jabs of his pen.

Singh sat with her hands folded calmly in front of her, offering rebuttals with the blandness of a person stating the obvious. The risk of persecution must be real, not speculative, she said.

Enough, Grace said. She was weary of these two as well. She turned to the interpreter. Ask how much she paid the agent.

Fifty thousand rupees, the woman said.

We have intelligence that people paid as much as fifty thousand *dollars*, Singh said.

I only had fifty thousand, and that is what the agent took.

And when you say the agent, you mean the smuggler, Grace said.

Fred had told her about the smugglers. International criminal rings that got rich off duping humanitarian countries. Shady and large, they had tentacles all over the world. Difficult to find and impossible to bring to justice.

The woman said, To us, the smugglers were like Good Samaritans.

Grace wanted to slap her.

Singh said: It is the Minister's opinion that the migrant is inadmissible on the grounds that she has aided and abetted a smuggling operation.

Grace said: I would tend to agree with you, Ms. Singh.

The woman's eyes widened. She swiveled in her seat, frantic, and shouted something in her language.

The interpreter said: There was no choice! Those men, those army dogs!

The woman's lawyers looked afraid. Their client had gone off the script and they had no control over what she said next. The reporters perked up.

The woman stifled a cry. Then she turned and faced Grace straight-on and yelled a string of invective, her rage breaking through the language barrier and slamming Grace hard in the chest. The woman's hands, balled into fists, were pressed to either side of her head. Her expression was wild.

Grace was momentarily stunned by the vitriol spewed in her direction. She closed her eyes, humiliated, then told herself to stop being unprofessional. It was her job to adjudicate the truth, not be a grief counselor. Abruptly, the woman stopped shouting and slapped a hand to her mouth.

We had to leave, the interpreter said in a quick, high voice.

The woman waved her arms to silence him.

Those dogs, the interpreter said. They hate us so much.

She vaulted across the table, her hands flailing at his mouth. The interpreter pushed back his chair.

Mr. Gigovaz! Grace yelled. Please restrain your client!

A dog. Grace had been called worse things in her life. She would not be intimidated by this woman's tantrum.

The young lawyer pulled the woman away from the interpreter. She said something, but her microphone was off and Grace couldn't tell for sure if she was even speaking in English. Now the three of them appeared to be having a side conversation in Tamil.

Grace slammed her hands on the desk and yelled, STOP!

There was an abrupt, contrite silence.

Mr. Blacker, Grace said. You are under oath to interpret faithfully. Please finish.

A dog. The insolence and disrespect. Grace would have it all repeated, in English, for the record.

The woman put her hands over her face and Blacker said: They raped my daughter.

The woman cried openly. Loud, gasping sobs projected in stereo. Gigovaz reached over and turned off her microphone. The rest of the room was still, everyone staring determinedly away from each other. Grace was confused. She tried to retrace the woman's words. *The dogs.* Not *a dog.*

Finally, Singh spoke up. This testimony deviates from what was told to Immigration at the port of entry.

Grace spoke to the woman directly: Is this true? Was your daughter assaulted? She could not bring herself to say the word *rape.*

The woman shook her head no.

Mrs. Sokolingham, Gigovaz said. Just tell the truth. Don't be afraid.

I do not know what happened, the woman said. She had turtled back into her sweater and was sniffling, swiping at her nose with her sleeve.

I know this is very difficult, Gigovaz said. Please, just tell us what you know.

The woman did not turn on her microphone when she spoke and Grace did not admonish her.

The interpreter cleared his throat. He said: Many of the army men were young. They must have been away from home, from their wives, for a long time. They liked to look at the girls in the camp. I saw things . . . girls standing at the fence and letting the guards do dirty things to them for presents.

Grace's pulse raced. Meg's scream came back to her.

They hated us, the woman said. But they were also men.

Grace wanted to put her fingers in her ears, order the woman to stop talking. She had asked the question, but now she didn't want to hear any more.

They were always prowling around with their guns, the woman said.

My daughters are fourteen and sixteen. I kept them inside the tent, but one night two men came. I tried to stop them. I tried to stop them, but they took my elder daughter . . . they took . . . Tara.

Meg screamed and the room tilted, blurring out of focus. Grace tensed and gripped the table, trying to master herself. There was no proof, none at all, that any of this was true. Her head cleared. The floor beneath her feet was concrete again.

When she looked back up, she saw the reporters. They were loving every minute of this. Grace could feel their excitement, the frenzied shorthand. They would print it up word for word: They took my daughter, the woman said, her voice flat, matter-of-fact. She came back in the morning. Her dress was torn. And those dogs, they had cut her hair.

All day the reporters had waited, patient through the bureaucratic monotony of detention reviews. And here, finally, was their reward: a perfect, sensational sound bite. *Those dogs, they had cut her hair.*

The woman spoke to the interpreter. Her voice was defiant. She didn't need the microphone to be heard. The interpreter turned to Grace and said: Tell them, if they try to send us back, I will kill myself and my daughters. Better to die here in heaven than go back to hell.

DON'T YOU TRUST US?

T he twins spent the whole ride trying to negotiate.
Ten thirty, Grace said, checking left then right before
rolling past a stop sign. I'm not changing my mind.

Brianne leaned forward from the backseat. All the other kids are
staying until the end.

None of your friends have curfews? Grace drove slowly, squinting at
the street names.

It's a grade eleven party, Meg said. She was seated next to Grace with
her nose pressed to the window. Over there, Mom. On the right.

And you girls are in grade nine. In two years, we can extend your
curfew a little longer.

The house was a modest two-story on a tree-lined street that had
traffic-calming circles in the middle of the road. Grace pulled up to the
curb and put the car into park. The driveway was empty. Where are
this boy's parents?

Taylor's a girl, Meg said. Her parents are at a concert or something.
They'll be back later.

The house was dark and quiet, betraying no hint of a bacchanalia.
Are you sure it's tonight? Grace asked.

Brianne's seat belt shot up. Meg reached for the door handle. Yep.
It's tonight.

A light in an upstairs room—a bedroom—turned on. Grace clicked
on the child safety locks. Wait, she said. How do you know this
sixteen-year-old?

From band, Brianne said.

She's second flute, Meg added.

Grace could feel their impatience, hovering just below the veneer of careful deference. Mom could change her mind at any moment, do a three-point turn and take them all home. Mom had been erratic lately; anything might set her off.

Grace weighed the odds. The benign blandness of the flute against the curtained glow in an upstairs bedroom.

A Mazda pulled into the driveway. Two boys emerged and Meg became very interested in something in her shoulder bag, letting her hair fall like a curtain around her face. The boys glanced at Grace's car before loping up the walkway. She scrutinized the taller one. Hair flopped flat across his eyes and a pair of twiggy legs. Skinny jeans and red high-tops. He was young and vaguely effeminate, which Steve had told her was the trend.

Emo is safe, Steve had said. No daughter of mine is going out with a hockey player.

But these were still boys with boy parts and boy strength. She thought of the woman at the hearing saying, *They hated us, but they were also men.*

Don't you trust us? Brianne said from the back.

It's not you I'm worried about.

Mom, Brianne said. Nothing's going to happen.

It's just a house party, Meg added.

She heard the undertone of exasperation. Crazy Mom and her paranoia self-destroy-ya.

I don't want you girls to feel like you have to hide anything from us, Grace said. If something happens tonight, for example. You can tell us. We'll understand.

Like what? Meg asked, flicking her eyes to the dashboard clock.

Just . . . anything. Heat rose up Grace's neck as she said this. She had not had the sex talk with the girls. She knew this was bad parenting—abdicating responsibility to the school system, to teachers and the locker room. The Internet. She tried again: If something happens that is confusing or maybe scary. You can come to us.

If there's any trouble with the Doritos, we'll let you know, Brianne said.

If we see something, we'll say something. Meg smirked, then seemed to remember the child safety locks. Sorry, Mom. Just . . . like, there's nothing to, like, worry about. For reals.

It's Taylor Barry's basement, Brianne said. It'll probably be totally lame anyway.

The front door of the house opened and a girl stepped out. Meg rolled down the window and called: On our way!

Mom, come on, Brianne said. This is embarrassing.

Yeah, we're probably creeping everyone out just sitting here like weirdos.

Grace depressed the parking brake and clicked the button to release the locks. Okay, go. Have fun.

Thanks for the ride.

Ten thirty, Grace called as the doors slammed in unison.

She waited before pulling away from the curb, watching the girls run up the walk as if fleeing her. They stepped into the lit entryway, then the door closed behind them and Grace did not know what was happening inside.

———

Grace leaned against the bathroom doorway and watched Steve pack deodorant and toothpaste into a shaving bag. The window and mirror were steamed up, Steve's wet hair plastered to his head. He wore plaid flannels and a Vancouver Canucks T-shirt.

He held out his shaving bag and made a face that was meant to be comical but came out as a grimace. Did I miss anything?

Grace crossed her arms and turned away. Surely you're a pro by now.

Come on, he said, following her into the bedroom. Don't be like that.

We had a deal, Steve.

This just came up. It's work. They need me.

The truth was, Steve liked being away with the team, sticking her with the weekend shift. While he slept in and ordered room service, she'd be chauffeuring the girls all over God's green earth, from violin lessons to swim practice to the grocery store for sleepover supplies.

On the bed, Steve's clothes were laid out in neat stacks. He unzipped his duffle bag and began loading things in. A three-day junket in California. Knocking back a pint and cheering from the press box. Tough life.

And by the way, thanks for backing me up on this "family history" thing, she said, emphasizing the air quotes. It's really great we can present a united front to the kids.

You're the one who's always saying they get too much screen time.

It's not right, she said. Obaachan would have hated it. And my mother knows that.

Kumi won't be with us forever, Steve said. That trip they made to Slocan back in August? That's something the girls will remember for the rest of their lives. Haven't you noticed how bonded they've become?

Grace had noticed all right. The three musketeers. They even sounded like Kumi, parroting everything she said. *The government keeps minorities down. Remember how they treated us.* This was exactly what Grace had feared would happen when they went prancing off to Slocan for the weekend. And now here they were donning the mantle of victimhood.

These are complex issues, she told Steve. They're too young to understand.

Well, I for one am glad they're spending time with their grandmother, he said. Instead of aimlessly wandering the mall. Anyway, questioning authority is part of growing up.

How convenient you're never around to be questioned.

Grace had an adjoining room off the master bedroom that she used as her study. When it became clear Steve had nothing more to say, that he didn't feel the need to defend himself, she returned to her work.

Before taking the girls to their party, she'd been reviewing the case she'd adjudicated that afternoon. Photos of the woman's daughters lay on the desk. The younger one wore her hair in Anne Shirley braids. She was fourteen but looked eleven. There was something juvenile about her expression, as if she might still play with dolls. Every migrant had a photo like this, taken shortly after arriving at Esquimalt. Most had smiled for the camera in a perfunctory way, an upturn in the corners of the mouth that didn't quite reach the eyes. But this girl's grin was open and unguarded, displaying an unself-conscious delight the twins had lost after puberty.

The older girl was sixteen and had very dark skin, a deep notch clefting her chin. *Tara.* Grace pushed the name aside and focused on the photo. The girl faced the camera head-on, eyes narrowed in a glower of reproach. Or was it weariness? Grace scrutinized the girl's expression, hoping to find some proof, of innocence or guilt, but all she saw was survival.

Grace knew she could call the girl in to give her testimony. She could order a psych evaluation. There were things Grace could do. What she wanted to do was forget about the case, about the whole boat and all these people.

Sisters gang-raped in front of brothers. Men brutalized until they became like animals. Color photographs of battlefields, naked bodies contorted in piles, all limbs and breasts and wide-open eyes. Their personal horrors, true or false, had latched themselves on to her and she could not shake free. She missed her old job. Ferries and highways, dispassionate assessments.

Grace knew this was not the right way to make the decision. Mitchell Hurst, with his Kenyan wells and his cyclones in wherever, would not let personal feelings color his judgment. Mitchell Hurst would compartmentalize. He would know that *IDP* stood for *international displaced people,* that IDP camps were refugee camps. He would not have had to consult the Internet. And if he wasn't such a smug arse, she would solicit his counsel.

Mitchell had conducted the woman's detention review that morning and caught up with Grace as she was finally leaving for the day. I'm ordering Mrs. Sokolingham's release, he'd announced. We have to start letting these people go.

The galling thing about Mitchell was how well he could pronounce all these foreign, impossible names. Was he trying to sway her? Grace wasn't going to be influenced by other adjudicators' judgments.

The Tigers had pioneered suicide vests. Their IEDs were so impressive al Qaeda tried to buy the technology. One woman, pretending her bomb belt was a pregnancy, had conned her way into prenatal classes at a military hospital to get close to a high-ranking target. Grace could not be too careful.

She held the photos side by side. Though their features were different, the girls shared that intangible quality that marked them as sisters. Or this was all nonsense that Grace had been primed to believe. Who was to say they were even related?

The whole family had arrived without a scrap of identification. Had they destroyed their papers, if not on the boat, then before they left Sri

Lanka? The cadre who had thrown her gun into the lagoon and run with them, maybe she was the "daughter" with the short hair.

These girls had been born into a country at war, in a place where children were given guns and taught to fight, where girls strapped on explosives and turned their bodies into weapons. A place where *suicide bomber* was the highest possible calling. They had lived unimaginable lives. While all the violence Meg and Brianne had ever known was confined to a video game.

Grace felt silly about overreacting in the car with the girls. A party in a suburban basement, what could be more innocuous? To have daughters was to live in perpetual fear of their violation.

From the bedroom, she heard Steve's duffle bag being zipped up. She could picture him tugging up the handles and swinging it off the bed. It landed on the carpet with a muffled thump.

It was nine o'clock and her daughters were in an unsupervised basement with boys who could drive. Grace fought the urge to phone them.

Have you heard of this Taylor Barry person? she called to Steve.

The flautist? he asked. Sure.

She studied the photos again. The elder girl's shorn hair kinked out in ragged, uneven edges, the longest hank barely reaching her chin. Grace touched her own hair, still up in a workday chignon, feeling the smooth strands, the outward bulge and twist of the updo she formed like a reflex every morning.

Men with weapons and displaced, vulnerable women. But women in the LTTE cut their hair short too. Grace knew what the lawyers would say: Circumstantial. *We must defer to the best-evidence rule.* Even in her imagination, Gigovaz's voice was grating. Best evidence. There was no evidence! Everything was down to what this woman said happened to her. And whether Grace believed it.

Steve was behind her, fiddling with the alarm clock. The flight is at eight, he said. What time do you think—

I have work too, she snapped. I had planned to put in a few hours at the office tomorrow.

Steve looked taken aback. His voice was wounded when he said: Why are you working on the weekend? I thought the point of this job was to take the pressure off.

Why on earth would you think that?

All the late nights and weekends, replying to e-mails at all hours . . . you were burnt out at Transport.

Burnt out? What are you—

All I'm saying is, I thought Fred was doing you a favor. But here you are stressing on a Friday night.

Work isn't the problem. You were supposed to be home this weekend, Steve. I expected to have tomorrow free to go into the office.

Can't you just work here?

Because that's how I want to spend my Saturday night—writing reports while ten teenagers squeal at top volume downstairs. How am I supposed to focus? She gestured to the files spread across the desk. I have to review the evidence and think carefully.

He peered over her shoulder, at the photos she was holding, and shrugged. They seem harmless to me.

WHAT TO DO?

Mahindan laid a hand on the window and felt the cold seep up the length of his arm. His yearning for Sellian was a physical ache, a low, vibrating hum deep in his bones. Outside, the sky was an unforgiving gray, the grass dead and tramped down inside the barbed-wire fence.

For months, he and Sellian had trudged along the roadside, the sun burning relentless. They had slept in open fields, longing for shelter, four concrete walls and a roof. Protection from falling shrapnel. A reprieve from the sun.

And now we might never see the sun again, Ranga said from the table. How can it rain so much in this country?

Ranga used a spoon to fish the tea bag out of his cup, wrapping the string around the handle. They were lingering over their toast, waiting for Prasad to return with a newspaper.

Word had come, the evening before, that Hema and her daughters had passed the admissibility hearing, and Prasad thought there might be a news story. Mahindan was glad, did not begrudge them their good fortune. Mr. Gigovaz had said all along they must be patient. Hema was proof there was hope to be grasped.

He wished Ranga would stop following him around like a stray dog, yapping on about his fears. *What if they come to find . . . ? What if they should ask me about . . . ?* What if. What if. What if. What if I had not helped you, Mahindan had finally snapped. What then? You would still be in that prison camp, no? Or a white van would have come for you. That had shut Ranga up. But only for a little while.

Red-and-green tinsel was strung across every window and doorway, despondent against the bland dining tables, the blank white walls.

Even his own skin was paler, grayer, these days. What Mahindan missed was color. The building that five months earlier had struck him as modern and clean now felt sterile and heartless, like the detached expressions on the judges' faces as they stared down at him from their thrones and denied him his freedom.

Prasad returned frowning, head bent over a front-page article. Mahindan saw the boat in an inset picture. It always gave him a strange jolt of half recognition to see it from this outside vantage— a rusting hulk in the middle of the ocean, heavy and listing to one side, blurred brown faces crowding both decks.

Looking back, he thought those had been his happiest moments. When the Canadian boats circled the ship and the helicopter's blades chopped the sky over their heads. Standing at the top of the gangplank, the sun gentle on his face, gazing out over the parking lot to see the crisp white tents, the Canadians in their comical face masks. Sellian light as a feather in his arms, waving ecstatically at the crowd and shouting: Hello! Hello!

That heady expectation, the profound relief, both felt distant now, far from his present reality. Windows that would not open. Guards at every door. Endless waiting.

Prasad swung his legs over the bench and sat down. His lips moved as he read. Mahindan tried to make out the headline upside down. He could only recognize the word *ship*.

They have taken a poll, Prasad said. He read in English, slowly so they could understand: Three out of five Canadians believe the vessel should have been turned away. Half of those polled think all the passengers should be deported, even if their refugee claims are valid.

They want to send us back? Mahindan was appalled.

He knew distrust and suspicion surrounded them, fears of Tigers hiding in their midst. Why else would they still be in jail after all these months? But he had thought, with time and effort, these fears could be allayed, that deep down everyone was keeping an open mind. Now to find this was how the Canadians felt. People he had never met hated him and wanted him dead.

How can these people be so wicked? Ranga asked. He rubbed his injured leg, stretching it back and forth under the table.

Prasad unfolded the newspaper and shook it open. He said, Just like at home, these things begin with the politicians. Prasad pointed to a photo of a man wearing a bow tie. He had round spectacles and thinning hair, parted at the side, sideburns that needed a trim.

This government minister, Prasad said. Just listen to what he has to say: The vessel and its illegal passengers are part of a larger criminal organization. Make no mistake, there are terrorists on board. We must not let the smugglers win.

Smugglers, Ranga said. How else to escape?

These politicians are very clever, Prasad said, his hand in a fist on the table. They know if they repeat something over and over, eventually people will believe them.

Mahindan could not understand it. Ordinary people he watched through the bus window while traveling to and from hearings, two women waiting at the corner for the light to change and one of them would have him deported. *Even if their refugee claims are valid.*

What to do? Ranga said, mournful. This is what they want to believe about us.

Then we must change their beliefs, Prasad said. He drummed his fingers on the table, thinking.

Prasad spoke to the guards and got his hands on a different newspaper. That evening, he read another article out loud to a group at their dinner table.

Outside, it was pitch-black. Mahindan wondered what the night air tasted like, what stars could be seen in Canada. At least they had been free on the boat. A two-month spell of liberty between the falling bombs and prison.

From the upper deck, the stars had been numerous, thousands more than he had ever seen from the shore. He and Sellian used to huddle together with a blanket, teeth chattering, and stare up until their necks hurt from craning. Sellian could trace the path of the seven sages and Mahindan pointed out the sages' wives—the Karthigai, six bright stars in the shape of an earring. When Sellian couldn't sleep, Mahindan would tell him the story of how the gods and demons had worked together to churn the ocean of milk, how for a thousand years they had toiled to release a nectar of immortality, only to find a terrible poison.

What stars could Sellian see now? Was Kumuran's wife telling him stories? Occasionally, he saw the women when he went to his hearings, and Hema had told him their jail was not so bad. There was a room full of toys where all the children played. Mahindan liked to picture Sellian there, racing cars and building forts out of blocks.

When Prasad read, he quoted the article in English first and then translated into Tamil: The Sri Lankan government insists there is complete peace and that the army went out of its way to minimize civilian casualties during the final advance on rebel-held territory.

Even before he had finished the sentence, men hissed and shook their heads.

The final advance, the man in the wheelchair said, from the end of the table. That is when they tried even harder to finish us off.

Complete peace! another man grumbled, lifting his shirt to expose a torso singed with cigarette burns. This is what the Sinhalese call peace.

The man in the wheelchair bobbed his head from side to side and flicked his palm in the air. This is some kind of peace, no?

This is my point, Prasad said. The Sri Lankan government is feeding the Canadians a pack of lies. We too must have a chance to tell our side of the story.

He set the newspaper aside and the man with the cigarette burns grabbed it up, scanning the article. Mahindan wondered how much he could read. He had tried earlier himself, with the newspaper Prasad had left behind on the breakfast table. He had stared at the incomprehensible text, picking out the handful of words he understood. *Ship. Tamil. And.*

These days, when Mahindan met with the lawyers, he tried as much as possible to speak in English, deciding what he would say in advance and rehearsing, whispering the words to himself quietly. But his literacy was limited to children's books. Whenever he felt he was making progress, something as simple as a newspaper would remind him of how much further he still had to go.

Prasad's idea was that they should write a letter. In English, he said. But expressing all our sentiments. And those of the women too. We can ask the Tamil Alliance to distribute it to the newspapers.

Mahindan admired Prasad's initiative, his ability to find solutions. Ranga, of course, had to throw cold water. He traced the scar on his cheek with his thumbnail, a habit that irritated Mahindan, and said: What's the point? They have already made up their minds.

If you cannot be helpful, just go, Mahindan snapped.

Prasad unfolded a sheet of paper from his pocket and said, Now see what I have written.

A guard interrupted with a message for Mahindan. He had a visitor.

Now? Mahindan asked in English.

It was 8 p.m.

It's your lawyer, the guard said, and Mahindan sprang up. Hema and her daughters were being released. The authorities must have reviewed his case and decided to let him go too. They walked down the hall, Mahindan's mind racing ahead. Soon all this, the heavy-soled footsteps in the dark, other people's night terrors, all this would be behind him. He would be reunited with Sellian and they could start their new life together!

It wasn't until they approached the private meeting room that Mahindan realized none of this could be true. He had failed his last detention review and the next one was already scheduled for the following week.

Through the little window inset into the door, he caught sight of Sam Nadarajah seated beside Mr. Gigovaz. For a moment, he wondered if they had come about Prasad's letter. But once in the room, he saw the grim expressions on their faces.

We have news, Sam said in English. Please sit.

Mahindan's head became dangerously buoyant and he fumbled to grasp the back of a chair. Something had happened to Sellian.

The door closed heavy behind him and he glanced back, full of an urgent, panicked instinct to run to his son. They had last seen each other on Saturday. He should have held Sellian tighter. He should not have let him go.

What is happening? Mahindan asked in Tamil. Sellian is sick? Hurt? Is he—

Sam pressed the air up and down with his palms. The boy is fine, he said.

Where is he? In hospital?

Illai. It is nothing like that. Sit down. Ukkarru, ukkarru.

Mahindan pulled the chair out blindly. *The boy is fine.*

Sam and Mr. Gigovaz conferred together in English while Mahindan stared at the table, unable to follow along. He tried to tamp down the terror, the adrenaline that had coursed in. Another frightening thought: They had come about the documents.

Sam spoke in Tamil: We have come from the women's prison. The thing is . . . Savitri is not well.

She has caught some illness? Mahindan asked. He took deep, steadying breaths. Alarm came easily these days and took great effort to dispel.

She has been very low, Sam said. Not eating, sleeping. It has been like this for some time. She cannot cope with two small children.

Okay. No problem, Mahindan said, using the English expressions. He saw now that the news, in fact, was good. It would be a relief to finally sever ties with that woman. He said, Sellian can come here.

Sam's eyes flicked away, past Mahindan to the wall behind him. The authorities believe the best thing is for Sellian to leave prison, he said. There is a couple who have agreed to take care of him. They live very close to here, thirty, maybe forty minutes by car.

Mahindan was confused. He glanced at Mr. Gigovaz and saw the grim expression on his face. To the lawyer, the actions they had to take were clear, nonnegotiable.

They want to put my son with another family? Mahindan asked Sam in Tamil.

Only until you are released, Sam said. It is just for the short term.

These people did not have their own children and now they wanted his son. Mahindan's voice shook as he said: I thought the Canadians hated us. They wish the boat had been sent away. Now it seems they want our children.

It is temporary, Sam said.

He remembered the Japanese judge, the stern expression that held tight to her face every time she looked at him, as though he was nothing, just a cockroach she would stamp under her heel. *She* must have done this to him. To punish him further.

The room swayed, the door, the walls, all of it grew fuzzy. There was one light overhead and then there were two. He blinked and his head was weightless, came unmoored.

Mahindan! Sam was at his side, pulling back his chair, pushing his head down gently. Deep breaths, Sam said. Deep breaths.

Mahindan, his head between his legs, breathing through his open mouth, had a single thought: NO. NO. NO. Ears ringing, he pushed back against Sam and sat upright. He struggled to speak, but when he did, his voice was loud, threatening to become a shout: Why can't Sellian come here? He's my son! How is he to live with these strangers who cannot speak our language?

He had lapsed into Tamil. Mahindan glanced at Mr. Gigovaz, who watched, impassive. If he could just convince Sam, together they might be able to appeal to Mr. Gigovaz, change the minds of the authorities.

He lowered his voice and turned to Sam, pleading: How will they know how to care for him?

Just think clearly for a moment, Sam said. In an English-speaking household, enrolled in school, imagine how easily Sellian will learn the language. He's still small, no? At that age, children adjust very quickly.

He will go to school? Mahindan said. The prospect was a glimmer in the darkness. He gripped the table and felt its stable surface. For months, he'd worried about Sellian falling behind, playing the fool instead of attending to his studies. To succeed in this country, he must have a good education.

A child should not be in jail, Sam said, switching to English. He should be learning his lessons and running around, playing outside.

With his father, Mahindan said, also in English, folding his arms across his chest. There was only one light overhead. His body felt more solid. He took a deep breath to be certain, puffing out his chest.

Mr. Gigovaz shook his head, as if to swat away an irritating insect. Remember why you came here, Mr. Mahindan. It was for your son most of all. Try to focus on what is best for him.

You have children? Mahindan asked in English. A son? A . . . a . . . girl?

Mr. Gigovaz shook his head again, his expression momentarily dimming, making Mahindan triumphant then furious. Who was this white man to tell him who and what he had come to this country for? What could a childless person know of parenting, what it was to be a father, to live in a constant state of trepidation for the well-being of another? He was angry at Sam too, who would leave in a little while and drive home to his warm house and his family. For Sam, this meeting was only an unpleasant interlude in an otherwise ordinary day.

Mahindan thought of Hema, and now he really was envious. Had she truly earned her freedom? Did she, who had never suffered separation from her daughters, deserve it more than him? What fortune it was to be a woman.

Savitri is keeping her son, he said in English. But mine is getting stolen. Because I am a father.

We will make sure he visits you, Mr. Gigovaz said.

Every Saturday without fail, Sam added. Point is, we have no choice in this matter. We must make the best of it.

I must make the best of it, Mahindan said bitterly in Tamil. *We* are not Sellian's fathers. Only I am.

Mr. Gigovaz leaned forward across the table. He wanted Mahindan to know he had met this couple personally. They were good people, a nurse and a school principal. They had a nice house, close to a school, across from a park. Priya and Charlika were taking Sellian there now. His son would have all the benefits.

What is wrong with them? Mahindan asked Sam. Why don't they have children of their own? Why must they steal my only son?

He felt the impotence of his rage. Already Sellian had been taken, and no one had asked his permission or even his opinion.

He remembered Ranga asking: *What to do?* The answer came to him in Sam's silence: nothing.

The Happiest Day

Chithra was curled on the settee moaning in pain. Mahindan rubbed circles against the small of her back and kissed her head, the floral scent of shampoo wafting off her still-damp hair.

A squeezing pain, she gasped. Squeezing, squeezing.

Mahindan had an eye on his watch. Thirty-three seconds, he said. Longest one.

His job was timekeeper. Later, he would tell their parents the exact time of birth and an astrological chart would be drawn. The child's entire future mapped out—auspicious numbers and days, best matches for marriage. Mahindan and Chithra were agnostic when it came to these things, but their parents were devout and this was the first grandchild.

What Mahindan anticipated most was the name-giving ceremony, when he would whisper the baby's name in its right ear. They had a few options chosen but hadn't yet made the final decision. When the elephant comes, we will know, Chithra said.

He peered out the window and prayed the dusky sky would remain quiet. Leaves shivered in the breeze. A stray cat slunk around the trunk of the mango tree. Every day for the past two weeks, they had asked themselves: today?

Today! The thought jolted him. Today they would meet their first-born.

Mahindan helped Chithra lumber off the settee. She made a slow, labored turn of the room, pressing a hot-water bottle to her back with both hands.

Get out, she said, speaking to the giant ball straining against her skirt, her navel popping out in a hard knot. Wicked child, you're evicted.

She was frightened but determined, jittery with nervous anticipation.

Nineteenth May, Mahindan said. Today is our child's birthday.

Let it be quick, Chithra muttered. Just let it be over.

Earlier, they had said a prayer to Parvati, and the sweet smell of incense still hung in the room.

On the radio, Chithra demanded, holding the back of a chair and practicing her squats. Must have a distraction.

The Voice of Tiger Radio was playing a drama about the ancient Tamil king Ellalan. The Chola King was renowned for fairness and good leadership, the narrator said. He was loved and respected by Tamils and Sinhalese alike.

There had been an uptick in nationalistic programming recently. LTTE flags were strung across streets and triumphant banners hung down the sides of buildings. Mahindan worried about the Sinhalese in their MiGs and Kfir jets overhead. Did the red flags only goad them?

Chithra groaned and Mahindan checked his watch. The pains were coming quicker now, each one closer on the heels of the other. He hoped labor would be swift. It twisted his insides to see Chithra like this, eyes squeezed shut, teeth gritted.

Paining, paining, she wailed.

Mahindan stroked her hair and told her he loved her. He wanted to siphon away her agony, bear some of it himself. He kissed her hot forehead and she reached back to squeeze his hand.

Why does it hurt so much? she asked in tears. It was not like this for Ruksala.

Ruksala had given birth six weeks earlier and Chithra had helped the midwife while Mahindan paced outside, a borrowed motorcycle at the ready. Ruksala scolded him for being overprotective, but the LTTE wouldn't send Rama home and it was all Mahindan could think to do.

Just as dawn was breaking, Chithra had come to find him slumped beside the cycle. She'd shaken the ball of his shoulder, and when he'd lifted his groggy head off his knees, she'd grinned and said: She's had a boy! Come meet Prem!

But seeing Ruksala through her time had only made Chithra more frightened. Now she eased herself back onto the settee with a grimace, wedging the hot water bottle behind her. On the radio, King Ellalan defeated his Sinhalese rival. I have conquered the Kingdom of Anuradhapura, the actor declared. In the name of the great Chola Empire.

Chithra's head fell back onto a pillow. I just want tonight to be over, she said. Then our baby will be here.

He was going to be a father! The prospect was absurd. What the devil did he know about raising a child? He watched Chithra, panting, eyes closed. Mothers had an instinct. He only had to follow her lead.

The tidy room was sparsely furnished, quiet but for the actors' voices and Chithra's shallow breaths, an owl hooting outside. In a few days, the whole place would be turned upside down by a squalling infant and mounds of dirty nappies. And in a few months? One chubby hand in front of the other, a baby crawling across the floor, then later, tentative steps, Chithra crouched with the camera. He could see his child's limbs, the soft creases and rolls, the gold drops in each ear if she was a girl, the thin bangle. He couldn't imagine the baby's face, though. Not yet. But soon. He caught Chithra's hand and kissed it. Soon.

Ominous music came through the speakers as Ellalan condemned his son to death. A grievous crime has been committed, the actor said. Atonement must be made.

My God, Chithra said. Who writes this drivel?

An involuntary cry escaped her lips and Mahindan, on his knees at her side, checked the time. Less than seven minutes! Hospital time!

A voice broke in on the radio, cutting the king off midsentence: We have breaking news from LTTE officials.

Chithra keened: Ehhhhhhnnnnnnnnnnn. Mahindan felt the bones of his hands being crushed in her grip. He tried to rub her back again, but she yelped: No!

The LTTE has declared a victory in Ratmalana, the news reader announced. A heroic martyr has destroyed seventeen enemies, including D. S. Samarasinghe, the Sinhalese minister for agriculture.

EHNNNNNNNNNNNNNNN, Chithra wailed.

Mahindan switched off the radio. The baby was coming!

At the hospital, everything moved in slow motion. An apathetic young man with a lazy eye presided over the waiting room where half a dozen desultory patients slumped in uncomfortable plastic chairs. Everyone gave a wide berth to the far corner, where part of the roof had caved in after an air strike. Orange pylons cordoned off the area underneath, where tubs had been set out to catch rainwater.

Mahindan filled in Chithra's name in a box while she white-knuckled the arms of a chair and groaned.

Will you call a doctor, please? he asked.

Have to fill out the forms first, the receptionist said without turning around.

He and everyone else in the waiting room were focused on the TV mounted behind the reception desk. It was tuned to the news on the local station, where a popular young journalist sat behind the anchor desk. She wore a red-and-yellow sari with a tiny black dot of pottu between her eyebrows.

. . . has praised the martyr's heroism and bravery, she said.

Mahindan filled in Chithra's birthday and wrote *none* under Allergies. Glancing over his shoulder, he saw her breathing evenly with her head resting against the wall behind her. His pen was steadier as he printed their address.

. . . the Tiger victory. Seventeen enemy combatants were killed, including the minister for agriculture.

He brought the form for Chithra to sign.

. . . young man from Jaffna . . .

Mahindan glanced at the TV while Chithra balanced the clipboard on her belly and scrawled her name.

A photo filled the screen. A boy no older than twenty with a smiling mouth and petrified eyes. What had possessed him to volunteer for this mission? And what had he thought as he drove into the airplane hangar? Did he close his eyes at the end, hands trembling on the steering wheel, foot on the pedal, speeding blindly to his death? Mahindan returned to the front desk, riveted by the television.

Now the Sinhalese will have their revenge, an old woman said loudly, and a few people hushed her.

Seventeen people at the Ratmalana airport. And only one politician.

The rest must have been civilians. Pilots and air hostesses, engineers working on a plane.

. . . Prabhakaran congratulated the hero before he left on his mission.

The young man was pictured in front of a bus shaking hands with the LTTE leader. Mahindan caught his breath. Red with a blue stripe across the front. Could it be the same one?

Hurry, Chithra called to his back.

Forms are finished? the receptionist asked, turning to Mahindan.

There was a rumble overhead and Mahindan tensed. The waiting room fell silent as heads swiveled to the ceiling. The ominous drone of an engine. Mahindan clung to the clipboard as the MiG bomber, loud and rushing, blocked out all other sound. It zoomed past and everyone exhaled. There was a colossal blast in the distance and the ground under their feet quaked.

Hands trembling, Mahindan handed the forms across the counter. He caught the receptionist's good eye and they shared a moment of mutual relief.

I'll call a nurse, the receptionist said. Please wait, sir. Only a moment.

Thank you.

The shock waves reverberated, juddering through his soles and up his legs. Seventeen dead in Ratmalana. What had he done?

Rolling wheels approached and a familiar voice called: Mrs. Mahindan?

The trainee nurse they had met months earlier held Chithra's arm as she lowered herself into the wheelchair.

I have finished my schooling, she said proudly as she led them to the maternity ward.

The walls they passed were patchworked with squares of what looked like gauze and packing tape. A long tube snaked down from the ceiling into a black bin.

But the doctor is here? Mahindan asked.

Oh yes, she said. How busy the obstetrician is tonight!

They entered a ward full of howling, bawling women. Women bent over beds while their husbands rubbed their backs. Women cross-stitching and chatting with their sisters. Women whimpering on their sides. All ripe to burst.

What were all these people thinking? What had he and Chithra been thinking? Seventeen dead in Ratmalana. What kind of world was this for a child? A visceral memory took him by surprise, the noxious smell of kerosene as he'd converted the bus's engine. He felt nauseous.

Four centimeters, the nurse said from between Chithra's legs. She stripped off her gloves and patted Chithra's knee. Getting close.

Please, Chithra said, catching hold of her arm. I want the painkillers.

Two hours later, Chithra was still in agony and Mahindan held her as she howled.

Must get through this part, she gasped.

Then the baby will be here, Mahindan said. The happiest day of our lives.

It was the consolation they had been repeating to themselves all night. He wanted to believe it was true, but he couldn't stop thinking about the bus, imagining the poor fellow driving through the doors of the airplane hangar and blowing himself up. Seventeen people.

None of the other women were in as much agony as Chithra, but the nurse said every mother was different and gave Mahindan a towel and a basin of water. When he pointed out the beeping monitors at some of the other bedsides, the nurse said equipment was limited. She wouldn't meet his eyes when she said this and he felt resentful of the lucky mothers.

It is too much, Chithra insisted. Can you not give me more painkillers?

The nurse was dismayed. Very sorry, Mrs. Mahindan. The embargoes, you know. We have to ration. If it wasn't for the shortages . . .

The pains are every two minutes now, Chithra said. Where is the doctor?

Be patient, the nurse said. Your waters haven't come.

She and Mahindan were helping Chithra onto the bed as she said this, and a flood of red gushed to the floor.

Chithra squeezed her eyes shut, cresting another wave of pain. Now will you call the doctor? she cried.

Mahindan saw the blood and the nurse's horror-struck expression right before she sprinted down the ward. Chithra squeezed his hand and screamed. He couldn't help staring at the pool of liquid, terrifyingly bright.

Thank God, Chithra said, panting heavily and lying back on her elbows. Worst one yet. Help me, will you?

Gingerly stepping around the seeping blood, he lifted her legs onto the bed.

Where has that nurse gone? she asked. Waters have come, no?

She . . . she . . . went to get the doctor, Mahindan said.

An orderly hurried in and pulled up the bedrails.

Please, madam, he said. Lie back.

Finally! Then she saw his face and asked: What's wrong? What's happened?

The orderly sped the bed through the ward. The cross-stitching woman glanced up as they passed. She gasped and covered her mouth.

Chithra clutched his arm. Mahindan?

The obstetrician met them in the corridor, shrugging blood-spattered surgical greens off her shoulders and letting them drop to the floor. The nurse popped out from behind a door and handed her a fresh gown. They had met the obstetrician twice before and Mahindan was relieved to see her competent face now. Chithra was seized by another contraction and moaned, uninhibited now, as they sailed down the corridor.

The placenta has detached from the wall of the uterus, the obstetrician shouted over Chithra's yowling. The orderly took a sharp turn and the foot of the bed bumped into a corner. The placenta feeds the baby, the obstetrician explained. Without nutrition, the child will go into shock. We must operate.

Corridors passed in a blur of doorways. Staff and patients pressed themselves against walls when they saw the bed coming. More people had joined them now—nurses, doctors, Mahindan could not tell.

A nurse called out: Thirty-seven weeks. First pregnancy. O-negative.

The baby, Chithra sobbed. Please save my baby.

Sooner we can get the baby out, the better, the obstetrician said.

Mahindan squeezed Chithra's hand. Someone arrived with a blood pressure cuff and he was elbowed out of the way.

Phone the blood bank, the doctor yelled to an orderly they passed. We need every unit of O-negative they have.

The mob around them was larger now, medical staff in scrubs and nursing uniforms, all racing to keep up. The operating theater came into view. Someone pushed a bundle into Mahindan's hands.

Stay here, the obstetrician ordered as the double doors swung open. The medical team surged forward, the bed in their center and Chithra with her knees up, gripping the rails and howling.

I love you, he yelled. Chithra! I love you!

But the doors had already closed and he was alone in the long, silent hallway. Looking down, he saw what he was holding. Scrubs. He pulled the oversized bottoms up over his trousers and pulled on the shirt. There was a cap and covers for his shoes. Tears streamed down his face. His child was going to die and it was all his fault.

Sir! A nurse in surgical gear scooped a hand through the air. Your wife is ready.

In the operating theater, Chithra was laid out like the victim of a magic trick. A blue screen hung between the two halves of her body. She had her arms spread in a *T* shape and a cap around her hair. The obstetrician and another surgeon stood behind the screen, covered head to foot in green. Chithra was attached to tubes and the monitors were lively, numbers flashing, a green line spiking up with a beep then plummeting to race across the screen. A plastic blood bag hung from a pole and rich red liquid shot through a tube into Chithra's arm. Seeing all the technology, the reassuring beep every time the green line peaked, the nurses bustling this way and that, all of it made Mahindan feel better. He sat on a stool by Chithra's head, took her cold hand, and kissed her clammy forehead.

No pain now, she said, but her eyes were sorrowful and her lower lip quivered.

Baby in distress, a nurse said.

She's bleeding, the surgeon said, and Mahindan thought: *she*. Their baby was a girl.

Chithra gave a juddering sob. Her mouth twisted with grief. He pressed his face against hers, forehead to forehead, nose next to nose. I'm sorry, he whispered. I'm sorry.

Where's the blood? The obstetrician's voice was a reprimand.

Mahindan wept, his tears mingling with Chithra's, her hand small and cold in his.

We have the last unit, a nurse called from across the room.

IV fluids, the obstetrician said.

The baby, Chithra whispered.

A boulder lodged in Mahindan's throat. I'm sorry, he sobbed.

At her side, the monitor beeped, each green mountain hitting its zenith a little quicker.

Heart rate, the surgeon said.

What had he done? What had he done?

Baby's in distress, the obstetrician said.

Mother's pressure dropping, the surgeon said.

The doors opened and an incubator rolled in. Neonatal team is here, the pediatrician called. The monitor was insistent, its beeps puncturing the hubbub. Mahindan thought of the bus and knew his daughter was dead. Karma like a boomerang had circled back on them, merciless.

Where are those fluids! the obstetrician demanded.

Don't have, the nurse yelled.

Norepinephrine, the surgeon said, his voice steady.

Chithra's chest had stopped heaving, but silent tears still leaked from the corners of her eyes, falling sideways and wetting the hair at her temples. Mahindan sniffed. It hurt to swallow. He pressed his mouth to her face.

Don't have any norepi, the nurse said.

The child had been cut off from her nourishment. Their daughter was in shock. He imagined the baby in suspended animation, her tiny mouth in an O of surprise. The utter disbelief. The sound and noise, the blast. It would have been over in a second. A blinding, wrenching instant. Life snuffed out.

God sakes, the surgeon said. Vasopressin, then. Just bring us something!

The baby? Chithra asked. Her voice was a whisper.

And Mahindan saw a long, wrinkled body, bloody and slimy. The black hair slicked to its head.

A boy, the obstetrician said.

Surprised, Mahindan thought: A boy! He nodded and smiled at Chithra, but she had closed her eyes. The room was silent now, everyone waiting, the only sound coming from the frantic monitor, and Mahindan, watching the creature in the doctor's hands, felt despair. The neonatal team swarmed in and carried the baby away. He saw their backs, gathered around his child, dead before he was born.

Mahindan couldn't face Chithra. What had he done?

Pressure still dropping, the obstetrician called. Oxygen saturation.

V-tach, the surgeon said.

Epi! the obstetrician shouted. Where's the damn epi?

Can't find it! Can't find it! The nurse sounded close to tears.

Chithra's hand went slack and he clasped it, instinctively, as the exhausted heart monitor gave up. The monotone sound when the person on the other end of the phone hangs up. Mahindan saw the flat line on the screen at the same moment he heard their son give a full and hearty wail.

C harlie drove them out to the suburbs of Maple Ridge. Priya was incensed at being roped into this errand, Gigovaz's last-minute order after she'd already worked late and was just powering down her computer and anticipating takeout sushi in her pajamas on the couch, passing out to some brainless reality show. But now they were heading east on Highway 1 and she had to swallow down her umbrage so Charlie wouldn't notice.

I can't believe they're doing this, Charlie fumed at the steering wheel. What's that expression you lawyers have?

Cruel and unusual, Priya said, staring at her dark reflection in the window, because it had struck her too.

Charlie turned onto the bypass road and Priya felt the familiar dread close in, the smothering gloom that lingered around the prison, a malignant force field that tightened its grip as they neared. The Women's Correctional Center was a gray, two-story box on neatly manicured grounds with a flagpole and a short flight of steps to the front door. But for the lack of windows, it could have been a school or a middle-tier pharmaceutical company. It struck her how punitive the name was. *Correctional.*

Charlie yanked up the parking brake and pressed the red button on her buckle so the seat belt reeled back with an angry zing. Truly, she said. This can't wait until morning? Why are we spiriting the kid away in the middle of the night?

Sellian was half-asleep and tearful when the guard brought him out, but he perked up when he spotted Charlie and hugged her hard, eyes squeezed shut.

He thinks he's going to see his father, Charlie said when they were back in the car.

Priya turned to smile at Sellian in the car seat, small and restrained under the convoluted crisscross of belts and clips. Though it was after 8 p.m. and he'd been roused from his bed, he was still wearing the government-issued track pants and sweater she always saw him in during the day.

Sellian asked a question in his high child's voice and Charlie replied, catching his eye in the rearview mirror. Illai, she said, shaking her head. Illai.

Priya knew this meant *no*. Sellian bobbed his head as he replied and the hope on his face required no translation. Priya caught the refrain: Appa. Appa.

It's no use, Charlie said. He won't believe me. She blew a hard breath, fluttering her bangs off her brow. But when she spoke to Sellian, her voice was cajoling, every sentence turning up at the end. What was Charlie saying, what words could she possibly find to explain where he was going and why?

Priya flipped through her paperwork as they drove, reviewing the business she had to conduct with the foster parents, the forms they had to initial and sign, the copies she must leave with them, the ones she had to take. There was a picture of the couple—Rick and Maggie Flanigan—and their bungalow in New Westminster. Priya twisted back and held the photos out to Sellian. These are the nice people who will take care of you, she said. And Charlie translated. Sellian clutched Ganesha to his chest and shook his mute head.

There are a dozen Tamil families who would gladly have taken him, Charlie said as she signaled to change lanes.

None of them are accredited foster parents, Priya said.

She'd already had this argument with Gigovaz. Haven't we learned our lesson on this? she'd railed. Stealing children from their *Native* parents and putting them in *white* homes? What's next? A special school run by pedophiles? She'd got so worked up, she hadn't even known what she was saying. A small voice inside her pleaded: For the love of God, woman, stop! But Gigovaz hadn't snapped or even taken his usual condescending tone. He'd only asked, with a bemused expression, Are you sure you don't want to work in refugee law? And that had shut her up. But then he'd given her this assignment and she knew it was her punishment.

Charlie waved an angry hand at the windshield and said, The government is going to all this trouble—jailing five hundred people in the suburbs, busing them to hearings, setting their lawyers on attack mode. They couldn't fast-track a few foster-parent applications and get our families certified?

Priya glanced over her shoulder at Sellian, wondering what he made of all this, Charlie ranting in English, and how much he understood. Imprisoned in the car seat, he sat quietly, holding Ganesha in his lap and petting his elephant head like a dog.

At the Flanigans', Sellian begged to be carried and Charlie lifted him onto her hip. When Priya tried to pat his back, he flinched and snuggled away.

The house had the air of a recent deep cleaning. Hovering under the potpourri was the sharp tang of something astringent, Lysol and Mr. Clean. Priya found her ability to hate the kidnappers—as she'd taken to privately denigrating them—flustered by this obvious effort and their benign, hopeful expressions.

Charlie introduced Sellian to his new foster parents in both languages, enunciating slowly in English: This is Mr. and Mrs. Flanigan. They are going to take care of you.

Maggie Flanigan put her face close to Sellian's and he began to cry, quietly, in half-suppressed sobs. Charlie, pressing on, suggested a tour.

See? Priya said. You'll have your own bedroom.

Sellian's new room had a trim of nineties wallpaper; a parade of cowboys rode their horses along the top of the wall. There was a plastic bin overflowing with trains and Mega Bloks, and Disney sheets on the bed featuring characters from an animated movie about talking cars. The Flanigans had laid out matching pajamas and Priya wanted to hug these strangers for their compassion. She thought of all the things Sellian would finally be able to do: hang from monkey bars, go to school. Though he didn't know it, he'd be better off here than in jail. But then she thought of Mahindan, who must be learning the news right this minute, and felt like a traitor.

Charlie was taking Sellian on a circle of the room, the Flanigans hovering behind. See all your new clothes? Charlie said, pulling back the door of the closet. She repeated herself in Tamil, but Sellian only pressed his face into her neck and whimpered. Priya's stomach sank. How were they ever going to leave him?

Maggie Flanigan suggested tea and they made stilted conversation in the living room as Sellian, in Charlie's lap, drifted off to sleep, their voices dropping lower and lower with his eyelids.

We only found out yesterday that Sellian was coming here, Rick Flanigan said. We would have tried to learn a little Tamil if we'd known.

We've been fostering for three years, Maggie Flanigan said, setting her tea down untouched. But this is our first time with . . . a language barrier.

There was a fleeting terrified expression on her face that made Priya and Charlie exchange a startled look.

He'll pick up English quickly, Charlie said. He's got a little bit already . . . his alphabet, the numbers up to twenty.

We've started the enrollment process for his school, Rick Flanigan said.

If you could just sign here, Priya said, holding out a pen.

Charlie put a finger to her lips and stood with Sellian cradled in her arms. He made a wakeful sound and she whispered, Shhh . . . shhhhh. Priya gathered up her paperwork and shook the Flanigans' hands, feeling complicit.

They were buttoning their coats when they heard a rustle in the bedroom and saw the doorknob turn. Charlie gave a quick shake of her head and jammed her feet into her shoes. The bedroom door flew open and Sellian barreled down the hall. Maggie Flanigan scooped him up and Sellian, struggling for freedom, reached for Charlie through the air, his face twisted into a piteous plea, begging in Tamil to the only person who would understand.

Get out! Charlie muttered to Priya. Go!

Outside, the suburban neighborhood was quiet. Across the street, a woman on a ladder hung Christmas lights. At their backs, Sellian screamed on the threshold, words blubbering out between sobs and tears as they fled down the walk, Priya's heart ready to break.

JEOPARDY

The lawyer who was against them asked: Is November twenty-seventh a special day for you?

Mr. Gigovaz had coached Mahindan to look the judge straight in the eyes. To keep his hands folded so they would not shake. Mahindan said in English: Twenty-seven November is Martyrs' Day.

Singh turned to the judge and said: A day to commemorate suicide bombers. Also called Heroes' Day.

Mahindan squeezed his hands. Martyrs' Day was for mourning— a day when Sellian stayed home from school and they went to the temple with Ruksala and Prem to say a prayer for Rama. In this country, he knew, they also had a Heroes' Day, in November. Something his grandfather had told him: History is owned by the winners.

Singh wanted to know how he observed Martyrs' Day, and he was forced to admit he lit lamps in the house and went onto the road to watch the dramatic reenactments.

And you took your son with you to these celebrations? Singh prodded.

Mr. Gigovaz interrupted: What would have happened if you had stayed home or not decorated your house?

How many detention reviews had he already endured? Was this the seventh? The eighth? Mahindan had the Japanese judge again, the one who he was sure had given Sellian to another family. Some judges wore their opinions like clothes; Mahindan could glean their thoughts in their furrowed brows, the way they either watched him or didn't. But he'd seen this Japanese woman more than anyone else, and she always had the same unreadable expression, mouth compressed in a severe line.

Mahindan told the truth: If we had not taken part in the celebrations, the cadres would have beat us up, forced me to join them.

Did she not know what it was like to have so little agency? To be faced with such cruel options it was as if there was no choice at all? These Canadians, with all their creature comforts, had such meager imaginations.

Duress, Mr. Gigovaz said to the judge, before turning to Singh and adding: Mr. Mahindan was a father and a widower living in an LTTE-controlled area. Would any of us have done differently?

Priya was not here today and Mahindan missed her presence. Just having her at the table—another person on his side—was a comfort.

Singh wanted to know why he hadn't left Kilinochchi sooner. Why didn't you take your son and move somewhere else—to a place that was not under Tiger control?

Mahindan swallowed back his frustration. He told himself it was good she was asking these foolish questions because he had prepared his answers and practiced them in English.

He said: In my country, there is no freedom.

Civilians living in LTTE-controlled areas required permission to leave, Mr. Gigovaz said. And after 2008, passes were heavily restricted.

Mahindan looked from Singh to the judge, back to Singh again, unsure of where to direct his appeal. Even with the pass, he said, where to go? Without a Sinhalese name, without knowing to speak their language? The Sinhalese, they hate Tamils. In my country, we are treated like animals. They just do not understand life.

Mr. Gigovaz appealed to the judge: The Sri Lankan government has engaged in systematic discrimination against its Tamil citizens ever since the introduction of the Sinhala First Act in 1956. This is all well-documented.

The judge turned on him: These specious arguments may hold water with some of my colleagues, Mr. Gigovaz, but please give me a little more credit. Your client was born into a country at war. He might have tried a little harder to leave sooner. She glared at Mahindan and added: Through legal means.

Mahindan panicked. All this time, he had thought the judge was bored; now, he realized she had already made her decision. Mahindan would never be allowed to leave the jail. His fate had been sealed before he'd walked in the door.

I held everything, he said, rubbing a palm over his sweaty upper lip. He cast about for the English words, mind racing. Money, house, business. I held everything, but I could not do nothing. He heard the tremble in his voice and hated that he could not control it. Kilinochchi, Colombo . . . no safe place to be a Tamil. Blood rushed in his ears. He had to do something! He had to convince her! There was a boat to Canada, he said. I took my chance.

The driver with the missing incisor, his pockmarked face leering in the shadows. The memory of it stopped Mahindan cold. Squeezing through a hole in the fence, alert for the sound of approaching guards. Sweat beaded the back of his neck. His stomach turned.

Singh pounced: How much did you pay the agent for your passage?

Mahindan knew better than to admit the true figure. He had not mastered the numbers yet and answered in Tamil: Five hundred thousand rupees.

The driver was a small man, hunched from years of stealth. Black as a devil, the whites of his eyes shining greedy in the darkness. The van already full and Mahindan still at the back of the mob, terrified the doors would slam shut in his face before he had a chance to scramble in. Sellian at his side, face pressed into his leg.

Five hundred thousand rupees, Singh said. She was tapping the edge of a folder against the desk as if she knew something and was drawing out the big reveal. Others are saying they paid more. Is there some reason the agent would give you a discount?

The judge was watching, curious now. His guts turned to liquid and he thought he might be sick. Mahindan took a deep breath through his nose and willed his face to show nothing but honesty. They all thought the agent who took their money was a man, that one person had coordinated the escape. They knew nothing. Not one single thing.

My wife used to say first price is worst price, he said. In Sri Lanka, this is the way. Always try and try until we are getting better.

Singh asked another question and Mahindan tried to follow, getting tripped up by her grammar and his own pounding pulse. He had to wait for the interpreter to explain.

Isn't it true the real reason you did not leave Kilinochchi sooner is because you were a member of the LTTE?

No, Mahindan said to the interpreter. Please tell them. Never.

He felt a little calmer. They didn't mind about the agent. Everyone on the boat had used an agent, and some of the women, at least, had been released from jail. It didn't matter what this or that person paid for the passage.

My client was a mechanic, Mr. Gigovaz told the judge, and Mahindan understood this meant he repaired vehicles. His vocabulary had improved, thanks to news programs and reward shows, Peter Mansbridge and Alex Trebek. *Jeopardy!* meant danger, but it also meant prizes.

When Singh said, Tell us about the bus you repaired in April 2003, he knew this was jeopardy.

There was a problem with the brakes, Mahindan told Singh, struggling to modulate his voice and make it sound calm. I had to replace them.

It was a marvel to him—the power of the Canadian police. Their ability to reach back in time and riffle through the minute details of his long-ago life. Mahindan had replaced the brake pads on countless buses over the years—minibuses, school buses, the number 4 public bus that ran the Kilinochchi–Jaffna route six times a day. That the authorities here could sift through all the Tatas and Leylands and come up with this one bus was terrifying.

This vehicle you worked on, Singh said. Did you do anything else apart from fixing the brakes?

They were in a different room than usual and the judge sat at a raised dais. She stared down at Mahindan, her expression shrewd.

Mahindan said: Only brakes had a problem. There was nothing else to repair.

He told himself it was all right. Mr. Gigovaz had warned him Singh would bring this evidence forward. He was prepared to answer her questions.

Exhibit F, Singh said. On May 19, 2003, the LTTE drove a bus rigged with explosives into an airplane hangar in Ratmalana, killing seventeen people, including three children and Sri Lanka's minister of agriculture. In repairing the bus, this man was directly responsible for the death of seventeen civilians.

Mahindan heard the triumph in her voice, the way she tried and failed to smother it at the end after realizing how it sounded—victory at the expense of seventeen dead foreigners. Everything about Singh spoke of her conviction, how certain she was that she could keep him locked away forever. *Seventeen civilians.*

Mahindan pressed his knees together to keep them from trembling and said very quickly, in English: Only I repaired brakes. I did not jig up no bombs.

When the bus was brought to your shop, did you know it belonged to the LTTE?

Mahindan shook his head. He was flustered by the injustice. Do work for the Tigers or be crushed by them. Give the Canadians a reason to deport him or tell a pack of lies. There was never a good option. He lapsed into Tamil and allowed the interpreter to be his mouthpiece.

I was a simple mechanic. I repaired motorcycles and cars and public buses. When the Tigers came to me, I did not have a choice. I repaired what was broken and did not ask questions.

Singh asked: It didn't bother you that the bus you fixed killed seventeen innocent people?

If he closed his eyes, he would see the green line again, hear the two doctors. *Heart rate. Pressure droppng.* His ears rang, the shrill so loud he could barely hear his own words. A cadre brought the bus and said to me, You repair it. If I had refused, he would have beaten me. If I had refused again, he would have killed me.

The impassive machines, the high, flustered voice of the nurse. *Can't find it! Can't find it!* Chithra's tears sliding sideways.

Chithra! he yelped.

He felt pressure on his wrist and saw Mr. Gigovaz, his face splotched red, his expression kind.

Chithra, Mahindan repeated, more softly. My wife was pregnant at the time. He appealed to the judge and said: With our son. The cadre would have set fire to our house, allowed my wife to burn inside. The things they did to us . . . you cannot imagine. Sinhalese army, Tamil Tigers . . . we were nothing to them.

He held the judge's eye and for a long moment there was silence. This was the judge who had set Hema and her daughters free. He held on to this nugget, this proof of her goodness.

Singh made a noise as if she was about to speak and Mr. Gigovaz cut her off: As a civilian making a living in a Tiger-controlled area, my client had no choice but to do work for the LTTE.

Mahindan said, When the bus came to me, I did not know nothing about a bombing. Only later, when it was done, only then I knew it was the bus I had repaired.

How often did you work for the LTTE? Singh asked.

Mahindan answered in Tamil: From time to time, changing transmissions, repairing engines, this kind of thing. No bombs, he added in English. No bombs.

Mr. Gigovaz said: My client has testified that he turned down offers to join the LTTE. And although Border Services has tried to suggest otherwise, there is no proof he ever trained or fought with them.

Fixing the brakes on a vehicle that is about to be used in a terrorist attack is as good as strapping on the explosives, Singh said. And by his own admission, your client continued to work with the LTTE even after he knew what they were capable of. She ignored Mr. Gigovaz and spoke directly to the judge: The migrant aided and abetted a terror attack. In repairing an LTTE-owned bus, he was party to a war crime.

Mahindan put his head in his hands and moaned.

WHY ARE YOU HERE?

There was a voice mail on Grace's BlackBerry. Keying in her password, she listened as she strode down the corridor, frowning when she heard her mother's voice.

Our house is on the market, Kumi launched in without any preamble. Guess the price. Just guess! Grace, I need you to . . .

Grace fumed silently. Kumi must think she had nothing better to do all day than respond to her mother's every whim. It wasn't enough that she had the twins tangled up in her mission—*the family history project,* they all called it—Kumi wanted to rope Grace in too. As if Grace didn't have evidence to parse and horror stories to sit through. Life-and-death decisions to make.

Grace was returning from a detention review. A widower with a small child in foster care. But he had also taken part in a suicide bombing. And he'd got jumpy when Singh brought up the agent. Did it mean something? I'm not a mind reader, Grace thought. And yet this job was all about being one, trying to guess at true motivations, to separate the deserving refugees from the ones who planned to use Canada as ground zero for a proxy war. She had denied the man's detention release. There might already be grounds for deportation, but that was a decision for the admissibility hearing.

Back in the summer, when she was still new to the job, she had told herself she just needed to learn the ropes, that she'd be ready to adjudicate admissibility hearings when the time came. But the calendar had caught up to her and she was still flailing.

So far, they were hearing only women's cases and she was deeming them admissible, setting her doubts aside and allowing the migrants to move on to the Refugee Board hearings. But in the new year, they would begin conducting the men's cases too. Already she found the prospect nerve-racking.

Grace replayed the voice mail. We need to trace the ownership back, Kumi said. Let the imposters claim the house is theirs. I still have the original deed.

As if Grace was a real estate agent! Her mother had no idea. None. Grace had worked herself into a temper as she stalked back to her office, silently seething. Mitchell Hurst was charging down the hallway on a collision course. He had a funny way of walking, as if led by his forehead. A ram charging, horns out.

At her door, Grace pulled the keys from her pocket and kept her head bent. She and Mitchell had fallen into a pattern of lukewarm pleasantries, acknowledging the other only when it could not be avoided. But today, Grace didn't think she could manage even that. *We need to trace the ownership. We.*

Ms. Nakamura. Mitchell came to a halt in front of her door.

Everyone else was Jill or Obi or Yee. She was the only one he addressed so officiously, as if he were the headmaster at a boarding school and she were a sixth-form girl. Be nice, she told herself.

Good afternoon, Mitchell.

I thought you might like to know I released Savitri Kumuran today.

I'm sorry? She slid her key in and unlocked the door.

He put his palm flat against her door and said, Mrs. Kumuran. She of the controversial necklace.

Oh. Right. I remember. Up close, she saw the tremor in his hands. He was agitated, full of nervous energy.

The expert sent his report, Mitchell said. He shoved the folder he was holding at her. Turns out his findings were inconclusive.

Oh. Okay. Grace took a step back. She wasn't sure why he was telling her all of this.

Inconclusive, he said. Imagine that.

Well, it sounds like it was an easy decision, then, she said. Trust Mitchell to have the good fortune of simple choices.

Mitchell's foot was tapping a mile a minute. Of course, anyone who knows anything about Tamil culture—

Mitchell, Grace said. Have I done something to offend you?

Offend *me*?

A door at the end of the hall opened and a group dispersed out. A couple of them glanced over and waved before going the other way.

Whatever I did to you, Grace said, it was unintentional.

Me? Mitchell said. He half groaned. Look around. He gestured to the copy room with the folder in his hand. You know what Obi used to do? He worked with stateless people in Madagascar. Yee was at the United Nations for five years. Jill has a master's in Refugee Studies. And then there are the others, adjudicators like you, he said, jabbing a finger so close it nearly poked her. Why are *you* here?

What the hell did Mitchell think, that this was how she got her jollies? By being subjected to war porn, an unstoppable reel that replayed in her mind when she closed her eyes every night? Even car horns made her jump these days.

What's gotten into you? Steve had asked one morning, when a sudden banging on the door made her yelp.

Who is breaking down our door? she'd said, chagrined. It sounds like a police raid.

Grace, they're only knocking.

And here was Mitchell Hurst, the little swot, accusing her of being here for—what? For fun?

I'm doing the same job as you, she said, keeping her voice level as she closed the door to seal them both in her office. Working the same hours, agonizing over the same decisions, losing the same amount of sleep over these cases. Regardless of our . . . *pedigree,* we're all here for the same reasons. So what exactly is your problem?

She moved behind her desk to put space between them. When Mitchell paced, he reminded her of Kumi. He clutched one hand in a fist at his mouth. Haven't you noticed there's a pattern to Singh's arguments? he said. It doesn't matter who the claimant is, the case against them is the same. He made air quotes with his fingers and said: Inadmissible on grounds of criminality. The Minister is of the opinion this person is a flight risk.

So?

Every claimant is supposed to be assessed individually, and yet it's clear Border Services has a standard evidence package. They're applying one set of vague arguments across the board against everyone. This isn't the way the system is supposed to work.

Can you blame them? Grace said. There are 503 people to process. You know how many asylum seekers we get at the border every year? Last year, it was fourteen thousand. So why is it the ones who arrive at the airport are evaluated on their own merits and these so-called boat people are treated as a generic mass? Why the double standard?

I—

Didn't know. Of course not. He stopped to fix her with a taunting stare. Don't suppose it came up much at Transport.

Grace, heat rising to her face, would have lost her temper if the phone hadn't rung. A familiar number flashed on the call display. I should really introduce them, Grace thought, pressing the button to mute the strident ringing and banish her mother to voice mail.

If you're going to stand there and abuse me, Mitchell, I'll have to ask you to leave.

Sorry, he said, addressing his apology to the floor. I shouldn't have . . . It's not personal.

Grace felt momentarily vindicated.

But then he said: I can't blame you for being ig—for not knowing the ins and outs of the system. I wouldn't either, if I'd just arrived a few months ago.

He was only stating facts, but Grace was stung. She told herself to rise above it.

Well, I appreciate you saying that.

And another thing, Mitchell said, worked up again, as if the awkward apology hadn't just happened. Why is Border Services calling claimant testimony into question? The jurisprudence directs us to presume honesty.

But that's preposterous! Grace said. How are we supposed to take claimants at their word? We don't know who these people are. They could be anyone, saying anything!

MacDonald v. Canada, he said. That's the precedent. Which of course you don't know because your entire career has been spent elsewhere!

She leaned forward across her desk, ready to snatch the bait, but he held up a hand and lowered his voice.

Every government does this, hands out adjudicator positions as if they're rewards. Vancouver, Montreal, Toronto . . . half the openings are filled by fund-raisers, communications directors, whoever. Listen, I'm just calling it like I see it. There are those of us who have spent our careers in this field and those of us who are well-meaning, perhaps, but neophytes just the same.

Okay, that's true, she said. And it's not like I haven't noticed.

Right. Well, then can you see it from my point of view? Without any background experience or understanding of case law . . . well, what are decisions based on without that foundation? What the Minister tells you, perhaps.

I haven't seen or spoken to Minister Blair in months, Grace said. And I resent the insinuation. Whatever you think of me, Mitchell, I do take this job seriously and I am making careful, considered decisions.

And what's Blair basing his decisions on, his public statements? Mitchell had resumed pacing. What's his experience with human rights and global conflict? With refugees? He's not even the immigration minister!

He *is* the public safety minister. Grace gestured to the newspaper in her recycling bin. The godfather was making headlines again.

Mitchell gave a short, sarcastic laugh. That mobster wasn't a refugee. He bought a million-dollar house a month before he got here. You want to stay up all night worrying about something? Worry about the millionaires who buy their way in. What are their ulterior motives?

The Fool

When Sampa came to collect his tractor, Mahindan told him: Brakes were worse than I thought.

The tractor was bright red, with two large driving wheels in the back, steering and seat in the center. Sampa circled, hands clasped behind him, inspecting the undercarriage.

Had to replace the routers and pads both, Mahindan said.

It's a good machine, no? Sampa said, now out of view on the other side of the vehicle. Solid construction.

A longtime customer, Sampa was proud of this tractor that he'd won six years ago through a Red Cross lottery.

Plus repair the transmission, Mahindan said. Oil and filter change.

He held out the paper where he had meticulously marked prices beside each repair. But Sampa had already climbed into the driving seat and was gripping the steering wheel.

To think how I used to slave with the bullocks, he said. All those years, nearly breaking my back.

Mahindan threw his fingers out from his forehead and said, Very difficult problem with the transmission. Took whole of yesterday *and* day before. Two days gone!

He was still holding out the bill, and when Sampa finally leaned down to read it, Mahindan braced for an argument.

But the thing is fine now? Sampa removed a roll of rupees from his pocket. I can use it?

Mahindan bobbed his head from side to side. Yes, can use.

Sampa drove away and Mahindan was left clutching the fraudulent invoice. He crumpled it up. The whole job had taken less than an hour.

Seven years he had run his business. Everyone knew his prices were set, that he wouldn't haggle or cheat. And until a few months ago, he had done neither.

There was only one vehicle left in the shop, a hobbled three-wheeler that belonged to another longtime customer, Kamal Joseph. Mahindan didn't know what to do with the thing now. All it needed was a little air in the front tire. But Joseph and his family were gone.

One day, Joseph's wife was seen taking her towels down from the laundry line. Next day, the girls were missing from school and the house was locked up. Mahindan pictured the family after dark, wheeling their cycles down the road, headlamps turned off, past the closed-up shops and silent houses. More and more people were doing this now, secreting through the jungle to avoid checkpoints, quietly defecting out of LTTE-controlled territory.

He and Ruksala had argued about it again the day before. Have to leave before it is too late, Mahindan had said. Soon, there will be no choice.

They were in the bunker, seated side by side on the padded concrete bench, the world outside falling to pieces with muffled thumps and thuds. At one time, this shelter would have been packed, but nowadays it was like this: an old woman snored in the corner, cotton wool stuffed in her ears; a trio of schoolgirls sat cross-legged on the floor doing their sums; five-year-old Sellian and his cousin brother Prem watched two amputees play checkers. Every few moments, Sellian tapped his man on the shoulder to suggest a better move.

How long before they send all the bomber jets at once? Mahindan whispered. You heard they took Mannar. The tanks will come for us next.

They won't flatten the city while the Americans are here, Ruksala said.

Ruksala worked at the United Nations compound, coordinating the distribution of supplies brought in by the World Food Program. As long as the foreigners had a presence in Kilinochchi, she thought they would be all right. Mahindan didn't like to point out that it hadn't helped Rama.

Instead, he insisted: Must go to the Sinhalese side before they come to us.

And then what? she muttered, glancing at the boys.

There were stories of Tamils who changed their names and passed themselves off as Sinhalese. But those were people who spoke the language, who didn't mind being Buddhist.

We'll be caught by the police, Ruksala said. They'll say we are LTTE. Who knows what they'll do to the children.

Stay here long enough and we *will* be LTTE, Mahindan said. You heard they took Chelva and his nephew. The boy is not even eleven.

The Tigers had stepped up their recruitment. One fighter per family was no longer enough. Ruksala made a noncommittal noise and watched a gecko scurrying across the wall disappear through a crack. Mahindan knew she was thinking of Rama. It had been a year since they'd had word and even longer since they'd seen him. Every evening after work, Ruksala waited in a plastic chair on her veranda, watching the lane, hoping for Rama to saunter out of the horizon with that duck-footed gait. If they left, it would have to be by stealth, like the Josephs. They'd never see Rama again.

A crash shook the bunker. Everyone glanced up instinctively, to the lightbulb quivering in the aftershock. Sellian and Prem clasped hands.

One of the checker players covered his head with his good arm. Day and night cooped up in a bomb shelter, he cried. For how long can we live like this?

Mahindan pondered the question now, as he locked the garage and wheeled out his bicycle. If Chithra were alive, she would say: What did I tell you? Should have left six years ago. He thought of his parents, how they must have agonized over this same decision when he was a child, in the late seventies and early eighties, as tensions between the Sinhalese and Tamils peaked and grumbles about property values escalated to rocks lobbed through windows. How long could they stay in Colombo, in the Sinhalese south? And how to move and start again in the unknown Tamil north?

We were brothers once, his Appa used to say. Tamil, Sinhalese, Burgher, Muslim, what is the difference? At one time, no one thought to ask.

Whatever Ruksala thought, Mahindan knew their situation was dire. The army was inching northward and converging from the west. Last month, they had taken the last Tiger stronghold in Mannar

District. Two weeks ago, word had come: Mallavi had fallen. Already, the refugees from Pachilaipalli had abandoned their mud huts and fled. Everyone knew Kilinochchi would be next. And if they dithered too long, there would be only one direction to run: east, until the army chased them into the sea.

Mahindan cycled down lanes lined with deserted houses. Squawking crows picked through moldering piles of refuse. Monkeys hung down from the trees, their bearded black faces mocking. Three puppies tumbled over each other, full of exuberance, thrilled to be alive. Mahindan felt the hot rubber of his slippers, dust settling between his bare toes.

He took the scenic route, purposely spinning out time. For months now, even as he wavered over the decision, he'd been making arrangements to leave. Taking money out of the bank, pocketing extra from unsuspecting customers. Today, he would sell Chithra's jewelry. He had it rolled up in a cloth and stashed in the bag on his back. It was crucial to get a good price. Once they left Kilinochchi, they would be strangers in a foreign land, with only the rupees to speak for them.

First offer is the worst offer, Mahindan told himself. No harm in asking for more. But repeating Chithra's maxims felt like donning another fighter's armor before battle.

What would she think if she'd seen him with Sampa and his tractor? Would she be proud or disgusted? He felt sullied by what he'd done, and annoyed with the idiot for being so gullible.

Mahindan joined the A9, a dual carriageway. Four lanes of traffic with a faded dividing line and trees on either side. Billboards promising the demise of the president. It was chaotic and noisy, buses and motorcycles, bicycles and three-wheelers all blaring their horns and jostling for space.

Mahindan overtook a girl on a cycle. She had a crate strapped down over her back tire, a pair of scales hanging off. A man led an elephant on a chain. An open-top lorry trundled along, bulging with mangoes and spewing diesel. A motorcycle roared by, father, mother, and two small children on board.

Kilinochchi's town center was a handful of bomb-scarred low-rises butting up against the highway. Colorful signs above the awnings advertised the Happy Corner Tea Shop and Ganesha's Fruit Stall. Tiger flags were pasted in every window. Half the shops were boarded up, the iron gates drawn across, cows lolling in front. Some had been looted, papers scattered on the floor, drawers yanked out.

Kumuran's shop was squeezed between the Western Union and the Internet café. The widow who ran the café leaned against an electrical pole chewing betel.

Mahindan rolled to a stop and got down from his cycle.

How Internet Auntie?

Not a dog in the street, she said, speaking out the side of her mouth.

Power is cut?

She shrugged and spit a gob of betel in an impressive arc. What to do?

The bell over the door of the jewelry shop tinkled as Mahindan entered. Inside, the place was dim, hazy with swirling dust. He was surprised to see Kumuran's wife, humming a love song as she swept. She set the ekel broom aside when she saw him and moved behind the counter.

Kumuran had got her down from Jaffna and there was talk her people were Burmese or Malay. She was an alluring woman, with skin so fair rumor had it her father had kept watch by the door with a gun while the family slept, to prevent an abduction.

You are searching for something particular? she asked, and Mahindan noticed that even now she maintained a regal air, her pottu neatly applied, lines drawn with kohl to accentuate her cat eyes.

He slung his backpack off his shoulder and removed the cloth-wrapped bundle. I came to sell. He glanced over her shoulder. Kumuran is in the back?

He's not here, the wife said. She reached out her hand and Mahindan pulled his away, wondering why she wasn't at school teaching.

When is he coming back? he asked.

Her laugh was bitter. He's gone to be a hero. Then she fixed him with a shrewd look. But you are still here, a young, healthy man. And with jewelry. She snatched the cloth roll out of his hand then briskly unfurled it, revealing bangles and chains, gold glinting in the gloom.

There was a shuffling noise. A pair of eyes shone out of the back room then vanished.

Kumuran's wife yelled over her shoulder: Be quiet, will you? She flicked her hand in the air. These children can't sit still for two minutes!

There were three boys, Mahindan remembered. He tried to soften the mood. How is your eldest? How is Sonal? Must be, what, thirteen by now?

The wife took a magnifying glass to Chithra's eardrops. Ten, she said. Children are still small.

Mahindan didn't challenge her fib. And your youngest? Clever boy. Same class as my Sellian, no?

She gave him a flashlight and said, Hold the torch.

On the wall behind her, six-headed Murugan, the god of war, sat on a peacock holding his two consorts. Mahindan gazed up at the deity, his serene feminine faces, the dazzle of feathers fanned out behind him, a hundred unblinking eyes. *First offer is the worst offer.*

Even after settling on a price, Chithra would slyly ask: Can you not do something more? And an extra vadai would be folded in paper, a spool of thread added to the bag. Always something with you, Mahindan would say, shaking his head in admiration and disbelief. She'd grin and turn her cupped palm to the sky. For me, there is always something.

Kumuran's wife took out a receipt pad and began writing sums. Her tongue stuck out of the corner of her mouth. Mahindan nudged a pendant toward her. It was a teardrop sapphire circled with diamonds, the pride of his mother's collection, which she'd given Chithra on their wedding day. *For my future granddaughter.* Kumuran's wife waved it away.

Five hundred thousand rupees, she announced.

Mahindan thought he had not heard properly. All Chithra's axioms flew from his head. For all this? he said. The eardrops alone are worth—

Very difficult these days to find buyers.

This was my wife's thali, he said, lifting the chain.

You want to keep it? She flipped her pencil around so the eraser nub faced the receipt.

What am I to do with a thali? Mahindan asked. He let the chain drop, irritated with his useless sentimentality.

Kumuran's wife tapped the pencil against the counter. Her face was inscrutable.

Mahindan said, My wife only wore twenty-two karat. This gold is top quality.

She shook a set of bangles and they made a feeble ting-ting sound. How thin these are! she said. Twenty-two karat maybe, but not much of it.

But the gemstones, he said, pointing out his mother's pendant.

Synthetic, she said. Colored glass.

Mahindan looked around helplessly, at the studded pathakkams and baby anklets displayed under the glass counter, the silver chains draped on an upright holder. This woman was determined to cheat him. But Kumuran's was his last option. Even the pawnshop was gone, destroyed a few days earlier by a shell.

If you don't like the price, she said, no problem.

For a moment, he assumed this was an invitation to haggle, but then she slid the bangles back into their zippered pouch and began gathering the chains. She folded the cloth into a rectangular package, the ends neatly tucked in, and held it across the counter in both palms, like an offering.

Wait, he said. All right, all right. Five hundred thousand. She counted the cash and he left quickly, disgraced and furious, Chithra's words in his ears: There goes the fool who was born yesterday.

Charlie was flying home for the holidays. Return of the divorcée, she said. Back to Scarborough, so my mother can Aiyo-Ah-Nay my marital status and accuse me of putting on weight while shoving vadai down my throat.

But Priya could see Charlie was excited. Family exerted a strong pull, always. From somewhere close to the navel.

Priya said Hema and the girls could spend Christmas with her. She made the offer spontaneously, and then agonized about asking her father. One Thursday at dinner, she bided her time, waiting in vain for a good opening, then blurted out the request as they tidied up.

They shouldn't be alone, she said, stacking dirty plates.

Priya had expected resistance or outright rejection, but what she saw on her father's face was alarm.

The more the merrier, Rat said, rolling up his sleeves at the sink.

Priya saw her father gearing up to say something, his mouth opening and closing in mute preparation, and rushed on: They're still shell-shocked. They won't leave the apartment by themselves, and Charlie's away for a week. They'll go stir-crazy.

What do you think, Uncle? Rat asked.

Uncle was spooning leftovers into an empty yogurt container. Priya had wanted to keep him out of this, get Appa to agree on his own. Uncle addressed himself to the curry. His voice was quiet, but his words were clear: I think we must give every kindness to these people.

Rat upended the dish detergent and squeezed. It'll be good to start some new traditions.

Last Christmas, their first without Ma, had been somber, haunted by an empty rattle despite their best efforts to put a good face on the day.

Yes, Appa agreed. New traditions.

Uncle bagged up the leftovers he had portioned out for Priya and Rat. Mutton curry in yogurt containers. Rice and dahl in margarine tubs. Rat attacked a pot with a clump of steel wool. Appa stared at the dirty glasses in his hands as if he didn't know what they were and Priya was pierced with an inexplicable guilt. Who came to the house, how they would celebrate—these decisions had always been her mother's purview.

Appa? she said, putting a hand on his arm. What do you think?

In this moment, she felt ready to capitulate. If he said no, she would drop the subject without a fight. But his shoulders just slumped in surrender.

Yes, of course, he said. Tell them to come and stay the night.

———

Hema and the girls were bundled head to toe and shivering on the sidewalk when Priya pulled up a little after nine in Charlie's borrowed car. Priya was in jeans and a sweater with the heat blasting and her coat stashed in the trunk.

Kaalai vanakkam, she said, cheery. Merry Christmas.

Such cold! Hema slammed the door shut and pressed her hands right up against the heating vent.

This is nothing, Priya said. She could see on the dashboard monitor that it was thirty-two degrees outside. She said, It is much colder in other places. Quebec . . .

Hema's expression was blank and Priya realized that, of course, she couldn't understand. Glancing in the rearview mirror, she tried to catch the eye of one of the girls, but they busied themselves with the seat belts.

Um. Okay. Well, let's go, she said, shifting the gear stick into drive.

It was a delicate sort of day. Dimpled clouds moved lazily across the mottled gray sky. Emptied of people and vehicles, Vancouver was a ghost town, full of a still, eerie beauty. *Closed* signs hung on every door.

Padmini, the younger daughter, piped up from the backseat: No people.

This is a treat, Priya said. To see the city like this . . . completely deserted.

Hema bobbed her head, but Priya wasn't convinced she'd

understood. The girls pressed their noses to the windows, their breath fogging the glass.

Theirs was the lone car on the wide, generous roads. On the Burrard Bridge, bracketed by English Bay on one side and False Creek on the other, Priya had the urge to drive in the center, straddle her tires over the yellow line, and speed down the straightaway, watching the silent towers of the city recede fast in the rearview mirror.

She was beset by a flurry of nerves, remorseful for how they'd all ganged up on Appa. Why had she forced this on him? She could have taken Hema and the girls out last night or even tomorrow, to gawk at the light displays downtown, the enormous tree at the convention center. Language was an issue, sure, but they would have muddled along.

The snow began as they sailed down Broadway. Fat white flakes splatting on the windows.

Oh! Tara said, her hand on the glass.

Snow, Priya said, turning on the wipers. It's snow.

On Christmas morning. Magic! Priya had barely pulled up the parking brake at her father's house before the doors were flung open and the girls tumbled out. Padmini grabbed a naked handful then yelped, dropping the snow and rubbing her hand up and down fast on her coat.

Welcome to winter, Priya said.

Her family was squeezed into the doorway.

Appa, this is Hema, Tara, and Padmini, Priya said.

When Appa greeted them in Tamil, their eyes lit up. But then Rat stepped forward to usher them in and Appa retreated with his head down.

Come, come, Uncle said in Tamil. Shall we have tea? Pittu? Soon, he and Hema were chatting away in the living room while Tara and Padmini marveled at the Christmas tree.

Priya found her father hiding in the kitchen. Appa, why don't you join us? She tilted her head in the direction of the living room.

Go, Rat said, tying on an apron. I got this.

No, no, Appa said. Must help Michael with the turkey. He gamely reached his hand into the bird to pull out the giblets, avoiding Priya's eyes.

Around noon, there was a break in the snowfall and Rat said they should take advantage before it resumed. The house had begun to feel claustrophobic with her father so awkwardly cloistered in the kitchen, and Priya was relieved to go outside.

They went to the park, everyone trudging single file, tamping down the snow on the unplowed sidewalk. Hema wore Ma's old boots and heavy-duty shoveling gloves. Tara and Padmini were kitted out in Priya and Rat's castoffs—snow pants they had outgrown, ski mitts they'd forgotten.

As they were leaving, Hema had asked Priya's father a question and he had answered quickly, then made an excuse to duck back into the house.

Now do you see what I mean? Priya whispered, tugging on Rat's arm as they plodded through the snow. I told you something was off. They walked close together, Priya behind him, bringing up the rear.

Yeah, Rat said, slowing down to let the gap between them and the others widen. But it's weird. He was agreeable enough last week.

Come on! We basically forced his hand. Priya watched her father, keeping his distance from the others, head down, shoulders shrugged up, the bottom of his woolen cap brushing the collar of his coat.

That's not what happened, Rat said. After you left, he asked if we thought turkey was okay, if they would like it or if we should also have rice and curry. And he got up early this morning to make pittu.

Priya hadn't known her father could operate the pittu maker. She pictured him layering rice flour and coconut flakes and setting it to steam over boiling water, Ma's cookery book at his elbow.

I assumed that was Uncle's doing, Priya said.

Nope, Rat said. We came down and he said, See what Santa has brought. Presents and pittu!

They arrived to find the park buried under several inches of virginal snow. Pine needles hung down, burdened under the weight.

Perfect snowman weather, Uncle said, using the English word *snowman* and demonstrating three stacking balls with his hands.

Breaking away from the group, Appa made his way to the swing set and Priya followed. She wanted to ask him what was going on but couldn't find the words, and instead said: Appa, why Canada?

Why Canada? he repeated. Why not Canada? It was the films.

Priya swung back and forth, her boots anchored to the ground. The tassels of her scarf pooled in her lap.

Your mother and I, we used to go to the cinema, he said. As often as we could afford. We liked the lumberjacks.

Priya snorted. This was so unlike her father, the man who meticulously read online reviews before buying a new toaster.

What did we know? I was a child during the '58 riots. They took the priest in Panadura, doused him in petrol, and set the bugger on fire. From an early age, I knew I had to go. Your mother and I, at the first opportunity, as soon as we had done our studies and passed out, we went to the embassy.

Priya watched her brother, knees bent and hunched over, pushing a giant ball of snow. She had in her possession only a foggy timeline of the civil war. Her parents had grown up in Colombo with citywide curfews *(If teachers caught us out after dark, they'd box our ears)*, but there had also been discos on the beach, parties that raged until dawn, intermarriages and close friendships between Tamils and Sinhalese. Her parents had left in '77, before the worst of it. The riots in the fifties were child's play compared with what happened in '83. Black July. We had a near miss, Ma used to say.

Hema and Tara were working on a snowball of their own while Uncle showed Padmini how to pack snow, turning it around in her hands until it formed a neat globe. He threw his (splat!) at a tree trunk and Padmini flung hers at her sister's face. Tara was shocked, snow in a Rorschach across her nose. Then she burst out laughing.

Now that's a nice sound, Priya's father said.

Thank you, Appa. Thank you for letting them spend today with us.

Tara went after Padmini, flinging snow and shrieking in Tamil. Padmini raced away, hands on her head. The snow made them awkward. It was like watching a chase in slow motion. Everyone cracked up.

Priya thought of her other clients, still trapped in prison. Even if they weren't Christian, they knew what the day meant, that all over the country people were celebrating with their families.

I read the article your people wrote, her father said.

It took Priya a moment to realize he meant the open letter Prasad had penned on behalf of the refugees. It had run on page three of the *Globe and Mail,* surrounded by holiday fluff pieces. Priya hoped its publication on Christmas Eve would inspire generosity.

Appa gestured to Tara and Padmini tussling in the snow and said, This is a good thing you have done.

He sounded so sincere, it made Priya want to tell him about the others, about Mahindan being separated from his son. Tomorrow, she would fill in for Charlie and take Sellian for his weekly visit. It would be the first time she went for a nonwork duty, and she was dreading it—the gloom that infected her at every prison visit, the relief and guilt she felt when their time was up, all of it intensified by Sellian's cries on the return journey.

Uncle was waving a hand, urging the girls to come back, he'd show them how to make a snow fort. He used the English word for *snow* and the Tamil word for *fort.*

There was a man called Subramaniam, Appa said. A friend of my father's who used to come to the house. He was a civil engineer, U.K. educated, very Westernized. He taught us to eat with forks and spoons. Mr. Subramaniam was the one who showed me how to knot a tie. My father didn't even own a suit.

Where is he now?

Priya had never heard of this person before and hoped her father would talk and talk, that his words would drown out the melancholy that had descended when she'd started thinking about Mahindan and Sellian.

But Appa stared straight ahead without speaking. The snowman was nearly finished and everyone had gathered around to watch Rat and Hema struggle the head into place. Tara had two sticks that would become the arms. Uncle held up a point-and-shoot camera, his mittens clamped under an armpit.

Mr. Subramaniam used to tell me: This country is no good. After Black July, they chased him away, back to Jaffna. My parents used to give charity to the temple—clothes, money—for the people who had really lost everything. The last time they saw him, he was drinking. The looters, they broke his son's hands. To hear that he had been brought so low, wearing my father's old cricket shirts . . .

Priya felt nothing, an empty void where pity should have been. Her clients had sapped all of it. She had nothing left for a man she did not know.

Hey! Rat called. You two layabouts!

Uncle waved the camera at them. Group photo!

Priya's father patted her shoulder and stood. Come, he said. It's Christmas. Enough of this sad-sad talk.

P riya had an idea. Ma's saris, she told her father. I'll never wear all of them. She thought, as she made the suggestion, that he might say no. To this day, Ma's toothbrush was still in the bathroom. But her father agreed, and Uncle, overhearing, offered to help.

Ma's almirah stood beside the window, in a shadowed corner of her parents' bedroom. Photos of Priya and her brother were stuck to the inside of the door—old three-by-fives with rounded edges, so washed out with age they were almost sepia.

Inside, the almirah smelled of mothballs and talcum powder, Yardley's English lavender. Clothes were neatly folded and stacked, quality formal saris on the bottom, everyday things on the top two shelves. There was a drawer full of pashminas and another for sari blouses.

Priya stood, almirah doors wide open, drawers pulled out, undecided for a moment. She touched the pendant at her neck and that made her think of Savitri.

One of our clients, Priya said. They took her thali away and claimed it was some kind of LTTE symbol.

Uncle snorted. What foolishness! Then, seeing her hesitate, he added, You don't have to do this. Or take any decisions now.

But Ma would have said, Keep all these clothes—what for? So Priya slid her arms under a stack of saris and carried them to the bed. They were the casual ones, nylon and polyester, slippery fabrics that refused to remain in neat piles.

Ma would want someone to wear these, she said. Hema and the girls should get some, and the Tamil Alliance can have the rest. She regretted not having done this sooner. Why was she hoarding a dead woman's clothes?

The formal saris were easier to carry. Starched and ironed after every use, they lay obedient, flat in her arms. These saris were familiar to Priya, yards of hand-loomed silk in rich, outrageous colors, the embroidery so elaborate it dazzled.

She chose six good-quality saris for Hema, Tara, and Padmini and decided she would keep the rest of the formal ones. It was too difficult to part with these memories—the pink faux-crepe Ma had worn on her fiftieth birthday, a peacock blue chiffon Priya had always loved, with diaphanous fabric that veiled the midsection and a heavy pallu with intricate resham embroidery.

The casual ones were easier to give away. These were things Ma wore years ago, before she'd swapped saris for slacks and sweaters. Machine-made with simple patterns, most were unfamiliar. She recognized only one—olive-green jacquard under magenta paisley, a garish thing Priya had always hated. Seeing it now made her nostalgic. She had a deep, overwhelming need to hug her mother again.

I'll just keep this one, she said, carrying it back to the almirah. The rest we can donate. What were you and Hema talking about on the walk home?

If she dwelled too much on Ma, the day would be ruined.

Fishermen, Uncle said. You remember those fellows on the poles?

The family had gone back to Sri Lanka on holiday a couple of times, to Colombo and the tea estates in Up Country, places unlikely to be bombed, during intervals when the situation with the LTTE was relatively quiet. In the south, they'd stayed at a beach resort where Priya watched the stilt fishermen. Bare-chested, in sarongs, they balanced on long wooden poles, waiting for fish to jerk at their rods.

Do you ever miss Sri Lanka? she asked. Since coming to Canada, Uncle had never gone back.

He sat on the edge of the bed, one knee angled up on the comforter, and watched her match blouses with saris. He said, Some things I miss. Others I don't. What I wouldn't give to taste a proper mangosteen again. But the troubles . . .

When her father was dreaming of being a lumberjack and filling out paperwork at the embassy, where was Uncle? Priya knew the details of her parents' emigration, how they'd scraped together the points and applied to several countries just in case, then waited to touch down before starting a family, ensuring their children's citizenship was a birthright. But Uncle's history was fuzzier. He'd arrived by way of Madras, where he'd been studying or working. Before that, he was in Jaffna, taking care of Priya's grandparents. But at some point, he must have lived in the capital too.

Uncle, were you in Colombo during the '83 riots?

The curfews and strikes, he said. The problems with the JVP. Shook! The JVP! You know about that?

The Communist insurrection in the south, she said. I know. But what about in '83?

He didn't answer, and Priya forced herself to be patient, using silence, as Gigovaz had taught her, to draw the story out.

Why are you bringing this up now? He grimaced and shook his head. These are old-old stories.

She could see his mind turning, going back over the terrain of whatever had happened, and that under the surface he was getting worked up. Priya fought her unease, the urge to change the subject and give them both an out. There was something going on here—she had not imagined it.

Finally, Uncle said: I was working at the Ceylon Bank, had just been promoted to assistant manager. I was never a strong student, not like your father. Our teachers would say Raja has the brains and Romesh has the charm. But work was easy—half the job was charming people.

Priya laughed. It was a long-standing joke that Uncle couldn't buy a paper at the shop without making a new friend. He wasn't gregarious, but he was a good listener and an unself-conscious joiner.

I was happy in those days, Uncle said. I was helping my parents, setting money aside, going to films and on holidays with friends. Once, a big group of us, boys and girls all, we hired a van and took it on safari in Yala. We were so busy watching for a leopard—I was hanging out the window trying to snap a good picture—we didn't notice the elephant until it was almost on top of us!

Uncle sighed. You know, Priya, we really were innocents. I could never have predicted what happened, even though there were signs. Big talk about the Buddhist nation, Sinhalese supremacy. They had

changed the country's name. Made Sinhala the official language.
But I thought, what of it? Of course there were quotas, limited
places at the universities, in the civil service, what we would now call
discrimination. We knew that as Tamils we had to work twice as hard.
But the thing is, I could. I spoke all three languages. I had a good
job, and so did my Appa. We were middle-class, not rich but very
comfortable. There was no reason to think this would ever change. The
riots in the fifties, the JVP, strikes and curfews—troubles were a part of
life. In these situations, when the temperature is turning up, turning
up, slowly, slowly, you never think you will be affected, not directly.

So he *was* there. Priya carried a pile of saris to the almirah,
keeping her back to him. If she didn't force him to meet her eye, to
acknowledge her presence, maybe he would keep reminiscing.

Behind her, the bed shifted and for a moment Priya thought he
would get up and leave.

Instead, he continued: I was coming home from office. From the
bus, we could see fellows were fighting. They were coming on and
demanding to know who was Tamil. The girls at least could cover their
heads and pretend to be Muslim. But the rest of us—God help you if
your Sinhala was poor, if someone knew you had a Tamil name.

Priya could picture it. The bus crowded with people, heaving and
close in the thick July humidity. A woman with her shopping, fish
in a dangling plastic bag. A schoolchild in uniform, his father in a
sarong and rubber slippers. The angry young men climbing the stairs
at the front, sleeves folded up, forearms bared. Everyone shifting
uncomfortably under their scrutiny, wondering who on the daily
commute was going to turn them in.

My Sinhala was good. When they asked my name, I said I was
Rupert Lakmanarachi. He was a Sinhalese friend from the office, first
name that came to mind. They didn't ask for papers, thank God. I
got down and took the lanes behind the buildings to Wellawatta. You
know Wellawatta? he asked.

Little Jaffna, she said.

All the fellows had run away, Uncle said, flicking his hand in the air.
Just left their kades and stalls and gone. The Sinhalese—young guys,
they would have been my age—were looting, throwing rocks through
windows. The doors weren't even locked. Mobs of thugs were arriving

by train, getting down at every lane. Understand, this whole thing was organized. These godayas from the countryside, who had never met a Tamil before and only knew to hate us, they were being brought in on purpose.

But what about the police? she asked.

Oh, the army soldiers were there, Uncle said. Just looking up and waiting, cheering the devils on. All of Colombo was burning. I was thinking only of Amma and Appa and rushing to get home.

Outside, the unplowed street was indistinguishable from the sidewalks—the whole of it buried under ten inches of unlikely snow. The neighbors were out, taking advantage of the last of the dying daylight. Priya heard shovels scrape against sidewalks, everyone calling Merry Christmas to each other.

She imagined Uncle hurrying through side streets, dodging stray dogs and rubbish piles and erratic trishaw drivers, checking left and right before emerging onto a main road. How did you get home without getting caught up in it, the mayhem? she asked.

I played along. A few times, passing the goons, I yelled, Sinhala first! Sri Lanka for the Sinhalese! This kind of nonsense.

Priya had never heard Uncle speak Sinhala before. From his mouth, the language was contemptuous, dripping with sarcasm. When he translated, she was surprised to find the English words almost harmless.

He continued: There was a petrol shed at the top of our road. They were giving fuel to the thugs. I got hold of a tire iron and cheered them on. Then I ran like a devil, fast as I could, to the house, waving the tire iron like a bloody maniac. Our neighbors refused to hide us. Would you believe it? For how many years did we know the Pereras? I'm telling you, the Sinhalese are friendly, but only to a point.

Priya didn't think this was necessarily true. Prasad had told her how often his Sinhalese colleagues protected him, how, when he was kidnapped, they'd paid the ransom and smuggled him out of Colombo. But she just played with the edge of a crochet wrap, rubbing a loop of lace.

We put all the valuables into a box, Uncle said. Amma's gold, all the money, car keys. We closed the shutters, locked the doors, and waited. It must have been hours. All the time, we could hear the looters getting closer. My God. It was so hot with the shutters closed. You know what is worse than violence?

Six months ago, she would not have been able to answer. But now she said: Waiting.

Uncle said, There were many moments when I wished I had already been killed, that it was finished. I still had the tire iron. I thought I could use it. Make it to be over.

This was a man she did not know. She idled by the window, rubbing a finger along the line of dust on a venetian blind, then tugged on the string to make the slats fly up.

We offed the lights, Uncle said. We had just a hurricane lamp on the floor, and we sat and waited. We heard helicopters and gunshots, big noise. Finally, they came for us. I could hear them calling from down the road. Kottiya, kottiya. You know this word?

Tiger, tiger, Priya said. She could imagine it, the young men with jerry cans and tire irons, voices soft and taunting.

Kottiya, kottiya, Uncle said. I made Amma and Appa hide under the bed. Amma was crying. In '58, they cut women's ears off. That was considered having a near miss. I went quickly to the front gate. There were three men and they had galkatas, homemade shotguns. The ringleader was a boy I had tutored in math. Fellow by the name of Suresh. Elder brother was my batchmate at St. Thomas's. Amma used to make us onion bhaji after school. I gave them the car keys, jewelry, money, everything. Some of the neighbors were standing at the windows and watching. The De Silvas. The Wickremasinghes. As if it was a tele-drama!

Priya wrapped her arms around herself and leaned a temple against the ice-cold window. Down below, Rat had both hands on the wide handle of a shovel, forcing it down the walk, snow gathering into the giant scoop as he pushed. Across the street, Mrs. Nowak raised a mittened hand and waved at him. Later, she would bring over a plate of amaretti and they would reciprocate with some of Priya's gingerbread.

I saw that Suresh did not want to know me, so I played along, Uncle said. If my father had been there, he would have said, Good evening, Suresh. How are your Amma and Thatha, are they well? Maybe he had even tried to pass by our house, but one of the other boys had the list. I could see it. Tamil, Sinhalese, Muslims, Burghers. We all lived side by side. But they knew which houses to torch and which ones to leave alone. Kandasamy—my old school chum—his house was on fire.

Later, I came to learn they had burned him inside. Meanwhile, that fool De Silva was standing in the window with his mouth gaping. One thing we did not hear that night: no ambulances, not a single siren.

I told them I was the only one home, Uncle said. One of the boys tried to push me aside. He said, Let us see for ourselves. He was filthy, big sweat stains. I don't think he even realized he was covered in blood. It was very hot that night.

The cast-iron radiators clicked to life. Tick. Tick. Tick. The streetlamps had come on. Christmas lights winked. Windows glowed warm, each one a tableau of happiness. Decorated evergreens, families playing charades. The snow made the street brighter.

I remember looking Suresh in the eyes and saying, I am alone here. The third boy was counting the rupees. He said, Come, let us see. He might have a pretty sister or a wife. I thought of your Amma then. Do you know, I was angry at your father when he left.

Priya turned to face him. You were?

I thought, if all the Tamils run away like rats, we'll only be giving the Sinhalese exactly what they want.

Uncle clenched and unclenched his fists, as if flexing for a fight, and Priya had an inkling like a shiver down her spine. For months, she had heard nothing but horrors—Ranga having his leg treated without anesthetic, Savitri running zigzags in the jungle with her son on her back. Had the inoculation prepared her? Uncle stared into the middle distance, seeing something that wasn't her. Something that happened long ago and far away. Priya readied herself for the story, whatever it was.

Uncle's eyes unfocused and he shrugged. The thugs continued on, he said. And next day, three of us got on a cargo ship and went to Jaffna. I never saw Colombo again.

Priya had known they had moved north. But she hadn't known it had been like this, in a panic.

That was their plan, you know, Uncle said. The government. They wanted us to leave the capital. They were the ones who arranged for the boat. They wanted all the Tamils in one small corner, trapped like animals.

Priya was confused. She had expected something else. This seemed anticlimactic. What is wrong with me? she wondered. Refugee law had made her morbid.

After we left, who took our jobs? Uncle asked. Who came to stay in our houses?

What do you mean?

Priya, what do you think happens when you terrorize a people, force them to flee, take away their options, then put them in a cage all together? Will they not try and break down the bars?

Okay. Yes.

He said, It is very convenient, no? These labels. *Terrorist.*

A pleasant smell wafted up from the kitchen, browning turkey, the skin starting to crackle and crust. Downstairs, Rat slammed the front door shut and stomped his boots on the mat. Water gushed out of the tap. Someone rummaged in the pots-and-pans cupboard.

You think the Sri Lankan government planned to turn the Tamils into Tigers? Priya asked. They wanted the LTTE to form?

Uncle stood up and Priya knew that now the story really was over. These buggers are all terrorists, he said. Only the innocent suffer.

The twins sat at the dining table surrounded by binders and pencil cases, their noses buried in books. Grace caught a glimpse of one of the covers and frowned. A blue-green dust jacket with a title in a garish orange font. *The Enemy That Never Was.* Thumbing through, she found reprinted photographs of prewar Vancouver. A tram on Powell; the Japanese Language School with its windows open; children playing double dutch, a girl midjump, hair and skirt flying. There was a silence in these images. The muted past in black and white, waiting for the future to impose its own interpretation.

What's all this?

Brianne tapped the side of her nose with one slow finger, a gesture she had picked up from Kumi, and said, We're following our noses.

She was slipping photocopies of old wartime notices into clear plastic sleeves. Under British Columbia's emblazoned crest, bilingual headlines screamed: NOTICE TO MALE ENEMY ALIENS. TO ALL PERSONS OF JAPANESE RACIAL ORIGIN. Grace grimaced as she read them.

Gran says they had to put these in the windows of the laundromat, Brianne said. She wiggled her fingers as if casting a spell. Ooooo . . . the yellow fear!

Don't say that! Grace snapped.

Mumsie, Brianne said, wide eyes aggrieved. I'm only being sarcastic.

It's an ugly thing to say, Grace said, her initial shock turning to dismay.

The girls exchanged a glance and Grace read its unsaid meaning. She knew she was being irrational and had been for weeks. She was enveloped in a gloom she couldn't understand, a churning, unspecified angst upending her usual equanimity. She'd been looking forward to the holidays, baking and family cheer, a break from war stories. And instead, she'd spent Christmas weekend in a funk, which she passed off as illness, too heavy-limbed to change out of pajamas most days.

The night before, the whole family—even Kumi—had gone to see a holiday comedy and Grace had stayed behind, wandering the rooms aimlessly. She'd sat on her mother's bed, surrounded by Kumi's things—the hand-me-down furniture, the framed photos on the wall—and sobbed for no reason, the flowered counterpane clutched tight in her fist.

Meg had her nose in a book, the end of a candy cane sticking out of one corner of her mouth. Mom, who's Mackenzie King?

Canada's longest-serving prime minister. A so-called Liberal. Grace turned to see Kumi in the doorway. She had a satisfied smirk on her face.

Canada should remain a country for the white man, Meg read. That's what he said!

Rain thrown sideways drummed a beat on the windows. It gushed out of the gutters, sogging the last of the Christmas snow. Grace wondered if the weather was to blame.

That was a long time ago, she said, taking the book from Meg and closing it.

World War Two. Not so long ago at all, Kumi said, laying an editorial cartoon on the table.

The twins leaned forward and Grace couldn't help doing the same. In the drawing, a grinning, androgynous character labeled *Jap* was wrapped in a kimono, hair in a high bun, with exaggerated slits for eyes, holding a bloody dagger over a bleeding figure named *Canada*. The caricature was at once comical and insidious.

This is who they accused us of being, Kumi said. Just like that, our country turned on us.

Kumi brought her thumb to her index finger and rubbed them together, concentrating. For a moment, Grace and the twins watched her, until Meg said, Like this, and snapped her fingers.

Never mind, Kumi said impatiently. The point is . . . the point is . . .

But how could anyone believe something so dumb? Brianne asked, gesturing to the cartoon. No one would fall for this now.

What about this business with the . . . the . . . Kumi searched Grace's face and said: You know what I mean. The letter in the paper . . . and it was Christmas Eve . . .

It's not the same thing, Grace said.

Kumi shook her head and rubbed her palms in wide circles over the tabletop. The twins waited patiently. When Kumi lost her train of thought, it was best to let her find her own way back.

Grace refused to help. Her mother had been harping on about that letter since it was published. She'd laid the newspaper on Grace's lap and demanded: And what do you have to say to this?

Well, of course they're going to claim they're innocent, Grace had replied, folding the paper and setting it aside. And I'm sure some of them legitimately are, but I make my decisions on a case-by-case basis, after considering all the evidence, not by blindly trusting something someone writes in their own defense.

It was the first acknowledgment Kumi had made of her new job. And of course it would be negative. Grace hated that she still needed her mother's approval.

Now Kumi mouthed something to herself, practicing before she said it out loud: Don't trust the government, girls. That is the lesson.

That's *not* the lesson! Grace said, appalled to see her daughters nodding like robots. Without good government, there is anarchy.

Kumi gave Grace one of her shrewd looks, the kind that seemed to see right through and shame her.

Everyone is doing their best, Grace said.

Everyone is doing their best, Kumi echoed. Their best was a barn on Hastings Street. She flipped through the books. Where is that letter?

What letter? Meg asked.

They agreed to the internment, Kumi said. They *agreed* to it as a show of good faith. All they asked was that families be kept together. She opened and closed binders, brushing away the girls' attempts to help.

What letter, Gran? Brianne asked.

The letter! The letter! Dear honorable sir. So *polite,* our people. Everything is always a *request.*

Is this it? Meg asked, pulling away the rings of a binder and extracting a plastic sleeve.

No, no. Kumi was blindly pushing and pulling books, scattering papers and sending pens rolling across the table. She put her hand on her head and appeared to waver. Grace, alert, hustled to her side.

Enough! Grace commanded, pulling back a chair. Sit down, Mom.

Kumi closed her eyes.

Deep breath, Grace said. And another.

Kumi's shoulders rose and fell under Grace's restraining palms. They inhaled and exhaled in unison, and Grace felt her own pulse slow.

It's scary, Brianne said. The government just deciding one day to take everything away.

I wouldn't let it happen, Meg said, and three binder rings snapped together.

Brianne said, As if you'd be able to stop it, idiot.

Meg gazed out the dark window, meditative, and Grace saw the devastation in her face—the injustice reaching forward three generations to latch on. How personal it felt, a nation's betrayal.

I wish you wouldn't expose the girls to this ugliness, Grace told her mother.

We're not babies! Meg said.

And you're not victims either, Grace said, crossing her arms over her chest. Nothing bad has happened to you.

It was a mistake to keep quiet all these years, Kumi said. I see that now. Over her shoulder, she held Grace's eyes. People who forget the wrongs that were done to them perpetuate those same wrongs on others.

The Japanese were here before the war, Grace told her mother. Our family were citizens. King was wrong to call them traitors. It's totally different.

Meg watched them. Different from what? she asked.

Nothing is different, Kumi said, turning to the twins. Not . . . distrust . . . of the . . . fear . . . fear . . . emotions are man . . . man . . . twisted up. She wound her fingers round and round, over each other, and mutely opened and closed her mouth.

Nothing has changed, Brianne prompted.

We shouldn't trust the government, added Meg, grinning at Grace.

Kumi's eyes flashed. Repatriated! My brothers and I were born here. What was Japan to us? May as well have been Timbuktu.

No Japs from the Rockies to the seas. A political slogan and a rallying cry. These words had no power over Grace or her girls, but when she thought of her grandparents, she cringed. And this was exactly what they would never have wanted: pity.

Swallow it down, little Gracie, Aiko used to say when the kids at school teased her and Grace came home crying. Never betray yourself by showing them your sorrow.

On the odd occasions Aiko had spoken of the internment, it had been matter-of-factly, in the same tone she used to describe dental surgery. *He removed two wisdom teeth. We were in Slocan for three years.* These were trials to be overcome rather than life-scarring traumas.

She mentioned this now, and added: Your great-grandmother didn't see herself as a victim and there's no reason you girls should either.

That generation was humiliated by what was done to them, Kumi said. Shame held their tongues.

What was she like? Brianne asked. Our great-grandmother?

My Obaachan was a proud woman, Grace said quickly, before Kumi could reply.

It was her grandmother who had raised her. While her parents were at work, Aiko packed lunches and took temperatures, helped her prepare for spelling bees. Once, on their way to the park, a kid had yelled out: DIRTY FOB! Grace could still see the boy, her age or perhaps a bit younger, pulling his finger out of his nose and pointing it at them. Grace had stopped, embarrassed. She had never heard the word before but understood it to be offensive. She had a strong sense, even then, of right and wrong, a scrupulous penchant for fairness.

I wanted to go to him, to yell or even hit him, Grace told the girls. He wasn't much bigger than me. But Obaachan just turned it into a joke. We came on a boat, she said. This is true. But we are not very fresh.

Kumi chuckled. That was my mother's favorite line.

She maintained a sense of dignity, Grace said, throwing her shoulders back and standing a little straighter. Obaachan knew there was nothing to be gained from being the injured party.

Mahindan stood in the cool of his garage, hanging his tools. Voice of Tiger Radio was playing an upbeat pop song and he had the sound on low. The garage was the tidiest it had ever been, equipment arranged on shelves, spare tires sorted by size. Even the floor had been swept and power-washed.

He rubbed a rag over his hands but only out of habit; they had been grease-free for weeks. It was only eleven, but he decided there wasn't any point in staying open. Might as well go home and be closer to the bomb shelter.

He was pulling the iron gate across when he heard the cacophony. Schoolchildren with their backpacks, lunch pails, and white uniforms spilled down the lane, girls in pinafores and boys in short pants. Sellian ran toward him.

What has happened? Mahindan asked, hands on hips.

Teacher sent us home, Sellian said with a shrug. Something is happening at the United Nations.

At the mention of the United Nations, Mahindan's panic whooshed in.

Sellian smacked his forehead with an exaggerated motion, a mannerism he had recently picked up from his grandmother. Ah! he said. Forgot my tiffin.

Doesn't matter, Mahindan said, fastening the padlock with shaking hands. Go to Appa's bicycle. Quickly!

He sat Sellian on the handlebars and kicked off. Sellian gripped the bar behind him and leaned his body out. The wind flicked through his hair as they sailed down the hill. Faster, Appa! Faster! he yelled, gleeful, as a pair of green doves in their path took flight.

Mahindan turned onto the main highway, quiet these days, only a scattering of bicycles and motorcycles and bullock carts spread out comfortably across the dual carriageway. Long gone were the days of congestion and traffic. There was plenty of room to overtake, and vehicles could change lanes without honking their intention.

They passed the Eelam Bank, where a mob crowded the teller's window. Mahindan pedaled faster. He had known this day would come. Why hadn't he acted? He thought of the cash he'd been hoarding, running through all the secret hiding places (bottom of the rice sack, between the pages of a romance novel, behind a photograph of his parents . . .) to calm his nerves. Veering around a pothole, he reminded himself that the important papers were safe in the almirah, the suitcase was packed and waiting under the bed.

His legs burned as he pumped hard, the pedals making quick revolutions. They passed the yellow water tower, standing watch over the city, then the bombed-out shell of an apartment building, the senior school where Rama had once taught, its west side gouged by an air strike. Kilinochchi, the proud Tiger capital. The Sri Lankan Army had set their sights on it.

Winded and sweating, the back of his shirt soaked, Mahindan turned off the main road onto a palmyra-shaded street. The United Nations compound consisted of several single-story buildings surrounded by a whitewashed wall and a ten-foot-high iron fence.

The commotion was audible even before the throng around the gate came within view. Women in saris. Men in short sleeves. Hands raised in protest, voices beseeching. Mahindan sailed to a stop and stuck his hands in Sellian's armpits to help him down, then pulled the hem of his shirt up and across his sweaty face.

What is happening, Appa?

Mahindan lifted him up on one hip and pushed his way through the desperate crowd. People reached around and over one another, everyone trying to squeeze their hands through the bars, waving and begging, hoping to be seen. The sun glinted off watch faces. The crowd pleaded: *Stay.*

He found a spot against the compound wall and from there he saw aid workers—white men and women in caps and sunglasses—packing boxes into trucks. All these days, all these days . . . He cursed himself for dallying. Sellian, his thumb in his mouth, buried his face into Mahindan's neck.

An Old Brahmin stood near them, bare-chested, with a green sarong knotted under his belly. He had a long white beard and was missing several teeth. We are begging you, he cried. Stay and witness our suffering.

Cupping a hand around Mahindan's ear, Sellian leaned in and said: I'm scared, Appa.

Nothing to be scared of, Mahindan murmured back. We are all here together.

Most of the aid workers returned inside, but one faced the protesters. He removed his cap and rubbed the back of his hand over his forehead.

The Old Brahmin called to him: Wait . . . we are not asking for anything else. Only wait and watch what happens. If you go, who will see?

Sellian pressed one ear into his father's shoulder. Mahindan covered the other with his hand. The aid worker raised his phone and panned it across the crowd. Mahindan imagined the scene he was recording— a crowd of people shouting in a foreign language, brown arms reaching through the gates. Holding tight to Sellian, Mahindan kept his own gaze steady, focused on the camera.

If you leave, we will all die, the Old Brahmin said. He raised both hands to his temple and flicked them down. The knife is at our throat. If you go, no one will see what happens.

Other voices chorused: Stay! Stay!

Would the white man later watch what he had recorded? Would he show it to a higher authority? An official in Europe or America? Would it make any difference?

Mahindan could feel Sellian's heart knocking against his chest. He pictured their important papers, identification cards, and vaccination records concealed in the folds of Chithra's wedding sari. He reminded himself of the changes of clothes—the exact shirts and trousers he had packed—the saucepans, the bandages, the new bars of soap. The tent poles, the sleeping mats.

Sellian poked his father's shoulder with a pointy finger. It's Ruksala Auntie!

Ruksala emerged from the main United Nations building with a group of local workers, dark-skinned men and women. They stood in an awkward jobless clump, watching the lorries being packed. When Mahindan and Sellian yelled her name, she came to speak to them through the bars.

Won't allow us to help, she said, and folded her arms across her chest.

They're leaving? Mahindan asked.

Government sent a fax, she said. Very official. Please be advised that we can no longer guarantee the safety of international workers.

The United Nations had their own bunker, and so far the MiGs and Kfir jets had given the entire compound a wide berth. It was the only safe place left in the city.

The Old Brahmin struggled his way out of the crowd, weeping. A young woman stepped into his vacated spot. She held her phone up to the gate. Fifteenth September, 2008, she said. This is the day the United Nations abandons Kilinochchi.

The aid worker was still panning his phone across the crowd at the gate and for a few moments they were like mirror images.

How can you do this? the young woman with the camera phone yelled. How?

They don't speak Tamil, Mahindan told her.

They understand, Ruksala said. She twisted her mouth to one side. They know what will happen.

And still they will leave us? Mahindan said.

They will go to Colombo and do what they can from there, Ruksala said.

A spark of hope: she could take Sellian!

But Ruksala shook her head. You think the Tigers will let any of *us* through the checkpoints?

A truck door slammed and Ruksala went to say her goodbyes. The gates opened and the crowd shuffled aside, keeping a respectful distance as the vehicles crawled through. Voices fell silent, everyone resigned to their fate.

With Sellian on the handlebars, Mahindan followed the convoy back through the town, keeping them in sight even as he fell behind. The small parade of vehicles was conspicuous with their yellow license plates and the blue-and-white United Nations flags that fluttered over the windows. All along the main road, people stopped to watch.

They left the town center and the road turned dusty orange, lined with low scrub and grass, the sparse landscape dotted with thin trees, their palms wild, hairy tufts. There was no one else here, just the lone cow in the shade flicking flies with its tail. The United Nations trucks slowed to a crawl, allowing Mahindan and Sellian to catch up.

The man with the camera phone sat in the passenger seat of the last vehicle, hanging out his open window. Mahindan pedaled up alongside until he was close enough to see the tears in his eyes. He said something Mahindan did not understand and Mahindan tried to think of some parting words for this man and his camera. But if there was no point in begging them to wait, what else was there to say?

They approached the wooden signpost that marked the entrance to the city. Kilinochchi's name was written in three languages: Tamil, Sinhala, and English.

Goodbye, Sellian shouted at the camera, one of the few English expressions he knew. Goodbye! Goodbye!

Mahindan braked at the sign and, standing there with one foot on the ground, the other on a pedal, he watched the convoy round the bend out of sight, the last blue-and-white flag flapping. Sellian was still calling: Goodbye!

———

The next day, they began their journey along the same route, the whole town with them, down Kilinochchi's main thoroughfare. Tractors, buses, three-wheelers, and motorcycles all laden with people and goods. The elderly sat in wagons with children in their laps while adults walked alongside, parcels balanced on their heads. Chickens complained from inside cages, beaks poking through the wire, feathers ruffling. People pushed bicycles, bundles of clothing, cooking pots, and burlap rice sacks tied down to the seats.

At their backs were the sounds of hammers and industry, the Tigers building a bund wall in a futile bid to hold the city. How long before the army descended? Weeks? Days?

Mahindan and his family were traveling light. Along with Ruksala and her son, Prem, there were Chithra's parents—old but mercifully still mobile. The adults pedaled their bicycles with the children on the handlebars. A wooden cart was hitched to each cycle and packed with bottled water, lentils, fruits, vegetables, tea, and biscuits. They moved slowly, part of a mass exodus, the last stragglers finally abandoning the town, Tiger cadres, weapons slung over their backs, flanking them on either side. There was no choice now. By staying till the end, they had thrown in their lot with the LTTE and could only go where the Tigers chose to frogmarch them.

The air raids the night before had been particularly vicious, but Mahindan had not gone to the bunker. He had fed Sellian two spoonfuls of gripe water to put him to sleep, then spent his last night in Kilinochchi in his own home, going through his cassette tapes and CDs, paging through old photo albums.

When the electricity had cut out, he'd lit all the hurricane lamps, luxuriating in the indulgence while he could, now that there was no need to conserve. It was dangerous—the house luminescent, an easy target. But Mahindan decided if they died here, tonight, in their own home, struck down by hellfire from the sky, it would be God's will, perhaps even a mercy. He'd drunk the last of the arrack and fallen asleep with the rush of jets overhead, wrapped up in Chithra's wedding sari. Picture frames rattled on the walls, but pressing his nose into the rich embroidery of the pallu, he felt he could almost get her scent again.

In the morning, he'd steamed idli, which they ate at the table with the fan spinning overhead. Mahindan told Sellian the story of how this table had come to them, a castoff from an uncle that he and Chithra had lugged between them from five streets over, laughing and teasing the whole way.

They didn't bother to clear the table or wash the plates, but Mahindan couldn't bring himself to leave the house unlocked. He had held Sellian's hand on the threshold and surveyed the space one last time, committing it all to memory, every crack in the wall, the beaded curtains dividing the rooms, the dusting of sand over the linoleum floor, his favorite rattan chair, the biscuit tin where they stored batteries and rubber bands and other odds and ends. Mahindan had kissed the key before slipping it into his pocket, praying the day would come when he would need it again.

Are we going to see Nila Auntie? Sellian asked now, when a female Tiger marched by.

Maybe, Mahindan said.

He couldn't recall the last time he'd had word from Chithra's sister. Beside him, Ruksala sobbed silently.

I'm sorry, she whispered.

They passed the water tower, felled and on its side, water gushing out. A bleeding giant. At the signpost, instead of heading south into government territory, as the United Nations vehicles had done the day before, they turned east.

SOLOMON

I t was a dreary Monday, the sky indeterminate, the air dense with mist. Priya wiped her face with her scarf as she stepped off the elevator. Her colleagues were turning on their computers and wriggling out of coats as they listened to voice mail. Everyone moved in the fog of lethargy with a post-holiday deflation, mocked by tinsel still drooping in doorways.

Gigovaz beckoned from his office and Priya slung her coat over her arm as she walked in. She was surprised to see Joyce inside, perched on the edge of the desk. Gigovaz skulked, hovering at her shoulder, a lumpy interloper in his own office.

Here's what we've come up with, Joyce announced. Corporate two and a half days a week, immigration two and a half.

Solomon had decreed it: Cut the baby in half. The office had been closed for the holidays. For ten days, Priya's BlackBerry had remained mercifully mute. When had they hatched this plan? Through text messages on Christmas Eve? Joyce in an apron surrounded by her family, Gigovaz with his greasy hand in a bucket of fried chicken? Already, Priya could see it would never work.

Newtown Gold rejected a buyout offer from CMP Russia, Joyce said. We think the Russians are going to bypass the company and go straight to the shareholders. And you know what that means.

A hostile takeover, Priya said.

That's why I need you, Joyce said. She handed Priya a stack of binders. Familiarize yourself with the particulars. I'm briefing the team at eleven.

Arms weighed down, Priya waited awkwardly for a moment after Joyce left, wondering if Gigovaz would assign her more work or clarify the arrangement. Two point five days—how exactly did that break down? But he pulled out his chair and waved her away. She left his office feeling that she should have thanked someone.

A buzz of tension surrounded the firm's law students. After three and a half years, they had rounded the corner on the last stretch of their education. Everyone was fretting, speculating on job prospects and worrying about interviews.

A twelve-month contract, Martha said, turning off the tap. In-house counsel at the City of Vancouver.

Isn't that part-time? Twyla asked, ripping a paper towel off the roller.

Tough economic times, Martha said. I'll take what I can get.

Eavesdropping from her stall, Priya cursed her bad luck. Everyone else had already taken their licensing exams, but hers had been scheduled for the last session. In March, she would return to the classroom for ten intensive weeks of preparation. And then what? Would the paltry work experience she'd amassed over the past seven months even qualify her for a job in corporate law?

Returning to her desk, she tried to squelch down her trepidation by thinking of Sellian, who had started school that day. A month in, and Sellian was still miserable in foster care. On Boxing Day, Priya had taken him to visit his father. He'd been cheerful enough on the way there, but the ride home was excruciating. Sellian was frantic, kicking and flailing while she strapped him into the car seat, then bawling all the way back to the Flanigans', begging her in broken English to turn the car around. She'd negotiated the highway with tears blurring her vision. Afterward, she'd sat alone in the Flanigans' driveway, with the car still parked, gripping the steering wheel and gathering her wits, knowing that as hard as Sellian cried and as distraught as she felt, it was Mahindan who suffered most.

The phone rang, startling her. Her father's number flashed on the display. This was odd; he usually called her at home.

Appa?

Ah, ah. You're there, he said, as if he had expected the machine. Good.

What's up? She turned her chair to the cabinet behind her desk, stretching the phone cord as she did, to multitask.

No, no, nothing, he said. Just wanted to call and . . . and . . . so? How? First day back everything is fine?

I'm working with corporate again, she said.

Oh.

Priya was bent in half, phone clamped between shoulder and ear, flicking through the hanging folders. Which is good, she prodded. Finally, what I've been wanting.

Ah-ah. Yes, he said, distracted.

Where are you? she asked. What are you doing?

Nothing. Just at home. Not doing anything. So, you're working with your Mrs. Lau again. Well done, pillai.

It's only half time, she said, pulling out a folder. Fifty percent corporate, fifty percent refugees.

Well, what to do, he said. They need you, no?

She had a troubling flashback to three years earlier, when her mother had phoned Priya in the middle of a lecture, then spent ten minutes recounting the mundane details of her day before dropping the atomic bomb: Doctor called this morning.

Priya became very still. Fear droned in her ears. Turning back to her desk, she cupped a hand around the receiver. Appa? Is everything okay?

Yes, yes. Fine, fine. Okay, I know you're busy. Just wanted to check you're coming on Thursday.

Of course, she said, scouring her memory. Had her father said anything about a doctor's appointment? He'd been healthy over the holidays, maybe a little tired, but that was all.

By the way, I was thinking . . . new year and all . . . there's some kind of group, is there? Working with these people . . . Hema and the others.

The Tamil Alliance?

Are they needing help? Want volunteers?

The ringing in her ears cleared. I imagine, she said. In fact . . . yes. Do you want me to get the details for Thursday?

No, no. Tamil Alliance? She could hear him rummaging and guessed it was for a pen.

I will call myself. No need to . . . Tam-il All-i-ance . . . no need to bring . . . to say on Thursday.

But—

Baba, I have to go.

Before he hung up, she heard the front door open and Uncle's voice in the background.

Mahindan watched, bemused, as a small bundle waddled in through the doors. It was a child, stuffed like a sausage into some kind of spacesuit, swaddled in head-to-toe red, a zipper down the center. The child's mouth was muffled by a long scarf. A band of blue wool covered his forehead. Only his eyes were visible. He walked stiffly, arms held out, marshmallow legs brushing together—swish, swish—his boots leaving damp tracks in their wake.

The child yanked off red mittens, letting them fall as he walked. The scarf unraveled, the hood was thrown back, and Mahindan realized with a start that this creature was his son.

I hate this stupid getup, Sellian said, flinging away the woolen cap and thumping down in a chair across from his father.

Ai! Mahindan admonished. Take care!

He jumped up to collect the discarded clothing. The fleece lining the mittens was soft. The warmth of Sellian's hand lingered.

See how well these things are made, Mahindan said. These are expensive, no?

Sellian bent forward, legs stuck out in front of him. His lip trembled when he failed to reach his boots, frustration threatening to turn into tears.

Mahindan crouched at his son's feet and ripped off the Velcro fastenings. No problem, he said quickly. No need to cry.

Mahindan had been awaiting this visit all week, but now they had something difficult to discuss. Sellian had started taking things—colored chalk, a classmate's ruler, the chocolates from schoolchildren's lunches. Nothing of value, just small-small things. They had found the box under his bed where he hoarded his treasures. Mahindan could not understand the motivation for this petty theft. Sellian lived with a middle-class family. He wanted for nothing.

Mahindan helped Sellian out of the winter costume, both of them struggling with the unfamiliar zipper, the cumbersome layers. Emerging from his straitjacket, Sellian was himself again, slight and trim, though Mahindan noticed his son had grown—but surely this had not happened overnight!—a sprout shooting up in the fertile Canadian soil.

Sellian's foster people had taken him to get his hair cut. It was slightly longer in the back and shorter in the front, the fringe spiky and subtly different, more Canadian. But when Mahindan ran a hand through, it felt just the same, fine and silky, still the hair of his child.

Sellian was mutinous. I hate the milk here, he said. It is like water, not even milk.

Arms folded and grim, he looked so thoroughly like his mother that Mahindan was overcome with affection.

You have a list? Mahindan said. All right. So tell me. He counted in English on his fingers: Number one, milk.

Number two, rain, Sellian said. Rain, rain, go away. Even the sun hates Canada.

Mahindan laughed and Sellian's expression was outraged. It was too delicious, this temper tantrum. It was Chithra all over again.

I hate that stupid Mrs. Ramamoorthy! Chithra used to fume after work. And to calm her down, Mahindan would make her itemize a list of grievances. (So bossy, know-it-all, her stupid finger, always wagging it at me. One of these days, I will bite it off.) What began in fury always ended in jest.

Point three, shoes. He kicked his foot out, knocked one boot over, and whined: I hate being made to wear shoes.

We never had shoes in Sri Lanka, Mahindan said, repeating one of his grandfather's stories, until the Portuguese came.

I wish they had never come, Sellian said. I wish *we* had never come.

What else? Mahindan asked quickly, not wanting to linger on this new grievance.

Meat loaf, Sellian said, and folded up his nose.

What is *mit loof*? Mahindan asked, pronouncing the strange English words with difficulty.

And they . . . I don't . . . I don't want to speak always English.

Mahindan understood his son's frustration because he felt it too. The language was exhausting, all the irregular verbs, the slow, tedious work of conjugation. Even the simplest sentence was an effort to construct. He labored over every consonant and vowel, stumbled over the silent *k*'s, acutely conscious of how awkward and tongue-tied he must sound, how different his pronunciation was from that of Canadians.

There was no need anymore to lecture Sellian about his English. Living with his new family, going to school every day, it was a natural education. Sellian could converse now with the guards if he liked, and Mahindan heard the offhand way he formulated sentences, his thoughts free-flowing, how he substituted Tamil words for the English ones he didn't know. Soon, English would be as good as a mother tongue. A foster mother tongue.

Everyone is saying your English is improving, Mahindan said. Why? Because you are speaking it all the time, because of this practice.

Sellian produced a small toy from his pocket—the Ganesha statue—and began tapping it on the table. I hate English. He kicked out and the other boot fell over. Stupid language.

These Saturday visits were the highlight of Mahindan's week. But their time together was never as he imagined, and afterward, he was always deflated.

Come now, pillai. Appa has to ask you something.

When Mahindan had first heard about the stealing, he'd been livid. But then he felt powerless, which was worse. If they were at home, he would have known what to do. One good caning to the backside and the boy would shape up.

These things happen from time to time, Sam Nadarajah said. The child has suffered a trauma. Do not be too angry with him.

Sellian would start seeing a special doctor. A psychologist, Sam had said. It is nothing to worry about.

Why did you do this thing, pillai? Mahindan asked now as Sellian refused to meet his eyes. You must be a good boy, Mahindan said. These people you are staying with, they are kind to you, no?

Secretly, he wanted Sellian to hate them. He begrudged having to say generous things about the child snatchers.

Sellian was sullen, still focused on Ganesha turning cartwheels on the table.

They give you a nice place to sleep and clean clothes to wear. They take you to school, where you play with other children. And this is how you thank them, by making trouble?

Sellian kicked his legs forward and back, as if he were on a swing. Where is Prem? he asked. I want to see Prem.

Hearing his nephew's name after all this time gave Mahindan a jolt. Prem is gone, no? Mahindan said, composing his face.

I want to see Prem, Sellian said.

I know. I want to see Prem too.

And Ruksala Auntie and Ammachi and Appachi.

Pillai, you know they are gone.

In the camp. I know.

He fiddled with the Ganesha statue, turning it around in his hands. The colors had faded, the blue skin much lighter, as if the god had taken ill.

Sellian said: I want to go back.

But Baba, you have forgotten how dangerous it was there?

No, Sellian said. Not there. Not the jungle. Not the camp. I want to go home. To my house. And my real school.

Baba, how to go back? They will have bombed the school and the house.

I hate it here. Maybe they will make us to go back.

Mahindan felt the air rush out of his lungs, as if someone had hit him hard in the center of his stomach. *Maybe they will make us to go back.* The fear that had lurked below the surface, trampled down after every failed detention review, was now flat on the table. Impossible to ignore.

He reached out to touch his son's hair again, sifting the fringe through his fingers, off Sellian's forehead. This brown-skinned child with his new haircut and winter costume who might pass like any other in a Canadian playground. Mahindan said, No one is going to send you back.

Sellian began to cry and Mahindan gathered his son up in his arms. No point thinking of what is in the past, he said, rocking Sellian. He inhaled the unfamiliar scents—laundry detergent, soap, and shampoo, brands he did not know. Foreign smells of an unknown life that now belonged to his son.

Now you are here, Mahindan said, whispering in his son's ear, trying to cut through the soft cries and sniffles. It is safe here. And you will grow to be big and go to school and get a job and marry.

And have a car, Sellian said, gulping.

Yes, Mahindan said, amused. A car you buy, not a car you steal! Sellian, listen to your Appa. Please do not take what is not yours. Borrow and return. But do not steal from others. This is the beginning of trouble.

He saw Ranga, in conversation with Sam, and looked away.

You are here now and there is a future for you here, Mahindan said.

HOARD

From inside his tent, Mahindan could hear a family building a shelter, erecting a frame of coconut planks and twine over the hollow they had dug in the ground. Their hammers kept a steady beat. The women called instructions to one another as they tied palm fronds together for the roof. *Tighter, tighter! No, that one is too small.*

Mahindan and his family had arrived a week earlier, here in Mullaitivu, the Tigers' eastern stronghold. A city on the coast, it was both a launching pad for the Sea Tigers and a manufacturing hub—turning out arms and ammunition, with a shipyard that supplied lightweight fighting vessels.

Mahindan, Ruksala, Chithra's parents, and the children had made a slow, months-long journey to get here, crawling down the A35, stopping along the way at one or another of the tiny hamlets that lined the highway. They would set up camp, exchange news with the locals, and stock up on whatever they could afford. But as settled as they became in any village, the sounds of fighting, advancing closer and closer, always spurred them on, the throng of people swelling as villagers too loaded their barrows and bicycles and took flight.

Close by, another group dug a protective trench. Their shovels made a ting! ting! sound whenever they hit stone. The clamor of voices and industry was punctuated by the distant thunder of artillery.

Mahindan lay on the floor of his tent and watched shadows play on the wall. Three child-shaped figures squealed as they ran past. Two men paused to greet each other.

How machan?

Small pain in my back. Otherwise, what to complain?

The men were elderly. Mahindan heard the croak in their voices, the small gurgle of phlegm in the back of one's throat. *What to complain?*

His legs ached. They had been swollen for days, bloated ankles indistinguishable from shins. Ruksala had taken the children to collect cockles. You have a rest, she said when he'd returned from temple. I will put these two rascals to work.

The day before, a couple had been felled on the beach while casting their nets. Mahindan was making an inventory of his catch when he heard the warning whistle. He had tensed, jaw in a clench, anticipating the detonating crash, the eruption of sand, the screams. Then he relaxed when he opened his eyes to find himself alive, limbs intact. Later, he had helped throw sand over the bodies.

Mahindan groaned. A mosquito landed on his arm and he didn't have the energy to swat it away. Exhaustion was a leaden weight; it pressed in from all sides. He longed for home, his bed in Kilinochchi. They had been on the run since September, the past three months spent like vagrants. Every morning waking up and wondering: Where to find water? What to eat? Was it safe enough here to stay another day? Knowing that all the worry and effort might be for naught. At any moment, calamity could fall from the sky. Even as he lay here, breathing in and out, barely thinking. Even as Ruksala and the children combed the beach for their dinner, wet sand like a sponge under their feet, the tide lapping at their toes.

And on top of everything else, Mahindan had lost his slippers. The next time they packed the tent and fled, he'd have to go barefoot.

The old men had moved on, their voices swallowed up in the hubbub of hammers and footsteps. Mahindan wasn't sure how long he'd been lying down, if he had dozed off. Sellian might come back soon.

With a great effort of will, he hauled himself upright, unbuttoned his trousers, and removed the money belt hidden under his waistband. It was a relief to release the clips and peel the cotton pack from his sweaty skin.

Then, removing the wallet from his pocket, he examined it properly for the first time. It was well made from supple leather, expensive. Inside, he found a thick wad of rupees. Mahindan had never seen money like this before, crisp new banknotes, each one stiff and unmarked. He fanned the money in his filthy hands, counting and re-counting, taking in the zeroes. Thirty identical bills, two thousand each. He squeezed his eyes closed. Opened them. Sixty thousand rupees. Could this windfall be real?

The two-thousand-rupee note was orange. It pictured the ancient rock fortress of Sigiriya. There was a legend of a bastard prince who usurped his brother's throne after murdering their father. He'd shoved the old man into a barrel lined with lime and rolled it down the hill. Then, terrified of retribution, the coward had fled, building his palace six hundred fifty feet in the sky, on Sigiriya. Lion Rock. Even at that time, the Sinhalese were wicked.

Mahindan rubbed the bills between his fingers, enjoying the feel of the newly printed paper. It was almost a pity they were his now, and would be kept in his money belt with the other rupees, each note creased and permanently sweat-dampened, so worn the paper was on the verge of disintegration. Sixty thousand rupees. The man in the car had been carrying sixty thousand rupees.

Early that morning, Mahindan and Sellian had gone to temple. Returning to camp, they took a meandering path away from the busy town center, Mahindan feeling the hot ground burn the soles of his bare feet. Entering a palmyra-shaded lane, they spotted the car. Abandoned on the side, it was a newer-model Toyota, sleek silver with a modern, aerodynamic shape. Even from a distance, Mahindan knew there would be no rust. Premonition tingled the tips of his fingers. It was midafternoon and the area was deserted. *Go!* Chithra whispered in his ear.

Wait here, he told Sellian. Close your eyes and let me hear how well you know your numbers.

The driver had his arms around the steering wheel, head cradled on the hub. He might have been asleep, pulled over to the side for a nap. Mahindan could spot no blood, no sign of injury. There was only the buzz of flies and stubborn rigor mortis. Sellian was well into the double digits. *Muppatti aru, muppatti elu, muppatti ettu.* The wallet was in the glove box. It was as easy as that.

Now, Mahindan stripped it. A driving license, a national identification card, two bank cards. With men, it was simple—one hand in a pocket and the wallet came out. Women carried less cash, but there was almost always a thali or a flash of gold at the ears. He hated the jewelry, the eardrops especially, the laborious process of unscrewing the backs, fingers brushing stiff, cold skin, insides roiling with the smell.

The first time had been surreal. The old woman under the tree, her sari blown up, a dog nosing around. Hungry dogs were unpredictable, but this one flattened its ears and slunk away when Mahindan brandished a stick. He had been alone that time, dragging his blistered feet from village to village, trying to find a stand where he could afford a little milk, a few eggs. Mahindan had only meant to cover the woman up, pull the sari down over her wizened legs. He said a prayer of thanks when he got closer, that his own parents had been allowed the mercy of heart attacks at home.

He'd felt hopeless in that moment and so hungry, his stomach groaning empty. Seeing the woman's clenched fist, the wrinkled skin around her knobby knees. Their lives meant so little, weren't even afforded the slightest dignity. The sun glinted off a bit of hardware at her waistband. The buckle of a coin purse winked at him. (*Take it!* Chithra urged.) He reached carefully to pull the sari down and felt his fingers grasp metal, then tugged. He held his breath, not daring to look around.

The purse was beaded. He felt the rough texture in his palm as he closed his fingers, the weight of the coins inside.

Dinner that night had been joyous. Ruksala fried eggs with a sprinkle of chili powder on top. The children, bellies sloshing with fresh milk, slept straight through the night.

Well done, pillai, Chithra's father had said as they washed the plates in the river. You have provided well today.

After that, Mahindan scavenged every chance he got. If Sellian was with him, he instructed the child to stay back, close his eyes, and recite a poem.

Keeping jewelry and cash was uncomplicated, but Mahindan was conflicted about the rest of it. The marriage licenses and school certificates, immunization records and passports—these paltry collections were all that remained of people's life stories. He could not bring himself to burn them in the cooking fire.

In the tent, Mahindan unzipped his suitcase and reached for the bag where he kept Chithra's documents. Her birth and death certificates, her laminated bus pass. Let the dead keep each other company.

The coins he set aside for food and new shoes. The bills he slid into the pouch, securing the belt around his waist. He didn't have a clear idea of what he would do with his hoard, only that it was security. He had left the garage and the house, all his tools, even Sellian's bicycle, behind in Kilinochchi. He had his son and he had nearly two million rupees. Could they secure a future with this treasure?

Mahindan heard familiar voices. He arranged his shirt just as the flap of the tent opened and Sellian strolled in, his hands behind his back.

How? Mahindan said. You and Prem found many cockles? We will have a feast tonight? Tell.

Ap-pa, Sellian said in a singsong voice. I have brought you a pre-sent.

Prawns? Mahindan asked, wondering what could be behind his son's back. A nice cuttlefish?

Sellian brought his arms forward with a flourish and held the gift out, beaming proudly. Straps worn but soles intact, near-perfect condition. A pair of men's sandals.

MODEL MIGRANT

At the end of January, with the women's hearings already under way, they began admissibility hearings for the men. Prasad, their model migrant, was first.

You're up, Gigovaz had told Priya.

Me?

Sure. You've researched the precedent. You know the case inside out.

Now, half an hour before the hearing, she loitered in the lobby with Prasad. Priya was preoccupied by a call they'd received the previous day, when Gigovaz hustled her into his office and put Singh on speaker. The Mounties had tracked down two of the people whose identification documents were found on the ship. They died in Sri Lanka, Singh announced. Last January.

Nervous? Prasad asked, nodding to Priya's unconsciously tapping shoe.

Sorry, she said, and planted her foot.

It was nearly one thirty and the entrance to the Immigration and Refugee Board building was busy with people returning from lunch, everyone in ties and slick blazers, twisting around to stare at Prasad in his regulation sweatpants and numbered shoes. Even without handcuffs, he stuck out. Priya felt ashamed of herself for being so self-absorbed.

Prasad patted her shoulder. You're a clever girl, he said. You'll do well today.

His English—already fluent on arrival—had subtly transformed over the past seven months. How's it going? he said these days, instead of How? In December, he'd given her the letter he'd written for the newspapers with a request that she remove the idiosyncratic turns of phrase.

Sri Lankan English is not Canadian English, he'd said. I've shifted here. Now I must learn the language properly.

Moved here, she'd corrected. Then added: But I like Sri Lankan English!

Prasad's open letter had been reprinted in all the papers over the holidays and inspired a flurry of goodwill on open-line shows and in letters to the editor. Charlie reported that donations to the Tamil Alliance had spiked. Priya had been impressed by the quality of Prasad's prose, the lines he had quoted from Niemöller *(First they came for the socialists, and I did not speak out . . .)*. She could see that he must have been a good journalist.

How are you? she asked. Are you worried about today?

Two people walked through the metal detectors, engaged in silent conversation. The woman signed at top speed; the man nodded his head, rapping his knuckles on an invisible door.

Prasad watched them as he spoke. When the president's thugs forced me into the trunk of their car, I feared for my life, he said. But today, this is only a hearing. What is there to be afraid of?

The couple strode past them, hands flying, one barely completing a thought before the other jumped in. The man tapped the woman's shoulder to get her attention then brought two fingers out, touching them to his thumb.

Mitchell Hurst is a good adjudicator, Priya said. He's fair.

The couple paused at the elevators. Priya read frustration in their mannerisms, in the signs she could not decipher. She thought of Charlie. Language was a superpower.

I read all your articles, Priya said. You wrote bravely.

Prasad looked pleased when he turned. Thank you.

They stared at each other, nodding, grins gradually falling flat, unsure of what to say next.

Priya took a chance. Prasad, do you know who left those identification papers on the ship?

He didn't answer immediately, and she could see him sizing her up.

Apart from pressing their clients for intel back in October, Gigovaz hadn't taken further action. There was nothing to do, he said even now, but hold their breaths and wait. And hope nothing came of it.

I'm your lawyer, Priya told Prasad. I have to keep everything you tell me confidential.

Those papers were not mine, Prasad answered. He didn't shake his head as he said this.

Do you know who they belonged to?

I have suspicions, he said. But not proof. I do not like to say more. They are only suspicions, you understand.

Two of those people died in Sri Lanka, she said.

I see.

They didn't get on the boat, and yet their papers did.

Working for a newspaper, Prasad said, what I learned is that sometimes what is suspicious is not bad.

She didn't tell him that, nefarious or not, if Singh found a way to connect those papers, even remotely, to any of the migrants, it would mean deportation.

The room was packed with reporters. Prasad's open letter had been left unsigned, but most of the media knew he was a fellow journalist and guessed he was the key author. They were all there to see how he would fare.

A full house for your debut, Gigovaz whispered.

Jump in if I start to drown, Priya said. Then she was annoyed with herself. She would never have shown weakness in front of Joyce Lau. But then, shareholder meetings and stock splits weren't life-and-death matters.

Mitchell Hurst walked in and took a seat at his elevated desk.

Okay, he said, turning on his microphone. This is how it's going to work. I'll hear from Border Services, then Mr. Prasad's lawyers, and we'll go from there. Please don't raise your voices. Please don't speak over each other. We're all adults here, so let's act like it.

Priya reached for her water bottle and took a deep breath. A low-grade tremor had gripped her entire body. She parted her teeth so they wouldn't chatter in her head.

Singh launched in with her usual terrorist spiel and Priya listened carefully, each familiar refrain a balm on her nerves.

She was relieved to have Hurst in the adjudicator's chair. He was frank and forthright and ran his hearings the same way, and though he didn't always rule in their favor, his decisions were never arbitrary.

What's the story with these adjudicators? Priya had asked Gigovaz once. Why are some of them so erratic?

They're in over their heads, Gigovaz said. And it shows.

Singh came around to the evidence: Prasad's articles. The migrant was well-known for his pro-LTTE stance, she said. I'd like to draw attention to Exhibit B, a February 3, 2009, opinion piece in which he compared the LTTE to freedom fighters and wrote that they were, quote, *working toward a homeland to which they are entitled.*

Priya had anticipated this line of attack. She fumbled through her papers to find the printout she needed. It was covered in Post-its and yellow highlights.

Hurst asked Gigovaz: Would you like to respond to that?

Priya leaned in to her microphone and said, Ms. Singh is cherry-picking. Her voice, magnified and distorted by the speakers, took her by surprise. She tried to ignore it and plowed through her practiced statements.

Read in its entirety, she continued, the article criticizes the extreme measures used by both the Sri Lankan government and the LTTE.

The stenographer was clacking at her keyboard, recording every word. Priya felt the sketch artist's gaze, hard, on her. She heard the reporters shuffling behind her back. *How do my clients do this?*

Priya held up her copy of the translated article and said, Exhibit B. Third paragraph, second line. And I quote: *This should not be read as an endorsement of the LTTE's methods. The Tigers are ruthless and bloodthirsty. No question, they must be eradicated.*

The migrant's reportage was overwhelmingly Tiger-positive, Singh said.

Priya heard the perfunctory tone in Singh's voice and was bolstered. Her hands had stopped shaking.

We have submitted other articles into evidence, Priya said. Our client is on record criticizing the Tigers for their tactics, including the use of child soldiers and civilians as human shields. The fact is, Mr. Prasad was balanced in his reporting.

Yes, I've read the articles, Hurst said. I'm not buying the terrorism angle on this one, Ms. Singh. So unless you have some other proof . . .

No? Okay, let's move on to the issue of protection. Ms. Rajasekaran, you're arguing for protection on the grounds of political opinion?

Priya felt slightly light-headed, high on the thrill of doing well. Don't get cocky, she told herself.

Mr. Prasad is a person in need of protection, Priya said, the voice in her head competing with the voice she heard, loud and declarative, addressing the room. (*Is that the way I sound?*) He was kidnapped and tortured, an incident from which he still bears the physical scars. His home in Colombo was sprayed with machine-gun fire.

The words were speeding out of her too quickly, a runaway train: His editor was shot in front of him and Mr. Prasad himself has received death threats. (*Slow down! Slow down!*) We have submitted photos, his editor's obituary, and the death threats into evidence . . .

She wobbled to a stop. Singh started to say something, but Hurst held up his hand and told Priya to continue. On her notepad was a message she had underlined to herself. *More than a serious possibility.*

It is our contention that Mr. Prasad will be tortured and killed if he returns to Sri Lanka. The prima facie evidence demonstrates there is more than a serious possibility of persecution.

Gigovaz wrote *AMNESTY INT* in large letters on the legal pad between them and Priya quickly added: Furthermore, Sri Lanka is a country with a notorious track record of suppressing journalists. Exhibits E and F are public statements to this effect from Reporters Without Borders and Amnesty International.

Hurst raised his brows. Finished?

Yes. Thank you. Priya heard her voice come through the microphone, small and embarrassed.

Someone behind her tittered. Gigovaz drew a happy face on the notepad. Joyce would never have done that, Priya thought, feeling grateful.

Hurst said, I'd like to hear from Mr. Prasad directly. Sir, I know this is difficult. Take your time. Please tell me why you believe your life would be in danger in Sri Lanka.

Priya sat back in her seat and reached for her water again as her nerves settled. She watched Prasad tell his story. The crowd at Priya's back sat very still. She tried to assess Prasad objectively and she saw a man who was earnest, credible.

I am not a terrorist, Prasad concluded. Believe me. I left my country to escape the terrorists.

Thank you, Mr. Prasad, Hurst said. Does Border Services have anything further?

Singh said, I'd like to ask the migrant a few questions about his journey.

Amarjit Singh, Priya thought, irritated. With your pretty brown skin. What are you even doing here? But then Priya asked herself: What am *I* doing here? And she felt slightly less antagonistic.

Singh said: You came with a passport.

I did.

So why not take a flight? Why use this irregular means of arrival?

I was being watched, Prasad said. They would have killed me if I tried to board a plane.

And you saw no issue with resorting to criminal means to sneak into this country? Singh said.

Prasad thought for a moment, then said: I am reading a book right now about a very famous railroad under the ground. I believe there is a long history in this country of . . . *irregular* arrivals.

The stenographer coughed to cover a snicker. Priya and Gigovaz glanced at each other, both of them folding in their lips. Even Hurst seemed to be forcing the corners of his mouth down. Model migrant, Priya thought. If only they were all so fortunate.

DEED

Kumi said the house had been altered. They've raised it
one story, see?

Is anything familiar? Grace asked.

They stood shivering on the sidewalk, appraising a modest house
on the corner of a residential street. An original craftsman in trendy
Strathcona, the real estate listing boasted. Tremendous curb appeal in
Vancouver's oldest neighborhood. Priced at $1.2 million.

There used to be a swing. Kumi pointed to the gnarly old walnut
tree with the twisted trunk. We weren't allowed to stand on it, but I
did anyway and one day I fell and sprained my ankle.

A family exited the house, and through the open door Grace saw the
front hall and a young man in a suit and tie, waving goodbye. Kumi
had the listing rolled tight in her fist.

You're sure you want to do this? Grace asked. She was nervous about
the deed in her mother's purse, ticking like a time bomb.

Let's go, Kumi said, head high.

Inside, there was rich wood paneling that must have been original,
and granite kitchen counters that most certainly were not. There was
an artificial scent in the air, aggressively floral and vaguely noxious.
Kumi went straight for the living room, leaving Grace to deal with the
real estate agent.

Multigenerational homes are popular these days, he said. There's an
in-law suite in the basement.

Oh, Grace said.

You could turn it into a rental, the agent said quickly. It has its own
entrance.

Okay, thanks. Grace had her eyes fixed over his shoulder as her mother disappeared around a corner. She took a step to the left and the agent mirrored her movement. When she moved right, he did the same. Excuse me, she said. I just have to . . .

The door behind her opened with a gust of cold air and the agent's eyes lit up. Grace scurried away.

In the dining room, Kumi stood, turning her woolen Olympic toque round and round in her hands. A young couple inspected the fireplace, one man kneeling with his head up the chimney while the other stood back to appraise the mantel. They matched in skinny jeans and ironic mustaches.

This used to be the kitchen, Kumi said. What have they done? Grace took her mother's arm and as they stood close together, Kumi squeezed her eyes shut and said: We had a black-and-white floor, in a checkerboard pattern. And there was a table here in the middle where I did my homework.

One of the young men glanced over, curious.

Mom, Grace whispered.

Kumi's voice rose with her certainty. My uncle built shelves, she said, gesturing to a wall. Floor to ceiling here. For our dry goods.

You lived here? the young man asked.

All the wainscoting is original, the real estate agent announced, leading a new arrival in.

Grace took the opportunity to steer her mother out and they walked down the hallway, Skinny Jeans close on their heels.

This isn't right, Kumi muttered.

It made Grace melancholy to watch her mother wandering from room to room, touching the tiled bathroom walls, the chair rail in the hallway, and finding nothing familiar, a nosy stranger trailing behind, feigning interest in the cabinetry, the plumbing under the sink.

On the drive over, Kumi had railed, indignant: It was practically the ghetto! No respectable white person would be caught dead where we lived. My father breaking his back in a labor camp, the rest of us sent to Slocan with only what we could carry, everything else auctioned for pennies. Thieves! That's *our* home. I should be leaving it to you.

But the house defeated her. A stranger in it, Kumi was too cowed by the unfamiliar rooms to fling the deed in the real estate agent's face.

What is that? she asked, pausing on the stairs and sniffing the air. Why does it smell like that?

A woman inspecting the banister gawked and Grace hustled her mother upstairs. In the smallest bedroom, Kumi put her hand on the window that faced the back garden.

Was this your room? Grace asked, taking in the pink princess bed with its teddy bear placed just so, the dollhouse in the corner, all of it professionally staged.

At a certain point, they made everyone register, Kumi said. You had to keep your papers on you at all times. I remember the day my parents went. They came home with black marks on their fingers.

The woman who had been behind them on the stairs started to walk in. Grace blurted: This room is occupied! The woman left muttering *weirdo* under her breath.

Kumi rubbed her right index finger with the opposite thumb, hard, as if trying to clean it. It took a week for the ink to fade, she said. Until the day she died, my mother kept her registration card in her wallet. Hers and my father's.

I didn't know that, Grace said.

Kumi shuffled to the bed and dropped down heavily. Grace looked at her mother, an old woman now, clutching a teddy bear under a canopy of tulle. What was this room like when Kumi was a girl? Grace thought of her own, ordinary childhood and how different her mother's had been. How instantaneously one's trajectory could pivot.

Excuse me. Skinny Jeans hovered in the doorway. I'm sorry. I couldn't help overhearing. Kumi gave him an encouraging smile and he joined her on the bed. You lived here, he said. Before the war?

How long had he been eavesdropping? Grace watched, horrified, as her mother opened her purse and brought out the deed. The paper was yellowed and delicate with age, creased deeply at the folds, the legalities spelled out in archaic cursive, all flourishes and swirls.

The young man treated it like the Magna Carta, unfolding it slowly and smoothing it out on his lap with care.

You lost your home during the internment. He reached out and touched Kumi's shoulder. His gaze was reverent and Kumi lapped it up.

The last days we spent here are the clearest in my memory, Kumi said. This disease . . . I can't tell you what I did yesterday, but I know exactly what I was wearing the day we boarded that train.

Mom, Grace said from the window. You're tired. We should go.

And my parents, Kumi continued. How calm they were, how carefully they controlled their emotions. Everything was quietly done—packing the suitcases, gathering all the things we had to turn over to the officials. My brother tried to hide a radio and my mother slapped him. Do what you are told, she said.

Was everyone so . . . so compliant? he asked.

Our community leaders urged cooperation. If there's one thing we Japanese do well, it's following the rules.

The stranger marveled at the deed, read out loud passages of its legal language. Kumi squeezed his hand and Grace was appalled at the naked gratitude on her face. Later, he'd tell his partner: *You won't believe what I just heard.* They'd put in an offer and the story would be a staple at their dinner parties. *This house has a history. I met the woman who . . .* Obaachan would be mortified, her private shame reduced to an anecdote.

It's an outrage what they did, he said.

Kumi had been tugging on the teddy bear's fur. She gazed at the young man, confused. Her lower lip trembled as she searched out Grace. What is this place? she whispered.

We have to go, Grace said, crossing the room decisively. My mother is not well.

Skinny Jeans looked abashed and Grace was glad.

Kumi revived in the car and asked Grace to take her to Powell Street. On the drive, she reminisced about growing up downtown, in the tight-knit community they called Little Tokyo.

Everyone knew each other, Kumi said. As long as it wasn't dark, we children could go anywhere we liked. She pointed to a delicatessen and said: That used to be a fish market.

Really?

When Grace was a child and would ask her mother, What was it like when you were growing up? Kumi always said the same thing: There was never enough money. We just had to make do.

Same for every immigrant, her grandmother Aiko would add. Hard work. Sacrifice for next generation. Nothing special about us.

Now, for the first time, Kumi was letting down her guard, telling another story.

We used to go to the fish market, me and my brothers, with our mother on Saturday mornings. It was my job to make sure the boys didn't get lost. Those little tricksters, the places they would hide!

They parked the car and walked, Grace with a protective arm around her mother's back. It was a cloudy day, threatening to drizzle, and people strolled all around them, collars turned up, complaining into cellphones about the cost of real estate. *It's these Asians. They buy up everything. Who can compete?*

Kumi stopped in front of a café and tapped her foot on the patch of sidewalk where they stood. We used to play hopscotch here, she said. Mr. Yanamoto was the greengrocer. He had big glass jars behind the counter, full of lollipops and Life Savers and Sugar Babies, and if we behaved ourselves, someone would buy us a treat.

Grace imagined a buzz of Japanese voices, little boys in short pants on their bicycles, girls skipping rope in Mary Janes, women sticking their heads out of windows, calling them in to dinner. The tram rattling by.

She saw police descending with their ugly posters, demanding business owners put them up. The notices would darken the windows, throwing shadows into every store and barbershop, her grandparents' laundromat. Then the curfews and raids, cameras and cars confiscated. What had it been like after the expulsion, when Little Tokyo was a ghost town, still and silent, a half-torn poster fluttering in the breeze.

It was disconcerting to think of her headstrong mother caught in the turmoil. A small, wounded child in a pinafore. A city girl bewildered by the long train ride deep into British Columbia's rural interior, the terrifying mountains looming overhead.

Kumi paused and blinked at the stairs that led to the café's door. She lifted a foot and held it in midair, clutching blindly, searching for Grace's arm. Low blood sugar, Grace thought. Another symptom.

Inside, the café had patterned cement tiles and dark wood shelving. Grace scoped out a round bistro table in the far corner with a view of the door. Recently, she had taken to sitting with her back to the wall in public places.

She brought Kumi a hot chocolate and a Danish. They're out of Sugar Babies, she joked.

The deed was on the table and Kumi fingered its edges. How different everything might have been, she said.

Mom, you need to eat, Grace said, and nudged the plate.

Kumi brought the Danish to her mouth and nibbled obediently, so Grace obliged her by pretending to examine the deed. She told herself it meant very little. Even if the war hadn't happened, the house would have passed out of the family's hands long ago, sold after her mother and uncles married and left home. Morose thoughts of Little Tokyo had made her despondent. It was a familiar in her life now, this niggle of despair that crept up from nowhere and threw a wet blanket over everything. Hormones, she'd decided, watching the twins bicker one day. They've returned.

My parents' generation, the Issei, they were so naive, Kumi said. That is the most galling thing. They thought if they made a show of good faith, the government would come to its senses. Such blind trust in democracy. Kumi ripped off a long strip of pastry and folded it into her mouth.

They did their best, Grace said, putting a hand over hers. They were trying to protect you.

Protect themselves, Kumi said. Save face. And see what . . . !

The MedicAlert bracelet dangled off her wrist as she lifted a napkin to cover her eyes. Grace turned her head slightly and waited, watching the door. A bulky man walked in, shoulders hunched, eyes concealed by a hood, hands hidden in his pockets. Fear hitched Grace's chest. The man raised his head and waved as a child ran over. When he pulled back his hood and sank to his knees, holding his arms out, his whole demeanor changed. Grace released a breath.

An unwanted memory intruded: a detention release Grace had denied. The migrant had a young son and his lawyer had played up the separation. *The boy is living with strangers who don't speak his language.*

Grace knew she had made the right call. There had been a bus bombing and the migrant was involved. She couldn't roll the dice on public safety, not when documents belonging to people who had died overseas inexplicably ended up on a boat here. No doubt, Mitchell and his *jurisprudence* would disagree with her decision. But what Mitchell didn't consider was that the process might be flawed. Let him be hamstrung by precedent. Grace would use common sense.

Twelve Montreal teenagers had conspired to bomb Parliament. At Heathrow, Coke cans jerry-rigged to explode were found on a flight bound for Canada. Every day, there was another terrorist threat in the news. Sometimes, pushing a grocery cart or standing in line at the ATM, Grace watched the people around her, blithely going about their business, and wondered how they could be so guileless, how a year ago she had been just the same.

Her mother cleared her throat and when Grace turned back, Kumi was sipping her hot chocolate, eyes dry.

Grace rotated the handle of her mug one way then the other. I didn't realize you were so angry.

Kumi sighed. Your father and I, we thought, at a certain point, the bitterness must end. You're Canadian. We did not want you to hate this country.

And the girls? What about them?

We were wrong, Kumi said. All through school, who were your friends, the man you married? You are Canadian in a way your father and I could never be.

Her mother was right, Grace thought. The twins could take a nuanced view, balancing the wrongs of the past against the good fortune of their present. Had this been her concern all along—that they'd turn against their country?

I regret it. By repeating our parents' mistakes, we did you a disservice. Kumi threaded and unthreaded her fingers, tugging her wedding ring on and off. How could it happen? she said. The internment? Certain people felt too rooted, too comfortable. They took it for granted that they deserved to be here more than us. Entitlement closed their hearts.

Grace saw where this was headed. Mom, please let's not start this again.

At one time, didn't they say terrible things about the Irish? They were dirty, they were poor, they had diseases. Energy revived, Kumi was on a roll. But after a while, the Irish came to be accepted. And then people who forgot the stones thrown at their grandparents threw those same stones at others.

We've been over this, Grace said, crumpling her napkin and reaching for her coat.

Just . . . just listen. Let me finish. I know you think I'm trying to tell you how to do your job.

And you aren't? Grace wound her scarf around her neck. It always came down to the same thing with her mother: critique. Nothing she did would ever be right.

That child who called you a FOB. Why did he do this? Kumi drew a line between their two sides of the table. Because he forgot.

Okay, okay, Grace said, holding out Kumi's gloves. Let's go home.

Kumi was irascible as they left. Don't treat me like a child, she snapped when Grace tried to help her into her coat.

Outside, it had begun to drizzle and the stairs were slick.

Get off me, get off me, Kumi said, waving Grace away.

The railing, Grace said.

I'm not decrepit yet, Kumi grumbled under her breath. Then she lifted her foot and missed a step. Crumpling like a marionette, she came down hard on one knee before pitching forward, headfirst, down the concrete stairs.

MOM! Grace screamed.

On the pavement, Kumi lay curled in a ball, one leg bent at a terrifying angle, perfectly still.

Come Clean

Balasingham Rangasamy, Singh said. Tiger name: Sammy. For ten years, between 1999 and 2009, this man smuggled weapons for the LTTE.

Even before Nigel Blacker could translate, Ranga sat up with a start. Priya's heart sank.

This man is not a low-level cadre, Singh said. He is a trained operative and a high-ranking member of the Sea Tigers, the LTTE's naval branch.

Priya was confused. How could Singh know all of these very specific things, and why had she not—

Gigovaz scowled at Priya and turned her microphone to face him. Excuse me, he said, but is there some evidence to support these accusations?

Singh slid a booklet across the desk toward Gigovaz. These documents only came to our attention an hour ago.

The booklet was two inches thick, the printed pages square-hole punched and bound with wire coils. There was a clear PVC cover and, underneath, a title page that read *Exhibit L*. At the front of the room, Mitchell Hurst already had a copy. An hour ago, and you had time for binding and a cover page? Priya wondered.

I did notify your office, Singh told Gigovaz, raising her brows at Priya.

Priya started to say: I—

Singh cut her off. The bottom line is, this man lied about his identity. On February 5, 2009, he captained a Sea Tiger vessel that attacked a Sri Lankan Army ship. The details are outlined in Exhibit L-10.

It's not an Exhibit if you haven't entered it into evidence, Priya fumed in her head. Border Services was at it again, withholding evidence until the last possible moment in order to catch them off guard. Back at the office, there probably was a message on Priya's machine. *This is Amy Singh. Just wanted to let you know . . .* How long had Singh watched the clock and waited, timing her call so the phone rang after she was sure Priya and Gigovaz had left?

Singh said: After a brief confrontation at sea, during which the migrant sustained a leg injury, the militants were captured. Five days later, he and two others escaped. This man is a wanted criminal in his native country. The Sri Lankan government has a warrant out for his arrest. Exhibit L-13.

Gigovaz was bent over the booklet, eyes flicking back and forth. The virgin pages crackled against each other as they turned.

There is a process to be followed, Priya said. Documentary evidence should be disclosed five days before a hearing. She knew she was grasping at straws, but she couldn't think what other objection to raise. This was not how things were done in a court of law. But then, this was not a court of law.

Singh said: I agree this is unorthodox. But we only received the dossier this morning and felt the information was too crucial to delay sharing. You will see, on page four, there is a copy of the migrant's passport. It was taken from him during his capture and is still in the possession of the Sri Lankan government.

Gigovaz turned to page four and Priya saw the familiar picture. Beard, full face, invisible mouth. A younger Ranga. Before the scar.

Singh had more ammo: Exhibit L-14, a translated copy of the Sri Lankan medic's report. I have highlighted the pertinent details. *A jagged piece of shrapnel lodged in the upper right shin. It is likely the patient will always have a limp.*

As Blacker translated, Priya watched Ranga, absently rubbing at his leg. The LTTE made us go here and there, he'd told them months ago. They used us for protection.

Months fleeing through the jungle while the army and the Tigers lobbed artillery back and forth over his head. Ranga, the innocent bystander, caught in the crossfire. A greengrocer. That's what Priya had thought he was. *You lied to me.*

Singh pressed on: We now have international corroboration for the migrant's true identity. As a longtime arms smuggler, he is known to authorities in India and Thailand. L-15, -16, and -17.

Singh rhymed off evidence without glancing at her notes, like someone who had spent the last hour committing her lines to memory.

We cannot possibly comment on evidence we haven't had time to review, Priya said, feeling wrong-footed and chagrined.

Hurst said nothing and turned the pages of the booklet.

Singh said, The direct evidence is overwhelming. This man has engaged in acts of subversion and terrorism for the past decade. Under Article 1F of the Act, these are sufficient grounds to deem him inadmissible. We ask that you issue an immediate deportation order.

Priya looked helplessly at Gigovaz. *Do something!* She pressed the button on her microphone, but before she could open her mouth, Gigovaz spoke up calmly. We request a recess to review this evidence and confer with our client.

Hurst turned to Ranga and asked: Do you have anything to say?

Blacker, in a deadpan voice: I am not a Tiger.

Hurst said: You are saying this evidence is false? That it has been fabricated?

Under the table, Ranga rubbed furiously at his leg. This man, he said, in English. This man no me.

At any time in your life, were you a Sea Tiger? Hurst asked.

Singh sat still, hands clasped, as Ranga dug his grave deeper.

No, Ranga said again in English. This man . . . this man no me.

I would request a short recess to speak with my client, Gigovaz said again. We have not had an opportunity—

We will break for the day, Hurst said. I too must review the evidence and then we can schedule a continuation of this hearing. In the meantime, Mr. Gigovaz, Ms. Rajasekaran, I suggest you urge your client to come clean.

———

Don't jump to conclusions, Gigovaz told Ranga as the guard locked the cuffs on his wrists.

Charlika translated, her words agitated and quick.

We can issue a challenge order in federal court or apply for a pre-removal risk assessment, Gigovaz said. Worst-case scenario, we appeal to the public safety minister.

Priya could hear the alarm in Gigovaz's voice, his lapse into legal jargon.

The guard locked Ranga's ankles together, then stood and said, Okay, let's go.

Charlika went with Ranga and the guard down the hallway toward the doors, still speaking in mile-a-minute Tamil.

Gigovaz turned on Priya. And where was your head in there?

I—

He slapped Singh's booklet against his hand. Too busy lobbying the government for mining execs? Get your head in the game! He stalked off, leaving her standing alone by the empty hearings room.

This isn't even my game! she wanted to yell at him. Idiot.

Priya walked toward the street, exhausted and defeated. She had spent the week before working late and preparing, lining up the evidence, readying her statements, drilling Ranga on his testimony. She'd been so confident walking in, telling herself she'd done the best she could. *This man no me.* Ranga would be deported. He was as good as dead.

Charlie was waiting for Priya on the sidewalk, one purse strap hanging off her shoulder, rummaging under her armpit. Are you okay? she asked.

Yeah. Well, better than him, Priya said. They watched the prison bus push off from the curb and ease into traffic.

Ranga's story had been so plausible, had lined up with everything Mahindan and the others said. The Tigers were known to use their own people as shields. Priya had gathered United Nations reports as corroboration. The Sri Lankan government itself had released videos showing the civilian migration. Hundreds of thousands of bodies surging across the desolate landscape, the images grainy but incontrovertible. Watching the footage, it had been possible to believe Ranga was somewhere in the crowd. Now, she just felt like a sucker.

They left the steel and glass of the financial district behind and headed downhill on Burrard, alongside cyclists and buses, the after-work rush. Straight ahead, Priya could see False Creek, the Burrard Bridge jammed with traffic.

Where are we going? she asked.

To my place, Charlie said. I know three people who will be happy to see you. You don't have plans, do you?

No, but—

No, listen, Charlie said. You don't even know. Hema cooks for me now, like 24/7. Tonight, it's lamprais.

Priya chuckled. Of course it is.

Woman can barely speak English, but she manages to find banana leaf, Charlie said. Don't ask from where.

They had crossed into Davie Village, where rainbow flags flanked the light poles and the garbage cans were painted bright pink. Every bar was jammed, everyone cheering the TV. The Winter Olympics had begun the previous weekend, while Priya was trapped in her apartment, held hostage by work. The Games had the whole city in the grip of a rare patriotic fever. Priya had put the live feed of the opening ceremony on mute as she wrote reports for Joyce, glancing up occasionally to see the crowds in red-and-white regalia thronging downtown. Taking breaks to catch up on the medal count while eating toast over the sink, she'd watched her homeless neighbors shuffling about in the square across the street. Alone in their shabby corner of the city, it was just her and the hoboes, the only ones untouched by the festivities.

She and Charlie walked in silence for a few moments, past tanning salons and payday loan shops, Priya still ruminating on Ranga. Earlier, at the office, she'd gone over the case file one last time and stared at his identity card. His face in the picture was fuller, less lined. Unlike the others, Ranga had not bounced back to his old weight.

He'd been more hirsute back then, with shaggy hair that concealed his ears, and a generous beard, mustache, and thick sideburns. There was something else that was different about the man in the photograph, something less substantial. Priya had thought it might be hope. The Ranga she knew was gaunt and haunted. Now she realized how naive she had been, to think she could divine a person's character from a tiny black-and-white image.

Is it true, arms dealing, all of it? Charlie asked.

Ranga says no. And I haven't had a chance to examine the evidence. But?

Priya shook her head. Border Services likes to play games, but this time I think they found something real.

So it's true, then. Charlie inhaled with pursed lips as they traversed the faded rainbow-striped crossing.

Ranga was the last person I'd have pegged for a rebel, Priya said. Especially in that long-term, committed, captaining-a-ship kind of way. He's always struck me as . . . well, the weakest one.

Who's to say what a person is capable of? Charlie said. If the government decided tomorrow to start hating on Tamils or Muslims or whoever . . . if they passed laws that disenfranchised us, limited our access to education, to jobs . . . if the '83 riots happened here in Vancouver . . .

I don't know, Priya said, thinking that it was difficult to imagine and that her first instinct might be to run.

If someone was threatening me, the people I loved? Charlie said. I'd fight back. With a knife, with my fists, M-16s . . . whatever.

Priya asked herself: What would I fight with? What weapons do I have? The law seemed impotent.

Charlie had run out of steam. She seethed in silence, veering around a fire hydrant.

How are Hema and the girls? Priya asked.

Picking up English quickly, Charlie said. Especially the girls. We're hoping to get them enrolled in school. It's too late for this year, but they can start in September and by then their English will have improved.

I really needed to hear that today.

Things aren't perfect, Charlie said. Any loud, unexpected noise makes them jump. Hema screams in her sleep. I've tried to talk to her about seeing someone, but no dice. And then, of course, there's still the Refugee Board hearing in July hanging over their heads.

How are they feeling about that? Priya asked. It struck her that in July she would no longer be their lawyer. It was jarring to think of all these cases moving forward, Gigovaz still struggling on, without her.

Depends on the day, Charlie said. Last week, Tara spent three days in bed. If one of them gets in a funk, game over. Have you heard anything about Savitri?

Her Refugee Board hearing is scheduled for late August, Priya said. We tried to give her as much time as possible to climb out of the depression. She needs therapy, maybe drugs . . . things we can't force on her.

Charlie shook her head. I *knew* this would happen. Didn't I say? They kept her in there for too long.

Charlie had a two-bedroom on Jervis Street, on the second floor of a redbrick low-rise that was past its best-before date.

I have to knock first, Charlie said as they walked down the hallway. Once, I came home early and they were waiting for me, knives out. She wrapped her knuckles one after the other like two plodding feet, five knocks, then stuck the key in the lock.

The apartment smelled of incense. The only light in the living room came from streetlamps and dusk fading through the window. The girls' faces were lit by the cool glow radiating off the TV screen. They sat on the floor, squeezing their fists and watching men's curling. Canada versus Norway.

Priya has come for dinner, Charlie said.

They waved distractedly.

Two more weeks of this, Charlie said as the girls chanted: Can-a-da! Can-a-da!

Don't speak English on my account, Priya said.

It's for them, not you, Charlie said. We only speak English here.

In the galley kitchen, Hema portioned out rice and curries in the middle of a flattened banana leaf. She flashed a wide, crooked-toothed grin at Priya and Charlie as they hovered in the doorway.

I tried to do this once, Priya said. But I kept overfilling the packets and splitting the leaves.

I am many years practice, Hema said. She deftly folded up the banana leaf like wrapping paper around a present, sliding in toothpicks to hold the ends in place. She said, Like a diaper!

She pronounced it *di-ah-per*.

From the other room, the detached drone of the announcers floated in. *His final shot. They're gonna have to drag this one. Will they get the angle? Nice brushing.*

The oven dinged to signal it was preheated and Hema slid the casserole dish in, five neatly packaged lamprais tucked inside. Finishing! she said.

Finished, Charlie corrected.

Hema rinsed her hands then held her arms out to grasp Priya's shoulders. Pressing her cheek to Priya's, she breathed in once before switching sides and repeating the motion.

Happy you are here, she said.

Me too, Priya said, and it was true. For the first time all day, she felt relaxed.

The match had ended and the girls wandered over. Padmini linked her arm with Priya's and peeked up at her shyly. Her hair was separated into two braids, each one looped at the end and held in place by a rectangle of cotton fabric tied into a bow. She had a black dot of pottu in the center of her forehead. Padmini was thin and flat-chested. She was fourteen but still played with dolls. When Priya compared her to the teenagers she saw, hanging on to a bus pole, thong strings sticking out of the back of their jeans like whale tails, an earbud in one ear, a phone pressed to the other, Padmini seemed an innocent. But she had endured horrors the girls chomping gum at the bus stop would never experience.

Tara stood by her sister, playing with a strand of hair that had fallen loose from her braid. Her hair was long enough now to tie back.

How are you both? Priya asked.

They stood silent and bashful until finally Charlie exclaimed: So, she's here! Talk, will you?

The girls told Priya in fragmented English about how they were filling their time: English classes every morning; math and science lessons at home to catch up on in the afternoons; long strolls drawing circles around the neighborhood, each day expanding their circumference of safety. They had gone to Coal Harbor to see the lighting of the Olympic cauldron on the weekend.

Not that we could see anything, Charlie said, emerging from her bedroom. She had changed into a skirt and a button-down plaid shirt. Her feet were bare, pleasantly plump and rounded, ten toes gleaming with red polish and a very thin gold chain circled around one ankle.

Such people! Hema said, bustling out with a stack of plates. How many are seeing this Olympic flame!

You are going? Tara asked Priya. Also to the flame?

Priya said she had spent her weekend working.

Hema patted her shoulder and said, Saving the people.

Priya didn't want to tell her that most of her time had been commandeered by the Newtown Gold takeover. Instead, she asked about their English classes.

Once the women started getting out of detention, the Tamil Alliance stepped up the schedule, Charlie said. Some retired schoolteachers have added daytime classes. And there are conversation groups around the clock. I met your dad and uncle, she added, answering the question Priya had not wanted to ask outright.

She learned that they were leading parallel Saturday conversation groups. Like Appa, Uncle had come to Priya in private and asked about volunteering. But neither had raised the subject again and Priya, following their lead, had also kept quiet. It was confusing to think of them driving there and back together, comparing notes on how their groups fared.

Ah! Hema said to the girls, waving a hand to the dining table. Clean, clean.

A Singer sewing machine sat on the table, surrounded by spools of thread and scraps of cloth. A pair of jeans hung over the back of a chair.

Hema got a job, Charlie explained.

At clean and dry, Hema said.

A dry cleaner, Charlie said.

Dry cleaner, Hema repeated, then mimed stitching and said, I am making hems, buttons, shorter, longer.

Alterations, Priya said. That's great.

We are helping, Padmini said, throwing the jeans over her shoulder and picking up the sewing machine by its handle.

The woman at the dry cleaner's can't understand how Hema gets work done so fast, Charlie said. Meanwhile, we've got a full-on sweatshop going here.

This was evidently a recycled joke, because Hema, Tara, and Padmini all laughed. A familiar intimacy hung cozy over the group— the way Padmini reached across her mother to gather up the spools of thread, the hip bump Tara and Charlie shared as they passed through the kitchen doorway.

Over dinner, they teased Charlie about a guy at the Tamil Alliance. Hema won't rest until I'm married off, Charlie told Priya.

Engineer, Hema said. Very nice boy.

You know the word *engineer*, Priya said. Of course you do.

Charlie shook her head at Priya, then whispered: Too bad he's gay.

TRUE OR FALSE

They were speaking quietly in their cell, waiting for Ranga to return from his hearing, Mahindan loitering in the open doorway while Prasad made his bed. Mahindan yawned loud and wide and a passerby who had turned to nod at him did the same. For the past two weeks, a recurring dream had been shattering his sleep. Every night, he ran through the jungle in maddening slow motion, the thunder of Kfir jets overhead, hunting frantically for Sellian.

Prasad smiled to himself as he shook out the bedsheet. Three days earlier, he had received good news: his detention release was granted and he had passed his admissibility hearing. On Friday, he was going to start living with Sam Nadarajah.

Just until I get on my feet, Prasad said, using the English expression, already thinking like a Canadian. He slid his fingers under the mattress to tuck in the sheet and said: But first I must find a job.

What jobs will you apply for? Mahindan kept his voice bright to mask his envy. When the first men were released, the mood had been celebratory, but as more were set free, those left behind grew increasingly bitter.

With one knee on the bed, Prasad leaned across to secure the flat sheet on the other side. I will work anywhere, he said. Just take any job washing plates or making french fries.

Mahindan snorted. These were not jobs for a graduate of the university.

Prasad folded the top of the sheet neatly over, forming an envelope into which he could slide. Don't make fun, he said. In these Western countries, our doctors drive taxis.

But don't you want to work at a newspaper?

Journalism was not my first career choice. Prasad shook out the blanket in Mahindan's direction, indicating he needed help. He said, The troubles at home, I thought someone has to speak the truth.

Mahindan bent to take hold of two corners of the blanket. And so now? What?

They walked away from each other then came back together, the blanket stretching and folding between them.

I would like to be a teacher.

Mahindan thought of how Prasad taught them English, the slow, patient way he corrected their pronunciation. Ah yes?

That is the job I would have chosen at home if . . .

If not for the war.

Yes.

Prasad laid the folded square at the foot of his bed. Mahindan had given up on his bed months ago. No matter how closely he tried to emulate Prasad's method, his own sheets were always creased and untidy.

You would be a good teacher.

Ah, but now we are here.

And so? Mahindan returned to the doorway and checked the corridor.

I have no qualifications and already schools will have teachers.

Mahindan watched Prasad sitting on the bed, staring at his hands, and felt exasperated. Days away from being released, and here he was, turning into another Ranga. What Mahindan wouldn't give to trade places with him. Was there anything he wouldn't do? He stared hard at Prasad, the tendon that stuck out on the side of his fragile neck, and thought, Yes, I would squeeze my hands around this man's throat if it meant freedom, reunion with Sellian. End an innocent man's life, even this I would do.

The certainty of his conviction—he could feel exactly how it would be, gripping and squeezing, skin on skin—lasted an instant, but it took his breath away. His hands trembled and he hid them quickly behind his back.

Prasad was watching him. What are you thinking?

Mahindan said, I'm thinking that is the point of coming here, no?

You did not marry because of the war. You did not become a teacher because of the war. Now you are here and there is no war. Therefore, no excuse.

Maybe I will marry, Prasad said, and then my children—

Don't, Mahindan said. It is a dangerous thing to live for your children.

He shook his hands at his sides, still feeling Prasad's throat in their grasp, and thought of Sellian instead, bewildered in his puffy red snow costume. *How to move around in this, Appa?* If only I could send him to live with Prasad, he thought, and the fantasy assuaged his guilt.

Anyway, Prasad said, brushing his hands down his trousers and standing up. One thing at a time. Fourteenth of June. The next bridge to cross.

Fourteenth of June. The hearing in front of the Refugee Board. Prasad's final test, and Mahindan knew he would pass that one too. Prasad's case was straightforward and the judges were sure to be impressed by his English. Out in the world, interacting with shopkeepers and bus drivers, working at some new job, by summer Prasad would have picked up the accent too. He would pass to the other side, while Mahindan remained stuck here.

Longing intensified his envy. Gone were the days when he could easily summon his better nature, believe Prasad's success foreshadowed his own. It was difficult now to hold on to any good feeling. Impossible even to pray, to repeat a mantra, without the interruption of some disquieting worry.

And after that, papers and permanent residency, Mahindan said. And then what?

After three years, I can apply for citizenship.

Freedom, Mahindan said.

So much optimism for everyone except yourself, Prasad said.

There were footsteps in the hallway and they both glanced toward the doorway, but it was only a guard.

Prasad retrieved a backpack Sam had given him. He'd been opening it regularly, decanting all its contents and laying them out neatly before packing them all back up. Now he unfurled the zipper, laying the two sides flat on his bed. Inside were two packages stacked one on top of the other. Socks and plain underpants, three pairs each, still sealed in clear plastic.

The clothes hanger on the back of the door, naked for months, was now dressed in a pair of folded black trousers and a checked long-sleeved shirt. On Friday, after his shower, Prasad would leave his jail clothes in the laundry bin and put on the things Sam had brought for him.

They're not new, Sam had said, apologetic.

They are new to me, Prasad replied.

Sam had clapped Mahindan's back and said, Your turn soon, machan.

But Mahindan was not so sure. Seeing Prasad's backpack made him remember his grandfather's suitcase and all the mementoes inside, his last tangible links to home. Would he ever get those back?

He craned his neck out into the hallway as Prasad placed all the items back in the bag. If Ranga succeeds at his admissibility hearing, Mahindan thought to himself, surely I will too.

It wasn't only men who were being released. Every week, there was good news from the other jail too. Many of the women and their children were out and, like Prasad, one by one were passing their admissibility hearings. After nearly eight months, the tide was turning in their favor.

Mahindan told himself to have faith. If it goes well for Ranga, it will go well for me. Freedom in Canada. He deserved it more than Ranga, who had grown lazy in his torpor, who whiled away days and weeks in bed instead of practicing his English.

It was a question of discipline, and Ranga had none, Mahindan decided. Not like Prasad. Not like me. This was a country of opportunity. Good fortune was available for those who would grasp on to it. But the assurances he had been repeating to himself for months had begun to sound empty.

There were voices coming down the hallway, footsteps. Prasad shoved the bag back under the bed and came to stand with Mahindan in the doorway. The three men who had left that afternoon were returning, Ranga bringing up the rear. His limp was more pronounced than usual, one leg lagging behind and his hand on its side, as if pulling it along. Shoulders hunched, Ranga stared at the floor, a convict on his way to the hangman. Mahindan's stomach sank.

Ranga came into the cell and Mahindan closed the door, standing against it with his hands behind his back.

They are sending me home, Ranga said without raising his head. Deportation, he said in English, then slumped on the lower bunk, elbows on his knees. His voice was flat, matter-of-fact.

Prasad sat beside him. They made a decision? So quickly?

Mahindan's pulse quickened. Prasad's judgment had taken weeks. There was no way Ranga could know his fate already.

I cannot go back, Ranga said.

Prasad put his hand on Ranga's shoulder. What happened?

They're saying I'm a Tiger.

To them, we are all Tigers, Prasad said.

Ranga clutched his hands in his hair. No! No! he yelled. His pupils were large, his expression wild.

Mahindan grasped the doorknob. Shhh . . . quiet, quiet, he said. Ranga could not know yet. He was being melodramatic.

There was a battle in the sea, Ranga said. Sometime . . . I don't know. The Sri Lankan Army and the LTTE. They are saying this is how I got my . . . my injury. They are saying I was a Sea Tiger.

Prasad took his hand from Ranga's shoulder. They have proof of this?

The identity card. Ranga howled into his hands.

Mahindan turned to the door and scanned as far as he could out the window. His knees trembled. *The identity card.* He had never considered . . .

It was not me, Ranga said. I was never in the LTTE.

Mahindan walked deeper into the room, blindly. The identity card. Ranga. The Sea Tigers. The thoughts pinballed around, refusing to be grasped. Light-headed, he dropped onto Prasad's bed. The springs squeaked, startled.

Prasad, Ranga said, looking him straight in the eyes. I am not a Tiger.

Then how can there be proof? Prasad asked. They are saying your identity card belongs to a Sea Tiger? Have they made a mistake?

Now he will tell, Mahindan thought. And everything will be finished.

It was not me, Ranga said.

The speaker in the ceiling crackled on and Mahindan jumped up. Prasad and Ranga turned to him. Prasad's brows were raised.

Dinner is available in the cafeteria until nine o'clock, the voice on the speaker said. Mahindan could understand all the regular announcements now.

Come, Prasad said, ducking as he stood to avoid banging his head on the upper bunk. Eat something.

Ranga crawled beneath the sheets and rolled over to face the wall. Under the blanket, Mahindan could see him kneading his injured leg.

Ranga, Mahindan said. I'm . . .

Ranga didn't move and Mahindan couldn't finish the sentence. He joined Prasad at the open door, waiting.

Just come with us, Prasad said. For company.

Men passed through the hallway speaking of inconsequential things, exchanging news about wives and daughters in the other jail, people who had already been released. *She has fallen sick again, but what to do? The child will not dress properly for this weather.*

Ranga, Mahindan said again. He rotated the doorknob back and forth. Ranga did not reply. He lay like a corpse, barely breathing. Prasad tilted his head in the direction of the hallway and they left.

Mahindan was anxious to hurry forward and catch up with the others, but Prasad measured out each step at a metronomic pace, wrapped in a blanket of ominous silence.

The identity card. Ranga. The Sea Tigers. Mahindan had never thought . . . Had Ranga said? The judge had not made a decision. It was all speculation.

The canteen was busy and the line moved slowly.

Chicken noodle, Prasad said, pushing his tray along the stainless steel rungs.

Just like Amma used to make, a man ahead of them joked.

Wednesday chicken noodle, Thursday spaghetti, Friday thosai, another man said.

Behind the counter, women in hairnets ladled soup out of black cauldrons. Steam unfurled in ribbons. Spoons clinked together. *Focus on this.*

Chicken and noodle, Mahindan repeated.

The orange-haired woman served him. She was big-made with friendly dimples. Mahindan handed her his bowl over the plastic partition.

Chicken and noodle, he said again, to himself. Noodle and chicken.

The woman passed his bowl back, her hands forming two Ls on

either side of the rim. She said, Careful. It's hot. And Mahindan understood.

Okay, he said in English. Thank you.

He set the bowl down carefully. The inside was ringed in condensation. He moved along toward the basket of bread rolls where Prasad stood, holding his tray between two hands, contemplating the little packet of butter and the knife beside it. Mahindan thought: This man has the power to finish me.

Almost everyone had been served and they were clustered boisterously around tables in the canteen's busy center. Mahindan took a step in that direction, but Prasad gestured toward a deserted corner and said, Let us go over there.

Mahindan couldn't think of a good excuse not to follow and they sat across from each other at a table by themselves. Prasad ate in an absent way, staring into his bowl. Sea Tigers. The identity card. Ranga's limp. Mahindan could see him circling around the evidence, sniffing, getting closer.

Mahindan's hand formed a fist around the handle of his spoon as he searched for a neutral topic. The soup was salty. Strings of noodles floated in the broth. The small orange cubes turned to mush in his mouth. They did not taste much like carrots. Canadian food was not bland, exactly. Its flavors were muted, like the colors outside. The green foliage, the blue skies, even the browns lacked a vibrancy that existed at home.

It's the sun, Prasad said. Here, we are far from the equator, and anyway, now it is winter.

Mahindan didn't know what the equator had to do with color saturation. Prasad bent his head over his bowl and Mahindan watched how he ate, how he held the handle of his spoon between two fingers. He wondered if this was something else Prasad had been taught at the university. He changed the position of his hand to mirror Prasad's then took another spoonful.

Soon, there will be appam for you, Mahindan said. And idli . . .

Never mind that, Prasad said abruptly. What about this business with Ranga?

Mahindan stared into his soup, at the swirls of oil floating on top. If they believe they have proof, what to do?

Do you think it is true, Ranga was in the LTTE?

You were always in Colombo? Grew up there, too?

Yes, Prasad said.

Mahindan let his spoon rest in the bowl. He said, In the north, there were two options. Join by choice or join by force.

He gazed toward the other tables, full of men joking and jostling. They had been following the Olympics and earlier that day had watched one of the snow events, boys balanced like surfers on boards rushing headlong down a mountain, winding in zigzags between flags. A man in the center of one of the tables was re-creating the demise of a German competitor. His hand crested the top of an imaginary slope and shot down.

I knew men who were proud to join, yes, Mahindan said. But for many, it was not like this. My cousin brother Rama, he was taken by force. My wife's sister, Nila, she went to the Tigers before they came for her, to protect her family, so they would let her parents be. Now, you tell me if this is voluntary.

And you? Prasad asked.

Mahindan was honest. If not for my garage, they would have forced me to join. It was only luck that saved me. I was worth more as a mechanic than a soldier.

Ranga says he was not in the LTTE.

Mahindan broke his bread in half. Then the authorities must be confused. It was someone else. Injured in a sea battle, he added, because he knew this would remind Prasad of the limp.

Prasad tapped his spoon against the edge of his bowl, thinking.

Saapidu, Mahindan said. Then in English: Eat before it is cold.

He dipped a piece of roll into his soup and watched the broth soak the bread. His stomach was hungry, but his mouth had lost its appetite.

The documents they found on the boat, Prasad said in Tamil. What do they have to do with all of this?

Who knows? Mahindan took a bite, forced himself to chew and swallow. If Ranga pointed the finger, he would deny it. Where was the proof? Kumuran's wife and all the others were gone from jail. There was no one else to speak against him.

Prasad contemplated the wall, staring over Mahindan's left shoulder as if avoiding his face. He ran through the possibilities, muttering to himself: Either they are right and Ranga was in the LTTE, or the authorities have made a mistake. Or someone wants Ranga to be sent back and has caused the mistake to happen. Or—

What is the point of guessing? This or that or a third thing, Mahindan said, using his upturned palms to demonstrate. What is important is not what is true or false. The important thing is what these people, the Canadian authorities, *believe* is true and false. What *they* want to believe.

Lady Doctor

The patient had hobbled in an hour earlier with a shrapnel injury that had become infected. The wound gaped. Pus oozed out. The leg was dead, everything black and liquefying.

This is a very bad case, the doctor said. It must be amputated.

Mahindan closed his eyes to summon a happy memory of Chithra, but she refused to oblige. He tried to muster up a mantra, the sound of Rama chanting, the fragrance of incense, but again there was nothing. Only this man and his putrefying leg.

In January, Mullaitivu had fallen and they had all moved here to Puthukkudiyiruppu, a small farming town eleven miles inland. The two-ward dispensary was already overrun, so the doctors had commandeered the school as a secondary hospital. The operating room was set up in one of the smaller classrooms. Four desks had been pushed together with a plastic sheet thrown on top. The patient was now lying on this improvised bed with his trouser leg cut off.

The doctor used the sink in the corner to wash her hands. She wore a paper mask and plastic goggles and pulled a yellow gown over her head to cover her cotton sari. Supplies were scarce and Mahindan and the other volunteer wore the same soiled gowns all day. They had taken what they could from the hospital in Mullaitivu; doctors, nurses, and ordinary people all working together to load equipment into wheelbarrows and patients onto bullock carts. Even the retreating cadres had pitched in, pushing the injured on their stretchers down the A35. A rare day of unity, everyone cooperating like a team.

In the hallway outside, patients moaned and gurney wheels rolled past. The lucky ones shared beds. Others were laid out on mats on the floor. There were five doctors and a dozen nurses in this improvised hospital, but most of the helpers were ordinary people like Mahindan, civilians who volunteered to escape the alternative. Every day, more and more people were conscripted into service by the LTTE, digging trenches, collecting weapons from dead bodies, or worse. Mahindan was thankful Sellian was only five, that near starvation had stunted his growth so he appeared even younger. Rumor had it they were taking children as young as nine.

There was a big green chalkboard set up on a wooden easel and children's paintings clipped to a laundry line along the back wall. Sunlight streamed in through the naked windows. It made Mahindan's skin crawl to be here.

The doctor had a small metal table on wheels where she laid out all her equipment. The doctor's hair was hidden under a shower cap. Yellow ducks swam in a line across her forehead. Mahindan and another volunteer stood on either side of the patient. The man was breathing hard. Sweat dampened his mustache. The infection bubbled away, corroding his leg. The smell was rancid. It burned in Mahindan's nose; his eyes watered.

He looked at the patient and tried to find something to hate—even disgust would make this easier—but all Mahindan saw was his own potential fate, how easily it could be him on this table, tomorrow or the next day, with no anesthetic and no consolation.

You must be brave, the doctor said.

The doctor said the patient's name often. She put her hand on his shoulder and focused on his eyes when she spoke. Mahindan tried not to learn anyone's names.

Have one of you a belt? the doctor asked.

The other volunteer undid his buckle and the patient clamped the belt between his teeth.

Keep him from moving, the doctor said. Please, sir, try to stay still.

The doctor held a scalpel; her attention was focused. The patient trembled and whimpered, lips folded into each other. Mahindan had one hand on the man's chest and the other on his arm. He ignored the queasy waver in his gut, the lightness in his head. He must not lose his dignity in front of the lady doctor.

She pressed the scalpel down, tip first. Drops of blood beaded up where blade met skin, a bright red line. Mahindan turned his head.

The world lay flat, pinned to the wall. Sri Lanka was a teardrop in India's shadow. America was green and, above it, Canada was orange. Large, unknowable countries oceans away.

The patient's head jerked off the table when he screamed. The belt clattered loose to the floor. Mahindan and the other volunteer moved quickly to press his shoulders down. When he muffled the man's shrieks with his hand, Mahindan felt spit and breath dampen his palm. The man's eyes squeezed closed. His wail was primal. Mahindan gritted his teeth as a memory assaulted him. Chithra gripped his hand and keened.

Ammmmmmma! the patient yelled.

Tears prickled Mahindan's eyes. He sniffed and bit down hard on his own tongue.

The incision was complete. The doctor peeled the skin back slowly, exposing muscle and sinew underneath. Rotten flesh fell away in clumps. The patient breathed in hot, hard bursts. Outside, a meal was being served. The smell wafted in—oats or gruel, something watery and insubstantial.

The doctor's gown was splashed with pus and blackened flesh. There was less blood than Mahindan had expected. He caught a whiff of something sweet and oddly familiar. A pile of bananas rotting in the sun, the smell of the body fermenting.

The doctor turned on the saw. Its blade whirred and vibrated. The man whimpered. His eyes were open again, wide with terror. Mahindan saw his pupils roll up toward his forehead. The body under his restraining hands went slack.

Fainted, the other volunteer said.

For the best, the doctor said, and bent over her work. The noise was a high-pitched whine.

———

The body, in death, was heavy and stiff. It took three men to lower it into a wheelbarrow. Mahindan struggled with the head, trying to rest it as gently as possible.

He's dead now, one of the volunteers said impatiently. Let's just finish this quickly. He shook his head and clucked his tongue against his teeth. Poor bugger. Who deserves this?

The two went ahead with the shovels and Mahindan was left to ferry the dead man through the hallways. He tried not to see the stump and its jagged stitches. Patients languishing on gurneys stared with blank eyes. The corridor to the back door was empty. An LTTE flag hung across the threshold. A yellow tiger burst out from a circle of bullets, its gaze following him.

Student artwork decorated the walls, a class project for Martyrs' Day. The students who had made these drawings were probably all dead. Mahindan could hear the sounds of the makeshift hospital around him—the clicks and clangs of moving equipment, the babble of voices as if from far away, and the wheel of the barrow rolling on the floor. The man's head was torqued, tucked against one shoulder. His intact leg dangled out.

He had grown feverish overnight, Mahindan was told. There were no medicines to give and nothing to do except let him shake and sweat, muttering gibberish. It had been hours before anyone realized he was dead. A complete and utter waste.

At the door, he stopped and set down the handles. After a furtive scan, he squatted beside the body and reached his hand into the man's pocket. The man wore jeans, which were stiff. It was a tight fit. Mahindan struggled to pull out a billfold. He caught sight of a five-hundred-rupee note before stuffing the money away. There was something else. An identity card, slimy but intact. He pocketed that too without glancing at the name, then stood, picked up the handles of the barrow, and walked forward with purpose out into the sunshine.

N aturally, it was Mitchell Hurst who got to order the first deportation. The evidence was overwhelming. A longtime weapons smuggler. A lieutenant high up in the LTTE. The Mounties, foreign intelligence, the Sri Lankan government, everyone agreeing: a cut-and-dried case. Black trying to pass itself off as white.

Fred was triumphant at the podium. This is a good day for public safety, he proclaimed. In its clear-eyed decision, the Immigration and Refugee Board has reaffirmed the nation's sovereignty and sent a message to the world. We will not, I repeat: We. Will. Not. Allow foreign criminals to steamroll over our laws.

In the lunchroom, Grace sliced her knife through the center of an avocado and nicked her thumb. She jerked, sucking in her teeth against the sting and running the cold water. Checking for blood, she rinsed the knife and ripped off a paper towel as a makeshift bandage.

She was bone-tired, her whole body rebelling against being upright. It had been a long day of admissibility hearings and she envied Mitchell's simple choice.

Slow progress on those illegals, Fred had said casually, the last time they'd spoken.

She hated disappointing him, but the evidence was spotty and inconsistent. Testimony conflicting with accounts given at the border, sincere-sounding migrants with improbable claims, or else the story was haphazard, impossible to verify. And Border Services was no better, putting forward spurious arguments with little hard evidence. Grace would return to her office with the meaningless affidavits, the newspaper clippings, the intelligence reports, and think the words: *dog's breakfast.*

And here was Mitchell Hurst with his virtuous fruit salad, watching Fred run his victory lap on the noon-hour news circuit.

This criminal is a risk to national security, Fred said. Today is a good day for our country.

Trust Mitchell to get the easy one.

Mitchell snapped the TV off. Your pal Fred Blair is a real piece of work, he said.

You're the one who ordered the deportation, she replied. But then she saw the anguish on his face, the hollow look in his eyes, the skin underneath beginning to bag out.

You know what? Mitchell said. I fucking hate this job.

He stared at her, haunted, and for once without enmity. The intimacy was unsettling. *You and me both.*

He's going to die, isn't he?

Isn't it incredible. Mitchell tossed his fork into his Tupperware container and jammed on the lid. I'm not a judge and we don't have capital punishment and yet I've just ordered a man to his death. Execution. Our citizens are too precious for that. But everyone else? They can all go to hell.

They were having a genuine conversation. After all these months, he was finally treating her like an equal. Grace put a fist to the small of her back, grinding her knuckles into the knots that had been tightening all day. She felt a heady urge to unburden her soul.

Does it *ever* get easier? she asked.

You get better at the job, Mitchell said. But it doesn't get easier.

Grace's eyes, under her contacts, burned. She'd spent half the night worrying about Kumi and wasted the other half tossing and turning. Every time she began to drift off, a rustle or thump would startle her awake. Grace bent over, head toward the floor, to ease her back. Her thumb smarted.

Are you okay? Mitchell asked.

She brought her toast and avocado to the table and took the seat opposite him. Do you ever wonder if it's the process that's flawed? she asked.

Definitely the process is flawed, he said. You could change everything and it would still be flawed.

Because fundamentally we're making impossible decisions, she said.

We have these black-and-white rules. If you've done A, B, or C, out you go, he said, and jerked a thumb to the door.

That part at least is clear-cut, she agreed.

But people's choices aren't, he said. Were they coerced? Is there regret? Who's a terrorist and who's a freedom fighter? How about child soldiers? There's no way to know if someone deserves asylum.

Or how they will act once we let them in, she said. The ache in Grace's back climbed up her spine.

Yes, he said. We can't predict people's actions. Or their children's. That's my fear.

You can't let fear rule you. His voice was almost gentle.

But Grace was piqued by his gullibility. You can't be governed by naïveté either, she shot back.

He shook his head like an angry bull, nostrils flaring. Just how many refugees do you think are criminals? Let's forget about the lucky ones who have family in Canada to sponsor them. Let's just consider the most desperate people, who come with nothing and make a last-ditch effort at asylum. That's who your buddy Blair is most concerned about, right? So how many of them go on to be murderers versus law-abiding citizens?

Grace's voice rose to meet his. Do you really have to drag the minister into this?

He's the party crasher! I'm still wondering what rock the immigration minister is hiding under.

Grace slammed her hands down and yelled, Must you antagonize?

Mitchell startled. In the silence, Grace heard the clock ticking, footsteps in the hall. Closing his eyes, Mitchell inhaled deeply. Grace did the same and felt her breath slow. She was disappointed in herself for letting him goad her into revealing so much emotion.

The vast, *vast* majority of us want the same things, he said in a quieter voice. Don't lose sight of that.

And a tiny minority want other things, Grace said. To attack our way of life. Don't lose sight of *that*.

———

Later, Steve pointed out: The man was a terrorist.

They were sorting shirts and folding towels, Steve standing in front of the washer and Grace crouching at the dryer, hot air radiating out of the drum. She peeled off her cardigan and cracked open the window. Cold February air blasted in, drizzly and refreshing against her bare arms.

They were speaking in low voices and Grace had one ear tuned to the room next door, where Kumi had been napping since three. It was nearly eight and soon Grace would have to make a judgment call. Which was more important: sleep or sustenance?

He smuggled in weapons, Steve said. Weapons that were used against civilians. There's no gray area here.

But does he deserve to die? she asked.

The doctor said Kumi was fortunate. Nothing had broken in the fall. The bad news was the concussion. She'd recovered from the delirium, but it had accelerated her disease.

They had moved her to the spare room on the first floor and found a woman to come in during the day. But these were not long-term solutions. Since the fall, Kumi slept more and her waking hours were often addled. There were places they could take her, benevolent spaces with bed rails and Foley catheters. Grace had the brochures the hospital had given her. Sign the papers and entrust your loved one to a higher power. The idea was seductive and unseemly. Why did it have to be her? Grace wondered. Why did *she* have to call all the shots?

Steve rolled two sports socks together. That's not what you're being asked to decide, he said. Does this man deserve to live here? *That* is the choice you're being called on to make. What happens when he returns home, that's for his country to determine.

I don't think it's like that, Grace said. Lethal injection. Or electrocution. Or anything so . . . humane.

Of course not, Steve said. They'll take him to a prison somewhere, torture him for a few days, then burn him alive. Or whatever it is they do in those places. But he knew the stakes going in. Why are you beating yourself up over the fate of a criminal?

Grace folded a pair of jeans, legs together, then hem to waist. She should wake her mother up. She should bring her some dinner. Life or death, there were things that had to get done.

I don't know, Grace said. I don't think I'm cut out for this—being judge, jury, and executioner.

When Priya showed up for family dinner, she found Appa, Uncle, and Rat surrounded by cardboard boxes. Books were stacked on the floor. There was a dismantled dollhouse on the coffee table. A Hula-Hoop leaned against the wall.

Priya hooked her scarf and coat on a peg and stepped out of her heels, rolling her ankles in relief. What's all this, she asked, early spring cleaning?

Rat folded pillowcases in a laundry basket. The TV behind him was on, volume muted. A Mazda 5 sped down the open road. Donations for the Tamil Alliance, he said. See what you've started?

What brought this on? Priya asked.

Appa was flipping through elementary-school readers. It's time to clean out all these things we don't need anymore.

Like three rice cookers, Rat said, hefting a box. Over his shoulder, bran flakes rained, slow motion, into a bowl. Did you know we have *three* rice cookers?

Priya crouched to help Uncle with the tape gun. What happened to not getting mixed up in all of that? she asked.

All of that is politics, Appa said, twisting both wrists upward. This is charity. How much help we got when we first came to this country.

Priya glanced at her brother and they both raised their brows. Growing up, they had routinely heard the parental refrain: We came with nothing and built all this ourselves. Hard work and education—the twin family deities.

Well, this is a new story, Rat said, indicating to Priya to come help him lift a Rubbermaid container.

It's the old story, Appa said. You children were too small to remember. When you were born, Michael, we hardly had anything. You slept in a box. Some people at my office got together and made a collection. Crib, clothes, children's shoes. So much we got!

All through this speech, Uncle silently carried things out to the car.

But what about when I wanted to join the Tamil students' group at school? she asked.

Priya. Her father flicked his hand out from his forehead. *That* is politics. Stay *out* of politics. All these protests and sit-downs—

Sit-ins, Rat corrected.

Sit-in. Sit-down. This and that petition. So-called activism, this is how trouble starts. Next thing you know, fellows are planting bombs on trains. I didn't want you children getting mixed up in all of that!

Finish school and work hard, Rat said, jutting out his chin and wagging his finger as Ma used to do. See how good this country has been to us? Don't complain!

They all laughed, even Uncle, and Priya felt an intense, fleeting contentment, as if her mother was still here, with them.

Nearly finished, Appa said, standing up to survey the living room, a hand rubbing the small of his back. Will you children order a pizza?

Rat, a pair of pink earmuffs around his neck like a DJ, had the takeout menu open. Ham, bacon, and sausage, he said. Large or extra-large?

Ever heard of a vegetable? Priya asked.

There's tomato sauce.

She stuck out her tongue, snatched the menu from her brother, and pulled out her phone.

Just don't order some low-carb vegan quinoa nonsense, he said, rolling a bicycle to the door.

The commercials ended and the anchor came on-screen, bald and sober behind the anchor's desk. Rat pointed the remote at the TV and Appa and Uncle turned to face it. Priya took her phone and the menu into the kitchen. She'd already watched Fred Blair deliver his self-satisfied sound bite several times. The sight of his smug little bow tie incensed her.

By the time she returned, the news had moved on to Afghanistan.

Well, that's a win for the Dark Side, Rat said, turning off the TV.

A good day for public safety, Priya mimicked. Reaffirmed the nation's sovereignty! Is it possible to hate a man you've never met?

What would you give to slap the smirk off his face? Rat asked.

I'd prefer to toss a Molotov cocktail into his office.

Rat clucked his tongue. You Tamils, all a bunch of terrorists.

This man they're sending back? Uncle asked.

He's one of ours, Priya replied. We didn't know about his past until Border Services blindsided us at the hearing.

If he did these things, Appa said, what choice does the government have?

Uncle grimaced and walked out with a box of books.

So it's true, then? Rat removed the earmuffs. He was in the LTTE?

Appears that way, she said. Of course, now this makes it harder for everyone else. The adjudicators know one person lied. And if one, why not all of them?

Okay, okay, Uncle broke in loudly, returning from the car. Michael and your father need to go soon or we won't have time to eat.

We'll be back in half an hour, Appa said.

He had a shoebox of cooking utensils under his arm. Rat looped the Hula-Hoop over his shoulder. Both were decked out in Olympic gear, red toques and wool mitts with white maple leaves.

If there's kale on that pizza, Rat warned.

Scram, Box Baby! Priya pushed him out.

Uncle closed the door behind them and Priya fell back into her father's recliner. A tight ache crept up the back of her neck. Her eyes burned, feverish. She'd spent the better part of the week on corporate. The battle between Newtown and CMP Russia was really heating up now and Joyce's team was all hands on deck.

I need Priya for the next few days, Joyce had told Gigovaz on Monday.

We're doing important work here, he'd said.

To which Joyce played her ace. Billable hours.

There was something unseemly about their tug-of-war. Like Jessica and Debbie in grade three, hands on hips in the playground, demanding of Priya: Tell us who you like better. Who's your real best friend?

Rumor had it the firm was creating a new junior position and

Gigovaz was hinting it would be on his team. But Priya knew all the partners would be jockeying to add a body, and there was no shortage of talent.

You're a rare find, Ms. Rajasekaran, Gigovaz had said (he'd finally learned how to pronounce her name). I can envision a future for you here.

Regardless of what he thought, it didn't change the fact that she wasn't cut out for refugee work. The emotional toll alone, never mind the quasi-legal mess of it—this was not what Priya had gone to law school for. Market volatility and the price of bullion, dispassionate motions filed by one company against another. And at the end of the day, everyone cashed their paychecks and went home. No hard feelings. *That* was why she'd gone to law school.

She was embarrassed for Gigovaz and exasperated with him whenever he passed her desk and muttered, conspiratorial: Don't worry. I've got a plan.

Priya's bar exam course began on Monday, but her future after that was still a question mark.

Uncle touched her forehead with the back of his hand. Shall I make you a milky tea?

I would love a milky tea.

He smoothed a hand over the crown of her head. Have a rest, Baba.

Priya reclined the chair back, her legs lifting up. If it wasn't a Thursday, she'd be alone in her apartment right now, overturning a can of Chunky Noodle into a saucepan, the beginnings of this same headache throbbing at her temples.

She closed her eyes and listened to the squeaky hinge of the spice cabinet, drawers rolling on their casters, Uncle's bare feet padding around the kitchen. Nothing had outwardly changed since their talk at Christmas, but she felt more protective toward Uncle now, as if their roles had been reversed and he was the child. It made her unsettled, the responsibility. Was this what it meant to grow up?

Your client, he called out after a while. How do they know he was in the LTTE?

They traced his identity card through Interpol, Priya said, joining him in the kitchen. We're talking high-ranking captain here, not just a foot soldier. He must have known they'd find out. I don't know how he played it so cool all these months. Now he claims he's innocent but offers no proof.

Uncle assembled a spice bouquet, arranging cardamom pods, fennel seeds, and cinnamon bark on a square of cheesecloth. Is there nothing left to do? he asked.

We can challenge the decision in federal court, but it's a Hail Mary. Even when people are innocent, fighting a removal order is a long shot. And anyway, our client's uncooperative.

She was furious at Ranga and frustrated by his obstinacy, his unwillingness to say any more, his deliberate blindness to the consequences of his actions.

The real victims are the people still waiting to have their cases heard, she said, thinking of Mahindan. Now anything they say will sound suspect. And Blair's making hay, riling up public opinion. This guy, all he's done is jeopardize everyone else's chances. It's so selfish!

Uncle removed his glasses and rubbed two fingers over his eyes. Priya, you remember what we spoke about at Christmas . . . about the thugs who came to the house and how the government had . . . how all the Tamil places were burning . . . ?

There was more to the story after all. Curiosity battled her desire to protect him, and she said: Uncle, you don't have to tell me if it upsets you.

You have a right to know, he said. To understand.

But then he didn't speak, and every tick of the black Timex on his thin, bony wrist was suddenly loud in the silence. Eventually, she prodded him along: You took a cargo ship north after the riots.

That first day in Jaffna, there were queues everywhere, Uncle said. Thousands of people had flooded the city, and there were no jobs. Rents went through the roof. One of Appa's nieces had a small house where we slept on the floor. We went to temple every day because it was one guaranteed meal, and counted ourselves lucky to not be in a refugee camp.

He continued: Private cars were banned, then boats with outboard motors. Eventually, even fishing was illegal. We couldn't go to the beach because there were cordons to stop the militants from getting supplies. Once, there was a forty-eight-hour curfew and we were trapped in the house, playing cards and waiting for the tanks to roll in. Soldiers banged the door in before we had a chance to open it; they turned the place upside down searching for weapons. My cousin's small girls were terrified. Appa and I stood in front to shield them. All the young men were rounded up for questioning. I was lucky to be sent home the next day, but my cousin's husband was interrogated for months. By the time he came back, he had lost his job. So now we were poorer, staying all day at home with nothing to do but drive each other crazy.

Uncle shook his head in frustration, then said: We thought there would be peace in Jaffna. At least there, our neighbors would not try to kill us. But when the Sinhalese had us all together, confined in one place, they attacked. Aerial bombing day and night, every morning bodies on the street. Sometimes, it felt we would spend the rest of our lives in a bunker.

Uncle bowed his head, palms flat on the laminate, folded lenses trapped under one hand. Priya waited, counting every breath.

Finally, without looking up, he continued: You know what a barrel bomb is? A wooden barrel packed with explosives and rubber and sawdust. Very cheap to make. Fellows pushed them out of transport planes with their feet, and from the ground you could see the thing twist and turn as it came down. It was like an earthquake when it fell. One barrel could knock out twenty houses. The worst was when the flaming rubber stuck to people's skin. If I close my eyes now, I can still hear the screaming. It wasn't human.

In high school, Uncle had helped Priya with her homework. They used to stand here just like this, on either side of the kitchen counter, while Ma puttered and fussed in the background, Priya with her eyes and fists squeezed shut and Uncle with the textbook open to the answer key, drilling her on irregular verbs and the Krebs cycle. The eleven factors that led to the Second World War. When her chemistry class learned the periodic table of elements, Uncle memorized them too. She had never bothered to wonder: What life had he led before this?

At that time, the army had control of Jaffna town, Uncle said. They were stationed at the fort and soldiers patrolled the streets. Uneducated boys, barely of age, were given uniforms and guns and allowed to swagger about like they owned the place. The Sinhalese had chased us out of the south because they said it was their land, and now their soldiers were occupying the north, *our* ancestral land. Setting fire to houses, businesses, beating people indiscriminately. No one could control them, or the Sinhalese didn't care to. They were constantly shaking us down just for being young men. They were paranoid we had weapons. In a way, maybe their distrust made what happened possible.

Priya was rankled by the injustice. The Sinhalese sent soldiers to terrorize Tamils and then cried foul when their victims fought back!

One day, I came upon a girl at a bus halt. Two soldiers were circling her. Just imagine, Priya, with their uniforms and guns, saying dirty things in Sinhala that maybe she could not even understand. For three years, I had kept quiet, avoiding their eyes, going around a corner if I saw the soldiers coming. But this one day, I could not stay silent. They had marked this girl out because she was alone and weak. I went and shouted at them in Sinhala. Hey! Why not pick on someone your own size? Some silly thing from a film. The minute the soldiers turned, I knew it was a mistake. One held my arms behind my back while the other punched. I screamed to the girl to run, but after the first fist slammed into my gut, I lost my breath. My whole body was being pummeled, but I couldn't feel the pain because all my focus was on trying just to gasp.

Uncle continued: By chance, some Tamil fellows arrived. A big group of them came out of a building or around a corner, I don't know, and the soldiers ran away. I managed to name the street where we were staying before fainting. They carried me from door to door until they found the house. Amma was hysterical. I had five broken ribs, couldn't open one eye for days. In time, my whole face would swell up. To this day, I am grateful to those fellows. I was in bed for more than a week and they visited every day. They were my age and most were Jaffna boys, raised in the north. Unlike me, they had never had jobs, had barely finished their schooling. Still, we got on like old chums. How many hours we spent discussing self-government and separation. When I think now, it seems like it was an all-consuming madness. But what else was there to do? At least there was hope in our plans.

They were LTTE? she asked.

At that time, there were different-different militants, he said. This group and that group. *The boys,* everyone called them. Out of all, the LTTE were the most powerful. Many people did not take them seriously. Amma called them low caste. She used to say: What do these uneducated godayas know about solving the Tamil problem? There was a real sense of fatalism among the older generation. This whole *what-to-do* attitude, their willingness to accept powerlessness, it frustrated me. It felt like collusion. My parents' generation, they had seen trouble brewing and put their trust in diplomacy and the political process, in Tamil politicians. But my friends and I, we could see how all that had failed.

Priya picked up the sports section spread across the counter and shuffled the pages back in order, then folded the newspaper in half, trying to keep her trembling hands occupied. The medal count screamed jubilant across the front page: OWN THE PODIUM!

Amma didn't like my new friends, Uncle said. I thought she was being a city snob. What did caste or even schooling matter when we were all brothers in the same fight? For three years, I had had nothing to do but let my rage fester. Twice now, Sinhalese thugs had nearly murdered me. I thought, if I must die, let it mean something. Let there be some honor in it.

Priya's first instinct was to leave the room. What was he saying? Surely he couldn't mean . . . Mouth dry, she croaked: But Appamma and Appappa. They stopped you.

My parents had begun talking about Canada, Uncle said. They too had given up on diplomacy, but their solution was to leave. Your father had started the paperwork to bring us all over. Every day, Tamils were emigrating, but I was twenty-five, twenty-six. How to talk sense to a person that age? The LTTE had just overrun the fort and liberated Jaffna. My new friends and I were all high on victory. Eelam felt inevitable.

Uncle's head was down, his eyes fixed on the counter. She saw the rise and fall of his chest and realized that she too was breathing hard. A thought crystallized like a boulder in her throat: My uncle was a Tiger.

You have to understand, Uncle said. We thought it would be a short-term struggle. One, two years maximum, and Sri Lanka would let us have our own country.

Uncle wore a shirt and tie to work and a sarong around the house.

He opened all the windows when he cooked because he didn't want
the house to stink of fried fish. The careless words Priya had let loose
minutes earlier returned to her. *I don't know how he played it so cool.*

I joined in '86, Uncle said. They gave me a rifle and a kuppie—
a cyanide capsule, you understand? By then, it was full-scale war. There
were training camps where we were taught how to use our weapons
and handle land mines.

And then what? she asked, her voice very small. She went to the sink
and filled the kettle with water, her hands still shaking. Why had she
opened this Pandora's box of old demons?

Then I just fought. Most of the time, we were running this way and
that, around in the jungle, contracting malaria and dysentery. Priya,
look at me.

She heard him turn as he said this, but she kept her back to him.
And shooting people? she asked quietly. The Sinhalese?

Priya. He came to the stove, where she was fiddling with the knob,
coaxing the gas to light, and, catching her wrist, forced her to face
him. It was war. I had to kill the enemy. He held her gaze and she
saw his irises, so dark the pupils were nearly imperceptible. Do you
understand?

Priya thought of Charlie then, the ferocity in her eyes when she said
she'd fight back with anything she had.

Yes, Priya said truthfully.

She felt his grip, firm and gentle, saw the high cheekbones, so like
her brother's, and the deep creases bracketing them, the gray wisps at
his temples. When she imagined a young man in camouflage, thick,
curly hair, a gun slung across his back, he looked nothing like her
uncle.

Releasing her wrist, he turned away and, shoulders slumping, said, I
hate burdening you with this.

You were right. I need to know, she said, terrified but resigned now
to whatever he might say. Tell me the rest.

Uncle poured milk into a pan and warmed it to a near boil,
skimming a spoon over the surface to tease off the thin layer of
translucent skin. Priya took out the mugs, falling in with the ritual,
relieved to have something to do, the certainty of action. They
returned to the counter and stood on opposite sides.

In '87, Uncle said, the government brought the Indians in to finish what they had started. For three years, their army occupied the north. So we fought the Indians. Idiotic, isn't it? I thought I was doing the honorable thing, taking up weapons and fighting for my people. But there is no honor in having your head blasted open by a grenade, in lying in the bushes with a kuppie between your teeth and a rifle cocked on your shoulder, shooting the legs out from under a man who cannot even see you. This is what Amma was trying to tell me: being a guerrilla was not the answer. Diplomacy wasn't the answer. The LTTE wasn't the answer.

Then what's the answer? she asked, almost of herself.

Nothing. There's just no answer. Only answer is to leave. See, your parents knew this all along. You know what your father said when I called to announce, like a fool, that I was going to liberate our people? He said I was selfish.

Priya winced, and Uncle said, No. He was right. But instead of listening, how did I act? He brought a fist to his temple and banged out each word: Selfish! Irresponsible! Ungrateful! Did I think of my parents, of the grief I was giving them? Did I think of your father? So far away, with a family of his own, and now he had to worry about his donkey of a brother.

He was still knocking his head with his fist. Uncle, Priya said, and gently pulled his hand away, holding it down on the counter, under her own, feeling his knuckles, how cold they were. Okay, she said. It's finished. It's over.

Your grandparents could have left. Your father kept saying: Come now, while the door is open. But they refused to leave without me. The last words I said to my father were that he understood nothing. And the last thing he told me was that he loved me.

Uncle flattened his hand. He turned his head to the wall.

By the time I found out, they had been dead and gone a week. My cousin told your father they had met with an accident, but you know how our people are . . . she might have made up a story to be kind.

Priya could not read his indifference—was it practiced or sincere? Perhaps time had healed the wound. Or the tragedies of those years were all of a piece, so awful you either let go or allowed them to drag you under.

The day I came to know about my parents, my unit was holed up in a hut on the outskirts of a village. We knew the Indians were nearby, but we didn't know how close. I volunteered to be a scout. Myself and another fellow we called Banu. Everyone had code names.

Priya took her hand back. She did not ask what his code name had been.

I was mourning my parents, furious at the Sinhalese, the Indians, our two-faced president. Uncle's fist hit the counter three times as he said: Selfish. Selfish. Selfish. It was easier to blame everyone else than be angry with myself. I was in a dangerous mood, shouting and cursing in English, about the motherfucking Indians who had no business on our land. Carrying on like a visaran as we went into the forest. Banu was begging me to keep my voice down. The jungle was dense in that area, and dark. The trees made canopies and blocked out the sun. The enemy could have been anywhere.

We had gone maybe forty-five minutes when Banu said he heard something. To this day, I don't know how he could have known the enemy was there. Maybe he didn't. Maybe he was just trying to make me shut up. Banu got down behind a bush and I climbed a wood apple tree. I went up so fast, the bark tore a hole in my trousers.

He rubbed his kneecap, as if remembering the chafing of the spiny trunk.

At first, I couldn't see anything. You know Vilam Palam? he asked, using the tree's Tamil name. The leaves are like ferns, difficult to see through. For a time, I thought it was a false alarm. There wasn't a monkey in sight. By then, even the animals knew to hide. After a while, I saw a small movement behind a coconut tree, then the green helmets. There were a dozen of them, every last one armed to the teeth. The largest, best-trained army in the world against two boys in broken sandals. I signaled down to Banu and took out my gun, but my hands were shaking and I couldn't get a clear shot. The Indians were moving from tree to tree, keeping their cover. I had the kuppie between my teeth, ready to bite.

Uncle rested his elbows on the counter and rubbed his hands over his head, fingertips pressing so hard the skin on his scalp creased. Straightening, he moved the things on the counter around—the folded newspaper, the spice jars, the mugs—thinking his own dark thoughts.

It occurred to Priya that this was a story no one else had heard. What did it feel like to be crouched in a tree, waiting for violent death?

They must have spotted Banu. One soldier stepped out with his machine gun. Immediately, he gave a shout and fell down. I almost swallowed my kuppie in shock. From under the bush, Banu had shot the fellow in the legs. All the Indians came out at once and Banu jumped up with his rifle raised. This is what we had been trained to do, fire and break through an ambush. My rifle was still in my hands, but I was paralyzed. I could swallow the poison or aim and take fire. I kept telling myself to do something, to pick a fate.

Banu was shooting in an erratic way. I don't think he was aiming at anyone in particular, or maybe he was just terrified like me and couldn't shoot properly. At the end, he screamed for his Amma.

Uncle shielded his eyes with one hand. Priya was sweating. Her right knee quivered, threatening to give out.

After Banu was dead, they all stood around, kicking his body. A better man would have pulled the trigger, had vengeance for Banu, for my Amma and Appa.

What did you do? she asked.

He turned to her and for a confusing moment she saw her father's face. I shut my eyes and waited until I heard them leave.

Priya was relieved. That nothing worse had happened. That the story was finally over. You were lucky, she said.

I was a coward. I returned my rifle and kuppie and never looked back.

The Tigers let you go—just like that?

At that time, it was different, he said. The fellows who came later, they were not so fortunate.

AN AFFRONT

Ranga insisted it was a lost cause. Deportation imminent. Nothing left to do.

He is giving up too easily, Mahindan told Prasad over the telephone. He says they will send him to his death.

Sam says there are options, Prasad said. There is still time.

The phone was mounted to the wall. Through the window, Mahindan saw the slim strip of grass where they took their daily exercise. There was a tall wooden pole carved with creatures Mahindan had never seen in Sri Lanka, fantastical beasts with long bills and giant wings. Prasad had told him once what this thing was called, but Mahindan could never remember the English word and there was no Tamil translation. Sellian would know. He would have learned the word in school. This and other Canadian things.

What is it like out there? Mahindan wanted to ask. He wished he could switch places with Prasad, be barefoot in Sam's house, open the window and feel the fresh air, and know that after this phone call he could go for a walk. Breathe in the wet Vancouver air and stroll down the streets, anonymous, with all the other Canadians. With Sellian.

Sometimes it overwhelmed him, this yearning for his son. The shower room was the only place he could surrender to his despair, away from the guards. He stood under the piercing spray, water pouring over his face, camouflaging his tears, his frustration at being trapped, the growing dread he'd made an irreparable mistake, his homesickness and grief for every single person he had ever known and loved, the pain of the water raining down like a thousand knives, all of it mixing together. It was the best time of the day, when he let loose his emotions, face contorting under the rain, his sobs drowned out by the rush, the wails of other men. One by one, the taps would turn off and, wet feet sloshing through the puddled tiles, they would pad into the changing room to towel off and dress, avoiding each other's eyes, each man pretending he was alone.

All is not lost, Prasad said on the phone. Sam and I will come and see you both tomorrow. How is Ranga?

What do you expect? He is depressed.

Stay with him, Prasad said. Keep an eye.

Mahindan was annoyed by the English expression. Who was the man to him? Mahindan didn't even know his name. And like a fool, he'd gone and got himself involved with this hopeless stranger.

Back in their cell, he repeated what Prasad had said. But Ranga said no. His chance was finished.

So you will go back? Mahindan asked. Just like that?

They have taken a decision, Ranga said. It has gone beyond my limit.

How to help a man who refused to help himself? Mahindan wanted to shake and slap Ranga. All this way you have come, he said. Only to give up?

What would you have me do? Shall I tell them the truth?

A shiver of fear made Mahindan tremble. Tell them you were forced to join, he said. Say it was against your will.

Doesn't matter what I say. They won't believe me.

Mahindan turned away, reassured and frustrated by Ranga's inaction. Anger was easier than guilt.

———

Word spread quickly and by afternoon it was all anyone could talk about.

How did this happen? someone asked Mahindan.

It was the hour for exercise, a dismal gray day, all the color sucked out of the world. There was a fine mist in the air, gradually settling, rather than falling, over everything. By the time they returned inside, their shoes and socks would be soaked. But it had been like this for days, and still it was better than being locked up indoors, so there they all were, hair pasted to wet foreheads, trying to make out the mountains through the fog.

Normally, Mahindan would be strolling alone along the fence, his fingers poking through the chain links, grazing free air. He liked to repeat English words he had learned. Or listen to the English CD as he walked, repeating sentences under his breath. But today, a crowd gathered around him.

Ranga had some bad connections?

LTTE. That is what I heard.

A man with a beard sucked at his teeth and said, Ah-nay, shame. How did they find this, how do they know?

They pelted him with speculation, greedy for information. He knew what they were really asking: How can I stop this bad fortune from falling on my head? No one dared ask Ranga directly. He was holed away in their cell and everyone gave him a wide berth, afraid to come too close in case his misfortune was contagious.

I do not think it is true, Mahindan said. About the LTTE.

But then he must go back, someone said. And demand a . . . what is it called, this thing?

An appeal, someone else said, using the English word.

The word *appeal* spread in a murmur through the group. If it happened to Ranga, it could happen to any of them. If it happened to one of them, it was less likely to happen to the others. Sympathy and relief. The unarticulated hope that one sacrificial lamb would suffice.

Mahindan was jittery. Ranga was a bomb that might at any second detonate. *What would you have me do?* He tried to tell himself it made no difference and reminded himself of Ranga's own words. *Doesn't matter what I say. They won't believe me.* He wondered about Kumuran's wife and the others who had thrown away their documents. All were already freed from prison. Had they heard about Ranga? Were they grateful about taking their decision? Was there any reason at all for them to point fingers? And if they did . . .

Mahindan extracted himself from the crowd to begin his usual round. A guard stood near the tall wooden pole. He was the one who used to bring Prasad newspapers. Mahindan practiced in his head a single sentence. At the pole, he stopped and said to the guard, Excuse me. Please, how is this thing called?

It's a totem pole, the guard said.

Mahindan repeated it: Toe-dem Pol. Toe-dem Pol. Thank you.

You're welcome, the guard said, smiling behind his spectacles.

And Mahindan thought: No, I will not end up like Ranga.

Ranga lay in bed, curled on top of the sheets, his eyes blank and staring. He hadn't moved an inch since morning.

Canteen is still open for another hour, Mahindan said. Please come and eat something.

Let me be. Ranga turned to face the wall.

Mahindan stood for a long moment, staring at Ranga's back, knobby spine visible through his thin shirt. Everyone else had gained weight, gaunt faces filling out, protruding wrist bones disappearing. Only Ranga remained painfully thin, as if he had never left the boat.

They were not supposed to take food from the canteen, but at dinner Mahindan had secreted a bun in his pocket. He held the bread out at Ranga's blind back and said, Eat something.

Leave me alone, will you? I have no hope. No hope tomorrow. No hope next week. No hope next year.

Ranga, please—

Don't call me that, he snapped. His voice was full of quiet ferocity, and Mahindan felt a chill of foreboding. A hopeless man was a dangerous man. He had nothing to lose.

Please don't, Mahindan said. I didn't know. How could I know? You have to believe me.

Ranga made no movement.

I have a son, Mahindan begged. Think of my—

Soon, I will be gone, Ranga said. And then you will have nothing to worry.

Leaving the bread on the bed, Mahindan walked out and closed the door behind him.

In the recreation room, everyone gathered around the television. On the news, pundits spoke about Ranga.

Deportation orders are permanent, an official said. Once a person is deported, they are barred from ever returning.

The man on television outlined the procedure. Ranga would be sent home in an airplane, a guard at his side to make sure he didn't run. *An escort to facilitate the removal.* He would be made to wear handcuffs. *For his own protection and safety.* He would be released in Colombo, free to go on his way.

What the official did not say was what would happen afterward. How there would be men waiting at the Bandaranaike Airport. Two thugs in uniform. Hello, sir, they would say. Please follow us. They would wear boots with heavy soles. Heavy enough to smash in a head. Or they would make Ranga drink petrol, then light him on fire. In Sri Lanka, there were many ways to make a bad death.

The news story ended and the room burst into chatter, everyone returning to the subject of Ranga, wondering when he would be sent back and what might be done to stop it.

It cannot happen, someone said. This is a good country.

But what did this one on the television say about . . .

Mahindan sat at the back and kept his own counsel. His conscience whispered: This is your fault. But no. Ranga was a grown man. He had taken his own decisions.

Someone switched the channel to a comedy program and Mahindan watched the screen without paying much attention. The words flowed over him and he was surprised to realize how much he understood.

A mother scolded her children for playing on the road. It is dangerous, she said. Don't you know you could die?

In Canada, they had a different conception of death. When a child was lost, his face was on the news every day. At home, everyone knew where the missing children went; there was no point in searching. In Sri Lanka, death was a fact of life. Here, it was an affront.

Mahindan imagined the foster people scolding Sellian for running in the road. He would not be permitted to wander on his own or climb a tree in his bare feet and knock down coconuts. No teacher would rap his knuckles with a ruler when he talked back in class. This was the life Sellian would live now, indulged and overprotected. Canada would make him soft. If something happened, he would not know how to survive.

During his trips downtown for detention hearings, Mahindan would stare out the window at the endless lanes of wide highways, the chains of cars, sun glinting off their shiny surfaces. At the spic-and-span sidewalks lined with trees and multicolored newspaper boxes, garbage concealed in cans. And he would imagine the city under siege. A civil war raging, rockets shooting from the mountains, glass blown out of houses, buildings gouged by bombs. Trees snapped in half, fires burning in the street, bodies crumpled, a car smoldering, all its doors flung wide open.

Mahindan's father had grown up in a nice bungalow in Colombo, with a maid who fed and bathed him and a man who came once a week to do odd jobs for his mother. It could happen so easily, in just a moment. The Immigration Building turning into a makeshift hospital. The whirr of the electric saw, blade on skin. A body bucking under Mahindan's restraining hands.

Sin, no? That poor bugger.

Mahindan startled. A man had sidled up alongside and was now watching him, expectant. His eyes were yellow. His mustache moved when he spoke. What will happen? he asked.

Mahindan scraped his chair and stood. I have to go back, he stammered. Keep an eye.

He left swiftly, bile filling his mouth. Chithra said: *Race!*

Through the jungle, they had raced, everyone hunched, hands over their heads, while artillery whistled overhead. Run! Run! R— Shouts cut short by a falling missile. Children crying for their parents. Bodies crumpling all around. Don't look! Sellian, my child. Do not turn your head. Keep your eyes straight ahead, watch the ground, do not trip and fall. Run!

Mahindan felt the coolness of the wall against his back and forced himself to take slow, deep breaths. I am in Canada, he reminded himself. I am here. From the other side of the wall, he could hear false cheer on the TV, people talking over it, being told to shut up. If any of them came out, they'd find him bent double and breathing hard, hands on his knees. He forced himself to walk forward, fisting his hands at his sides, one foot in front of the other.

He focused on the white, unmarked walls, the bright lights overhead, and told himself: I am in Canada. The hallway was deserted. More and more people had been released from detention and the jail was quieter these days, its population thinned out. Eventually, his breathing slowed and his head felt blessedly calm. Passing by open doors, he saw empty rooms—made-up beds, silent sinks. Up ahead, his cell door was closed. The fluorescent light glinted off the handle. He had a fleeting impression of being alone, the last man left in detention.

No, he thought fiercely. I *will* get out.

Mahindan saw the legs first—the gray track-suit bottoms, elastic gathered at the ankles—then the ribbed white socks. One shoelace had come undone; the two ends hung separate. There was a half second of confusion, and then understanding. A body dangling in midair.

Illai! Mahindan screamed in Tamil. The door handle was jammed. His heart slammed in his chest. Illai! Illai! He banged on the window and frantically searched his memory before the English word came to him: Help! Help!

Heavy soles thundered from all directions. Guards shouted into their radios. The corridor was chaos and commotion, but inside, the cell was silent. Ranga's body was still. Mahindan couldn't breathe. Invisible hands tightened around his throat. He choked and gasped for breath, still pumping the useless door handle and screaming NO! in Tamil.

Ranga's head lolled. His mouth was open, tongue hanging out, his last gasp dead on his lips.

Lions and Tigers

A United Nations convoy had finally arrived in the village, the first one Mahindan had seen in months: forty covered trucks and aid workers in flak jackets and helmets. They kept their voices low and their eyes on the uniformed cadres circulating among the masses, M-16 rifles slung over their shoulders. The aid workers were jumpy, flinching at every thump and sudden movement, as they handed out packets of rations—rice, beans, a bit of cooking oil—and in return requested information. How long have you been on the run? Are you injured? What supplies do you have?

Drones hummed overhead. From the A35 came the din of artillery, the army and the Tigers exchanging fire. A child ran in a looping figure eight, her arms held straight out like an airplane. Mahindan stepped out of her way to avoid a collision.

The government had dropped flyers, a warning written in clumsy Tamil that they should move, with directions to the No Fire Zone, and Mahindan and his family had arrived here three days earlier. They had come from Puthukkudiyiruppu with thousands of others, trudging on foot, pushing barrows and cycles bundled high with belongings, Tiger cadres marching grimly beside them, everyone heading east together, ducking and jumping into ditches at the whistle of incoming fire.

The village was tiny, two dozen concrete bungalows and a pockmarked temple. A tiny carving of Ganesha riding his mouse lay upside down at the temple door, no bigger than a stone. Sellian had picked him up and kissed his elephant head, then slipped the little statue into his pocket for safekeeping.

They were hemmed in on a narrow spit of land, the Indian Ocean on one side, a lagoon and the army in the jungle on the other. Every day, more people surged in, with their tractors and their cows and their last resorts. They slept in fields and coconut groves, in tents along the sides of dirt roads. They squeezed in where they could, occupying spaces left empty by the dead.

The village heaved, swollen with the fears and exhaustion of thousands upon thousands of refugees. The sun burned, relentless, day after day. Those without tents constructed shelters out of sticks, plastic tarps slung overtop. Others had only a mat, not even a tree under which to shelter. Saris had been cut up to make bandages. Scraps of fabric were used to patch tents and sewn into sandbags, bright splashes of pattern and color against the mud-brown landscape.

Mahindan balanced a saucepan over a fire and squatted in a circle with his family. When the meal was cooked, they passed the pot around, eating straight out of it with their hands. Ruksala had one plantain left. It was big enough for everyone to take a bite.

They had a bottle of silty water from the lagoon that they used to wash their hands and another of drinking water from the well that they shared between them. Mahindan let Chithra's mother have the last drop and ignored the shooting pains in his gut.

Some people had set up camp in the playground around the tiny infirmary and Mahindan felt fortunate to have found a space for their tents here. The clinic's coordinates had been transmitted to the army. A red cross was painted on the roof. In its shadow, they would have some safety.

The Tigers had mobile artillery units: long-nosed cannons mounted on wheeled planks that fired off blasts of orange-gray smoke. The army had multibarrel rocket launchers. The Tigers shot off five shells; the army hit back with forty. But by the time they returned fire, the Tigers had hitched their howitzers and rolled off to a new location. The horizon exploded in shellfire flashes and smoke plumes. Every day, the shelling crept nearer.

The last food packet had been doled out and the United Nations convoy was leaving, the vehicles snaking away like a slow-moving caterpillar, down the highway and back toward safe government territory. The field beyond glowed, lit up by a thousand cooking fires. In the playground, people swarmed all around, their legs brushing by the small family circle. They called to each other, groaned over injuries, and soothed crying babies. A murder of crows soared overhead in a sweeping circle then settled in the trees. Men wheeled out barrows through the back doors of the infirmary. No one had strength any longer to dig proper graves.

The playground equipment was dented and rusty. A little girl stood on the rubber seat of a swing, squealing, her plait flying out behind her. Boys swung like monkeys, reaching past the missing bars. The children shrieked and yelled. They tripped each other in jest, fell, and jumped back up unhurt. The children were indestructible.

Sellian had been eyeing the seesaws, and the moment one was free, he and Prem jumped up and ran to it. A Tiger cadre toured the perimeter of the playground with a megaphone. She wore fatigues and a cropped haircut. Her tone was calm and even, a soothing cadence. There is no reason to worry, she called out. Our line is secure.

There was a burst of machine-gun fire in the distance, an angry retort. The army, relentless, had finally chased them here, to the eastern edge of the island, penned in a cage with the soldiers bearing down. From the aid workers, Mahindan knew the army had used the United Nations convoy as cover to move their line forward. They were now reportedly closer than ever.

You must go, Chithra's mother said.

Take the children to safety, Chithra's father agreed. We are old. You must leave us.

They spoke quietly, all of them leaning into the circle, holding their hands to the fire as if to keep warm.

They will shoot us if we try, Ruksala said.

The Tigers had cadres stationed along the length of the lagoon. People said they were firing at defectors. But there were other rumors too. People spoke of a counterstrike, another Tiger victory to embarrass the government. The United Nations convoy had revived hope of international intervention. Standing in the food line, Mahindan had heard an old man weep: Will no one help us? But the convoy had left and Mahindan knew in his heart no one else was coming.

Anyway, we will die, Chithra's father said. Carry the children. Run fast. Go to the army.

Do it first thing in the morning, his wife agreed.

There were land mines in the jungle and there would be more shelling. And then, of course, even if they made it, there would be the Sinhalese.

We do not know, Mahindan said, what it will be like over there.

Might be safer on the government side, Ruksala said. Might be more dangerous.

Mahindan watched his son, straddled on the wooden board, suspended in midair. He'd long ago lost track of the days but thought it might be May now, maybe even Sellian's birthday. The seesaw was painted in camouflage with a tiger-stripe pattern. There was a wooden toy rifle affixed to each grip. The boys were playing their favorite game: Lions and Tigers.

Tamil Eelam! Prem shouted. We will have freedom!

Sellian imitated the juddering blasts of an AK-47. I will rape your mothers, he yelled to his cousin. I will eat your dirty Tamil babies.

There is no reason to worry. The cadre's voice came to them again, magnified over the cacophony. The Tigers will protect you. You are safe here.

They watched her pick her way around playground equipment and cooking fires. Bits of bright silk and paisley fluttered in the breeze. Children had made kites out of palm fronds and sari scraps. One had got caught in a tree and a boy climbed up to retrieve it, feet spread apart, bare toes gripping bark. His mother stood below with her arms out. Come down, she called. Aiyo! This child! You will fall and break your neck and then you will die!

Let us not speak of this now, Ruksala said. Tomorrow we will take a decision.

Mahindan pitched his tent in the last of the evening light. A million stars shone in the sky. This was the tent he had inherited from his father. As a boy, he had strapped it to the back of his bicycle and gone to the ocean with his cousins. They had camped on the beach and woken up covered in bites, angry red bumps all over their arms and legs. At home, the mothers had yelled: Look what these foolish children have done now!

Life was always high drama. The mothers were martyrs and their sons were visaran, tiny lunatics, fashioning trouble from mud and sticks and garden snakes. But in unexpected moments, the mothers would soften. Frying onions or pumping water, they would suddenly pull the boys against them and squeeze until they yelped. Amma! I can't breathe!

Sellian stumped over, his whole body sinking under the weight of exhaustion. The rush and excitement of a cooked meal and the seesaw had faded and he was ready for sleep. They called good night to the others in the tents beside them and Chithra's mother blew a kiss. Ruksala's eyes were red and raw. The gunfire had gone silent, but they could still hear the drone high in the sky. Mahindan lay with Sellian in his arms, wishing Chithra was with them and thankful she was not. He was asleep in moments.

———

A scream pierced his dreams. Mahindan clutched his son instinctively. Shells and rockets crashed all around, the ground under them quaking. Shouts of fear and anguish were drowned out by the whistle of incoming fire and the thud of falling debris. The tent shook. Mahindan was terrified it would come unmoored.

Sellian whimpered. His eyes were wide open, blinking with panic. Mahindan kept his arms tight around his son. His son who was still whole and unharmed. Every second was another scrap of life. Every second, they were both one moment closer to death.

The shelling went on for hours. Sellian would drop into sleep only to be jerked back awake by a crash. Mahindan rubbed circles on his back. He felt the wild thumping of his own heart, clamoring to be free of his body. He was desperate to know if the others were safe. People were dying all around them. Let it be fast, he prayed, holding his son. Let it be fast.

All these months they had spent limping across the country. What had it been for when now, at the end, they were all consigned to share this ignominious death? Here, huddled like animals, in an open graveyard. Pawns for the Tigers. Spoils for the Lions.

A shell exploded so close the whole tent shuddered. There was an almighty boom, then a bright orange flash, and for a split second everything was illuminated: the blue mat under them and the small brown suitcase. On the walls of the tent, the outside world was reflected in grotesque shadows. Shapes flung through the air. Then both sight and sound were extinguished.

Mahindan felt the heavy thud of rocks raining to the ground. Something large landed on part of the tent, the fabric collapsing under its weight. He gathered his son closer, turned his head away. This was death, this was how it came, with a great noise and then abrupt, hollowing silence.

He moved his jaw and heard nothing. The earth beneath them had stilled, as if it too had surrendered to death. Finally, finally, the shelling ceased.

Sellian's whole body was damp with sweat and tears. He had wet himself. The smell of urine was sharp. But he was alive. They were both alive. Outside the tent, all around them, was the agony of the dying, and Mahindan's consolation was being deaf to their cries. Ruksala, Prem, Chithra's parents—dead? alive? injured? He was paralyzed by fear and horror and the slow wash of relief settling over him. His vision closed in, his consciousness grew faint. A black hole yawned open, and he gave himself over to it with gratitude.

———

Sound was the first sensation to reach him—a rooster's grating crow. The tent was riddled with tiny tears and holes, singed by flying shrapnel. Pinpricks of light dazzled in. Mahindan left Sellian sleeping and crawled out.

The world, on fire all night long, now lay smoldering. Smoke made his eyes water. The stench filled his nose and mouth. Charred flesh, shit, and the metallic tang of blood. He choked, doubling over, and, opening his eyes, saw a finger on the ground, severed, a gold band still ringed around it.

He stumbled away in horror and saw the wreckage through the haze, the earth gouged, tents ripped to shreds, sandbags blasted open. A man, his clothes in tatters, limped past in a daze.

People were slumped in trenches, dead in the graves they had dug for themselves, their clothing blood-sodden. The swing set lay on its side, two people pinned underneath. The dead were dead now and the survivors wandered, aimless, crouching in front of bodies, turning over debris. No one called out to their loved ones.

There was a crater in the ground where his family's tents had been. Bits of steel, flesh, and clothing were sprinkled like confetti all around.

His hearing was pitch perfect now. The slap of his sandals, the rusty gate of the playground squeaking back and forth, the tortured sounds of a crow dying in a bush, and the mournful caws of its compatriots perched on the infirmary's roof. It was all very loud in the weak morning light.

Trees were snapped in half. A mother sprawled dead on a mat, two babies at her bared breasts, one still mewling. Another child, naked, hung flayed on the chain-link fence.

At the base of the slide, he found Ruksala's torso, her hands cradling Prem's head. Chithra's mother had her arm slung over a tree branch, her husband's upper body with it, sliced clean at the waist.

Mahindan remembered the amputation, the grinding saw, the man bucking, his eyes rolling back. Ruksala's terrified eyes were open. Mahindan turned away and dry-heaved.

A voice came to him from the jungle, far away but crystal clear. Amplified by a megaphone, it rang out in Sinhala. Mahindan heard the foreign words and understood their message. The war was over. The army had won.

How's your mother? Fred asked. Did you get her in at Willow Lake?

Grace unwrapped a wedge of Camembert and sniffed. It was a bleak Saturday afternoon and they stood in her kitchen, Grace arranging crackers and cheese on a cutting board.

We moved her in last week, she said. Mom hates it.

You can't blame yourself, Fred said.

She threw her drink at Steve, Grace said.

Kumi had been arguing with Grace, demanding to go home, when Steve strolled in with a cheery good morning. Grace had seen her mother's arm reel back. Duck! she'd yelled. DUCK!

She couldn't help laughing as she relayed the story. You should have seen it, she said, pulling back her hand to lob an invisible projectile. I swear it flew in slow motion, then *splat!* Strawberry meal replacement all over the wall. And poor Steve. I feel bad for laughing, but it was so absurd. Grace put her hands on her head to demonstrate how Steve had cowered on the floor.

She's a crackerjack, Fred said. I'll have to visit.

Oh, I wouldn't, Grace said, taking two beers from the fridge. She's pretty confused.

She didn't tell him how Kumi had pointed an accusing finger as Steve scuttled out. That's the man! she'd yelled. He's the one who took everything from us!

Balancing her beer on the cutting board, Grace led the way to the conservatory. Built as an addition, it had floor-to-ceiling windows and a sloped glass ceiling. The room had inherited Kumi's ferns and philodendrons, but without her tending they'd begun to brown. Steve had left the weekend papers out, scattered across the wicker three-seater.

Sorry, Grace said, tidying them away.

Fred scowled at the headlines. A terrorist decides to kill himself and now we're being crucified for it.

It had been two weeks since the suicide and the media were still having a field day. The Opposition were demanding an inquiry. Every evening, pundits weighed in at televised round tables. The ship was once again on the front page. There were more reporters at hearings now. Vultures, Mitchell Hurst called them. Circling around in hopes of a copycat. Grace felt the added pressure of their gaze as she struggled to deliberate cases.

Fred filled her in on a bill he was drafting to crack down on human smuggling. The agents are the real villains here, he said. We have to encourage people to go through the proper channels and not just jump on the first boat that sails into the harbor.

Grace rocked in her favorite chair and watched the sun burning white behind the clouds. The garden was soggy brown, strewn with twigs and dead leaves, blown-in candy wrappers and soda-can tabs.

How? she asked. The claimants all say they were fenced in at a detention camp before they left. And travel was restricted during the war. It sounds a lot like East Germany, to be honest.

We're using Australia as a model, Fred said. Our generosity is being abused by phony refugees. We can't continue like this.

Grace remembered something one of the migrants had said, at a hearing months ago. *To us, the smugglers were like Good Samaritans.* At the time, the statement had incensed her, but now she thought she could understand.

But if the High Commission is in the capital and people can't physically get there, how do they apply? And then, of course, the situation is dire and people are desperate.

Exactly! Fred said. That's what the smugglers are counting on, desperation and a soft-touch country.

The sun broke through, flooding the conservatory with an unexpected warmth.

We should airlift people out, she said.

Airlift? Fred choked on his beer and a gremlin inside Grace smirked.

Hear me out, she said.

We're dealing with international criminal networks, Fred broke in. Drugs, prostitution, racketeering. Human smuggling is just one cog in the wheel. You should sit in on some of these briefings. Then you'd understand the magnitude of the—

I agree with you, she said, holding up a hand. So let's put the agents out of business. We'd still vet people, of course, but at least—

The fact is, the system is broken, Fred said. Look how much time is tied up in monthly detention reviews.

Well, that's true, Grace conceded.

After several months of contesting releases, Border Services had finally run out of steam—used up all their bogus arguments (that was Mitchell's opinion)—and only the most questionable migrants were still behind bars.

The detention reviews, just like the smugglers, were a distraction from the real issue, Grace felt. Were these people dangerous? That was the million-dollar question. After the suicide, Grace had gone back over her files and discovered she'd adjudicated two of the dead man's detention reviews. Both times, she'd denied his request, but only out of caution, because no one else had yet been released. She could see in her notes that she'd thought him harmless, and that made her question her judgment, all the people she'd deemed admissible, all the potential terrorists who were now one step closer to citizenship. She didn't dare confess her misgivings, but they haunted her as she lay awake every night, as she listened to the news in rush-hour traffic and wondered where the twins were. What if?

The pouches under Fred's eyes were more pronounced than usual. As they carried their empties to the kitchen, she noticed the sheen of sweat on his brow. He dabbed at it with a handkerchief. Grace could have offered ice water or turned on the fan, but she felt spiteful and didn't.

We need to renovate the system so bona fide refugees can be processed faster, Fred said. He brought the side of one hand down on the palm of the other. Mandatory detention for irregular arrivals with reviews twice a year instead of every month.

Grace hooked her fingers around the necks of the empty bottles and opened the cupboard door under the sink. Who's a bona fide refugee?

she asked. What's the definition? I've been at this nearly nine months, Fred. And I have to tell you, the evidence isn't so neat and tidy.

You don't know everything, she thought. And the realization made her feel both superior and disappointed.

What's going on with you, Grace? Are they making you soft over there?

Of course not, she said quickly, avoiding his eyes. But consider a hypothetical. A man admits to doing mechanical work on a car that's later used in a suicide bombing. Maybe he had his hands on the bombs and maybe he didn't. Maybe he was coerced to do the work or maybe he wasn't. There's no evidence either way.

He aided and abetted a terrorist organization, Fred said. Deport him. End of story.

What about a doctor who operates on a Tiger?

Did he know who he was treating? Did the patient go on to fire a missile?

You make it sound so simple.

Who do you want in this country? People who share our values, or warmongers who bring their fights here?

Meg wandered into the kitchen. She loitered in front of the open fridge, nibbling her thumbnail, the door resting against her hip, the light illuminating her face.

How may I help you? Grace asked.

I just want a drink, Meg whined. She took out the carton of apple juice and twisted off the cap.

A glass, please, Grace said.

Fred was on a roll, speechifying as if the cameras were on him. Five hundred illegals arrive en masse, having destroyed their documents, and it's impossible to identify them or separate the legitimate from the criminals.

Grace was aware of Meg, lolling with her back against the counter, watching Fred.

Don't you have homework? Grace asked.

It's a free country, Meg said. She raised her glass to her mouth, stared at Fred over the rim, and mumbled, Unless no one wants you.

Megumi Jane Flynn!

I should go, Fred said, dabbing at his forehead then pocketing his handkerchief.

I'm so sorry about that, Grace said at the front door. She's going through a phase. *Both* of my children are going through a phase.

You're speaking to a veteran, Fred said.

Back in the kitchen, she asked: Was that really necessary?

Meg turned away to set her glass in the sink. Gran says he's the kind of person history will judge.

That's an ugly thing to say! Minister Blair has been a friend to this family for years.

He would have sent us to Slocan first chance he got, Meg said. He likes people best when they're behind bars.

Grace was infuriated to hear Kumi's words, her irrational prejudice against the government, aped so unthinkingly by her fifteen-year-old daughter.

Little girl, Grace said, turning to leave. Talk to me in twenty years, when you've learned something about the world.

They had taken Ranga away in a black body bag. Mahindan had watched, disbelieving, a crowd gathering around him, as the doctor shook his head and pulled up the zipper.

When Priya came to visit, he'd nearly confessed.

All my fault, he cried, his hands covering his face.

You can't blame yourself, Priya said. She must have thought he didn't understand, because she said it again, enunciating slowly: It is not your fault.

I did not keep an eye, he said, venturing a partial truth.

Ranga wanted to end his life, Priya told him firmly. He would have found a way.

There was so much compassion in her voice that a wicked part of him wondered if this tragedy could somehow work to his benefit, if it would sway the judges to also take pity. And after that, he lost his nerve and said nothing else.

As Ranga's roommate, Mahindan became his de facto next of kin, the undeserving recipient of the other men's sympathy. They carried him off to the recreation room, where the chairs were pushed aside and an improvised funeral was held, everyone in a circle on the floor, singing hymns and chanting. Mahindan recognized this was for his benefit more than Ranga's, everyone's goodwill for the dead man now concentrated squarely on him. The shame of it made him wretched.

It was after Ranga's death that the real exodus began. The judges, as if pricked by their consciences, began granting people freedom in earnest. Five men would go to their detention reviews and four would return happy. But there were more deportation orders too. By April, a month after Ranga's death, only a few dozen men remained and Mahindan found it possible once again to venture thoughts of the future.

What he daydreamed about most: having his own flat, playing cards, and making food after work, listening to Sellian tell stories about school. He knew every inch of this imaginary new home—the deadbolt on the front door, the mattress on the floor he and Sellian would share.

Sometimes, he thought of Sellian older, graduating from the university or married with children, whom Mahindan would visit. They would call him Appappa. Two or three little girls, all of whom resembled Chithra. A time in the future when all of this—the irritating fluorescent lighting, the regulation gray trousers, the detention reviews, the heavy metal doors and exposed tubes of piping—would be a distant memory, all of it worth it.

But then, another setback.

They are moving you, Charlika told him apologetically.

The remaining group of migrants was small enough to be accommodated with Canadian prisoners in the hulking main jail. The price they would pay for the freedom of the others.

Priya and Charlika came together to break the news to him. Priya had another update: his admissibility hearing had finally been scheduled. May 14, six weeks from now. This was a critical test, the most important one so far. The first—and possibly last—chance he'd have to lay out his case. And if he passed! Priya explained they would then have a stronger argument for ending detention. He'd have Sellian back and there would be only one final hurdle to overcome, the Refugee Board hearing. But if he failed . . . Admissibility hearings were not like detention reviews. Failure meant deportation. There was no second chance.

Don't give up hope, Priya said. We are still fighting.

Still fighting, always fighting. Like the cadres firing off rounds as the army closed in. Still fighting. Until they weren't anymore.

The men were marched single file into an aging building with capricious plumbing. Floors and floors of barred cells, the paint on the bunk beds peeling off in flakes. Mahindan saw the metal bars and thought: Now we are truly being punished.

The prison was enormous, and Mahindan and his compatriots were separated and assigned to quarters throughout the building. His cell was on the second level. On the first day, he stood at the railing, watching the crowd of strangers milling below, all six feet tall with menacing biceps. They were giants, these Canadian criminals. Mahindan felt the woozy wave of vertigo and squeezed his hands around the railing. *One little shove and I would go headfirst to my death.* He stepped back quickly.

His cell had a bunk bed, two square metal lockers, a sink, and a toilet bolted to the wall. Mahindan took in the smooth walls and ceiling, the bars that formed the door of his concrete tomb. The building was older but made of superior construction. There were no overhead bars from which to hang yourself.

The cell was lit by a bare bulb. The string hung down, swinging back and forth like a pendulum. He watched it for a moment, hypnotized, seeing Ranga's lifeless limbs. It had taken two guards to cut him down, one hugging his legs while the other stood on a chair.

I have done nothing to deserve this, Mahindan thought. I am not a criminal. But then he remembered Ranga and knew it was no use. He deserved every ounce of this bad fortune.

Doesn't matter what happens to me as long as Sellian can have a future, Mahindan told himself. But he thought of the grandchildren he had imagined and knew this too was an empty platitude.

A stranger entered, startling Mahindan. He gave a gruff nod and Mahindan understood this was his cellmate. He had a shaved head and invisible eyebrows. His T-shirt sleeves were rolled up and Mahindan saw tattoos inked along the length of both arms, alarming images, pythons entwined with devils. His width seemed to take up the cell. Mahindan flattened himself against the lockers and pretended to organize his exercise books, the CD player, and the two language CDs. He could see the man's things—a deodorant stick, a calendar with a picture of a lady in a swimming costume. Mahindan's own possessions struck him as childish. He wished the lockers had doors.

Lights out in five, a guard called, his boots striding heavy down the hall.

The springs of the upper bunk complained as the man heaved himself into bed. He didn't remove his boots.

Mahindan taped the drawing Sellian had made, months earlier, to the wall by his bed, a crayon talisman. *Home,* it declared in Sellian's clumsy hand. Red mangoes hanging ripe from their trees, the hammock swaying in the hot breeze. If he closed his eyes, Mahindan could still picture their house exactly. Could Sellian?

He crawled under the covers just as the lights were abruptly extinguished, and lay awake, petrified, listening to the bedsprings shift ominously above him.

———

Mahindan did not know where they kept the other Tamils. From time to time, he'd see five or six others—in the fenced yard outside or in the canteen, on the bus going to and from hearings. They'd converge on each other then linger, awkward and wordless, after their paltry supply of news dried up.

More deportation orders had been issued. One woman had screamed for so long they had taken her to hospital. But others had been released; many were already in Toronto. Mahindan thought of them often, safe in the interior of the country. He could pick out Toronto on a map now, and had mastered the provinces and their capitals. Not that it mattered.

His admissibility hearing was still four weeks away. We're preparing the evidence, Mr. Gigovaz told him. But we won't start coaching you until closer to the hearing.

Whole days passed when he had no one to speak to. Days of lonely meals, solo circuits around the chain-link fence. Nights when he'd struggle to stay awake, his eyes open in the dark, listening to the snoring above him, alert for trouble. He noted the days on the calendar. How slowly they passed, his life trickling away at a tedious drip.

He remembered Ranga's broken stride, the hitch in his hips as he dragged his injured leg forward. How arduous survival must have been. Ducking in ditches, driving tent pegs into the parched ground, waiting in line for food, for medicine, the latrine, every blessed thing ten times more difficult with an injured limb. How had Ranga been wounded? Did his leg pain him? Mahindan had never bothered to ask, only turned away. An ounce of kindness, how little it would have cost him. And how much it would have meant.

Mahindan yawned, missing his morning nap. He had taken to

sleeping during the day, at times when he knew he would have the cell to himself. At night, he would fend off sleep with thoughts of Sellian. Increasingly, these were memories of the past. Sellian as a baby wailing in frustration when he couldn't summon the momentum to roll over. The sweet innocence with which he had slept as a newborn, eyes squeezed shut, a single finger crooked on his chin. This one is a thinker, Mahindan had joked. It was impossible for him to picture their future now, the flat he had once imagined for them.

He lived for Saturdays. The weight-lifting relief of that moment when his son walked into the visiting room. Mahindan arrived early and sat, agitated, watching the doorway. A young woman entered, her eyes cast down, clutching the sides of her jacket together. An old gent with a cane hobbled behind her.

A jovial black man came in. He grinned, pointed with an outstretched hand to his friend at the back of the room, and knocked his fist twice on his chest. Then a harassed mother, a child latched to every limb.

Sellian did not like the new prison. The visiting area was full of surly strangers. The metal tables and chairs were bolted to the ground. Here, they did not have a Coca-Cola machine. Sellian had been thirty minutes late for his last visit and when he'd finally come in, Mahindan could see the residue of tears, eyes faintly pink. Priya was reluctant to admit what had happened, but later she confessed they'd witnessed a confrontation outside between a guard and a prisoner. We had to go back to the car for a little while, she told him. Mahindan worried Sellian hated the prison so much he'd refuse to keep visiting.

A man in a suit entered carrying a briefcase. Mahindan felt sorry for the prisoners whose only visitors were lawyers.

Then a small head appeared, jet-black hair. Mahindan exhaled. Charlika popped up behind Sellian. She waved when she saw Mahindan, then discreetly faded away.

Sometimes, if some of the other men were around, she would stay to speak with them. If Priya was with her, the two would leave the visiting room. He didn't know where they went, only that their return signaled the end of the visit.

Today, Sellian wanted to talk about swimming. The foster people had enrolled him in lessons and he had just come from the pool. Sellian described blowing bubbles, how he'd learned to paddle

his hands and feet like mad to keep his head above water. He
demonstrated the technique while panting like a dog and Mahindan
laughed, though his heart wasn't in it. He'd have loved to have seen it
firsthand, his son's floundering attempts at this new skill.

Sellian had stopped bringing Ganesha to his visits. He spoke
of friends Mahindan had never met. On Sundays after church, he
practiced hitting baseballs in the park. When Mahindan asked about
cricket, Sellian said no one played that here. Then he told Mahindan
about ice hockey and announced in winter he would learn to skate.

How are your studies? Mahindan asked now.

We learned a song in French, Sellian said.

He sang a little tune in his tinny, off-key voice. Mahindan heard the
string of indecipherable words and thought: Another language to learn!

Something crashed to the ground and they both startled. Sellian
jumped up, ran around the table, and gripped his father's leg. A chair
lay on its side. A man glared at a cowering woman.

Two guards sprinted across the room and seized the offender by
his shoulders. Mahindan recognized the man, who was a friend of his
cellmate. He was bald with a dagger tattooed down the right side of his
neck. Mahindan's arms circled his son's back, protective.

The man struggled against the guards. He yelled a word Mahindan
didn't know. The woman clutched her handbag across her chest like a
shield. She flinched and backed away as the guards hustled the man out.

Sellian had Mahindan's leg in a vise. His eyes were big with fright.

It is finished now, Mahindan said, soothing, as the chatter in the
room gradually returned. It is nothing to do with us.

Mahindan pulled his son into his lap. He didn't say anything
when Sellian stuck his thumb in his mouth. Tell me about hitting the
baseballs, he said. Are you improving?

Where is Charlika Auntie? Sellian asked. Let's go see what she is
doing. He sat up and scanned the room, as if expecting to find her.

She'll come now, Mahindan said. And what about your new
friend . . . Mahindan struggled to recall the boy's name.

Let's go outside, Sellian said. He jumped off Mahindan's lap and
tugged on his arm.

What happens when Charlika Auntie comes, hmm? And we're not
here? What will she think?

I want to go outside. Sellian yanked harder. His voice rose to a grating pitch.

Sellian had acquired a whine. A demanding petulance Mahindan did not recognize. Those foster people must be spoiling him. Six years of good parenting and it would all be ruined by child snatchers too soft to give proper discipline.

I don't want to stay here. Sellian crossed his arms and glowered at his father, defiant chin pressed to his chest. When can you leave this place, Appa?

Mahindan glanced at the clock. Charlika really would return soon.

Sellian, Mahindan said. Be a good boy, now. Hmm? Another five minutes and Charlika Auntie will be here to take you back.

Discipline was a luxury for full-time parents.

And come, he added. I'll tell you a story.

No, Sellian said, and stamped his foot. No! No! No! He furiously shook his head. I hate it here! I hate it!

A few people glanced over. A woman sitting nearby clucked her tongue.

Mahindan put his hands on Sellian's shoulders and tried to catch his eye. A story, he said. Don't you want to hear about the time your father nearly drowned?

Sellian flung his head back. He pressed his knuckles to his eyes and gasped through fake sobs. I hate it! I hate it!

All conversation stopped. Mahindan felt the entire room gawking, their curiosity and judgment.

Pillai, pillai . . . Mahindan couldn't think what to say.

Sellian let loose an earsplitting scream. His face reddened with the effort. His eyes squeezed shut. Mahindan looked around helplessly. People covered their ears. Several winced. Mahindan picked his son up, clasped him close, trying to calm him down, desperate to muffle the sound. Sellian jerked away, but Mahindan held tight. His throat constricted. Tears made his vision swim. Sellian flailed and kicked, and still Mahindan held on. He took deep breaths then stopped when they threatened to become sobs. Gradually, the scream died down, replaced by genuine tears. Sellian's body went slack, docile in his arms. Mahindan pressed his mouth to the top of his son's head, relieved. He got a hold of his own emotions, forced them down. And when he

dared speak, whispered the only words that came to mind: You are
loved. You are so loved.

———

After Sellian left, Mahindan felt wrung out, wanted nothing more
than a long, dreamless sleep. It was midafternoon. The time of day
when Mahindan's cellmate played cards with some other prisoners. But
when Mahindan returned to the cell, the man was there, pushing and
grunting, facedown with the floor. Mahindan, astonished, stumbled
to a halt and watched his bare back, the hard rounds of his shoulders,
flexing while his body, flat as a plank, pumped up and down.

His head and neck were flushed an angry red. His back was
covered in a terrifying pattern—intricately drawn roses and crosses
and fish-tailed women, a dizzying mix of the pious and profane.
Mahindan picked out a dolphin, its back fin slipping out the left eye
of a skull.

The man was all muscle and ink, his biceps like water barrels, thick
veins jutting out. The sight of them made Mahindan queasy. He
performed his exercises with precision, one arm now held behind his
back, his body rising and falling in a straight line, every muscle taut.

Mahindan felt awkward hovering, but the cell was narrow and he
didn't have anywhere else to go. The man glanced up and Mahindan
looked away, embarrassed.

Something had altered. The things on the shelf, the color of the
walls, he couldn't work out exactly what it was. The lady in the bathing
costume leered from the calendar. The man's shirt was slung over the
bedpost. The toilet, bolted to the wall, gaped open.

Mahindan's focus narrowed in on a blank patch of wall to the right
of his bunk. He took a step forward and touched the folded square of
masking tape. Sellian's drawing was gone.

He turned as the bald man stood. The man rolled his wrists, flexing
his fingers in and out of fists. His boots were heavy as he approached.
Mahindan broke into a cold sweat. The hallway was deserted. No one
would hear him scream. The man was an arm's reach away, just one
extended fist. Mahindan could see, up close, the angry vein throbbing
on his bicep. He leaned forward and Mahindan flinched, reflexively
bringing his hands up to protect his face. Bending, the man reached

around and under the bed, then straightened and held out Sellian's drawing.

Dropping his hands, Mahindan stared at the picture. One corner was bent. The man pressed the drawing to the wall where the tape was, banging hard at the middle of the paper. The side of his fist thumped twice over Mahindan's crayon avatar. Grabbing the shirt off the bedpost, the man pulled it over his head and left the cell.

Nest Egg

Rumors percolated through the government prison camp. At night, in the tent, in the early morning queue to collect water. Hushed voices that went silent when the Sinhalese soldiers came in sight.

A man, everyone agreed. With connections. The ship was in Trincomalee Harbor. Or in Batticaloa. They had to get to Mannar. People must decide quickly. Give the agent the money and let him make the arrangements.

A vehicle would come to collect them at night. Look for a green van, a new Toyota HiAce with all the passenger windows covered up. No, the van would be black. The Rukmani model, older and less conspicuous. Don't be foolish! As if the soldiers wouldn't notice a strange van. No, it was the United Nations vehicle, the one that brought food and medicines, that would smuggle them out. Children hidden in empty burlap sacks. Adults lying flat, everybody quiet. Everyone knows the United Nations vans are never inspected.

Except they were. Mahindan had seen soldiers force the doors, slash the bags, then kick sand over the scattered grains with their boots as the aid workers helplessly watched. But here was the choice: stay and take a chance or go and take a different chance.

They will send us home soon, a woman said. She pulled a squirming three-year-old into her lap. President Rajapaksa has promised. Eighty percent resettlement by the end of the year.

Rajapaksa has promised! The man she was speaking with turned his head and spat.

Mahindan wished he wouldn't do this in the tent where they all ate and slept, he and Sellian and these six complete strangers, the woman with her children, the man and his lame wife who lay in a corner, asleep or dead.

The government-issued tent was a crude construction of tarpaulin and sticks, the whole thing sheathed in useless mosquito netting. At night, the furious wind flung up dust and stones that tore holes in the tarp so that when it rained, water dribbled in. In a few months, their shelter would be in shreds. And then what? Then nothing. They would just have to make do.

Unit 75, Block 42. He and Sellian had been assigned here after being processed. After the last, worst bombing, when the remaining Tiger cadres had stripped off their uniforms and tried to run away. They had watched the army advance, trudging through the lagoon in slow motion, their weapons raised and loaded. And Mahindan had thought then: This is the end. Now they will finish us.

Instead, they were herded like cattle into the back of a windowless van and driven fifty miles inland to Menik Farm, an enormous holding pen entrapping a quarter of a million people, all the Tamils the army hadn't yet managed to kill. Seven hundred acres of clear-cut jungle, surrounded by ten feet of razor and barbed wire, the sun blazing down and not a tree left for shade.

Soldiers with rifles and batons patrolled on foot. Armored vehicles came and went, throwing up dust like clouds of mosquitoes. At night, young people were forced into white vans and never heard from again. The week Mahindan and Sellian arrived, six girls who had gone missing were found dead in the river, their bodies facedown and naked. The Sinhalese called this a welfare village.

There are land mines, the woman insisted. The child wriggled free and she caught him by the waist. Once they are cleared, we won't have to stay. Mrs. Clinton is coming. I heard someone say. Mrs. Clinton is coming to close the camp.

Mahindan scratched up and down, a hand on each leg, feeling the relief of his dirty nails and the raw burn of his sores, mosquito bites that had burst open and bled. At home, he would have split an aloe leaf and let the gel ooze out, a cooling balm on his skin.

Mrs. Clinton! The man spat again. Why should the Americans care what happens to us?

In a corner, his wife stirred feebly under a thin sheet.

You think you can have your house back? the man asked. Place would have been looted by now. Sinhalese would have moved in. Your house, my house. How do you think they are paying all these soldiers?

The woman didn't reply as she carried the child outside. Three days earlier, a white van had come for her teenaged son.

Leave her alone, will you? Mahindan said as he got up. Can you not see she is worried about the boy?

Outside, Sellian was one of a group of children clustered around the canal, egging each other on. The biggest boy stepped back several paces then took a running leap across. The canal was shallow and brown, everyone's dirty water heading, lethargic, downstream, a buzzing layer of mosquitoes breeding on top. In this death camp, insects were the only creatures allowed to thrive.

Sellian had been up all night whimpering with nausea and burning with fever, heaving over a bucket, ropes of bile coming out. Mahindan had rubbed his son's sweat-drenched back and felt his burning forehead, terrified of malaria. But when morning came, Sellian was in a boisterous mood, ready to play. Mahindan had given up on warning him against this game at the canal. Sellian knew to take care when the soldiers were nearby, to avoid eye contact and get into the tent as fast as possible. It was enough.

Mahindan put his head down and walked by quickly, before Sellian could notice. The child had grown clingy.

The woman sat ten feet away, beside a broken-down barrow, still struggling to hold on to her son. She stared blankly with watery eyes as he kicked his thin legs in protest and pointed at the canal. Mahindan's stomach made a mournful noise. He had fed Sellian their last packet of biscuits the day before yesterday. He gave the woman a wide berth as he passed. There was enough to worry about without getting involved with other people's problems.

By the supermarket, two children tugged on their father, one at each beleaguered arm. Appa—just one icy-choc. Apppppppppaaaa!

As Mahindan passed, the man grumbled, They won't stock anything useful like an ax or a sun hat, but Ribena and ice cream? Those they will happily sell.

The Lak Sathosa was a shiny new building, papered with ads of fair-skinned women drinking ice-cold Coca-Cola and three flavors of

Elephant House ice cream. People said it was the first thing built here, even before they brought in the tents.

Six hundred rupees a kilo! Mahindan said, gesturing to the display of oranges in the window.

The United Nations is banned from bringing fruits and vegetables, the man said, raising his voice over the hollering of his children. All so this Sinhalese chain can rob us.

Mahindan had become adept at idle chatter, striking up fleeting friendships with strangers. He chose people carefully, picking out targets in advance while holding his breath in the early morning latrine queue, following them around surreptitiously.

People like this man were good candidates. He had children, maybe even some money to be loitering outside the Lak Sathosa. But Mahindan sought out the desperate too—women with teenaged daughters. He made small talk for a few days, watched carefully before approaching. *Let me do you a favor.*

Up ahead, a small boy squatted in front of a pot, eating with one hand and swatting away flies with the other. He wore a T-shirt and nothing else. When a group of soldiers came into view, the boy scuttled away and Mahindan veered between two tents toward a back lane.

Most customers were grudging, waiting until the last possible moment before handing over their money, unhappy about having to adopt different names, learn strange birthdays. But some were relieved to don new identities.

A new name for a new country, one woman had said. It is like reincarnation.

Next life, please God, may we be anything but Tamil, Mahindan had replied.

An advertisement for the Ceylon Bank blared over the speakers. Who in their right mind would entrust their money to the Sinhalese? Mahindan wondered. He touched the heavy bulge at his waistband, surreptitiously. The nest egg he'd been incubating. Soon, it would hatch.

He took a circuitous route, checking over his shoulder from time to time until arriving at Unit 17, a rudimentary hut. A bedsheet was strung across the entrance and a man lounged in front.

Hot, isn't it? he said.

Better sun than rain, Mahindan replied, scratching at a new bite on his wrist and wiping the blood on his sleeve.

He had given himself over to it—the dirt and the filth. Water was a precious commodity, reserved for drinking and cooking. To wash his face or slosh a mouthful, *to spit it out,* to clean his teeth, would have been a waste.

Sometimes, he dreamed of a proper body wash. Squatting on the tiled floor of his bathroom, upending a basin of water over his head, then attacking his skin with a hard pumice, scraping off the layers of grime.

There were a couple dozen people in the hut. A young woman held court behind a wooden table. She was dressed like a Westerner in jeans and a shirt with thin straps that bared her shoulders. Her hair was frizzy, a thick fringe across her forehead. This was not the agent Mahindan had met the week before.

The air was ripe, heavy with fear and perspiration. A few people fanned themselves with newspapers. Mahindan wondered again, for the umpteenth time, whether this wasn't a ruse.

After all, what had he been doing all these days if not perpetuating his own deceptions? Profiting from fear, the atmosphere of half-truths and misinformation. Proper identification, he'd learned to say in a practiced, authoritative voice. More documents you have, easier it will be.

He'd hit on the idea when he overheard some strangers talking. What's the use of sailing all the way to America or Canada without a passport or papers? one had said. They will only send me back.

For months, Mahindan had been carrying mementoes of dead strangers for no better reason than sheer superstition, only to find there had been a purpose all along. His posthumous gift from the dead: a one-way ticket out of hell.

Mahindan caught sight of a customer, the man's injured leg dragging behind at an angle. He had done this stranger a favor, given him a discount when he was five thousand rupees short. It was a spontaneous action, a moment of weakness brought on by the knowledge that it was his final sale, that even with the price reduction he had enough for two fares. Now the man waved and Mahindan turned away, irritated. This is what he had learned from his short-lived business: Treat a man like a customer and he will see you as a professional. But do a man a favor and he will think you are his friend.

Next to the man was a face Mahindan recognized but couldn't place. Fair-skinned. A woman. Had he seen her in Mullaitivu? In Puthukkudiyiruppu? Hunger fogged his memory.

The agent called the meeting to order. The boat is nearly full, she announced. Her warning echoed through the group in a murmur. *Nearly full. Nearly full.*

An old woman spoke up: But so much money! How to afford?

The young woman pursed her lips and Mahindan thought she would make a sharp retort. But when she spoke, it was with insistence rather than anger.

Ammachi, she said. What do you think? She ticked the points off on her fingers. First is the cost of transportation. The boat, the vans to sneak past checkpoints. How much fuel do you think is needed for such a long journey? And then you must eat. And have enough water. We are arranging a cruise, and here you are saying you want to come on board for free.

The old woman shook her head as if in rebuttal but lowered her gaze, contrite. Mahindan's belly gave another empty grumble. He thought of appam—of ladling the batter into the chetti, cracking an egg and turning up the flame, watching the edges turn golden and crisp up.

The young woman wasn't finished. Her voice rose, indignant: Do you think we are doing this for a profit? What about the risk we are taking? If any of us gets caught by the authorities—

Speak quietly, will you? someone snapped.

Mahindan could just recall the taste of it, doughy and soft, the yolk, runny and yellow, in the center. His mouth filled with water.

The young woman flicked her eyes to the aluminum ceiling. The goons are nowhere near. Anyway, they don't know our language.

They don't need a reason, someone else said.

Fried eggplant. Crab curry. Fresh chapati, hot from the iron griddle, ripping a piece off and watching the steam rise. Mahindan's stomach rumbled expectantly. He chided himself to stop dreaming and pay attention.

We Tamils must take care of each other, the young woman said. I'm not scared of the Sinhalese.

Mahindan saw it was the truth. She was too young to be afraid. Or her heart was stronger than his, armored with more valor. A fleeting thought: I could turn her in. The soldiers were constantly on the lookout; there were rewards for Tamils who pointed fingers. See how stout her courage would be when they came for her in the night— three men with their batons and their leers. It occurred to him that she might be working with them. That this was the source of her fearlessness and the boat was a ruse to ensnare them. How to trust a woman who put her shoulders on display?

The pains began again, cutting like knives through his belly. Not enough water, an aid worker had told him. Your kidneys need a drink. He had secreted Mahindan an extra bottle. That was four days ago.

One million rupees, someone said. This is the final price? Can you make an exception for small children?

Is there a third-class fare? someone else asked.

Even here, in hell, every price was negotiable.

Mahindan had conducted business on his own terms, set prices, and refused bargain hunters. And from the start, he'd been meticulous, studying the tiny photos every chance he got and scanning faces, alert for similarities, singling out customers, choosing only those he was sure were discreet.

But his final sale had been careless. He'd been observing the limping man for days, watching as he left the Red Cross stand with a single food packet and waited alone in line for the well. This man with the wounded leg was one of the few who went into the Lak Sathosa and emerged with a striped plastic bag. A man with money, alone in the world, and Mahindan only a few thousand rupees short.

The transaction was doomed from the start.

It can never work, the man had said, scratching his thumbnail down the scar on his cheek. I have heard stories. These boats are not safe.

The blankness of his expression, the insistence on defeat— Mahindan instantly regretted his choice. But now it was too late. The boat was due to leave any day.

Here is not safe, Mahindan said. He waved his hand toward the fence and added, The boat might be a little dangerous, but at least it is a *chance*.

I have never left this country, the man said. Being on the water, it makes me vomit.

Mahindan was incensed and terrified. How had he survived, this man whose only instinct was to lie down and die? And now his defeatism threatened to kill Mahindan too.

These agents are our people, Mahindan said. We can trust them.

A truck rounded a corner, uniformed soldiers sitting on the flatbed, their weapons held across their chests, legs dangling, ready to leap down at any moment. The soldiers had been chatting, but as the truck approached, it slowed to a crawl and they grew silent.

Mahindan and the stranger didn't speak. They looked away from each other, away from the soldiers, at nothing in particular, holding their breaths.

Out his open window, the driver yelled something in Sinhala. Two of the soldiers responded. A third laughed. Mahindan's heart pounded. He chanced a glance and one of them lifted his rifle, pointing the barrel straight at Mahindan's chest. As the truck passed, so did the soldier's aim, from Mahindan to the other man, who wavered on his feet as if in a faint. The soldier grinned and barked a single word. The truck sped off, flinging dust and stones in its wake.

The man bent over, his hands on his knees, and retched. Mahindan put a hand over his face and squeezed his eyes shut. Blood was pounding loud in his ears, but he was also thinking. He waited until the man had got control of himself, then, very quietly, he said: Stay in this death camp and your story is finished.

After that, it was almost too easy.

Now, Mahindan saw the fool still grinning at him. The woman whose face was a mystery called out to the agent: What about jewelry? Will you accept gold instead of money?

And with a jolt, Mahindan recognized Kumuran's wife. Stripped of her kohl and pottu, her brows unkempt, she was haggard, unrecognizable. But her voice was just the same, the authoritative tone of a person who was certain of getting what she wanted. Embarrassed, he shuffled, trying to cloak himself in the crowd.

The agent bobbed her head in an okay-we-can-see way. Bring your money and your jewelry, anything you have. Remember: boat leaves tonight.

People rushed forward, crowding in around the table, but Mahindan hung back. He felt the reassuring heft of the rupees under his waistband. Was he willing to hand them over?

Kumuran's wife was speaking with the agent, passing her a drawstring bag. She touched her thali, fingering the pendants as the agent peered into the bag, pulling out chains and bangles, coins and cash. Was Chithra's thali in there? His Amma's pendant? Or maybe she had sold those pieces long ago and was now using the profits—his money—to purchase her freedom.

Kumuran's wife made her transaction and left, and gradually so did the others. He was alone in the hut with the agent, and still his uncertainty remained. Two million rupees. Think what else he could do. How he and Sellian could make a new start if they were released. What they could eat.

The young woman counted, her fingers deftly transferring bills from one hand to the other. She was comfortable with large sums, a professional. Was this reassuring or suspect? Mahindan felt an itchy movement and sank a hand into his hair. Head lice. All these bodily demands on his attention. It was impossible to think!

For how many? she asked.

Myself and my son. He is small.

She held out her hand and he hesitated. If you're not interested, she said, irritated.

He caught sight of the bag Kumuran's wife had given the agent. He remembered Chithra's bangles, the dust-swirled air in the jewelry shop.

My son and I are ready to leave, he said. There is nothing for us here.

He saw something different in her expression then. Resignation.

No, she agreed. There is nothing left here.

How old was she? Twenty? Maybe younger. And where were her people? He thought of Sellian and felt sorry. At least they had each other. Otherwise, what? All this effort and trouble. It would have all been in vain.

Outside, Kumuran's wife was waiting for him. He scowled and tried to walk away from her. He felt light but not unburdened. The young woman had given him a receipt with a few enigmatic words: *One adult male, one child male.* When he'd asked for a ticket, she'd said it was unnecessary. *I know you.* He wanted to get to a quiet place where he could pull the receipt out and peer at it—the young woman's flippant scrawl, the dubious flicks of her pen—and search for a sign of legitimacy. *One adult male, one child male.*

Kumuran's wife hurried along beside him. You don't remember me?
I remember you.

A man inside said you helped him, she said.

I don't know any man, Mahindan said.

But now he was worried. How much did she know? She could run
to the main road, flag down a soldier, and . . .

He said you have papers, she said.

I don't know anything about papers, he said. She had no proof, he
told himself. The money was gone. All he had was a meaningless note.
One adult male, one child male.

I lost our identity cards and documents, she said. In the jungle,
during a shelling, I lost everything. And now everyone is saying how to
arrive without papers?

The past two weeks had passed excruciatingly slowly, in the grip of
nerve-racking paranoia. Approaching people, affecting a false authority,
conducting furtive exchanges under the nose of the authorities. The
final sale had been a relief. He hadn't even been tempted to sell the
remaining documents. Now, he reminded himself: why goad fate?

But they were nearing the Lak Sathosa and he remembered the
oranges, the children begging for ice cream. He could taste the cold
cream melting on his tongue, the citrus tang of the orange, the spray
of the juice when his finger dug into the peel, pulled it away. He could
buy Sellian bananas, chocolate biscuits. A big bottle of water!

If you do not help me, she cried, then this will be useless. She held
up her fist and he saw a slip of paper rolled inside.

Could it be Kumuran's wife was sincere?

Come, he muttered, and took her elbow. Don't talk like this in the
open.

They left the main road and found shade behind a row of huts, by
the imposing chain-link fence. The landscape on the other side was
bare and flat. They might be anywhere. Mahindan felt sure now the
Sinhalese would never allow them to leave. The boat was their only
chance.

I will give you papers, he said, feeling cruel. Only thing I want is my
Amma's pendant.

Her eyebrows jumped in distress and she held out empty hands. I
don't have—

I hope you got a better price than I did.

I had to give it to the agent, she said. I didn't have enough money for the fare.

He blew out a frustrated breath and shook his head. After all this, she didn't even have money for him!

You must help me, Kumuran's wife pleaded. She tugged on his forearm.

He thought: Let the boat leave without her. What do I care?

Impossible, he said. I don't have documents for three children.

One child, she said, and dropped his arm. Only my youngest. Same age as your son.

Mahindan remembered the eyes in the back room of her shop, how she had lied about her children's ages. The bank's advertisement blared over the speakers *(Trust your savings to a leader in private banking)* and Mahindan felt all his hatred, so powerful moments earlier, dissipate. He did not wish this hell on anyone.

Kumuran's wife stepped closer and took his hand. His instinct was to flinch away, but then her fingers squeezed around his and he allowed himself to relax. It was so long since he'd been touched by a woman, he'd forgotten the sensation. The promise of softness.

I don't have money, she said. But maybe there is something else you want.

She looked down coyly and the slant of her eyes was still alluring, the lashes thick and exotic. She moved his hand over her breast. It was small but well-formed. A handful, just enough. Physical pleasure was a surprise, an old friend long forgotten. He felt a stirring in his abdomen and a stiffening lower down. If this was a trap, he had already fallen in.

When she glanced up again, her eyes were very dark but also empty. Like the vacant stares of the women who stood at the fence and let soldiers fondle them in broad daylight. A fly buzzed in Mahindan's ear. He asked, Have you any food?

One Day

The upside to being back at school was having her weekends off. It was luxurious to lounge in bed till noon with a trashy novel, then meet Rat at the seawall. They sped along on their Rollerblades, the green slopes of Stanley Park on their left, the mountains and water on their right, discussing the bar exam and her job prospects. The downside to her newfound freedom: more time to worry about the future. Unemployment wasn't an option, but the way things were going, it was the most likely outcome.

This isn't like you, Rat said as they veered into the bicycle lane to bypass two men with a stroller. To sit around doing nothing and expect something to fall in your lap.

I've been studying, she said. No point in landing a job if I don't pass the licensing exam.

But this was a lie. It was easy to find time for revision. The truth was, she had been on the job boards. But when she saw the postings—in-house counsel for an insurance company, junior associate at a boutique law firm, filling in a maternity leave for a real estate agency—she felt paralyzed. It should have been simple to write a cover letter, attach her résumé, and hit apply, but something held her back.

She didn't tell her brother this, but she did confess it to Charlie.

I can't apply to jobs, Priya said. I can't physically make myself. . . . Is that crazy?

It was early May, and they were driving out to New Westminster to see Sellian. Priya was almost a regular now for his visits to his father, joining Charlie most Saturdays. Approaching the gates of Mahindan's new prison was even more daunting than before, and though Sellian no longer cried when they left, this only depressed her more.

She'd begun volunteering at the Tamil Alliance too, leading a conversation group on Tuesday evenings. She'd told Charlie it was because she finally had time to herself again, but this wasn't the whole truth. Really, she wanted to stay connected to her former clients. But everyone was on different schedules and she had to satisfy herself with the scraps that filtered down through the grapevine. Savitri was still mired in depression and her son was being bullied in school. Prasad had a newspaper route and was applying for an entry-level job at the *Vancouver Sun*.

After Ranga's death, she had gone to temple with her father and uncle to say a prayer. Afterward, she'd seen Appa squeeze Uncle's shoulder and the two nod their heads at each other in unspoken understanding.

Sounds like you don't want to be a lawyer, Charlie said, turning down the volume on the radio and accelerating past a truck.

No. I definitely want to be a lawyer, she said. Of this one thing, Priya was certain.

They were cruising down the highway, windows cracked open, and had just passed the exit to Burnaby. Vancouver was greening up nicely, all of nature encroaching as if to envelop the city.

All these ridiculous detentions and hearings, Charlie said. I wouldn't blame you for having second thoughts.

Priya made a noncommittal noise and stared out the window. The cherry blossoms were in full bloom, branches weighed down in explosions of pink. The tree limbs stretched across the streets to form canopies, scattering shadows and petals across the asphalt.

Sellian was waiting by the front window, jacket zipped up, shoes on and laced. He was bursting to see them and spoke in rapid-fire Tamil about his day. He'd had three whole chicken strips at lunch! And all of his peas and carrots! They'd checked his height and he was one inch taller! He'd learned a new song in Sunday school! Did Charlika Auntie and Priya Auntie want to hear it?

The Flanigans waved goodbye at the front door. They were nice-enough people and were happy to consent to these outings, but Priya couldn't help resenting them anyway. What were they playing at, taking the boy to church?

Sellian chattered away happily as they walked to the park, a hand in each of theirs. It had rained that morning. Cars rolled wetly down the street. Freshly laid mulch mounded up around rosebushes. The air smelled of wet, dark earth and greenery, blooming flowers.

Charlie insisted on speaking Tamil during these visits (*What if he has to live with those people forever?*), and Priya was glad, even if it meant she was mostly shut out of their conversations. If she paid close attention, she could usually work out what they were saying, but it was easier to walk along with her own thoughts for company. Mahindan's admissibility hearing was scheduled for Friday, and she couldn't help wondering how he and Gigovaz were preparing.

Her mind wandered in the classroom too. While the lecturer droned on about injunctions and writs of execution, Priya speculated on how Savitri would survive her Refugee Board hearing, how Prasad was coping while waiting for his. At lunchtime, she would hurry into the hall to check the messages on her phone. It was always a little deflating to see nothing from Gigovaz.

The Flanigans lived down the street from a large city park. There was a baseball diamond and a soccer field, two playgrounds, and a splash pad. Sellian wanted to see the sheep, so they went to the petting farm first.

There were new lambs in the pen, which caused a flurry of excitement. Two little girls had got there first and Charlie had to remind Sellian to wait his turn.

Sellian, your birthday is coming, she said to distract him. How old will you be?

Aaru, Sellian said, then counted out six fingers and held them up.

Elu, Priya corrected. Seven.

Sellian crouched to peer through the chain-link fence at the piglets wallowing in the mud.

Illai, he said. Then, in English: Six.

Priya frowned and did the math in her head. Seven. She was sure of it.

How many candles on your last cake? Charlie asked in English.

Ainthu, Sellian said, holding up a handful of raised fingers. He added in English: Orange cake and chocolate frosting. He became dreamy at the memory of frosting.

Priya opened her mouth, but Charlie shook her head in warning.

Good, Charlie said. Then you'll have two birthdays this year. First cake with six candles. Second cake with seven candles.

Two cakes! Sellian was transported. After that, he didn't care about lambs or pigs. He only wanted to plan his party.

Balloons? he asked, jumping up and down.

For sure balloons, Priya agreed. You can't have a birthday without balloons.

Two cakes, he said again. He turned in happy circles until he made himself dizzy, then stumbled into Priya with a laugh. And Appa must feed me the first piece!

Priya grabbed Sellian and tickled him until he squealed. If everything went in Mahindan's favor on Friday . . .

Good news, Charlie said. The lambs are free.

Priya's phone beeped while they were heading back to the city. She was momentarily excited, thinking, irrationally, it would be Gigovaz. But it was a text from Joyce Lau. She was at the office. Did Priya have time to stop by? There was a matter to discuss. It wouldn't take long.

What is it? Charlie glanced over from the driver's seat.

Can you drop me off at the office?

After two months away, Priya felt a little self-conscious walking through the tall glass doors. She brushed off her jacket and checked her soles for grass clippings. The building was deserted and silent. A clandestine meeting. It could be bad news. Joyce might want to break it to her gently.

She stopped on the seventh floor first. Gigovaz's door was open, but the windowless office was dark. An air of neglect hung over the room—the untidy desk, precarious towers of files on the chairs, books scattered across the floor, deterring the cleaners from ever venturing in. The lingering smell of stale coffee had seeped into the walls.

Joyce was on the phone when Priya peered tentatively through her half-open door. Joyce waved her in, still speaking into her headset. She nodded, as if to the caller, then rolled her eyes at Priya. The conspiratorial gesture gave Priya a little thrill.

She admired the office while she waited. It was spotless and airy, the desk uncluttered by tchotchkes. A suit sheathed in dry-cleaning plastic hung on the back of the door.

Being in Joyce's presence always filled Priya with a mixture of trepidation and awe. This was what she wanted: a nameplate on the door, an audacious flower arrangement on the desk. The tiger lilies were in bloom, exuding a heady perfume.

We won, Joyce said, following Priya's gaze. She removed her headset and rubbed her hands as she stood.

I saw the news, Priya said. Congratulations.

In a surprise decision, the government had stepped in to block CMP's takeover. Newtown Gold is an important Canadian institution, the industry minister had said. A foreign sale would not confer a net benefit for Canadians.

It's partly down to you, Joyce said. You helped us build the case.

She gestured to a chair and Priya sat, then didn't know how to cross her legs, this way or that? She laid her feet flat on the floor and smoothed her skirt over her knees, feeling like a schoolgirl.

Joyce took a seat beside her and leaned in. I'm going to cut right to it, Priya, she said. Peter and I are in agreement on this: Your work has impressed us. We think you're an asset to the firm, and on Friday, we lobbied the other partners to create a position and keep you on board.

Priya pressed her knees together to stop them from trembling. The fog around her future cleared. Thank you, Priya said. I don't know what to say—

Joyce waved away her thanks. For the moment, it's a one-year contract, she said. But continue the good work and we'll see what we can do.

This is what I've wanted from the start, Priya said, to begin my career here.

Joyce patted her shoulder and nodded. Good! And I want you here too. Everyone wins. Joyce stood, and said offhandedly, You should know Peter's angling for the position to reside in immigration.

I'm sorry? Priya had assumed the new position would be a continuation of their previous arrangement, splitting her time fifty-fifty between Joyce and Gigovaz.

Joyce moved behind her desk and, with her back to Priya, said: I just wanted to give you a heads-up, but HR will call on Monday to make it all official. Just tell them you want to work with corporate and they'll draw up the appropriate paperwork. Joyce appeared to think the meeting was over. Powering down her laptop, she unplugged it from its port.

Priya stood in her confusion. I have a choice?

Joyce looked up, her eyebrows close together. I've no doubt Peter's been a fine mentor, but you've paid your dues, Priya. I've made that very clear to him. When you pass the bar, you'll return as a colleague, not a student. I think you've earned the right to choose your specialization.

Joyce Lau in her Herman Miller chair, mountain vista in the background, telling Priya one day all this could be hers.

Joyce, I can't thank you enough. Truly. *You've* been my mentor. But if it's my choice, then I . . .

Priya thought about Prasad, about Savitri's thali, which hadn't been returned, and about Sellian, who believed he was still five. Uncle Romesh saying, *Fellows who came later* . . . How to explain any of this to Joyce? *You've earned the right.*

Priya drew herself up and said, I'd like to continue my work with immigration and refugee law.

You would? Joyce was baffled.

We have a client in detention and three others who still have to face the Refugee Board. I'd like to see those cases through.

But Priya, you know that could take years. And this position is only guaranteed for one.

I know, Priya said. She spied the lilies out of the corner of her eye. *One day.* The thing is, she said, they need me.

OLD BAIT

Kumi had visitors. Two women her age sat on either side of her bed, their hands and expressions animated.

Tomorrow, one said. Can you believe it?

And of course, we're happy, the other said.

But how unexpected! There's still so much to organize.

The women spoke in quick, excited voices, interrupting to finish each other's sentences. Kumi's head swiveled like she was watching a Ping-Pong match. Grace followed the dinner cart in. She could tell Kumi was struggling to follow the conversation from the bewildered half smile on her face.

Grace never knew what state she'd find her mother in. On her worst days, Kumi reverted to Japanese, grasping her hand and in a piteous voice begging for things Grace couldn't decipher. Sometimes, in the clutch of 3 a.m. insomnia, Grace would be seized by a fear: what if her mother was dying, and none of them were there? Her last moments would be spent in a fog of foreign language, surrounded by strangers.

Chicken divan, the porter announced, and Kumi's friends left in a flurry of cheek kisses, one pressing Grace's hand on her way out. Your mother is very dear to us, the stranger said.

Now, Mrs. Nakamura, the porter said, arranging her meal on the tray table. Will your daughter be helping you?

No one helps me, Kumi said, furrowing her brows. You do your work, she ordered after the porter left, and Grace obliged, knowing her mother couldn't manipulate utensils and carry on a conversation at the same time and hated when people watched her eat.

Grace yawned. Exhaustion bore down like a fifty-pound weight. She was on the tail end of a round of admissibility hearings and was looking forward to putting the last one behind her the next day. That was the cycle: three weeks of hearings, one week to write decisions. Then the whole process began again. Sisyphus, hands braced on knees, panting at the top of the hill, while the rock rolled to the bottom.

The corridor at her back was full of dinnertime sounds, wheels rolling down linoleum, knocks on doors, jolly women calling out to their charges. *Broccoli, Mrs. Miller, your favorite.* The smell of chicken and overcooked pasta permeated everything, mingling with the urine and antiseptic.

Grace rubbed her eyes then forced them to open wide. She had brought an Evidentiary Package with her and spread the exhibits over two chairs. She recognized the migrant from previous hearings. Thirty-six and widowed with a son. Admitted to having worked for the Tigers and implicated in at least one major suicide attack. *I was a simple mechanic. When the Tigers came to me, I did not have a choice.*

While the lawyers lobbed their arguments and their precedents, Grace sat in admissibility hearings and focused on the claimants, her mother's words echoing in her ears: in another time and place, we were those people. She'd seen an amputee earlier in the week. One pant leg folded and pinned up, he'd rolled himself forward with great effort, pushing off with arms and torso as if he might propel his whole body out of the wheelchair, a futile bid for freedom. This man was new to Grace. She wondered how on earth he had survived a sea voyage and why he had even tried.

They have ulterior motives, Fred had warned during an unexpected phone call earlier that day. Make no mistake. We're living in a new age of terror. Subway bombings, 9/11, teenagers conspiring to blow up Parliament! These people and their boats, they bring their problems here.

Those kids were born in Canada, Grace pointed out as she stretched a foot to kick shut her office door. She felt uncomfortable about this call, made to her cellphone in the middle of a workday.

Exactly, Fred said, and she could hear him striding down a corridor somewhere in Ottawa. We're being attacked on all fronts. That's why we must stay vigilant.

Mitchell Hurst would write this off as hyperbole. Kumi would say . . . No, it didn't matter what she would say. Her mother conflating unrelated incidents, Mitchell's cavalier attitude toward safety, Fred and his grandiose pronouncements—the only thing worse than feeling out of her depth was being subjected to the unsolicited opinions of all and sundry.

Grace was doing her part, whatever Fred might think. She'd issued her share of deportation orders and learned to steel herself against the emotional backlash. If someone joined a terrorist militia, that was on them. They had made their choices and she refused to lose sleep over hers.

More nerve-racking were the ambiguous cases, the ones where there was more conjecture than solid evidence. Don't you ever worry about letting the wrong person in? she'd asked Mitchell once. To which he'd replied: I worry about sending the wrong person back.

She had to admit, the possibility troubled her too. But she disciplined herself against rumination. If it was a choice between a stranger and her family, Grace would always choose her family. We have to take care of Canadians first, she'd said to Mitchell. That's the priority.

Utensils clicked together. Kumi chewed and swallowed, clearing her throat before taking a drink. On good days, she ate well. It was the bad days, more frequent since her move to the nursing home, that were the problem.

I'm so tired, Grace thought, hopeless. She longed to lie down, right there on the floor, and close her eyes. Every night was a race. The faster she could get dinner on the table, harangue the girls about homework, the sooner she could go to bed. A zombie all day, stifling yawns and struggling to focus, she'd crawl under the covers only to feel drowsiness dissipate, insomnia take its place and snuggle up against her.

Kumi wiped her mouth with her napkin then used it to cover her divided tray. She hated having the remnants of her meals inspected—how much she'd eaten, what was left behind—and Grace was scrupulous to avert her eyes.

Imagine, Kumi said, struggling to sit up and waving away Grace's attempts to help. At this stage in life, to become an activist again.

She filled Grace in on the visit from her friends. The Nisei group had achieved a success. They'd convinced city council to issue a formal apology.

It's happening at the council meeting tomorrow, Kumi told Grace. I'm going.

Let's wait and see, Grace said. They had been cautioned to take each day as it came.

The doctor said I could go, Kumi said. Not that I need anyone's . . . anyone's . . .

Permission, Grace said.

The girls are coming too.

Grace was going to object, then remembered the teachers had a professional development day and school would be closed.

There will be a plaque unveiling afterward, Kumi said. Finally, an ack . . . ack . . . say what they did. That's all we want. An . . . an . . . say sorry.

That's great, Mom. All your hard work is paying off.

Resistance was futile, Grace decided. If Kumi was set on this course, she might as well be supportive. Odds were she'd be addled in the morning and the whole thing would be off.

Let me show you, Kumi said. She groped at her nightstand, slapping Grace's helping hand away.

Everything Kumi did happened in slow motion these days, but being scrutinized only made her cranky, so Grace returned to the evidence. The migrant had worked for the Tigers for years, performing innocuous repairs by his account, planting bombs by Singh's. No definitive proof either way. His lawyer claimed duress, that his client had never been paid. A widower with a child to protect. If this was the worst Singh could dig up, was it really so bad? High-minded scruples, Grace knew, went out the door when children walked in.

Kumi twisted to dig deeper in the top drawer and pushed her tray table aside. It caught the corner of one of Grace's papers and she snatched it up before it fluttered to the ground. A photocopy of the migrant's Sri Lankan identity card. It reminded her of the documents found on the ship. She was sure now they were proof of some larger conspiracy and didn't understand why this line of interrogation wasn't pursued at every hearing. To Grace, this was negligent.

Hold, Kumi said, forcing a book into Grace's hands. She emptied the drawer, piling all its contents on top of Grace's files. Exhibit L disappeared under a manila envelope labeled *Photos*. A pair of socks landed on a set of newspaper clippings.

We c-c-com . . . com . . . paid. We paid a foundry in Richmond.

Let no one say we are a . . . a . . . wasting public . . . taxes . . . dollars. Kumi squeezed a tangerine in her hand as she hunted for each word. Hold, she said again, pressing the fruit on Grace.

When Kumi thumped another book down, some of Grace's papers slid to the floor and she leaned over to retrieve them. Singh hadn't entered the suspicious identity documents into evidence, signaling she wouldn't raise them tomorrow either. Never mind, Grace thought. She'd question the migrant herself and gauge his reaction. If even one Tiger was allowed in, if it happened on her watch . . . Grace couldn't risk that kind of blunder.

Finally! Kumi said. She produced the drawing with a flourish. This is the design.

Very nice, Grace said. The plaque was bronze, with the city's logo. There were hundreds of these memorials around Vancouver, all identical and equally unremarkable.

Yuki's husband is a lawyer, Kumi said. He greased the wheels.

Greasy lawyers, Grace joked.

We were banned from practicing law, Kumi said. I always h-h-hoped you would become a lawyer.

This was decades-old bait and Grace knew better than to take it.

There are memorials to everything in this city, Kumi said, sighing heavily, running her hands over the computer-generated image. But not one com-com-com . . . to show what happened to us.

Grace gathered up Kumi's things, separating stray fruit and books from government evidence, and crammed them back in the drawer.

We don't ad-ad-ad-vo . . . advocate. We don't speak up for ourselves. My parents' attitude was *it can't be helped*.

Grace bristled. But Mom, what were they supposed to do? You're acting as if there was a choice.

The worst part is, that . . . those . . . their gen . . . gen . . . Issei blamed themselves, Kumi said. The dishonor was a sta . . . sta . . . like a mark . . . could not rub it out. But we can do some-some . . . this. We can do this. It's not too late.

And you *are* doing something, Grace said, wondering how her grandmother would have felt, her disgrace etched in bronze, on permanent display for every passing gawker. Grace motioned to Kumi's binders and photo albums on the bookshelf, and said: All your research, the information you've compiled about our family history. It's a good legacy.

Kumi fixed a gimlet eye on Grace. Come with us tomorrow.

I have work, Mom. She gestured to her documents and files, now all in a muddle. I have a hearing to adjudicate first thing in the morning. It'll probably go all day.

Kumi waved her hand dismissively. Get someone else to cover for you.

You have no idea what I do, Grace said, her patience finally snapping. She began packing her things. If her mother insisted on goading her, Grace would go home.

I know what your job is, Kumi said. Making history . . . history . . . making it happen. And happen. Again. Again.

This is totally different! These people are . . . we're fighting a war on terror.

Yes, yes. War is always the excuse. Real war, fake war. Either will do.

Fake war! Forty-five years and they were still caught in the same impossible loop: Grace working hard to make her mother proud and Kumi scornful of all her best efforts. Grace told herself not to fall into the trap of anger. She silently counted to three, then said: You know very well it's not the same thing. This is a new kind of war, one we've never seen before. The country's security is at stake. It's *my* job to protect us.

Kumi pressed her lips together and pushed them out. The incisive look in her eyes made Grace feel as though she were fourteen again.

Don't fool yourself, Grace. You're not that important.

M r. Gigovaz was distracted. He kept tapping his foot and glancing at the front doors. It only made Mahindan more nervous. They were in the lobby of the government building, waiting for his admissibility hearing, sitting close to the water cooler because Mahindan had to keep refilling his paper cup. When he contemplated the magnitude of what was about to happen, his thoughts zinged in all directions and his mouth dried up.

It was summer again. On the journey downtown, Mahindan had gazed longingly out the bus window at the sailboats anchored in the creek. Sunlight glittered on the water and shone off the blue-green glass of the staggered office towers. On the sidewalks, women wore skirts and men strolled with jackets slung over their shoulders. Mahindan had pressed his hand hard against the warm windowpane, thinking if only it would open, he would jump down and join them.

Don't forget the details, Mr. Gigovaz said. The details are important.

They had been through all of this already, rehearsing answers to every question they knew the other lawyer would ask. But Mr. Gigovaz believed in last-minute revision. You have come to a place where the people are spoiled, he said. It is easier to call you a liar than believe what you say is true.

Mahindan could still smell the lingering scent of sandalwood in the folds of Chithra's wedding sari, feel the rough silk between his fingers as he pulled out the packet of certificates and identification papers, the hoard of rupees rolled up in a rubber band.

They had been on the run for so long, days and months all blurring into each other. The firelight of a hundred thousand campsites at dusk. Kilinochchi's toppled water tower lying on its side and bleeding like a fallen giant. The gates of the United Nations building gaping open, looters in the windows. Machine guns submerged in the lagoon. Children wailing in shallow trenches.

But these were only fragments and they would never do. This was Canada, where they made the water to fall inside, where they drew a straight line between right actions and wrong. Messy and fragmented was how you ended up like Ranga. Neat was Prasad making his bed every morning, folding his dirty clothes before giving them for washing.

Mr. Gigovaz glanced at his watch then toward the mouth of the corridor that led to the rooms where the hearings were conducted. After his admissibility hearing, Mahindan would have another detention review. The twelfth one since he'd arrived? The thirteenth? How many failed reviews were already behind him? At some point, he'd stopped counting.

In his darkest moments, Mahindan thought he'd never get out of prison. The file the judges opened whenever he had to face them, it would drop to the floor, fall behind a cupboard, into oblivion. Mr. Gigovaz and Sam and Sellian would all go on with their lives, even his cellmate with the tattoos would one day finish his sentence and leave, and Mahindan would be left in the cell. Solitary and forgotten.

Mahindan pressed his jittery feet down firmly. He had arrived with his papers in order. He had learned to speak English. He had stitched the pieces of his life together and re-formed them into a whole. He would tell the judge a good and compelling story and pass this hearing. They *would* release him from jail. They *would* allow him to stay.

You don't have to speak English, Mr. Gigovaz said abruptly. Let the interpreter do his job.

I have been in this country nearly a year, Mahindan said. It is time to open my mouth. As much as I can, I want to speak and be heard.

Mr. Gigovaz always had a rebuttal at the ready, but something caught his eye and his voice relaxed. Look who has come to see you.

Appa! A body hurtled forward in a blur of blue denim.

Mahindan's mouth fell open. He jumped to his feet and held out his arms. Over Sellian's shoulder, he saw Priya and Charlika ambling up, grinning.

Appa! They didn't tell me you would be here! Are you coming with us?

But what . . . why are you here? Mahindan asked. Why are you not in school?

No school today, Charlika said. Priya had the idea we might surprise you.

To spend time with his son, outside the prison, without even handcuffs and only one mild-mannered guard standing unobtrusively to the side . . . what luxury! These women are angels, he thought.

Sellian bounced on the balls of his feet and pumped Mahindan's arm up and down. His words tripped over each other in their rush to come out. He was spending the day with Charlika Auntie and Priya Auntie! They were going to hear stories at the library! They were going to the park! There would be whales and sea otters!

He said *sea otters* in English and Mahindan tried to imagine what such a thing could be.

And then we will ride bicycles! Sellian said.

And if he's good, there might be an icy-choc, Charlika said, and winked.

Mahindan was glad. This is who Sellian should be spending time with, he thought. Our kind of people.

Sellian was still enthusing. And they have big tanks with different-different fish, he said. And sharks! Appa, have you ever seen a shark? Sellian's eyes bugged out, transfixed at the prospect of being in close range to such a terrifying creature.

You are lucky to have such nice aunties, Mahindan said. Did you remember to say thank you?

Sellian kept a tight hold of Mahindan's hand, unwilling to let go. Will you come with us, Appa? To see the sharks and ride bicycles?

Your father has a big meeting today, Charlika said. He needs to stay here and speak with some important people.

Is it about the future? Sellian asked. He grew still. The word *future* was totemic, heavy with importance. A word he knew in both languages.

Yes. Mahindan stroked his son's head. Appa is here to make the arrangements for our future.

Sellian considered this for a moment, a crease forming between his eyes. His tongue worried at something at the back of his mouth.

Mahindan lifted his chin. What are you eating?

Loose tooth, Sellian said. He opened wide and Mahindan saw a new gap in the bottom row—another baby tooth gone.

It had happened two nights earlier, Sellian explained. He told a bewildering story that Mahindan only pretended to understand, about a creature that had crept into his room at night to take the tooth from under his pillow and leave a coin in exchange. Mahindan wondered if his son was developing unhealthy fantasies. Did that special doctor Sellian was seeing know about this? He would have to ask Sam.

Soon I will have different teeth, Sellian said.

You'll be a new boy, Mahindan agreed.

His overbite might disappear. Already, Sellian's face was different. His cheeks had filled out over the past several months and his teeth didn't protrude as much.

Through Sellian's whole life, Mahindan had spent nearly every day with him. He had grown from infant to toddler to child so gradually Mahindan had relied on photographs and visiting relations to notice the changes. But now, restricted to weekly visitation, he brooded on every small alteration—new gestures whose provenance he couldn't decipher, unexpected haircuts.

Mr. Gigovaz asked about school and Sellian switched to English. I like math the best, he said. And recess.

Mahindan didn't know what a recess was, but the others seemed to think this was a joke, so he laughed along.

Mr. Gigovaz said they used to play cops and robbers when he was in school, and Sellian told him about soccer and ice hockey.

It took less concentration to understand Sellian's English. His pronunciation was clear, every syllable enunciated. Mahindan wondered if that too would change with time, if Sellian would soon swallow consonants and merge vowels like Charlika and Priya and other native speakers. They pronounced their *t*'s like *d*'s. Bri*dish* Columbia instead of Bri*tish* Columbia.

Mahindan watched Sellian with wonder, this boy who was his son but looked and spoke like someone else's. How fluent his English had become in just a few months! The child, in whom Mahindan had once glimpsed his own youth, his wife's idiosyncrasies, was growing mysterious to him. Soon, he would be wholly inaccessible.

Yesterday at school, I won a race, Sellian told Mr. Gigovaz. He was still hanging on to Mahindan's arm, absently patting and stroking. First time I won, he said. Then he wistfully added: But there was no gold medal.

The others chuckled and Mahindan had the urge to grab his son and hold tight.

Sellian wanted to show his father how fast he could run.

Not here, Mahindan said. This is a place for business, not playing.

Come outside, Sellian said.

I must stay here, Mahindan said. His mouth was parched and he took another swallow of water. Have you forgotten I have this important meeting?

Sellian stood and tugged on Mahindan's arm. Come outside, he wheedled. Come see how fast I can run. His voice jumped an octave. The whimpering threat of a tantrum hovered. Come, Appa, let's leave this place.

Priya turned to Mr. Gigovaz and asked: No one will mind if he runs here, will they? It's pretty quiet now.

Show us how fast you are, Charlika said, also in English. She pointed. Run to the elevators and back. We'll time you.

His gripe was forgotten in an instant and Mahindan was both grateful and chagrined. It was *his* duty to discipline his son, to break him of petulance. Sellian crouched, one knee to the floor.

Be careful, Mahindan said. Don't knock anyone down. Mahindan glanced at the guard, then scanned the lobby. But Priya was right. Apart from themselves, the place was deserted.

On your mark, Charlika said, consulting her watch.

Priya held out her arm in front of Sellian like a barrier.

Ready, Charlika said. Steady . . .

Sellian bit his lip in concentration. Even the guard watched, doting.

Priya raised her arm as Charlika said: GO!

From where had Sellian learned to run like this? He sprinted like an athlete, arms at right angles, slicing the air, soles kicking high. Mahindan tried to recall how he had looked in the Kilinochchi playground, at school game days. He remembered nothing. Had he been dreaming that whole time? Squandering precious moments of parenthood he should have been storing up for later.

Sellian's fingers grazed the panel of buttons on the elevator and he wheeled around. From the back, in his new summer clothes, hair and limbs longer, he had been unrecognizable, but when he returned, the triumphant expression on his face belonged to his mother.

Priya and Charlika cheered at low volume, pumping their fists in the air like cricket fans. Mr. Gigovaz held out his palm for a victory slap.

Record time, Charlika said.

Future Olympian, Priya added.

Well done, pillai. Mahindan ruffled his son's hair.

In the corridor, a door opened and Mr. Gigovaz said: That's our cue.

Wish your Appa luck at his meeting, Charlika told Sellian in Tamil.

How abruptly their time together had come to an end. Now it was Mahindan who held on to Sellian, reluctant to let go. Sellian put his arms around his father's neck, squeezing hard. Good luck, Appa, he whispered. Just do your best.

Mahindan choked up at this, the words of encouragement he used to dole out before tests and sports matches returned to him. I will, he promised. He felt Sellian's hot breath in his ear, smelled his now-familiar scent of Canadian soap and detergent. Be a good boy, he said. Don't give any trouble.

Break a leg on Monday, Mr. Gigovaz said to Priya.

Thanks, she said. I'll text you when I'm out of the exam.

The women held out their hands and Sellian took one with each of his. Mahindan remembered that first parting at the dock, how hard Sellian had fought against separation, beating feet and fists at the guard.

Shall we go to the library? Charlika asked in Tamil.

Sellian flashed a glassy-eyed, gap-toothed grin and Mahindan could see his thoughts had already sprung forward to the rest of his day—bicycle rides and sharks. How docile he was now as he called goodbye in English.

We'll bring him to see you on Saturday, Priya said.

Mahindan could only nod, a boulder choking his throat as Priya and Charlika walked off with his child between them, all three in jeans and T-shirts, appearing for all the world as if they belonged to each other. As if they *belonged*. They went through the glass doors and into the sunshine and Sellian did not look back.

At the hearings room, Mr. Gigovaz stopped, the corners of his eyes creased with concern. Are you ready?

Inside, there were murmured voices, chairs scraping. Mahindan glimpsed the judge, the interpreter, the blur of reporters, everyone waiting. Light-headed, he grasped the door frame. *How am I to do this?*

He closed his eyes and saw the red earth of Kilinochchi, mellow dusk closing in. Chithra's arms circled him from behind, chin resting on his shoulder. She pressed her face against his neck and hummed.

Just take a breath, Mr. Gigovaz said.

Mahindan inhaled and felt Chithra, her warmth so familiar, pressed at his back. *It is time,* she whispered. *You must go.*

I'm ready, Mahindan said, and stepped over the threshold.

AUTHOR'S NOTE

In October 2009 and August 2010, the *Ocean Lady* and the MV *Sun Sea,* two ships bearing together just over 550 Tamil refugees from Sri Lanka, arrived in British Columbia. Those vessels and their passengers were the inspiration for this novel.

As a writer, I'm interested in people, and as I combed through the articles and news reports about the two ships, I searched hard for clues about the asylum seekers and their journeys. What lives had they led? Whom had they lost? And what did they make of this unwelcoming new land?

Just as in the novel, there was a publication ban on the newcomers' names, a necessary precaution to ensure their safety. But anonymity and silence also stripped these people of their identities. It was left to others—politicians, journalists, Internet trolls, armchair pundits—to frame their narratives, to conflate them into a faceless mass labeled "terrorists" or "refugees." Occasionally, I came across something an actual claimant said—statements made at hearings, in rare media interviews, or in footage recorded from inside the war zone. These words, raw, heartbreaking, struck me as precious, so I borrowed a handful and put them in my characters' mouths. I hope that by using the words of these anonymous individuals, I have, in a small way, given their voices a microphone.

For all the press coverage and opinion pieces, details about the actual people who made the voyage were scant and the bread crumbs I found—a claimant's profession, another one's jewelry, the fact that children were separated from their parents and placed in foster care—were so sparing and bland that I was obliged to rely on my imagination. As a result, the characters in this book are my own and entirely fictitious. Physical appearance and family dynamics, personal histories and motivations, these were all invented along with the specifics of each refugee claim.

Early in my research, an article about a migrant who had been a mechanic in Sri Lanka, where he was alleged to have done work for the LTTE, caught my eye. His situation made me question the notion of free will. How is personal morality maintained in the face of certain death? Mahindan was created as I wrestled with these questions; I put myself in his slippers and pondered how I'd act. Mahindan is a fictional character, of course, but sometimes I think he is me, or the person I might have become if fate had been different.

Fred Blair is a wholly fictional character. If he seems familiar it is because there are politicians like him in every country and era, their rhetoric predictable and unchanging.

Ranga's suicide was inspired by stories from around the world of migrants who have taken their lives while languishing in detention and refugee camps.

The Boat People is a work of fiction, but many of the circumstances depicted in both Sri Lanka and Canada are based in fact. Gordon Weiss's *The Cage: The Fight for Sri Lanka and the Last Days of the Tamil Tigers* and director Callum Macrae's investigative documentary *Sri Lanka's Killing Fields* were crucial to my understanding of the war's final days. The chapters "Witness" and "Lions and Tigers" are particularly indebted to these sources. A February 2009 Human Rights Watch report titled "War on the Displaced: Sri Lankan Army and LTTE Abuses Against Civilians in the Vanni" gave me further insight into the civilian toll.

For insight into life in the LTTE-controlled north, I turned to *In My Mother's House: Civil War in Sri Lanka* by Sharika Thiranagama (chapter one), *Rebel Rulers: Insurgent Governance and Civilian Life During War* by Zachariah Cherian Mampilly (chapter four), articles by memoirist Niromi de Soyza, and a particularly helpful first-person account by the late K. Mylvaganam that appeared on the now-defunct website sangam.org.

The Sri Lankan civil war, and the incidents leading up to it, has been recounted as faithfully as possible in the novel, with one exception: the length of the ceasefire that began in 2002 has been compressed for dramatic effect. While in the novel it lasts only a few months, in actual fact an uneasy truce held for four years.

For a crash course on Canada's legal system, I relied on *Refugee Law* by Martin Jones and Sasha Baglay, "The Complexity of Determining Refugeehood: A Multidisciplinary Analysis of the Decision-Making Process of the Canadian Immigration and Refugee Board" in the *Journal of Refugee Studies* (volume 15, no. 1, 2002), and "Refugees Who Arrive by Boat and Canada's Commitment to the Refugee Convention: A Discursive Analysis" by Alexandra Mann in *Refuge* (volume 26, no. 2). "*Sun Sea:* Five Years Later," a report by the Canadian Council for Refugees published in August 2015, is an eye-opening account of how the government dealt with the arrivals of the MV *Sun Sea* and the *Ocean Lady*.

Several articles, discovered in the earliest days of my research, set the novel's tone: "Tamil, Tiger, Terrorist?" by Fathima Cader, *Briarpatch* (July 7, 2011) and "Strangers by Sea: A Tale of Canada's Boat People" by Michael Valpy, *Globe and Mail* (August 13, 2010). The expression "arrival of the fittest" is borrowed from Rachel Giese's excellent piece of the same name published in *The Walrus* (June 2011).

Key sources on the Japanese internment were *The Politics of Racism: The Uprooting of Japanese Canadians during the Second World War* by Ann Gomer Sunhahara and *This Is My Own: Letters to Wes & Other Writings on Japanese Canadians, 1941–1948* by Muriel Kitagawa.

The character of Prasad was partially inspired by Lasantha Wickrematunge, a brave Sinhalese journalist who was assassinated in Sri Lanka in 2009 for his fair-minded reporting. His haunting final essay, posthumously published in the January 13, 2009, issue of *The Guardian,* provided fodder for Prasad's work, as did some of the facts of the intimidation campaign that dogged his career and life. Please read it.

The novel's Tamil characters have a dangerous habit of dismissing all Sinhalese people as villains. The truth is, there were heroes on the other side too, men and women like Wickrematunge who, at great personal risk and cost, protected Tamils and advocated for their rights.

GRATITUDE

Thank you to the talented writers of The Port Authority whose fingerprints and red pens have been all over this project from the start: Melissa Barbeau, Jamie Fitzpatrick, Carrie Ivardi, Matthew Lewis, Morgan Murray, Gary Newhook, and Susan Sinnott. There are no words in this language or any other to convey just how much you mean to me.

Stephanie Sinclair has been *The Boat People*'s best and loudest champion. More than an agent, she is a wizard, making the magic happen behind the scenes.

My editors, Melissa Danaczko and Anita Chong, asked all the tough questions and made me sweat for every sentence. Margo Shickmanter provided invaluable feedback on the crucial final drafts. Thank you to Emiliano Ponzi for the stunning jacket illustration and to Pei Loi Koay and Emily Mahon for the beautiful text and design. Thank you Bill Thomas, Rita Madrigal, Sarah Engelmann, Charlotte O'Donnell, and everyone at Doubleday U.S. who laid out the welcome mat, gave *The Boat People* a home, and made my biggest, wildest dream come true.

I'm grateful for the brave readers who critiqued early (dreadful) drafts: Kristen Romme, Lisa Pickersgill, Annamarie Beckel, and my mother, Swarna Bala.

Lisa Moore likes to say: "Put your characters in peril." Thank you, Lisa, for your wisdom and generosity. I have done my best!

Nadra Ginting told me that decomposing flesh smells like rotting fruit and then, in patient, excruciating detail, explained how to perform an amputation. "Lady Doctor" is for you, Nads.

This book owes a debt to the vibrant and supportive literary community in St. John's, to the more established writers who held doors open, and to the organizations that nurtured my work: the Writers' Alliance of NL, ArtsNL, the Arts and Letters Awards, the Literary Society of NL, and Memorial University. May we always have the benefit of well-funded cultural institutions.

Important parts of *The Boat People*'s narrative grew out of my family's experiences during the '58 and '83 riots. I am thankful to my father, Mohan Bala, who shared those stories.

Deep and sincere gratitude to those who took my writing seriously before it was a career, and in particular my extended family of Baird and Pickersgill in-laws, a smart and loving clan with impeccable taste.

Tom Baird makes all that is good in my life possible. He is my first reader and chief supporter, the giver of unlimited shoulder rubs. He believed in *The Boat People* before anyone else—before even me.